dead man
Airbrushed

dead man
Airbrushed

Ieuan M. Pugh

First impression: 2014
© Ieuan M. Pugh & Y Lolfa Cyf., 2014

Cover painting: Ieuan M. Pugh

ISBN: 978 1 84771 831 0

Published and printed in Wales
on paper from well-maintained forests by
Y Lolfa Cyf., Talybont, Ceredigion SY24 5HE
e-mail ylolfa@ylolfa.com
website www.ylolfa.com
tel 01970 832 304
fax 832 782

Foreword

The art student draped in the flags of age stoically guarded his lack of success
For his mission had changed from upholding the truth to promulgating the quest.
Threatening desertion his soul weighed its options with a remarkable air of disloyalty,
For ignorance drowned in a surfeit of scorn washed by his enigmatic folly.

Tempting canvasses filled the studio, generating storms of capricious views:
His conscience self-defiled a fractal striptease of society's flexible values;
Convention exposed his malady by conjugating the verb to humiliate,
Construed to oppress the courtly judgement, fashioned in squalor, salvation too late.

Losing his appeal the art student withdrew as tears fell in an autumn of crocodiles,
So his lonesome soul was buried alone while the carcase was left to philander.
Given no option the delusion took flight to the land of mahogany shadows
Where flags of age forlornly waved goodbye, goodbye, for God's sake *do* goodbye.

Ieuan M. Pugh
Kerry, Powys, 2014

1
Interviews

THE GHOST OF Johannes Taliesin's initial conditions painted a turbulent muddle in his late teens, thereafter setting a direction in which unmanageable consequences increased in perfect symmetry to the effluxion of time. Sentenced to a statute of natural limitations he clambered between dire consequence and fortuitously clement circumstance. Hitherto, any tentative grasp he had of life's challenges assumed the benefits of adult management to be a given. But during the final year in grammar school Johannes discovered that deciding on a career and its consequent course of study brought for the first time the shock of personal responsibility. In the meantime, school was an experience that he endured if, for no other reason, it created the means by which he could eventually escape the meagre and struggle of the farm.

Johannes had always disliked the cheek-by-jowl conditions demanded by the school regime. But matters improved immensely on entry to upper six: the art master gave him permission to use a space secluded behind screens in the nether regions of the art room for additional studies in art. The sanctuary perfectly suited Johannes's idiosyncratic character. Wherever his timetable stated 'preparation' or 'option' he would make for the obscurity of the sanctuary, working in splendid isolation to produce drawings of The Clapping Faun, bust of Roman Centurion, plaster cast of Shell Girl and the like. The sanctuary had an additional advantage: by manoeuvring the working position to afford a vantage point through a slit in the screens, he was able to view art room comings and goings while retaining anonymity.

Towards the end of the final year his off-beam thinking was laid bare by a deceptively innocuous interview. On the particular day in question Johannes was busy producing his umpteenth study of Roman Centurion, when the art room door opened and in walked the headmaster's secretary.

'Sorry to interrupt your class, Mr Davies,' she said, 'I am looking for Johannes Taliesin. His form master says he spends his preparation periods here in the art room. Is he here today?'

'*Uh-oh,*' Inner Voice sighed.

'Yes, he is here in his usual squirrel's dray,' Mr Davies replied, 'Johannes!'

'Sir?'

'Headmaster's secretary to see you.'

'*Crickey, what does the headmaster's secretary want us for?*' Inner Voice squeaked.

Johannes broke cover and confronted the secretary, in front of the class of gawping juniors, of all embarrassments.

'Johannes, Mr James would like to see you in his study immediately,' she said, 'and you had better look sharp because I've spent an age finding you – don't want to keep the headmaster waiting any longer, do we?'

'*Heck! What does the headmaster want to see us for? Bet it's about PE.*' Johannes had developed a life-long dependency on Inner Voice's readiness to offer advice, albeit pessimistic.

He headed off at a pace for the headmaster's study, located at the opposite end of the campus to the art room. Arriving somewhat short of breath, Johannes gave the door a timid tap.

'Enter!' the crisp boom of the headmaster's voice resonated.

'*Oh God.*'

He crept in.

'Ah, Taliesin! How long ago was it that my secretary located you?'

'J-just now, Sir, in the art room; I came immediately.'

'Sit down! You seem to be breathing heavily – why are you so unfit?'

'This is it, fitness. Bet Hopkins has told him we mitch PE. Oh God, here goes.'

'D-didn't realise I-I w-was unfit, S-Sir.'

'Mr Hopkins informs me you systematically miss attendance of PE classes. Is this correct?' Headmaster James wasted no time in getting to the point.

'Oh God, we knew this moment would arrive.'

'Y-yes, S-Sir,' the faithful stutter had returned.

'I take it your avoidance of PE is supported by a sound reason. Can you provide a reason, Taliesin?'

'Um…'

'This is awful… a sound reason. One minute we are enjoying our solitary confinement; next we're being interrogated by the headmaster for mitching PE. Why hadn't we invented an off-the-shelf foolproof reason before? Oh God.'

'Well, Taliesin?'

'A sound reason… the sound reason of last resort could always be tinea pedis. Here goes.'

'I… um… I… I've got t-tinea p-pedis, S-Sir,' Johannes's response lacked that certain conviction of one who really suffered the discomfort of tinea pedis.

'Hmm… tinea pedis… hmm, a contagious fungal infection. Do you have a medical certificate to substantiate the existence of this malady?'

'If we had one we would have shown it to Hopkins jolly quick. How do we answer without saying no?'

Johannes's head was spinning.

'Um… n-no, S-Sir.'

'*What in God's name did we have to go and say no for?*' Inner Voice did not always enjoy firm contact with Johannes's central nervous system.

Headmaster James glowered, 'You will report to Mr Hopkins with a valid medical certificate or, failing that, you will arrange with him a timetable for normal attendance at PE classes.'

'Y-yes, Sir,' Johannes acknowledged with relief, and got up to leave.

'*Phew, that went easier than we… perhaps telling the truth works…*'

'Where are you going, Taliesin? Come back and sit down! That is not the reason I sent for you, although it is sufficient for a reprimand in its own right –'

'*Oh God! There's more!*'

' – The reason I have called to see you is because I have been reviewing this year's university applications, and find the only name not on the list from upper six is yours, Taliesin. Please advise me why.'

'*Oh God, there we were thinking the PE thing went easy; now our case takes a plunge…*'

'Um.'

'Well?'

'Um… because I intend applying for a short-service commission in the Royal Air Force, Sir,' Johannes blurted stutter-free.

'*No stutter, got to be a catch*'

'WHAT?'

'Because I intend app –'

'I heard you,' Headmaster James interrupted, holding Johannes in an indefatigable glare of horror.

An enormous silence followed, during which time Johannes was greatly intimidated to note unflattering thoughts etching their way across the headmaster's face: 'How could we have registered such an idiot on the matriculation roll?' followed by, 'Beynon Jones Latin was right all along' and, 'Ardwyn's university entrance record will take a nosedive this year.' But none of these were externalised. Instead, the headmaster asked the deceptively innocuous, 'Have you discussed this with your father?'

'Um… n-not yet, S-Sir,' the stutter came back.

'It would be interesting to witness his response,' the headmaster said, knowing Taliesin Senior to be a Quaker conscientious objector unfortunately possessed of an incandescent temperament that was incompatible with his pacifist proclamations.

'Y-yes, S-Sir,' Johannes's response carried a note of hopelessness.

'Had you not considered an academic route?'

'Y-yes, S-Sir.'

'And?'

'I… um… I… um…'

'Be honest – tell him we are no good at academic subjects.'

'I-I'm not very good at ac-academic s-subjects, S-Sir.'

'Are you capable in any line, Taliesin?'

'Come to think of it, we are not very good at anything,' Inner Voice capitulated.

'N-not very good at – perhaps drawing, S-Sir.'

'What about art generally?'

'I-I like to think – but n-no, S-Sir, only drawing.'

'Oh dear, let us hope drawing comes to your aid when the Royal Air Force rejects your application.'

'W-will they re-reject me, S-Sir?'

'No doubt about it, Taliesin; that is, if your father permits you to apply in the first place. Report back to my study following consultation with your father on this topic, and report to Mr Hopkins regarding a medical certificate for your tinea pedis. Dismissed.'

'Th-thank you, S-Sir.'

'Boy, are we in a pickle. Going to the doctor without tinea pedis will result in no doctor's note, which will take some explaining to Hopkins and the headmaster, some awkward questions to answer… then there is the RAF thing… breaking the news to Daddy, may as well test the farm petrol store with a lighted match… boy, are we in a pickle.'

As he returned to the art room Johannes thought about the many horns of his quandary. At the end of every thought lay an explosion of one form or another. He decided to hide away in his sanctuary and brood about things for a few days before taking any action, a strategy that had been successful once or twice in the past…

'Whichever action we take the outcomes appear eminently undesirable, horns of a dilemma stuff.'

Of course, delay in such circumstances had a limited shelf life: it would not be long before the headmaster would despatch his secretary to collect Johannes for another grilling; or his mother would recognise brood mode and demand an explanation, whereupon his father would enter the arena, steam pouring from every orifice; and no doubt the headmaster would have tipped off Hopkins to expect Johannes Taliesin bearing a sheaf of medical certificates, with his feet bandaged to the knees…

Before any of these eventualities took their course, Johannes plucked up what little courage he could muster and delivered himself to Hopkins at the male gymnasium.

On setting foot in the gym's entrance the stench of male sweat repulsed him – having long since signed a pact of immunity to his own stench – and was reminded why he had embarked on a policy of mitching all that time ago. He presented himself to Hopkins.

'Who are you?' Hopkins demanded.

'This bodes well, but, God, he's an obnoxious little creature.'

'Johannes Taliesin, Sir.'

'Who?'

Years ago Johannes had decided PE teachers were a cut or two below the intelligence plimsoll line of other academic teachers. Hopkins illustrated this prejudice perfectly, so instead of going through the rigmarole of identification, Johannes went straight to the point.

'You informed the headmaster of my mitching gym, Sir, and he ordered me to report to you.'

'What form are you in?' Hopkins was still attempting to clear his mind regarding the newcomer.

'Upper six, Sir.'

'Upper six?'

'That's what we said.'

'Yes, Sir.'

'When did you join this school?' Hopkins, if nothing else, was tenacious at pursuing a futile line of enquiry.

'In form one, Sir.'

'Why is it I have never seen you before?'

'True he has never seen us in this shape before: we are about three times the height we were when we attended PE last. There's a chink of light here, but knowing how to capitalise on it is the trick.'

'You did, Sir.'

'When?'

'Wh-when I took gym,' came Johannes's feeble reply, losing his grip on capitalising on the chink of light.

'When did you take PE classes last, Taliesin?' Hopkins was slowly getting his act together.

'At… at the end of… um… at the end of form two.'

'FORM TWO!' Hopkins exploded, the news implying as much trouble for him as for Johannes.

'*The headmaster will carpet Hopkins for errantly losing one of his flock for five years. There's hope for us yet.*'

'Sir.'

'How many years ago was that, Taliesin?'

'About um… about five, Sir.'

'And you have been in attendance at this school in the meantime?'

'Yes, Sir.'

'What about games?'

'Also, Sir.'

Hopkins sat down, putting his head in his hands.

'*Errantly losing one of his flock…*'

'Where have you been hiding all this time?'

'I… um… I haven't been hiding as such, Sir. It's just that… um… whenever I saw you coming, I would skip in the opposite direction…'

'For five years, Taliesin?' Hopkins's voice had grown strained.

'The way you put it, Sir, it seems a long time.'

'And you are now in upper six?'

'Sir.'

'This could be some sort of record – what has been your excuse all these years?'

'Tinea pedis, Sir.'

'That has got to be a contradiction, Taliesin; do you have a medical certificate?'

'Er – no, Sir.'

'In which case how do you know?' Hopkins demanded.

'*He's using his limited intelligence to its extreme capacity; he'll have a stroke any second.*'

But in spite of Inner Voice's bravado this was the moment Johannes dreaded; he gave a desultory shrug.

'Let me examine your feet,' he said crisply and, unzipping a section of disinfectant gauze from a roll, placed it on the floor, 'take off your shoes but stand on the disinfectant gauze, as tinea pedis is an infectious fungus.'

'Oh God, we've got holes in our socks!'

Johannes hesitated.

'Get on with it, Taliesin.'

'Ask him if he really wants to go ahead with this,' Inner Voice suggested.

'I've got –'

'Get on with it!'

Johannes removed his shoes to expose socks with more holes than material: dirty, smelly rags, bent over at the toes in order to draw down leg sock to disguise the multiple holes at heel. The stench of rotten cheese wafted up. Hopkins, who must have experienced prime examples of sweaty feet in his time, visibly swayed.

'Remove your socks,' he gasped, 'but don't step off the disinfectant gauze.'

Johannes reluctantly obliged.

'Heavens, Taliesin, if only I could see through the dirt... can't make out – don't step off the gauze!' he bellowed, 'Certainly you have some angry-looking redness between your toes, amongst the dirt. I should order you to the showers immediately, but you might contaminate the floors; put your socks and shoes back on – don't step off the disinfectant gauze until the shoes are firmly in place. Do you not have a whole pair of socks?'

'No, Sir.'

'You are in upper six, you say?' Mr Hopkins consulted his files for some time, 'Ah here is your name, "Johannes Taliesin": I reported your absences to the headmaster at the beginning of your form three. Then I crossed out your name, assuming of course that you had either left or been dismissed from Ardwyn.'

'The headmaster must have a remarkable memory, Sir.'

Hopkins winced.

'Might I suggest, Sir – this is not meant to be rude – that you leave my name in its crossed-out state?'

'Out of the question, Taliesin!' Hopkins barked, 'Snag is, Headmaster told you to report to me, therefore Headmaster will require a resolution other than a deleted name from me.'

'Remarkably good thinking for a PE master.'

'Remarkably g – I see your point, Sir. I'll visit my doctor.'

'That's one down, two more – Daddy and doctor – to go. We think it should be Daddy next, as the outcome might preclude a visit to the doctor, and future attendance at school for that matter.'

The period of turbulent muddle took a distinct turn for the unexpected when Johannes broached the subject of Royal Air Force intentions to his father.

'WHAT?' Taliesin Senior exploded.

'I will be an officer, Dad, as it is a short-service commission I intend applying for.'

'But the RAF is a military organisation designed to deliver death before that final solution is reciprocated by the enemy, imaginary or otherwise.'

'Daddy's been reading too many war histories.'

'That's only in wartime, Dad.'

'It's the potential mission of dealing death that I am talking about!' his father continued to roar.

'Daddy's not talking, he's roaring.'

'But they pay a salary from the first day, Dad,' Johannes bargained.

'Pay a salary?' the voice moderated and steam retracted.

'Why didn't we plea-bargain the salary thing straight away?'

'Yes, and I can't afford to go to university, so it's a better option.'

'Don't bring the I-can't-afford-to-go-to-university into it,' the roar resumed, 'fact is your academic achievements are so dismal that entry to university is out of the question. Besides, that nosey crowd down at county hall are not getting any of my financial details under the pretext of deliberating over a grant application for my son, and that's that!'

That indeed was where Johannes's father left the subject. Clearly, being paid a salary from day one was a clincher. Money was so short at Troed-yr-Henrhiw Farm that even conscientious objector principles were brushed aside when it came to an opportunity to avoid financial declarations to county hall officers, with the bonus of one less mouth to feed. Johannes could hardly believe his good fortune.

'Phew! That's two down, one to go.'

Upon presenting his sweaty rash-infested feet to the family doctor, with the aroma of fetid cheese filling the surgery and no doubt squeezing itself under the door into the crowded waiting room, Johannes was surprised by the speed at which both a prescription for an anti-fungal solution and a medical certificate excusing him from PE for the remainder of the summer term were thrust into his hand.

'Your feet have a propensity to sweat excessively, Johannes. Perhaps if you were to wear socks they would help absorb perspiration, thus alleviating its acidic tendency to scald the mucus between your toes that provides the ideal breeding ground for tinea pedis. Read the instructions carefully and make sure you abide by them. Avoid walking barefoot at home otherwise you will contaminate the rest of your family. I disagree with this modern youth affectation abandoning the wearing of socks, as good wholesome wool is a proven absorbent of perspiration –'

'Not wearing socks another one of our brainwaves, almost a touch of genius, but our socks could hardly be called socks.'

'– Are you eating properly, Johannes?'

'Yes, doctor.'

'I mean, do you eat everything your mother puts in front of you?'

'We wolf it down.'

'Yes, doctor.'

'You look a bit thin for your height to me; in fact, emaciated would be more accurate. How tall are you?'

'Six foot two in my st – in my bare feet, doctor.'

'Hmm, try eating more bulk carbohydrates. Incidentally, have you visited your dentist recently? Your halitosis is a little oppressive, Johannes.'

'Thank you, doctor.' Johannes's gratitude was not at all directed at the advice given, but for the delivery of the medical certificate, which piece of paper would go a long way to re-establishing his regime of undisturbed solitary confinement at the back of the art room.

'I cannot understand it, Taliesin, your father acceding to such an outlandish career as the Royal Air Force after maintaining you at grammar school for seven years.' Headmaster James muttered upon receiving the information from Johannes, 'I suppose we have to reluctantly accept you are a university non-entrant statistic. Incidentally, Mr Hopkins has advised me that you have produced a medical certificate confirming your condition as being tinea pedis.'

'Yes, Sir, I have to wash my feet twice a day in an anti-fungal solution that the doctor prescribed for me,' Johannes chirped blithely.

'Had you paid a visit to your family practitioner regarding the fungal malady on any previous occasion?'

'Watch out! This is a trick question: no, we're damned, yes, we're damned; avoid both.'

'Um… I, um… um.'

'Let me make it easy for you, Johannes – yes or no?'

'Oh God, thought we had resolved our problem.'

'Haven't been to the doctor since I broke my arm, Sir.'

'When would that have been, Johannes?'

'When I was nine, Sir.'

'In which case you self-assessed your tinea pedis, Johannes; this could be classified as remarkable except tinea pedis is a fairly obvious condition.'

Clearly, Headmaster James was unimpressed with Johannes and must have academically written him off the moment it became apparent the RAF venture was alive and well.

'Might I say in defence of my father's Quaker beliefs, Sir, that I persuaded him on the basis that as an officer on a short-term commission at the Royal Air Force I would be in receipt of a salary, which would excuse his having to maintain me.'

'Did you use that as a bargaining ploy against your father, Taliesin?' the headmaster asked, aghast.

'Uh-oh, the Johannes has metamorphosed into Taliesin.'

'Eventually, Sir.'

'Hmm, I'm inclined to believe you only use your brainpower when a solution is required to escape a problem your natural indolence has allowed to accumulate about you, Taliesin. Dismissed.'

'Thank you, Sir.'

'Why is it that everybody, but everybody, has to take a parting negative kick at us? Perhaps we should kick back…'

In spite of his best efforts to enlist in the Royal Air Force, Johannes landed upside down behind a haystack in a college of art: the events crucial to this dramatic change all occurred inside one week. Although his participation in the decision to pursue a career in art reached no further than a confused shrug of the shoulders, once set he allowed the notion to swell that he had skilfully orchestrated a destiny in the creative plastic arts. However, his outraged father and bewildered mother, knowing their son's propensity for believing intuition to be the console of caprice, were strongly of the view that, as art colleges ranked fairly low on the scale of Quaker moral orthodoxy, forces other than Johannes's questionable power of objective analysis had been in operation. From Johannes's perspective, a career in art detracted from his fervent but failed attempts at gaining access to the career of his first preference, the Royal Air Force.

Johannes eventually applied for entry to the Royal Air Force. A three-day selection exercise at RAF Uxbridge followed, which starkly revealed his unsuitability for entry to Her Majesty's armed forces. In an astute act of self-preservation that ensured Johannes Taliesin was kept a safe distance from their expensive equipment, the Royal Air Force hit upon a career appropriate to his temperament. In short, the RAF took the liberty of applying on Johannes's behalf for entry to a college of art for full-time study in art. As with many events in Johannes's life where he had entrusted decisions to others, the path that eventually took him to the college of art had begun with different intentions. The instance of the RAF persuading his malleable mentality vied for, and gained, pole position in his catalogue of sloppy thinking, which rendered an outcome profoundly at variance in purpose to Johannes's emotional inclination.

His decision to apply to the Royal Air Force had been based on nothing more profound than a fleeting incident when a fighter aircraft flew spectacularly low over the Taliesin farm; so low that Johannes later swore he saw the look of sublime heroics on the pilot's face. Be that very much as maybe, the fleeting moment hooked him on an ambition to fly a war machine. Johannes's application to the RAF was for a specific short-service commission in 'general utilities'. Although unaware of its implications, the title appeared simultaneously impressive and catch-all, which seemed perfectly good reason to merit ticking the box on the application form.

It will never be proven as fortunate or otherwise: Johannes

failed all practical and written tests conducted at RAF Uxbridge, the examiners having been struck by the magnitude of evidence that indicated by an awesome margin the applicant's inappropriateness for the RAF. The letter of refusal was expressed as a circular in the usual convoluted terminology of the armed services. Both the refusal and unfamiliar language floored Johannes. Although the communication advised that refusal at RAF Uxbridge meant refusal for entry to the RAF generally, Johannes engaged a special bumpkin form of denial.

'There has to be some kind of mistake; they mean Uxbridge and General Utilities. Daddy will laugh his head off, which will make Mammy cry her head off… ignore the letter and apply again.'

'Unsuccessful' was quickly confined to Uxbridge geographically and 'general utilities' specifically, the message failing to penetrate deep enough into Johannes's sporadic thinking. His inability to grasp the meaning of 'no,' even bluntly delivered as in the RAF case, frequently propelled his despairing father into becoming seriously apoplectic; but all this was to no avail.

The unexpected direction Johannes Taliesin's life took from thereon owed a good deal to his casual misunderstanding of the generality of the RAF letter of refusal. He resolutely re-applied, this time for a short-service commission in 'armaments' at RAF Fighter Command Hornchurch. The arbitrary choice of 'armaments' was meaningless in the greater turning of Johannes's reasoning but nevertheless his Quaker conscientiously objecting parents were lost for words.

'Armaments' had been chosen as a change to 'general utilities' in the hope it would imply the applicant was serious regarding the quest to become a member of the Royal Air Force; but following the RAF Uxbridge debacle the choice of department was immaterial: even catering, camouflage or mowing the airbase lawns would have been deemed too much of a liability and his application would therefore have been ruled out of the question.

Upon receiving the second application, alarm bells rang at RAF Central Command. No doubt the applicant was unable to grasp the meaning of rejection, but there was also an outside chance that he was a young communist with an ulterior motive, considering the Iron Curtain had descended across Europe only a dozen years previously. The report regarding his field tests at Uxbridge was revisited. It reminded recruitment officers that Taliesin displayed an unequivocal ineptitude in technical management; a very low register in interpersonal skills; a psychological inappropriateness never before plumbed at RAF Uxbridge Assessment Centre; and an inability to collaborate in teamwork activities exacerbated by poor grasp of group dynamics. Johannes was aware of these elements, as on his day of departure a trainee staff officer had related them with an ill-disguised smirk. Taken as a whole the report indicated beyond reasonable doubt that Taliesin's presence should never again be entertained on RAF premises, leave alone in a supersonic fighter aircraft armed with missiles. Clearly, a second aptitude test was deemed a waste of time for both parties. The Royal Air Force had decided to take no chances, and a well-tuned strategy of lateral evasion disguised as cordial public relations was implemented.

Johannes Taliesin was summoned to RAF Recruitment Headquarters Swansea for a discussion regarding general logistics and dispositional tactics. Without applying sufficient analysis of an invitation of this nature Johannes's thinking did not progress beyond the point of being thrilled that his second application was eliciting a serious response.

At Swansea he met with a friendly staff sergeant who evidently possessed a unique facility for dealing with enthusiastic rednecks where their capabilities did not match aspirations. Shortly after the interview had commenced Johannes became confused. The friendly staff sergeant talked about alternatives.

'*Alternatives?*' Inner Voice leapt awake.

Obviously Johannes had not been listening properly. To add to his confusion, he was more mesmerised by the staff sergeant's wide and waggling handlebar moustache than that which was being explained, and wondered when the subject of armaments at RAF Hornchuch would come to the fore. Then, suddenly, Johannes's confused mind was abruptly cleared of all its daydreams.

'So you see, Mr Taliesin, we at RAF Recruitment believe your abundant talents would be better put to training in art,' the staff sergeant breezed.

'*What does he mean, abundant talents better put to training in art?*' Inner Voice yelped in alarm.

To Johannes's recollection he had not been called 'Mr Taliesin' before, but that touch of larding only succeeded in coaxing him further from the point. Whatever devastating RAF decisions had been explained by the staff sergeant prior to this point had already been lost in the daydreams, but the term 'better put to training in art' woke him from his torpor.

'Um... I, um,' Johannes mumbled, 'I, um... I was hoping to go to, um... armaments at RAF Hornchurch.'

'Perhaps not RAF Hornchurch, Mr Taliesin. Actually, I happen to know from first-hand experience they are a right shower at Hornchurch,' the staff sergeant replied in the grand manner of indiscreet theatre, 'and you with your abundant talents in art would soon find armaments not to your creative sympathy, and quite probably your contemporaries there would be out of your class, old sport.'

This had the desired effect of flattering Johannes, although indeed over the years people had found this process to be never too difficult.

'*We should be suspicious of the direction this one-sided discussion is taking, or perhaps on the other hand...*'

'Do you think so?' Johannes asked, waking up, and suddenly feeling a little more positive or, perhaps, a little less negative, about the one-sided discussion. Obviously the staff sergeant's assessment of Johannes's talent in art related to the Grade E in A level art he had included in his applications to the RAF.

'Oh! Undoubtedly, Mr Taliesin,' the staff sergeant's moustache waggled its agreement.

'*We are suspicious...*'

'Um,' pondered Johannes, de-coupling his imagination from 'armaments' in Fighter Command RAF Hornchurch to attach it in turn to an imaginary college of art. This was a most alarming turn in events, of which Johannes was certainly not in charge. The full implication that his enthusiasm for fighter aircraft had been redirected in a matter of seconds to the innocuous activity of art at college would take some time to meld with his fantasies.

A short pause followed, as Johannes speculated the implications of the dramatic change to his ambitions the staff sergeant had initiated. Although Johannes was unaware of such subtleties, pausing in a discussion with an experienced RAF staff sergeant was fatal, as a pause provided the opportunity for a pounce on the prey.

'We have taken the liberty of collecting an application form on your behalf from the famous college of art up the road.'

'Um... famous college of art up the road?' Johannes fumbled; that a college of art existed up the road was revelation enough, leave alone a famous one.

'The famous Swansea College of Art, no less! Don't tell us you have not heard of the most famous college of art in the whole of Wales?' the staff sergeant feigned surprise, his handlebars theatrically lifting skyward.

Johannes had not heard of Swansea College of Art or, if he had, the name had never registered with him. He knew of the name Swansea and its geographic orientation through maps, today being the first time he had ever visited the place. Swansea College of Art, however, had never made his consciousness.

'We haven't heard of Swansea College of Art, but don't admit it to handlebars,' Inner Voice piped defensively, *'he's probably testing our general knowledge to illustrate our determination to go to RAF Hornchurch.'*

Certainly there was no fear of Johannes admitting his ignorance to the staff sergeant. One of the finer points of his rural gaucheness was to avoid admission of ignorance at all costs.

'Oh, Swansea College of Art. Hmm… of course,' he said, emulating the staff sergeant's jauntiness.

'Thought so, old sport, just a momentary lapse… we have filled in the application form on your behalf from information you had kindly furnished in previous correspondence,' the staff sergeant breezed, opening a drawer and whipping out the form. Johannes had never seen an application form to a college of art before until one appeared out of the drawer, duly completed save a signature.

Realising his application to RAF Hornchurch had been seamlessly airbrushed off the meeting's agenda, Johannes's heart sank into a bottomless pit. His future with armaments and fighter aircraft had been shot down, and would never come to pass.

'Wh… what happens now?' Johannes asked, bewildered.

'What happens now is that you check the application form to ensure we have included all of your particulars, and in the right place,' the staff sergeant replied, sliding the form across to Johannes.

Hardly giving Johannes time to read the first line, he added,

'You sign here with your normal signature,' indicating with a finger, 'as I understand it, art colleges enjoy a surfeit of pretty women, which is more than can be said for RAF Hornchurch,' the staff sergeant flourished, the while his indicating finger still hovering, ensuring no last-second wavering.

The staff sergeant's nonchalant 'as I understand it, art colleges enjoy a surfeit of pretty women' delivered to a callow country bumpkin whose first line of choice would have pretty women surrounding him for ever, was nothing less than an inspired masterstroke. Clearly the RAF staff sergeant chosen to deal with Johannes occupied a unique calibre of his own. His psychology had the desired effect: pretty women emerged with crowding enthusiasm to the point of Johannes's confused mind. Without any further hesitation he hastily signed, in case the staff sergeant should have a change of mind. From that moment Johannes displayed the air of one whose purpose in travelling down to RAF Recruitment Headquarters Swansea had always been to sign an application form for entry to Swansea College of Art. The look of relief on the RAF staff sergeant's face was akin to Colonel Hall's upon receiving the news that Sergeant Bilko was to be transferred to another camp.

'Rest assured, Mr Taliesin, RAF Recruitment Headquarters will ensure your application is delivered by hand to Swansea College of Art,' were his parting remarks, while hardly able to conceal a gloating job well done, promotion in the offing or it could have been simple relief written all over his waggling moustache.

Back at home in rural mid Wales late that night Johannes was relating the events of the day to his parents. He reached the point in the narrative explaining his decision to transfer his ambitions from armaments in the RAF to an art college –

'WHAT?' his father exploded, 'you mean the RAF *persuaded* you to change your plans! At least you would have been paid in the RAF, but an art college –' the appropriate words failed to come out. His father had read the situation accurately having witnessed Johannes's dithering followed by a precipitous switch of intent on umpteen previous occasions; then, 'it sounds to me you have been coaxed out of the fire and thrown into the iniquitous frying pan of living in a garret and mingling with guttersnipes'. Clearly, Taliesin Senior held a dismal view of art colleges, as he was comparing them unfavourably with a national institution whose existence was contrary to his pacifist beliefs.

Regardless, from thereon matters proceeded apace. A plethora of obstacles seemed to sidle into the background whereas in other circumstances any one element taken in isolation would have prevented progress: the RAF application to Swansea College of Art could have been rejected in the first instance with Johannes's academic qualifications too low in both quality and quantity; the academic session too far advanced to allow catch-up; the RAF's confidential report should have been damning. However, none of these matters dissuaded the college of art from inviting him to interview. Johannes had to repeat to himself: he had been invited to interview at Swansea College of Art!

Obviously, the advanced stage of the academic year accelerated the interview process, with all procedures undertaken in great haste. For successful catch-up Johannes depended upon many assumptions, not least being that the level of his practical ability should match that of the students already established on the cohort for which he – or rather, the RAF – had applied. Many other concerns of equal importance clambered for attention, but as he had entered one of the most exciting fluster episodes of his life, they did not remain at the point of his brain long enough for resolution. Johannes's panic regarding the impending interview and its outcome went off a scale he normally reserved for private worry, but his pride reached even beyond that stellar limit to permit being seen in such a state. His standard approach to all matters of this nature was to bury the panic and muddle through. If the muddle method proved unsuccessful then a touch of accelerated bluster rarely failed to make headway of sorts as God was clearly on his side, bestowing upon him endless future sanctuaries when pickles could be resolved.

Johannes's lack of preparation, amongst other glaringly obvious blunders, was the genesis of most of the problems that were ever to haunt him. He did not so much engage the interview and manage its hidden variables as he allowed the interview to manage him. It charged at him like an enraged bull, butting details such as appropriate intellectual planning out of his cerebral coliseum. Matters that were beyond his grasp at the time were a blur of contradicting improbabilities, such that no one item entered the arena long enough for serious consideration. The speed at which events had developed overwhelmed his otherwise placid rural muddle by introducing a strong uncertainty principle that unfortunately bore no relation to science.

The occasion was the first time Johannes became fully aware in living perpetrations that the road to hell was paved with other persons' intentions on his behalf: previously adult intrusions were intended to pull him back onto a straight and narrow path, but now he was on his own in an entirely new circumstance. Hailing from a social class of meagre rural alternatives, his options were limited. A haze of diminishing returns hung between the administrations of the two operating bodies, namely the RAF and Swansea College of Art. The RAF simply wished the back of an unsuitable candidate who had persisted in applications of a futile nature, while the college with best intentions wished to avoid delay in the interview process due to the advanced stage of the autumn term.

Johannes naively assumed persons other than he were responsible for important details such as fees, maintenance grant, lodgings and materials. He erroneously assumed the RAF, as the agent sponsoring his application to the college of art, would embrace all matters of infrastructure. It did not dawn until far too late the true nature of RAF interest was simply to remove his name from their recruitment register; but at that stage in his adolescence Johannes's level of meagre naivety was at despair proportions. His father was so deeply involved in fighting the vagaries of small farm existence in a seriously wet part of Wales that he gave little time to deal with such matters. When the subject was broached the night before the interview, which Johannes had assumed was ample time for decisive action on such matters, there followed the usual hullabaloo that passed as family discussion in the Taliesin household. In other words, most matters were not resolved; others went unmentioned. The collision of Johannes's unworldly naivety and his father's raging obduracy were a perfect recipe for inaction.

Left to his own devices Johannes did not have a clue regarding formal application to the Cardiganshire Granting Authority and the need to generate additional maintenance income. He was also clueless regarding the college purpose – its courses, levels, their status and outlets – and possessed no useful information regarding the nature of the course to which he – or, rather, the RAF – had applied. Belatedly, he realised the responsibility to instigate proper administrative procedures was his. It did not help that his application was out of the normal routine. A gigantic cock-up developed with Johannes struggling to regain compatible oxygen zones. The case of impressing upon his father the need to submit the appropriate grant forms to the county granting authority duly filled, signed and submitted without a moment lost perfectly illustrated Johannes's last-minute modus operandi: an ineptitude of gargantuan proportions that conspired with a poor sense of timing undermined by a sublime panic.

The elephant in the ointment was his father's disinclination to return forms that would disclose his financial business, least of all to Cardiganshire Granting Authority, many of whose members knew Taliesin of Troed-yr-Henrhiw Farm. Here lay the genesis of Johannes's weakness in eliciting a fair grant requirement. Collaboration with his father was more or less relegated to the any-other-business item of the agenda at the most accordant of times, but matters financial removed the item altogether. Being under twenty-one, communication with the granting authority was not Johannes's responsibility, even if he had at the time been aware of it.

Failing to obtain a prospectus was a serious oversight. As the RAF had procured the application form, the prospectus committed to that form most probably lay in a rubbish bin at RAF Recruitment Headquarters Swansea.

'*Prospectus?*' Inner Voice had wondered at one inspired moment, '*How can we possibly know what the RAF applied for without a prospectus?*'

Unfortunately, due to Johannes's last-minute tendency, time did not allow for a prospectus to be requested, even if he had known what to pursue. Certainly such a useful tool had not been mentioned as he signed the application form at RAF Recruitment Headquarters Swansea with a surfeit of pretty women crowding the point of his brain.

The omissions were so numerous and of such major importance individually that any normal applicant would have aborted the interview until such time that they were better prepared. But Johannes was not normal. Imbued with an enormous impulse accelerator saw him head over heels in love with the idea of being an art student just the day after the RAF meeting. Thus delay was out of the question, but in fairness delay might have removed the opportunity for an interview forever. Hindsight would demonstrate that the major omissions in planning due to his negligence and incompetence would return to haunt him, and were a major cusp in his life of meagre and struggle.

'*We are heading into an enormous mess, as time will tell,*' Inner Voice was clear, but at the time he avoided constraining his recently liberated psyche with such matters. Art college seemed so much more sophisticated than armaments at RAF Hornchurch, that he wondered why it had not occurred to him sooner.

Johannes was ever the naive optimist; these matters of major importance hardly dented his headlong charge into uncharted realms. Besides, he was already imagining himself returning home as an art student, which exciting thought transcended all considerations already relegated to any other business of the prosaic. It was therefore with a whirl of heady flux and little else that he set off by train from Aberystwyth to Swansea.

The invitation to interview requested examples of recently produced artwork. Not possessing a folio for transportation of two-dimensional work was of academic consideration only, as Johannes had left any two-dimensional work worth presenting at school six months ago. He possessed several three-dimensional clay models, however, which had been rescued from the farm rubbish tip by his mother, either as an act of far-sightedness or just Quaker conservatism for toils completed. In all probability it was the latter, as the announcement that he had been called for interview at Swansea College of Art came like a bolt from the blue to his mother. Although Johannes had dumped the pieces having belatedly awakened to their forlorn mediocrity, his mother's rescue mission was nevertheless met with eternal gratitude. The work had been produced for the A level art course at grammar school when Johannes had experienced a burst of recreational energy, his art teacher more through optimism than judgement referring to the work as expressing the zenith of Johannes's mediocre talents, but forlornly shaking his head at the non-realisation of greater truths.

To protect these delicate fired ceramic items – *Rock and Roll Group*, *Bust of a Child*, *One-legged Parrot* and so on – Johannes had requisitioned cork dust from barrels that had hitherto contained Greek grapes. He reasoned if the stuff could protect grapes that had travelled all the way from Greece, then surely it would protect ceramic models; so he had poured copious amounts of it into his snakeskin-veneered cardboard suitcase until the fragile articles were buried under its compression.

'*A singular brainwave, for once,*' Inner Voice proudly crowed, but then, '*pity we can't apply the same acumen to other matters like maintenance grants, prospectus, vital pieces of administration and other loose ends.*'

Clattering along in the Swansea-bound train gave Johannes time to reflect on the momentous occasion of attending an interview to enter a college of art. Nothing could be more different to his background of rural poverty, except of course fighter aircraft armaments in the RAF. He had yearned for several months for a position in the RAF, while consideration of a future in art was all of nine days old. His knowledge of the art world was as scant as that of the armed forces, so he decided the best policy was not to dwell on the matter.

He reflected instead on the financial and administrative chaos regarding a maintenance grant for support and lodgings, and immediately decided to shoo that idea out of his mind as well.

'*Don't go shoo-ing these matters out of mind, confront the bloody things!*'

He decided to shoo the matters out of his mind as well, as

he was enjoying the view through the window and the glorious warmth of the rattling carriage, chugging to a new adventure.

From the first hearing of Johannes's abrupt diversion from RAF to college of art his father had been adroitly opposed to the notion. Enrolling at a college of art, of all things! The idea of his son as an art student was beyond thinking about, although the son of a conscientious objector applying for a post in RAF Fighter Command had fallen into a different part of the same category of the unthinkable. From his father's point of view it appeared Johannes was exercising two extremes in order to inflame the brain, and he was beaten in trying to resolve which choice delivered the greater risk of apoplexy. In previous days, lectures poured forth from his father describing a figure eight in presentation, with repetitive phrases like 'narrow intellect,' 'stupid' and 'end up in the gutter' being regularly crossed over. Unfortunately for Johannes the arguments were indefensible.

'*The ramshackle dereliction of our squalid farmhouse takes some equalling when the threat of ending up in the gutter is preached,*' Inner Voice whinged in an attempt at self-justification, '*but for God's sake don't draw Father's attention to that anomaly in his reasoning. He would do us great damage, no doubt.*'

His father's assessment of art colleges was based upon a single sighting of a photograph adjoining a scurrilous article in *The Daily Mirror* concerning scantily clad female art students attending the notorious Chelsea Arts Ball. For Taliesin of Troed-yr-Henrhiw Farm this was evidence enough to support the leap to his lifelong conviction that art colleges were 'dens of licentious iniquity'. Upon being informed of scantily clad females at arts balls Johannes's emotions took the same pathway as with the RAF staff sergeant's remark regarding a surfeit of pretty women at art colleges, and he ineptly expressed delight, which of course succeeded in hardening his father's Quaker resolve.

Johannes's ineptitude assumed a stride yet further when he

countered with the reasonable argument that the social events of a college need not necessarily reflect its academic content, which sent his father's temper rocketing, as this reasonable argument was in danger of obstructing his father's strongly held prejudice.

'That was a blunder! We should know by now not to put facts between Father and his prejudices,' Inner Voice regretted.

Meanwhile, amidst these reflections, the train steamed into Swansea, which put an end to Johannes's self-flagellation. Compared to the squalid little poke teetering upside down behind a rotting haystack that was home, Swansea's sprawling industrial complex presented itself in utopian finery. The broad Sargasso swathes of Alexandra Road were breathtakingly grand after the weed-strewn cart track that slouched past his muddy home. He was undeservedly in another world; rampant Quaker guilt weighed heavily. It was all relative of course but in contrast to Johannes's slummy environment almost anywhere appeared as metropolitan nirvana, so Swansea was high on the list of quivering plinths.

Johannes gazed in wonder at the red brick and dressed Portland stone edifice that was the Glynn Vivian Art Gallery with its important yet solemn windows. An immense sense of secure stability seemed to emanate from the edifice. In time he would discover artists worthy of admiration in the Glynn Vivian Collection – it was never referred to as the art gallery, always as the 'Glynn Vivian' in proud tones similar to 'The Tate' or 'The Ashmolean' – artists such as Fred Janes, Ceri Richards, Evan Walters, Herman Shapiro and Joseph Herman. The gallery embraced the mists and atavism of a grander past bringing its reference through history to small admiring people of the day.

Opposite the Victorian facade of the Glynn Vivian in Alexandra Road was Swansea College of Art – the most famous art college in Wales, was the staff sergeant's sale patter. The college building was similar in age to the Glynn Vivian, sharing a similar brick and dressed Portland stone structure, but taller, built in the booming years of Victorian enterprise. Occupying the same street quadrant was the Deffett Francis Library together with the Central Police Station. He considered the relations the police must have with art students, their respective activities being in such close proximity.

Johannes gazed in the wonder of one so short on travel and experience, so long of meagre and struggle. The whole appeared to his bumpkin naivety as formidable and majestic, an image of a by-gone era oppressively apparent, filled to its edges with facade. He felt important to be visiting Swansea a second time inside one week but his euphoria was levelled by the familiar creep of intimidation, over which he had little control.

Swansea College of Art stood undamaged on the periphery of a devastated Swansea centre that had been razed to the ground by hideous Second World War bombing, almost his age ago. As the rubble had long since been cleared away, an empty landscape stretched beyond. Every quadrant was a car park, but demand was low owing to the shortage of cars. Post-war poured-concrete monstrosities were being erected in Swansea centre. It was difficult to discern the difference between Hitler's handiwork and the architectural pride of the Post-war School of Concrete Brutalism. Or at least that was how it appeared to Johannes, although his naive knowledge of architecture had not developed beyond the appreciation of farm buildings and the new block at grammar school.

'We don't possess the necessary architecturally educated eye to appreciate the intense beauty of these concrete pillboxes they call shops. Our bumpkin eye cannot make a valid judgement. Perhaps in time…' Inner Voice trailed away.

Everything about the college of art appeared massive. The faded Windsor-blue double doors were multi-panelled and exceptionally tall, curving into a Norman arch. Each panel was centred with a bolt head. All edges were rounded off, belying generations of repeated over-painting, apart from two giant ornate brass doorknobs. Johannes had seen bigger doors, but only in pictures. One half-door was open. The cause of Johannes's lingering to stare around in wonderment was to a large degree his fascination with the buildings of Alexandra Road, but a nervousness to enter the college building also played its part.

'*Better go in,*' Inner Voice nagged.

The wide tree-decked pavement alongside the college was devoid of students. This surprised Johannes as he had expected art students to be to-ing and fro-ing through the main door like cows to a milking parlour.

He entered, his nervousness swelling to the usual base panic. A broad and cavernous stone stairway rising from the entrance's wide assembly vestibule was similarly quiet. Perhaps the date was wrong after all, and the whole college was away for the day, like St David's Day at grammar school in Aberystwyth. He pressed on, lugging his heavy snakeskin number up the endless flights of stairs, higher and higher, looking for a door off. Whereas Johannes had approached the interview at RAF Recruitment Headquarters in a casual almost relaxed manner, things had gone so radically different to expectation that this time he was nervously awaiting the unexpected.

Eventually, after two mini landings and much hallowed silence he reached a larger, more accommodating, landing on which sat a bench and a magnificent replica of Michelangelo's David. He recognised the statue from pictures in a book on Michelangelo in Aberystwyth Library. A set of double doors, replicating the entrance doors in both design and colour, led off. A singular lack of directional advice added to Johannes's anxiety. He applied guesswork, never his strong point even when not in a high state of nervousness, and pushed on the half of the door that seemed most polished by hand use. It gave, stiffly.

It was during his ungainly clamber through the strongly sprung door that Johannes first noticed a new clumsiness had visited itself upon his snakeskin suitcase. The confounded thing was bulging; not the decently proportioned snakeskin number he had when setting out in the rain from home, but bulging horribly.

'God! It's bulging! How come we hadn't noticed that incumbency before?'

Consideration of the causes of his suitcase's metamorphosis from slim to heavily pregnant in the course of the journey from Aberystwyth to Swansea were quickly forgotten as he was confronted by an amazing sight in the corridor beyond.

'What about the bulging suitcase?' Inner Voice wondered, but immediately lost interest upon sighting a motley crowd of art students in the corridor,

'My God! Look at –'

Johannes's heart gave a leap into a place that was quite unfamiliar to him.

Students were lounging against the walls, lounging on benches, sprawling across the floor; they were chattering, laughing, smoking, drinking coffee. Johannes could but articulate his best country bumpkin gape at the wondrous exhibition of art students. He had never knowingly met with art students before, and now he was confronted by at least a hundred of them, trailing down an endless corridor into the dimness of the smoky haze.

'My God! We had no idea,' Inner Voice stuttered, *'who would have –?'*

The austere and silent exterior of the grand Victorian edifice contained within it a surprising collection of the excesses of the student species. Johannes gaped in wonder, having never before experienced anything like it. This was an awful lot for his limited experience to take in at one glance.

'Look how they dress! We are clean out of fashion!'

Whereas through his meagre and struggle he strove to dress up, these people dressed down.

'They're sitting on the floor. The girls –'

Whereas Johannes would sit properly on a bench – feet together, back straight – these people ignored the conventional benches and were sitting on the floor.

'The smoke, smoke everywhere –'

Whereas Johannes dared not smoke, these people belched like chimneys.

'Hair! But look at the girls!'

Whereas Johannes was forbidden to depart until his mother had clipped his hair to the contours of a pudding basin, here all the males wore their hair shoulder length –

'Just like Daddy's hair! Right, that's it, from now we let our hair grow. Look at the girls, the girls!'

Whereas back in cow dung Ruritania any display of the female body beyond approved conventions raised both eyebrows and tempers.

'Practically naked!'

Here the amount of female flesh exhibited between casually unbuttoned garments gave leave for the release of a dangerous hypertension whose precise anatomical location Johannes was in no state to identify.

'Our God!' Inner Voice squeaked a change of allegiance, *'It's too much! They must be... the RAF staff sergeant was right!'*

The corridor with its high ceiling seemed to travel on forever, but between Johannes and forever was a thick pall of smoke from the belching industrial chimneys – Balkan Sobrani, Three Nuns, Disque Bleu, de Maurier. Indeed, anything but the common Rizla roll-your-own that his father could barely afford.

The collective smell was both informative and exotic, a blending of coffee, cigarette smoke, heady perfume and Scandinavian turpentine spirit. Figuring large were the corridor's different functions: apart from buzzing egress and access, it also doubled as a gallery and coffee bar. An ethos of excited tension embraced its length. Benches hugged one side and lockers the other – faded Windsor-blue – upon which sprawled art students. Paintings hung on both sides. The coffee bar consisted of a mysterious hole-in-the-wall from which a boiler-suited arm repeatedly extended to provide eager customers with drinks.

Johannes amazed at the relative grandiosity, enthralled by the minutiae, consumed to the full the new visual experiences. His darting eye caught a graffito high up on the galleried corridor ceiling in an inaccessible place no ladder could hope to reach, reading, 'roy cant spel'.

'Roy cant spel, we ask – this is it, Swansea College of Art, the roy cant spel college of art,' Inner Voice was enchanted, but nevertheless Johannes's Quaker guilt conjured an image of his father's growling disaffection. The scene was straight from Kafka: sprawls of students decorating the floor in an imaginary courtroom of 'The Trial'. A blinding array of new sights! What a dream for a bumpkin. The staff sergeant had been so right: here was indeed a surfeit of pretty women.

One of the beautiful women stood out from the rest: she was practically naked in the shortest of dressing gowns displaying her long legs with a casual exhibitionism. Johannes presumed she must be a life model, although his limited experience had not included previous sightings of such wondrous entities. He knew of their existence from studying A level art history, but had never before seen one pouring out of an unbelievably short dressing gown.

The art students were dressed in clothes that had demanded a fine art in selecting inappropriateness. Sweaters down to their knees, leather flying-jackets, drainpipes, short skirts with non-functional patches attached. They reminded Johannes of his batty Aunt Hanna and her eccentric dressing, although the females being centuries younger looked wondrously better in their clothes. He was immediately smitten by the unusual presentation of beautiful women, and true to form, he desired the unattainable: his lusts held no feasible tenets in logic.

'*Think of it, we'll be able to sha – er, no, second thoughts, we'll fail; forget it,*' Inner Voice performed a sudden volte-face, reverting to its normal objective role and, having achieved the seamless change, proceeded to prattle about his father's distemper.

'*Perhaps Daddy's distemper is justified, Chelsea Arts Ball and all that...*'

The atmosphere was intoxicating to a bumpkin as gauche as Johannes who, just a handful of days previously, had mendaciously bluffed his knowledge of Swansea College of Art's existence to the RAF staff sergeant. Now circumstances had thrust him in a whirl into the midst of a world so very different to his narrow agricultural background. He was at the most famous art college in Wales! Wow!

Part of the intoxication was due to the students seeming so happy, a mood he had rarely experienced in rural Cardiganshire. He felt he was growing up by the second, but inwardly acknowledged the unimaginable distance to be traversed; an outsider intruding uninvited on a happy family circle, but nevertheless allowing a reckless wave of euphoria to flood his feelings. He imagined he had come upon a world for which he had long been searching. Inner Voice tempered the euphoria.

'*Don't get carried away,*' it prattled logically, '*ten to one we will not be accepted, Taliesin's Law of Cussedness and all that... atmospheres of attraction and desire possessing a half life of no time at all… cunning knack of self-destruction… well founded in many practical examples.'*

So, true to his nature of swinging moods, his heart promptly fell.

All these whizzing thoughts had occurred in the few seconds from the moment of clambering clumsily through the door. The buzzing crowd turned as one to stare at him. He was immediately recognised as a visitor, for obvious comparative reasons: pale spotty complexion, bright ginger hair styled in the rural basin crop, snakeskin suitcase possessing peculiar dimensions, orthodox Co-op clothing department sports jacket, grey flannels, non-ironed collar and tie knotted too tightly, skewed aside after the journey.

Due to the social intimacy of the college of art anyone not family was immediately classified as alien. But in their intimate security they were to a degree tolerant and friendly towards aliens. Johannes's natural timidity desired acceptance any place, and this delightful place was indubitably desirable. He stood beside the door, rearranging his features from those of gawp to a nonchalant form of squirm. A beautiful Audrey Hepburn lookalike asked him if she could help. She wore a sweater that must have been knitted with fence poles the thick wool stitches were gigantic. She was obviously not wearing a bra as a nipple protruded precociously through a knit-hole to stare absent-mindedly at the country bumpkin. This was too much for Johannes: his nerves jangled and promptly fled the scene.

In attempting to state his purpose for being there, his stutter, which he erroneously assumed had gone since the interview with Headmaster James, made an untimely reappearance.

'I-I-um, in-interv –, interv,' he stuttered in the most relaxed tone he could muster, while nursing his freshly returned handicap.

'Not now, for God's sake!' Inner Voice raged.

Johannes began to perspire.

'Int – interv –,' he stuttered.

Students in his vicinity stopped their various activities: not every day a perfect example of rural atavism walked in.

'*Bugger! The bloody stutter is back! Now of all times,*' Inner Voice, recognising the malady had returned, was beside exasperation.

Fortunately Audrey Hepburn understood, as if she were well practised in dealing with stuttering bumpkins.

'You need to see the principal's secretary; I'll show you where she is,' she said, leading the way, 'she's down the bottom end of the corridor. Where are you from?'

'Tr-Tr-um, Tr '

'Tredegar?'

'N-n –'

'Trefeglwys?'

'*For God's sake get a bloody g-grip!*'

'Troedyrhenrhiwfarmincwmbrwynonearaberystwyth,' Johannes exploded.

'Gosh,' Audrey Hepburn responded calmly, 'and we're already halfway down the corridor. That's the principal's office there,' she pointed as they passed, 'have you always talked funny?'

Johannes caught 'PRINCIPAL' set on a door.

'N-n –'

'Never mind. We had an art college social dance in the Antique Studio last night. Everyone got drunk and had a fabulous time. Ken Hendy drove his motorbike along the corridor and went down the stairs the other end. He's in hospital but Mike says he'll be out by tomorrow. He's a wag. Why is your suitcase bulging?'

'Be-because it, it –'

'Yes, it poured here as well first thing.'

Audrey Hepburn's manner was so relaxing and friendly that, by the time they had reached the office of the principal's secretary, Johannes had irreconcilably fallen in love with her. This circumstance of the heart did not help his stutter. He attempted to distract himself from the buzz by studying the artworks hanging on the walls. They were students' works, yet so classy, accomplished. Two caught his attention: graphic images *When the Rain is in the Wind* and *The Red Noise*. Johannes was enchanted by their poetry.

'Here we are,' his beautiful guide pointed to a little door tucked down a few steps off the corridor, 'good luck with your interview; you must be very brave applying so late in the term. You never told me your name,' and she skipped on her heel and was gone back up the corridor before Johannes had time to stutter a reply, no doubt relieved to have offloaded such a freak. Johannes watched her go, and was dismayed to hear her clearly say to a fellow student,

'They're interviewing some weird ones these days, dredging the barrel, it seems,' thumbing over her shoulder at Johannes.

'*Fine start, b-bloody stutter. Get a grip! That's better,*' Inner Voice was plunged with the weakness.

Such was the emptiness of Johannes's little life and the shallowness of his social provenance that he readily went to pieces when confronted by anything new, or by the objects of his fantasy and fleeting desire. His innate deprivations vied for denigrating attention with the narrowness of his academic education. A well-tuned spoiling mechanism existed between his conceptualising such circumstances and their practical manifestation, unerringly ensuring his best intentions would never come to fruition. Even his well-practised statements fell at the feet of his inarticulate expression. This handicap was abetted by his lack of planning, inappropriate transaction, social ineptitude and plain clumsiness, liabilities faithfully accompanying Johannes on arrival for interview, exacerbated by the threat his returned stutter could be worse than temporary.

So it was that a battalion of disadvantages conspired to screw up Johannes's earnest endeavours to make amends for the debacle of the RAF applying on his behalf for a studentship at Swansea College of Art.

His limited reading on the contemporaneous subject of late 1950s art colleges advised they were among the most self-centred and elitist environments in the world of higher education, where their inmates possessed an intrinsic assumption their right to receive full support: parental, institutional, governmental, financial, moral, emotional – gratis. All the elements Johannes had failed to apply for or were non-existent in his meagre and struggle. His personal flagellants were abandoned upside down behind a wet haystack on a muddy farm lost in a gloomy valley in upland Cardiganshire, where one stormy night his panhandled galleon had jumped its mooring. Little wonder Inner Voice diverted at the drop of a metaphor into parabolas of cynicism and pessimism.

But the proximity of the little door to the principal's secretary office tore him from dwelling on his innate disadvantages. Attending to the task at hand, he took a deep breath, and tapped on the door.

'Min, the door's open,' a little voice trilled from beyond.

He entered and immediately recognised from the geometry that the room had been a broom cupboard in grander days of yore. But it was now an office. The principal's secretary was busily working at a typewriter; she looked like a well-dressed sparrow. He could not negotiate his suitcase through the little door so had no alternative but to leave it on the bottom step of the short flight.

The principal's secretary asked his business. As his mental stability eventually caught up with the postulates of his imagination, Johannes slipped deeper into inferiority mode. In announcing himself, Johannes recognised that the stutter had elected itself as the spoiling mechanism of the day, at least as he best judged for the moment for, upon opening his mouth to speak, nothing but rubbish came out. The confounded stutter was a faithful companion to his inner tensions. Not to worry, it would disappear when circumstances possessed no importance.

'Yo-yo Tal-Taliesin,' he announced.

'*We said the name wrong, idiot!*' Inner Voice cringed.

'Jo-Joh-annes T-taliesin,' he repeated.

'*Huh.*'

Then, in order to re-establish conscious sanity over spoiling mechanism, he attempted to repeat the attempted correction.

'Jo-Johannes Taliesin,' he insisted, but in a louder voice.

The principal's secretary stared, blinked widely, and said something that sounded like,

'You the candidate for interview?'

Johannes did not understand a word she said owing to her unusual accent. It could have been 'You the idiot representing the RAF?'

'*Her sentence was not that long, but she trills quickly, though. Perhaps she said they laid the land waste and called it peace; or, canned idiots pour in here like rain through the flue – ah! We've got it – candidates pour through the flue.*'

Johannes fidgeted, blinked narrowly and uttered a non-committal,

'I-I-th-think s-so.'

The principal's secretary stared again, computing: obviously, she must have been well conversant with idiots pouring through her broom cupboard. Then, like all canny secretaries, decoded his fluster.

'Wait here,' she said, and like a little sparrow disappeared up the corridor, having had to first hop over Johannes's ill-dumped suitcase.

Johannes did as he was ordered, head still buzzing from the motley scene in the corridor. Presently, Miss Sparrow returned and ushered him back into the corridor, which was now empty. Audrey Hepburn had gone. Grabbing his bulging suitcase, Johannes followed the hopping back up the corridor. Passing an open studio door a few bars of what Johannes recognised as Delta blues wafted out on a sea of oil painting unguents. The magic of this new environment continued. They stopped at the principal's Windsor-blue door, which had the name, KW Hancock, ARCA, beneath the PRINCIPAL title. Windsor-blue must have been the agreed institutional colour. On being sent in by Miss Sparrow, she announced 'Applicant' from behind him, and left.

Principal KW Hancock's office was in reality a painting atelier. Clearly, it was Principal Hancock who would be interviewing him. Johannes wondered if the principal interviewed all candidates, or was it due to the late stage of the term, or was he singled out as a special case considering the RAF had been involved? Regardless, his heart gave a jump at the thought of being interviewed by the principal of all people.

How different was Principal Hancock to the staff sergeant at the RAF Recruitment Office! He was middle-aged and greying. His face was long and gaunt with a goatee beard and moustache similar to the one worn by the *Laughing Cavalier* of Frans Hals repute, except the principal's facial hair attachments were grey and no remnant of smile appeared, leave alone a laugh. He was tall and spare, almost haggard-looking, but draped in the flags of dignity. Over a Harris Tweed jacket he wore a flowing faded Windsor-blue painting smock that was covered from shoulder to hem with multicolour smudges and wipes of oil paint. It reminded Johannes of his father's clothes when he sprayed the farm implements red to the foreground accompaniment of a raging storm. In contrast to his eccentric father, the principal was calm and quiet.

In due course Johannes would learn that the principal of a college of art wielded enormous power that needed judicious despatch. He was not expected to be a Chancellor of the Exchequer or an economist or a stock market whiz kid in red braces, but an artist with gravitas, who practised his sublime profession in an atelier that tolerably doubled as an office. The butchers, bakers and candlestick-making members of the board of governors, the political chatterers of the Local Education Authority and irritants such as Her Majesty's Inspectorate were all kept at a dignified arm's length, and treated with deferential contempt. These bodies were obliged to pay tribute to the principal, never the other way round. Principal Hancock, set in the midst of his atelier, strewn with easels and canvases and works-in-progress, appeared no different to the general countenance of art college principals.

Johannes Taliesin the rural bumpkin was assaulted by a variety of visual images; beyond their general level some demanded special attention. The atelier hung with what he assumed to be Principal Hancock's paintings; the pleasant aroma of oil paint, linseed oil, fixative and Scandinavian turpentine spirit hung everywhere. The whole studio was a set piece from the neoclassical period – Ingres, David – with huge drapes, models' screens and plaster casts of classical figures. Johannes had never experienced the like before.

Two large oil paintings were works-in-progress, resting on sturdy easels set around a rostrum upon which stood a draped chair. The easels were fairly dripping with paint, fresh and unguent, their shelves loaded with huge tubes of oils in various stages of utility. A well of linseed oil clung precariously to one of the easels; many worn but clean brushes were stacked in pots. A large palette showing signs of recent cleaning hung on a side hook. Standing alongside the nearer of the paintings was a high mixing table.

The stunning quality of the paintings so shook Johannes that he momentarily forgot the purpose of his visit. He froze in wonder before them, gawping in naive enthralment. Never before had he experienced such living paintings in the act of progress.

'*Superb, stupendous! Oh our God, wish we could paint like this,*' Inner Voice despaired.

The underlying draughtsmanship secured Johannes's wonder; its form was awesome. Johannes continued to stand and stare, clutching his bulging suitcase, frozen in wonder. The further of the two paintings appeared complete. It was a half-length portrait of an elderly gentleman wearing official robes. His bucolic face possessed the smug pretentiousness of someone affecting the grandee but failing to disguise the ravages of excessive living, and Principal Hancock's observation had poked clean through the facade. One eyebrow arched and screwed above an arrogant eye; the other brow smooth, straight and serene with the eye below un-belonging and lonely, pleading of the viewer,

'Please don't be harsh in your judgement! I am pretending to be someone I am not.' Johannes could but wonder how the principal had captured such characteristics in oil paint.

'*Our God! Wait till we tell them back home...*'

And that was it. Mr Hancock's brush had not allowed the slightest detail of character to escape. His discerning eye and skilful hand had caught every visual incident that displayed the man's pretentiousness, securing them forever in oils as a testimony to his subject. This was so far beyond Johannes's ability, beyond his dreams... the brushwork simply stunned him.

At school he had read a book on John Constable, and

recognised Principal Hancock favoured the same rose madder ground used by the old master. The warm colour sparkled through here and there to exciting effect, encouraging the portrait to scintillate with life. Principal Hancock's brushstrokes were authoritative and assured, long and unhesitating in stroke. It seemed his colours were absolutely right and precisely in the right place, all related to a cool quarter of his palette; yet every passage was fulfilling its purpose. Timeless.

Johannes had spent long hours scrutinising reproductions in the school library. He recognised Titian, Rubens, Ingres and, especially, William Etty in the principal's work. Draughtsmanship skills in the portrait easily matched those of Augustus John and Russell Flint at their best.

'We resolve here and now we are going to paint with the courage and authority of Principal Hancock,' vowed Inner Voice rather recklessly.

The nearer canvas was a full-length study of the female nude. From the face he immediately recognised the model as the one pouring out of her mini dressing gown at the coffee kiosk. The study was breathtaking! What an amazing representation! The oils glistened all over the canvas with freshness and vivacity. Colours from all quarters of the palette represented flesh, hair, shadow. The lustre of the painting fairly vibrated.

'The draughtsmanship beneath the oils... could we ever draw like that? Could we ever?'

The powerful draughtsmanship was controlled beyond Johannes's imagination. What amazing versatility! Principal Hancock's brush had represented an air of provocation, of lasciviousness, the nature of the model. Johannes was stunned: a naked woman free of artificers and a crumpled old man pretending to be someone else. Johannes, lost in wonder, had still not engaged the reality that he was in the office-atelier for the purpose of an interview; instead he continued to stare from one painting to the other. But he had the gumption to recognise that he was in the company for the first time in his life of a brilliant painter in oils. The experience had a dramatic and lasting effect upon him.

In the midst of his admiration Johannes heard a calm and ice-cold voice calling him out of his dream.

'Please take a seat… take a seat.'

It was the principal, who had been patiently waiting goodness knows how long, motioning to him to sit in a chair set before his large desk. Johannes gulped, dropped his bulging suitcase and, coming back to the reality of the interview, scuttled to sit down in the paint-strewn chair.

'It's probably wet paint,' Inner Voice, as pessimistic as ever, warned.

But Johannes did not care. In fact he fairly yearned to be daubed with some of the oil paint, a token of being part of the wonderful work in Principal Hancock's atelier; anyway, as this was an art college the idea of sitting down in wet paint gave an immediate feeling of acceptance. But perhaps it was not wet, as he had been instructed to sit in the chair by the principal, and it was the only chair this side of the desk.

'I-I-th-th-think y-your paintings are g-great, S-sir,' he fumbled.

'Perhaps they are not his paintings.'

But a connection between the colours on the canvases and similar colours on the principal's painting smock put Johannes's mind at rest, at least regarding his unsolicited praise. Johannes noticed a silk handkerchief flowing out of the breast pocket of the principal's Harris Tweed jacket.

Principal Hancock did not acknowledge the clumsy compliment; instead, he began reading from a bundle of forms before him, which indicated to Johannes the interview had begun.

'We bet the damaging Report from RAF Uxbridge is included in that lot,' Inner Voice prattled.

'We have received this application form,' the principal spoke quietly in the clipped tones of well-educated English, but with undertones of dignified suffering Johannes had never before encountered, 'submitted by the Royal Air Force Recruitment Office here in Swansea, but nevertheless signed by you on the nineteenth of this month.'

At which early point the principal stopped reading and looked up at Johannes. The RAF involvement was an issue Johannes would have preferred avoiding, given the option. On the spur of the early moment he chose to wait for the principal to continue, hoping the subject would run away from the cause where the RAF had hijacked his life. Alas the principal did not continue, as clearly he was keen to determine the unusual genesis of the application, so did not detract from staring inscrutably at Johannes.

'He wants us to admit the RAF made the application, and we had no say in it. Bluff it out,' from the start this advice from Inner Voice was remarkable in its unhelpfulness.

Johannes set about a glut of mental prevarication. Was the introductory remark a question or a statement, as the principal's intonation described baffling patterns? Johannes waited.

'Well, did you sign it?' The principal asked regally.

'Aha! That's an easy question to answer safely.'

'Y-Yes, S-Sir.'

'But we must *try to stop this bloody stuttering.'*

'Why could you have not completed the form in the conventional manner?' the principal enquired, not unreasonably.

'C-c-con-conventional m-manner, S-sir?'

'Independently,' the principal helpfully tutored, still in amenable frame.

Clearly, Principal Hancock was seeking substantiation of the application form's bona fide nature. Erroneously, Johannes believed it to be of paramount importance to avoid disclosing the information the principal's line of enquiry sought, deciding the best tactic to gain success in the interview would be to obfuscate. After some moments of consideration, Johannes uttered one of his better examples of inane obfuscation.

'I-I'm not sure, S-Sir,' he blinked evasively.

There was indeed a degree of truth in Johannes's reply. His vacillation related to the 'independently' bit rather than the 'submitted by the Royal Air Force' part, but clearly the identification of his fuzziness was both lost and immaterial to Principal Hancock.

'Not sure! Good heavens, young man, then are you saying you signed under duress?'

'We gave the wrong answer.'

No doubt Johannes's reply was unsatisfactory from the principal's point of view.

'N-No, S-Sir, not exactly d-duress, but I was there to s-support a d-different application —'

The principal half-rolled his eyes, allowing the visage of dignity to momentarily slip.

'Where was there?' he asked grittily.

'The R-RAF Recruitment Office here in S-Swansea.'

'What was the different application you were supporting?'

'Oh God,' Inner Voice groaned.

'A short-s-service c-commission in armaments at R-RAF Horn-Hornchurch.'

Principal Hancock let out a deep intentional sigh and stared for what appeared to be an age at Johannes.

'Hmm. Regretfully I see,' he eventually conceded.

'There's something he doesn't like. His attitude to us reminds us of Daddy's attitude to us.'

Principal Hancock shared with Johannes's father the propensity to become impatient when having to confront needless obfuscation, reason for which was always transparent to everyone but its perpetrator. Johannes obfuscated more from mental disorganisation, grinding fear and the consequences of truth, rather than anything deliberately designed to irritate the interrogator.

'And what ideology were you intending to aggrandise in armaments at Hornchurch?'

This floored Johannes. The Royal Air Force staff sergeant at the Recruitment Office Swansea asked him questions about art. The principal of Swansea College of Art was asking him questions about armaments in the Royal Air Force. He gathered second thoughts and wondered if this was to his advantage.

'*No. We are incapable of answering questions on either subject.*'

It seemed the interview was not going well from the start. Johannes felt the urgent need to elevate his performance above the mundane clumsiness or it was goodbye to Swansea College of Art and Audrey Hepburn.

'*And all the other beautiful women.*'

So he hit upon a new tactic.

'C-Could you r-repeat the question, please?'

In any other circumstances this could be identified as a brainwave, but perhaps not in these. Principal Hancock winced, and perceptively narrowed his eyes. Generally, the principal managed a cool and kindly face, if perhaps a little inscrutable when confronting governors, HMI, aliens from another planet, those sorts of things. Now however Johannes Taliesin was a commodity that effected change in lifelong habits. Johannes could but think of the oil painting of the old man in official robes, pretentiousness exposed, but it had little to do with clumsiness. He was getting deeper into the quagmire.

'Just admit you are confused. Can't answer questions, won't admit the truth. Just admit the RAF led you by the nose. Admit it, for God's sake... growing up in a squalid little farm in rural Cardiganshire. This lot is a metropolis...' Inner Voice lectured on spuriously.

Principal Hancock altered his features to an arrangement of compassionate aloofness. It had not taken him long to identify the reason for the RAF's enthusiasm to reject Johannes Taliesin. Here before him was an astonishing calibre of stupid obfuscation that befell his luck to interview. The principal cut his losses.

'Let us start again at the beginning,' he said with a disposition of intense patience and, taking a deep breath, asked, 'How-did-it-come-about-the-Royal-Air-Force-filled-in-the-application-form-for-you?'

He spoke very slowly, emphatically, patiently, with hyphenated words, as if dictating to a young child.

'B-Because I-I had-re-re-applied-for-a-sh-short-s-service-commission-this-time-in-armaments-at-Horn-Hornchurch,' was Johannes's mimetic albeit stuttered reply.

'And?'

Johannes stared giddily, realising with a rush of embarrassment that his obfuscations had not furnished the principal with anything closely resembling enough information to satisfy the questions.

'Don't tell him you failed at Uxbridge.'

Johannes was avoiding admitting the truth. Admitting that he had failed the psychology and field tests for his original choice in 'general utilities' at RAF Uxbridge, thus highlighting the inappropriateness of an application for entry to RAF Hornchurch in 'armaments' fighter command would expose so many defects to the principal that the end of his art student daydreams would be upon him soonest.

'The r-raff office was d-different,' he declared, on a parabolic curve of evasion.

'I presume by 'raff' we are still discussing the RAF?' the principal alluded patiently.

Johannes quickly nodded, hoping speed would camouflage the stupidity of his evasive answers, and continued, 'This time it was S-Swansea; the f-first time at Ux-Ux-um-Uxbridge. I s-spent some time at Ux-Ux-Uxbr –'

'Uxbridge,' the principal patiently completed.

'Uxbridge,' Johannes said successfully, 'b-but I-I… I…' his narrative faded away. To complete the sentence required the single word 'failed'. But Johannes could not bring himself to say the word, regardless the stutter block, and strove to find an acceptable word that would supplant it. His mind was buzzing with panic and embarrassment. Inner Voice was aiding and abetting the cover-up.

'We think we are doing well, apart from the stutter and avoiding admitting the truth…'

Oblivious to the principal's patient forbearance, Johannes glanced about the atelier, searching for clues. This was a bad move. In moments of high tension he was easily sidetracked, the most recent instance being the ease with which the RAF staff sergeant flummoxed him. But Johannes famously paid no heed to lessons hard learnt. Apart from being engrossed in Principal Hancock's wonderful oil paintings, he had noticed little else.

The atelier was filled with the accoutrements of art business: racks of antique books, shelves of painting materials, old apothecary jars containing coloured liquids, brass ornaments and a wonderful Glynn Vivian poster advertising Fred Janes's portrait of Dylan Thomas.

Two tables were placed beyond the rostrum upon which sat plaster castes of hands, feet and a nose. Standing beside them was a caste of the lower half of a clapping faun, which he recognised because one stood in the art room of the grammar school. Then he became aware for the first time of a large window reaching to the high ceiling, and outside he could see the roof of the Glynn Vivian. Behind it a hill climbed precipitously with rows of terraced cottages rising higgledy-piggledy, tier upon tier, to its top. Clothes lines hung in their tiny stonewalled gardens, their washing dancing in the wind, clapping their hands with glee at Johannes's predicament. He quickly looked away and back to the principal, who was waiting with his usual face of inscrutable patience.

'Better say something pretty damn sharp.'

God! This was awful. He needed a word, a magic word that would satisfy the principal whilst simultaneously avoiding communicating any sense of failure. He thought of the word 'withdrew' but that would have been untrue. He dismissed the word 'deselect' on the grounds it was another way of admitting failure. He boldly thought of 'I decided to apply to an art institution instead, and the RAF advised Swansea College of Art was the best art college in Wales' but that could not preclude his application to RAF Hornchurch, or that the RAF had undertaken the formal process of applying on his behalf. What a pickle!

A flight of desperation took him to 'I accidentally killed the commandant's dog at RAF Uxbridge and was court-marshalled in disgrace. Although found guilty I was nevertheless treated as a hero because the dog had persistently bitten airmen and visitors alike.' There was a thin streak of truth in this, i.e. the commandant's dog had bitten Johannes, but in fairness to the dog it was self-defence. However, as the confounded stutter had returned he would have spent the rest of the day getting it out and, anyway, the elaboration was too precarious, so he decided against it.

Suddenly, amidst Johannes's scrabbling round for a suitable excuse he became aware that the principal was tapping his desk, waiting for the sentence to be completed. So Johannes pointed his brain forward in a most determined fashion to confront the dilemma but, as on most other occasions, it had little effect. As a last desperate fling he thought 'I was advised that the Thames Estuary air is bad for chests, so I promptly opted for Swansea College of Art,' but immediately recognised the flaws in this approach. This was indeed awful: 'failed' was unavoidable.

Johannes was still scratching round for a convincing phrase that would avoid using the f word when,

'Go on,' the principal firmly measured, jolting Johannes back to reality, 'we are still waiting.'

Here Johannes was caught on the horns of his psychological weaknesses: an inability to manage the consequences of telling a lie but simultaneously lacking the courage to admit the truth, while all along lacking the wit to articulate a plausible outcome. The result was almost invariably a good deal of dithering followed by an impulsive outburst. No amount of soul-searching would identify the operative moment he slipped into such muddles, as the tools of analysis were themselves the cause of his problems.

In matters such as this Johannes panicked and as usual when panicking his Quaker upbringing took over. He blurted out that which should have been admitted in the first place,

'I-I failed!'

'God! What possessed us to say the truth? That's it! Curtains!'

'At last,' the principal said with a huge sigh of relief, 'yes, we know.'

'Y-You know!' Johannes inadvertently spluttered.

'Yes, we know,' the principal repeated calmly, casually looking down at the papers before him, a look of Balthusian ennui on his gaunt face.

Johannes's immediate worry, although of no material influence on his dismal performance, was the principal's prior knowledge of the failure,

'And who are the we he persistently refers to?'

What next? A committee of academics filing into Principal Hancock's atelier and subjecting him to a cross-examination regarding his intentions in armaments? Or, heaven forbid, would he be conducted to a life-drawing studio and ordered to produce a drawing at least as professional as one by William Etty?

The confirmation dawned on Johannes, somewhat belatedly of course, that the bundle of papers before the principal contained all sorts of information other than just the application form he had signed in the RAF Recruitment Office. Amongst others, the damning report on his Uxbridge failure must lie among them. This nugget of common sense set Johannes's mind to worrying about the long list of blunders he had performed during the selection procedure at Uxbridge,

'Failure to use commodities to build an emergency bridge, sleepwalking, out of bounds in the women's quarters, wrong written answers, wrong verbal answers, levity during serious moments –'

There were so many…

Principal Hancock had achieved his objective in the most subtle of ways: to oblige the applicant to admit his failure at Uxbridge. Johannes felt relieved that the thought of having to admit failure was by far more painful than the act of admission itself. But then the principal dismayed him by returning to the RAF theme.

'Why did you persist, this time in 'armaments' of all things, if you had already failed the selection test in 'general utilities' at Uxbridge?'

'At-at that t-time I had always wanted to join the RAF,' Johannes replied, almost devoid of stutter, 'but n-not now,' he hastily added.

Johannes was proving to be a most unconvincing applicant,

and the principal was communicating his sound belief in this fact through, amongst other things, strained facial expressions.

'It appears to us the move from 'armaments' in the Royal Air Force to a studentship at a college of art is a somewhat dramatic leap to say the least, would you not agree?'

Johannes shrugged his shoulders, nodded his head and sat in silent compliance, convinced his interview had reached a stage when it was pointless proceeding.

'*Curtains,*' Inner Voice snarled, '*say goodbye to college of art.*'

But, amazingly, the principal did not seem to be drawing the interview to a close, which in the very least indicated that it was not curtains just yet. Or perhaps the principal could have been a closet masochist. Certainly, he had alighted on Johannes's weakest interview points, that art had not been remotely his first choice and the application to a college of art was a makeshift modus operandi out of an unsuccessful venture in the RAF. The application to Swansea College of Art was following a similar negative route as had those to the RAF and his new, if but just over a week old, dream to enter the world of art seemed to be fading fast.

'*This is unbearable,*' Inner Voice groaned.

'Would you not agree?' Principal Hancock repeated, to Johannes's astonishment.

Obviously, Johannes's shrug and nod had not been sufficient to communicate his agreement with the principal's observation.

'Yes, S-sir.'

'Armaments of all things.'

Whereupon the principal sighed audibly, as of one who knows a greater truth underlying the matter at hand. Obviously he was a pacifist. With Johannes's father a Tabor Quaker and conscientious objector, his mother a Hero of Conscience

Quaker and now the principal a pacifist he felt under siege by the forces of appeasement.

'Can we imagine if they all met what notes they would swap about us?'

The principal perused the papers before him and, thumbing them through, perceptively shook his head.

'Yes, indeed,' he said quietly, talking to the report, agreeing with something the RAF had written, no doubt. Whatever it was, he was not about to share it with Johannes. Then he wrote something on the application form with one of those wonderful old-fashioned dip-in-the-ink quill pens. He wrote and wrote, dipped and wrote.

Johannes could not make out what the principal was writing, as an array of obstacles stood in the way: giant sticks of charcoal for use on coarse canvas, Chinese bamboo watercolour brushes, several dry-point etching needles in an ornate jar, many vases of pencils, graphite sticks and Conte crayons, an airbrush head. So he gave up attempting to decipher the few passages of italic copperplate that were visible and decided instead to concentrate on the principal's face. Not that either of the exercises helped him: what would have been of help would be to have cleared his head in readiness for the next questions; but that was relying upon a mentality that was not in the ownership of Johannes, at least not during interviews.

The principal's face was a study in measured patience. One eyebrow slowly arched high into the forehead as his steel-blue eyes scrutinised the written notes. His mouth, surrounded by moustache and goatee beard, was arranged in a near-grimace. Johannes drew the conclusion that Principal Hancock would prefer to be finishing his wonderful painting of the nude, or unblocking a toilet, or even entertaining ten idiots from the local Nonsense College, than interviewing a galoot from the Welsh hinterland.

After writing in silence for some while, Principal Hancock gently laid his quill pen down and fixed Johannes with a cold stare. Then he spoke, calmly,

'Very well, Johannes Taliesin, given that your aspiration to study at this institution is merely the outcome of two unsuccessful attempts at joining the ranks of the Royal Air Force, I still nevertheless have to satisfy myself that your knowledge of the wider art world is at least alive and well.'

Johannes did not have a clue what was coming, but his heart began to sink all the same.

'We shall pursue the history of art for a few minutes,' the principal confirmed the nature of the wider art world he was referring to.

'Did you study the history of art at school?'

'*Oh God…*'

'Yes, S-sir, s-some.'

'Good. We will explore the extent of your limited study.'

Johannes's heart completed its sinking. At school he had never felt at ease with history of art. He had woolly memories of the neoclassicists and the French Impressionists, but preferred not to be questioned in any depth about those periods. He winced and waited.

'Let us consider a well-known generality in art history. Let me see… what in your estimation can be acclaimed as a memorable example of Renaissance painting?'

This floored Johannes; for him at that moment it was the world's worst question. He had never been able to separate Renaissance from Reformation or Baroque from Rococo with any degree of confidence and in any case had not studied these periods. At best he confused the lot with the neoclassical. Renaissance was neither here nor there in his memory banks. So, instead of admitting his confusion, Johannes hazarded a guess, but beforehand needed to attempt an elevation of his previous objectives. This no longer mattered one scrap but was in truth a diversion.

'I-I joined the RAF on a s-selection course as a sh-short s-service commissioned officer, S-Sir, not the ranks,' Johannes amazed himself his audacity.

The principal looked at him uncomprehendingly. To him ranks and short-service commissions were two facets of the same delusion, being all part of war games and killing. The expression on his gaunt face explained a complete disinterest in the differentiation.

'Go on,' he said, as if the information Johannes had given was part of the answer to his question on Renaissance painting.

The diversion had exhausted all of Johannes's alternatives: now he was up against it.

'By now we are sure he knows we don't know,' Inner Voice was most encouraging.

'Um – *C-Cupid and S-Psyche* by Canova,' Johannes blurted.

An excruciatingly painful silence followed. The principal presented his usual countenance of inscrutability. When at last a response came, Johannes's guess at a Renaissance painting had elicited a reaction that could best be described as mixed.

'Hmm,' Principal Hancock pondered calmly, rearranging his features to display timeless patience overburdened by the duty to educate those beyond the calling, 'while I agree with you Antonio Canova's *Cupid and Psyche* is a memorable work, it is unfortunately not a painting, having been carved from marble, and Canova's work and dates fall into the neoclassical period. The Renaissance predates this by a century or so.'

Johannes had been let down gently, which served to exacerbate his intense feeling of embarrassment and isolation. The principal was about to ask another question, hesitated, and then abandoned the idea altogether. He returned to writing on the application form. Again silence descended upon the office-atelier. No doubt the principal was amassing evidence that would justify an unsuccessful application.

Looking up, he asked, 'Have you brought along any examples of work?'

Johannes was greatly relieved the subject of art history was finished with, but the prospect of showing his suitcase-load of mediocrity failed to sustain the relief.

'Y-yes, S-sir,' he said in a voice riven with apprehension.

'Where are they?'

'Here, in my s-suit- in my s-suitcase.'

The principal frowned.

'Very well, though a somewhat unorthodox mode of transportation, let us see them. Place your suitcase on that stand.'

He indicated the stand near the painting-in-progress nude. In fact, the stand was perilously close to the painting-in-progress. Johannes's heart sank further.

'*He intends comparing our work with his superb life study in oils.*'

Once he had balanced the bulging suitcase on the stand the principal ordered,

'Exhibit your work,' in clipped tones.

Up to the point at which Johannes was asked to exhibit his work the interview had progressed on a steady downhill trend to a circumstance Inner Voice best described as,

'*Hopeless.*'

It had reached such a lamentable low in Johannes estimation that, despite his outward optimism, he could muster no enthusiasm for a successful outcome. The only shred of hope could be gleaned from the sign that the principal had not already drawn the interview to a close. Johannes had the clear impression that the principal was exercising to the full his enormous expertise in endeavouring to extract fragments of sense from an applicant of such country bumpkin status but, notwithstanding the principal's patience and perseverance, the applicant had said nothing of academic value conducive to being accepted on a study course at Swansea College of Art.

The obfuscated evasions regarding failure at Uxbridge: awful; the switch from armaments in the RAF to art: no plausible justification; Canova's marble *Cupid and Psyche* as a Renaissance painting – in an art college of all places: blunder of the first order. Johannes's ability to respond appropriately to the challenge of the moment was, to be charitable to his meagre talents, undeveloped. He was pessimistic that the interview was not progressing at all well when suddenly matters took a dramatic turn for the worse.

The journey from Troed-yr-Henrhiw began in pouring rain. As long as Johannes could remember this meteorological fixture was normal for Wales, but especially in late November as the Taliesin Law of Cussedness guaranteed, especially if one was setting off with a parcel or satchel or a cardboard suitcase that should not under any circumstances be exposed to water. On the occasion of this interview day he and his suitcase were soaked. The rail journey from Aberystwyth to Swansea allowed drying out in a sporadic kind of way. The coal-driven train meant the passenger compartments were steam heated, alternating between unbearably hot or uncomfortably cold. No happy midway existed between these two extremes as the temperature was entirely dependent upon the engine producing excessive amounts of steam as it struggled up the inclines, or nothing at all as it freewheeled frantically down the other side.

On several occasions during the course of the journey Johannes's compartment filled with belching steam from a leak beneath the seats. This did not worry him in the least because being a wimp to the cold he was comforted by a level of tropical swamp that would send normal mortals into a faint.

He was grateful for the intervals of excessive hot steam and enjoyed the Turkish bath between the periods of Arctic cold. The soaking by rain and steaming by Turkish bath had had no effect on Johannes. But the same could not be said for his cardboard suitcase where an excess of water both liquid and gaseous imposed a profound effect on the absorptive nature of its cork content, which in turn exerted undesired dynamics on the exterior form. Walking from the central station to Swansea College of Art, Johannes had from time to time been a little concerned about the morphological metamorphosis of his cardboard snakeskin suitcase, but being bowled along by the many new sights he had not given the matter much thought. Not much serious thought that is until the moment of opening it in Principal Hancock's office-atelier on the stand next to his painting-in-progress of a nude.

The suitcase bulged to such a horrible dimension that it contradicted steady seating on the stand. Johannes's head swam as the cause of the swelling dawned. His discomfort was exacerbated when he noticed the paper snakeskin had begun to peel off the cardboard. At this vital moment the idiosyncrasies of cardboard suitcase fasteners entered the act. Due to extra pressure on the lid catches, they would not release: after all, the cheap cardboard receptacle was not adorned with quality catches. These tinfoil affairs were as cheap as the cardboard they were meant to secure and were not fabricated to withstand overdoses of rainfall, hot steam and excessive pressure from within. The tension on them contrived the impression that they were locked.

Knowing the catches were not locked, as he had lost the key during the RAF Uxbridge debacle, Johannes engaged in a measure of vigorous handiwork. Conscious that the principal was waiting, he gave the catches a determined and ultimate wrench, cursing his luck the while.

'*Everything goes wrong! Story of our life, every bloody thing goes wrong!*' Inner Voice expressed with frantic exasperation.

On this occasion Inner Voice's pessimism was justified. The lid burst open with an awful explosion. The operative gremlin playing quantum entanglement with Johannes's unlucky star that day ensured the cork dust should react very badly to being drenched in the rain, cooked in a steam bath, compressed absolute by the shrinking cardboard and finally released with a jolt. Johannes had no time for a detailed analysis of the disaster at the moment of turmoil; it was too late a realisation. As the lid exploded so clouds of cork dust – effervescent neutrinos, sastrugi with a mind – billowed everywhere.

'*Bloody hell! Bloody hell! Our disasters are always major!*' Inner Voice snatched enough time to reflect.

The dust storm spread with amazing speed, heading, as cork dust will, for wet surfaces. It readily alighted on the wet surfaces of Principal Hancock's painting-in-progress of a nude, and on the paint-dripping easel; it stuck with glee to the palette, and to the wonderful 'Old Holland' paints; it jumped onto the principal's treasured brushes, and furred up the palette knives; it settled on the surface of the raw linseed oil in the well clinging perilously to the easel, leaped into the pot of pure Scandinavian turpentine spirit, interfered with the paint diluter and changed the nature of the accelerator medium. It swirled about as a cloud, momentarily dimming visibility in the atelier. Johannes felt a wave of hysteria coming on, so quickly adopted evasive action: he decided the calamity could not be happening.

Clearly the nude was the painting Principal Hancock had been working on most recently, for the cascading cork determined within a nanosecond a method for differentiating wet oils from dry oils on a canvas.

'Should try patenting this technique, bloody good method for detecting painting activities in an atelier before a murder had taken place.' Inner Voice was prime.

Time slowed down, as time does in moments such as this. The atelier went dark and whizzed round and round; bells began chiming; Johannes's head spun and he began losing his already tenuous grip on reality. At that moment he realised with searing embarrassment the last passage Principal Hancock must have been most recently working on for, in place of deft brushstrokes representing pubic hair, a neat triangle of cork dust hung fig leaf fashion. Johannes began recruiting every ounce of fortitude to fight back the hysteria.

His head swished determinedly. Inner Voice swam around in the vast lakes of his empty brain.

'Don't panic! We've been here before... nothing new in this latest of our catastrophes... perhaps it's a bad dream while broad waking... we'll wake up soon in homely Troed-yr-Henrhiw, listening to the mellifluous tones of Father and Mother quarrelling.'

The other blunders of Johannes's interview paled into insignificance: it was difficult to hold a steady handle on his latest catastrophe.

'Why us? Why us?'

Listening to his parents quarrelling would have been a pleasant alternative; even having teeth pulled would have been preferable. Johannes was in the grip of a conscious nightmare.

'S-S-Sorry, S-S-Sir, the s-suitcase must have shrunk in the rain.'

'Go on, blame the rain.'

Damaging Principal Hancock's best artist's materials was bad enough, but the heinous crime of desecrating his oil painting-in-progress was beyond atonement. Hideous bile welled up in his throat, and the growing panic gave rise to an urgent need for a toilet.

Principal Hancock stared inscrutably at the disaster, the while maintaining a dignified silence. Although Johannes's shaken disposition was hindering objective observation, he nevertheless gathered the impression that Principal Hancock was displaying signs of the onset of something seriously life threatening. The principal's gaunt face paled and a shaking hand clapped his perspiring forehead. He held the pose, muttering something, sotto voce, details of which the buzzing hysteria in Johannes's head superimposed, sounding vaguely like,

'Damned-something-or-other' or it could have been 'Damned late entry applicants' but it really sounded more like 'Damned maintenance of the group dynamic' of which Johannes could not make any sense, so he reverted to believing 'Damned late entry applicants'.

'S-Sorry, S-Sir, the s-suitcase sh-shrank,' Johannes burbled, reason having escaped what remained of his mental processes.

'Damned inconsiderate of the suitcase,' the principal clearly enunciated.

'For God's sake stay calm. Take the principal's good example. Calm. Just tidy up the damned mess. Calm,' Inner Voice commanded.

'The rain and the s-steam on the t-train I-I th-think, S-Sir.'

'Damned inconsiderate of the rain and the steam on the train,' the principal replied, superbly maintaining his dignity throughout.

Johannes had three concerns: that he would successfully fight back the hysteria; that he could control is bladder; and the principal would not suffer a stroke on account of his clumsiness. Then Inner Voice, mostly the sober partner in Johannes's varied mentality, decided to take leave of reason, having such tendency to occur during extreme crises.

'The principal is not saying that at all. What he is saying is we should patent that method of differentiating wet oil paint from the

dry rest, while admiring our innovative method of transporting rubbish.'

Ignoring both the principal and his inner clarion, Johannes compulsively embarked upon cleaning up the cork dust, scraping and scratching with his fingers – a hopeless task. He could not bring himself to look again in the direction of the cork triangle, which was far too embarrassing to face. His brain had gone numb to reason. Presently the principal joined Johannes at the epicentre of the cork storm. He looked with dismay at the cork triangle, but then turned his gaze to peruse Johannes's examples of artwork in the suitcase, now exposed due to most of the cork having fled the scene. The look of dignified dismay turned to horror. Turning swiftly on his heel, the principal returned to his desk and sat down.

'For heaven's sake come and sit down, Taliesin! Stop fussing and leave well alone before we have another incident. I have seen sufficient of your work,' he said, his enormous reservoir of patience showing signs of exhaustion. He waved a dismissive hand in the direction of the suitcase containing Johannes's models. Johannes obediently abandoned his hopeless cleaning task and sat down before the principal.

'I recall the work when I marked it for the WJEC Advanced Level award. I take it you have produced nothing new?'

'This is q-quite new, S-Sir,' Johannes stuttered, stifling the thought his mother had rescued it from the farm rubbish tip.

'Nothing in addition to your Advanced Level scripts?'

'N-No, S-Sir, I've been in the raff – um, RAF.'

'This is indeed correct. From the reports I have here your involvement with the Royal Air Force took less than one week. The Advanced Level scripts were photographed and submitted in early June. It is now the fourth week in November, time enough to produce additional work by one so keen to study at an art institution, do you agree?'

'Y-Yes, S-sir.'

Without another word the principal picked up his telephone receiver and pressed an intercom button.

'Uh-oh! He's going to call someone to escort us off the premises.'

'Could you please ask Cornelius to step into my office?' whereupon he replaced the receiver.

'Oh God, this is it!' Inner Voice had abandoned all hope.

The principal wrote some notes on Johannes's application form.

'No doubt he's writing 'the need arose to have the applicant escorted off the premises by Cornelius' in the 'for official use only' section of our application form.'

Meanwhile it took a little longer to dawn on Johannes that the principal had been the A level art examiner, who gave a grade 'E' for the work. What a memory! Quite understandably, the principal did not want to see *Bust of a Child*, *Rock and Roll Group* and *One-legged Parrot* again. At the time Johannes was unable to reconcile a grade 'E' with the mediocre quality of his work, little realising the marking system in art had more to do with peer-group orientation than with established absolute values in what must have been a low-standard cohort.

A tap-tap on the door signalled Cornelius had arrived.

'Min.'

In walked a prim middle-aged man wearing a navy blue boiler suit. Johannes recollected the arm that served drinks through the hole-in-the-wall coffee shop was also garbed in a boiler suit. Cornelius was the college caretaker and general factotum. Johannes held his breath.

'You wanted me, Sir – oh my God, Sir! What happened?'

'Yes, for a matter of some urgency, Cornelius. Could you please clean this lot up as best you can. Leave the painting.'

'Phew! We are not to be escorted off the premises yet.'

Amazingly the principal continued with the interview in the presence of the college caretaker, and Johannes resumed the better-mannered position of presenting his face to the principal.

'Oh, my God, Sir' Cornelius groaned, 'how did it happen?'

Johannes swivelled round. A look of horror clutched the caretaker's face as his eyes were adjusting to the difference between oil paint and cork. Johannes caught him staring at the cork triangle.

'The damage to your painting, Sir!'

'Yes, Cornelius, leave the painting please. Try clearing the rest as best you can,' the principal said, labouring to maintain his patience.

The look on Cornelius's face impelled a strong urge in Johannes to erupt into giggles, a sure sign his faithful hysteria was close to the surface. How he wanted to go to the toilet!

'Don't start our hysteria now of all times as we will pee our flannels.'

Except for a vague hint of irascibility, an ashen complexion and a glazed expression of disbelief at what was happening to the tranquillity and perfection of his office-atelier, the principal appeared to remain largely unperturbed. He spoke slowly and quietly, as if sipping a glass of poison. Seneca the Elder would have been proud to welcome him into the Brotherhood of Stoics. How the principal retained his presence of mind was beyond Johannes's understanding. Before him was such an opposite character to his father: Johannes was brought up in an atmosphere where the Sword of Damocles that hung day and night over his father's head was attached to the hair trigger of his utter lack of patience. Johannes mentally retracted any similarity he had assumed the principal shared with his father.

Principal Hancock took a deep breath and closed his fingertips as if in prayer.

'A student on the first year of the intermediate course has recently withdrawn for domestic reasons,' the principal began on another tack, 'Her tutors advised us of their best endeavours to dissuade her, but to no avail due to her forthcoming membership of the League of Young Mothers.'

Johannes hardly heard the words. His head was buzzing. His Inner Voice was prattling and all the colours of the rainbow were making noises in his head. He was waiting for the hammer blow. As he had not been escorted off the premises he expected the principal to whip out from a drawer an application form on Johannes's behalf for a vacancy as a coal heaver on a tramp steamer at Swansea Docks that was ready and waiting to depart that night for Patagonia.

'Unfortunately,' the principal continued, 'the student in question had great talent and potential, and would have been an asset to us in our hour of need.'

'*Hour of need? Great talent and potential; we think we get it,*' Inner Voice prattled.

Obviously, Principal Hancock's preamble was phrased to underline Johannes's lack of talent; however, he was fully aware of his shortcomings and dwelling on them at this juncture was neither here nor there. Undeniably, he was finished and this was the principal's professional method of informing him.

'Alas, the League of Young Mothers' gain is our loss. Your good fortune, Taliesin, is that the education department insists –'

The principal broke off abruptly and, looking over Johannes's shoulder, called out to Cornelius,

'Not the package, Cornelius; the package belongs to the applicant. Yes, leave that.'

Johannes swivelled round on hearing 'belongs to the applicant'. To his horror Cornelius was about to bin *One-legged Parrot*.

'Thought it was damaged beyond repair, Sir,' Cornelius muttered and, with measured reluctance and a look of utter disbelief he replaced it in the suitcase. It was the sort of look that said he binned work far superior to this every day in the studios, that sort of look.

'Anyway, what did Hancock mean by 'package'?

'– that the college maintains numbers of the group dynamic…'

'Ah! That's what he said: 'damned inconsiderate of the group dynamic,' now it makes sense.'

'… it is a complete mystery what goes on in the heads of the elected members, especially as they are furnished with the advice that taking on numbers simply to maintain quotas has a deleterious effect on standards. Personally we and the trustees have to disagree with the Ministry of Education's insistence on maintaining fixed numbers for each group –'

He interrupted his peroration yet again and, looking beyond Johannes, called to Cornelius.

'Thank you, Cornelius, leave the painting, thank you.'

'– regardless of standards, but there again…'

The principal paused, and let out a great sigh. Obviously he was troubled by a ministerial decree that had the potential for lowering standards in colleges of art. It appeared he was intent on absolving himself of responsibility for lowering the standard of Swansea College of Art in particular, but the implications were beyond Johannes's comprehension, although he was aware of his own dismal standard as an applicant. The principal seemed about to divulge further confidences regarding the Ministry of Education but after giving Johannes an odd look, thought better of it. Clearly he felt enough information had already been divulged regarding the Ministry of Education that was running the risk of swamping Johannes's intellect. He changed tack.

'We have before us reports from the Royal Air Force

Recruitment Office here in Swansea concerning your failed selection for 'general utilities' at RAF Uxbridge. It appears that the psychometric tests and character assessments have been borne out with remarkable accuracy. Perhaps the Royal Air Force should have retained your services after all and transferred you to Bomber Command, but all in all and in the interests of peace in our time we believe the right decision has been taken,' he cleared his throat and swallowed hard, 'Nevertheless, unfortunately for this institution through an application sponsored by the Royal Air Force you have presented yourself to Swansea College of Art, and are therefore a statistic. We hope it will be a salutary lesson to the Ministry of Education and their confounded group dynamic policies. We hope also it will not have a deleterious effect upon our institution.'

'*What does he mean, "deleterious effect upon our institution"? What's he getting at?*' Inner Voice quizzed.

The principal paused, held his breath and then, in a distinctly strained voice, revealed that which had pained him to arrive at.

'Very reluctantly we are obliged to accept you –'

'*ACCEPT?*'

'– Please be aware it is not due to your academic qualifications, which fall short of the institution's entry requirement; nor your tendency to obfuscate where no reasonable alternative is of material use; nor the merit of your work, which I feel bound to say is not remotely up to the required standard of entry to this institution; nor the depth of your knowledge of history of art; nor your frankness in accepting matters of fact; nor your deportment in delicate environments; nor even our compassionate consideration of your speech impediment. Quite frankly –'

'*Speech impediment?*'

'– I am at a loss to list any positives from this interview. Unfortunately our considerations are restricted to the need to maintain the group dynamic of the intermediate course. We take it you will elect to commence in the first year?'

Johannes could not believe what he was hearing, and promptly forgot the whole list of negative points.

'Accept us? Don't believe a word of it, there's got to be a catch.'

The 'very reluctantly we are obliged' did not settle into Johannes's brain for some considerable period after. At that moment he was so deeply enthralled that he omitted to answer the question, so the principal decided for him.

'You shall enrol in the first year of the intermediate course. As you have already lost an appreciable part of the term, one hardly need say the sooner you commence the better. The chances of your catching up with the peer group level, given your lack of aptitude and poor knowledge base, can charitably be deemed as indeterminate. You shall start on Monday. See my secretary regarding enrolment details,' and with a brusque swing of his chair he turned away to address Cornelius,

'Now, Cornelius, are we having any success with this calamity?'

Even if Principal Hancock had realised that the disaster inflicted on his atelier was a fleeting harbinger of things to come, he did not show it. That he held serious doubts regarding Johannes's fitness for enrolment at Swansea College of Art was never in doubt, as indeed was his strong resentment in complying with the political decree to maintain numbers regardless of talent. But little did he realise that accepting Johannes Taliesin as a full-time student would do nothing other than contribute to the grand decline of Swansea College of Art.

Johannes's delight in being accepted against all odds generated an uncontrollable rush of hot excitement; fortunately he located the toilet in time. Having reported to the principal's secretary to announce his triumph, she took a few details from him, confirmed he start on 'Monday,' and that he report to her first thing on that day. She then wished him a pleasant journey. He made his way to Swansea Central Station in a haze, and was soon chugging home.

Euphoria and pride buried the official reason for his acceptance deep in the denial paddock that housed his very best friend the ostrich. Settling down in the snug compartment on the train home Johannes took the opportunity to devise a plausible reason for his acceptance at Swansea College of Art, as the principal's 'very reluctantly we are obliged to accept you' would not be well received at home. When he was satisfied he had aggrandised carefully selected minutiae from the interview miles beyond recognition of the facts he fell into a fitful sleep.

Notwithstanding the exciting development in his otherwise calamity-ridden life Johannes's sleep was far from contented. All sorts of images and colour sounds whirled through to the rhythmic clatter of the steam engine. His normal dreams of falling and metamorphosing perspectives superimposed the day's exciting events. Johannes was a little boy who wandered in wonderment past huge buildings woven with strangely dressed people chased by bulls with goatee beards. God was there as an artist dressed in a Windsor-blue smock busily painting everyone's legs green so they could fly away. Enormous shadows from a little candle twinkled, water dropped from the sky straight through the roof, untouched bells clanged spontaneously, cats scratched at a stroke. God had thoughtfully placed these entities before him to challenge his fitness for no purpose that made sense.

'The moral is you do not easily fit with either yourself or other people,' Dream interposed.

Johannes called down a saviour of spreading wings, anything but divine, and he could fly, which marked the end of effort. Thenceforward he buried his head in clouds at the hint of a problem, so he comforted the conviction short as his attention pertained that impossibility had been conquered for the duration.

'Your first forays were climbing out of a cot,' Dream continued the narrative, 'reaching a doorknob, staring at patterns on the floor, erroneous stuff of monumental unimportance. It rendered down to a measurement of ineptitude. Your degree of attainment is nearer the dismal end of an already damned narrow group dynamic spectrum.'

'So this is where it started going wrong,' the little boy proclaimed to Dream.

'In whirling time it will take you decades to realise your grasp of colour and line will always evade your best efforts,' Dream haunted.

'I think I don't know,' the little boy responded.

'You enjoy an intimate relationship with your shortcomings,' Dream nagged.

'No, I don't,' the little boy protested.

'You possess unique assets unfortunately run through with irremediable flaws,' Dream continued, undeterred, 'your compulsive, optimistic, dysfunctional mindset is wired by a tangle of uncomprehending elves that will not join the sparkle.'

'What?'

'Although bright on sporadic calendars, your flares of invention are lost in the mechanism necessary for transferring thoughts to the road of social intercourse.'

'So this is where it started going wrong,' the little boy repeated.

'Damned inconsiderate of the group dynamic,' Dream preached, 'for in this dream, when your thoughts successfully reach the road, your navigating system fails to obtain.'

'Or perhaps here?' he sought.

'Thought so, old sport, just a momentary lapse. Blue moons bring all exciting events together, best art college in Wales, but this rare success is ruined by the useless productions they cause in others, and the events have before and after datelines attached to them...'

'Conwyl Elfed... Conwyl Elfed,' a halt-master's voice interrupted the dream. The train squeaked to a halt but Johannes knew the Halt was far from Aberystwyth so he did not open his eyes. A few doors banged, a whistle sounded and they were off again. Johannes clung to his dream...

'... As a consequence your life is beset by great calamities,' Dream continued, 'from which you are ever striving extrication.'

'Perhaps not RAF Hornchurch, Mr Taliesin.'

'No one would be more surprised than me if my plans worked for a change,' said the little boy.

'It is straining the concept of trust to believe the existential tenets of parabolic coherence in strategic planning are involved, for most occasions happen without conscious planning. You learned at an early age to suppress outward signs of incredulity, lest you betray awareness of your dire uselessness. Regardless, you take for granted that challenging the impossible is a genuflection to Creation, even though for your mundane... even though a transfer to bomber command, but peace in our time... even though for your mundane mind normalcy operates at a refreshingly primitive level... even though years later you have come to realise such single-minded thoughts at the age of four manifested the relative peak of optimum output for your cerebral capacity, since which apogee a grand decline has been in progress. In those early dawns your frail psyche engaged a delusion from which it has rarely retreated: that each ensuing quantum of knowledge would add empirically to your fortress of intellect –'

'I don't understand any more,' the little boy complained.

'– enabling, amongst other benefits, easier despatch of

conundrums. Unfortunately this fatuous delusion inflates in consort with your gathering years. Two matters are acutely apparent. One, the more knowledge you accumulate, the less you will be at ease with yourself; two, the magnitude of your delusion increases inversely by the effluxion of time. God know what is going to happen to you at Swansea College of –'

'Aberystwyth, Aberystwyth! Wake up, young man, the train doesn't go any further – oh, it's you! Don't forget your cardboard box.'

'I've been accepted!' he declared on bursting through the door at home.

'What?' his father was no academic judge of artistic skill, but he recognised rubbish when it was being married to cork in a snakeskin cardboard receptacle or, rather, when he saw it upside down on the farm tip.

'Accepted,' Johannes repeated, all signs of the speech impediment gone.

'Cripes, I can't believe it! There's got to be a catch somewhere.'

'Lucky I rescued your accidentally discarded artefacts,' his mother diplomatically contributed, proudly.

'Yes, thank you. The principal remembered marking them for the WJEC A levels. I was accepted on the basis of my potential, and for recognising works of beauty from the neoclassical period.'

'I think I smell the inklings of fantasy,' his father growled.

Upon spouting his unofficial reason for acceptance, Johannes realised he was lumbered with it.

'*That's sold your soul to the devil,*' Inner Voice growled, '*What happens if Daddy has to talk with the principal on the phone? Fees, grants, maintenance allowance, lodgings – there must be a thousand reasons he will need to talk with the principal.*'

The unofficial reason passed the test, albeit with a knitted brow of incomprehension by his mother and a scowl of deep scepticism from his father. But as the unofficial reason had not met with an explosive rejection, it had passed the first and main hurdle; so living with the lie from now on would not present too much difficulty. Johannes was readily able to adjust to his false declarations and, as usual, allowed his euphoria to carry him away into the territory of imprudence.

'The principal quoted from the RAF report, and accepted their intention to sponsor me for study at a college of art because they recognised my artistic aptitude from the start,' Johannes spouted, 'the principal, Principal Hancock, that is, said that instead of armaments at Hornchurch, bomber command would have been grateful for my services.'

That last embroider was an embellishment too far.

'WHAT?' his father exploded, 'Did you BREAK something?'

'No, I didn't break anything,' Johannes truthfully denied, albeit feebly.

'I'm not so sure! Bomber command indeed!' his father growled, 'ten to one I'll get a bill from the principal. I can't believe a son of mine is going to enrol at an art college! Holy mackerel, it's out of the fire into the frying pan, mark my words! Worse than the fire, I've just talked my friends round to your joining the RAF of all things, now I have to tell them you are going to an art college! Bring me a bowl of water, I'm going to wash my hands.'

2
Enter One Untalented Student

DURING THE HECTIC days following his interview Johannes
contacted county hall several times, either by telephone or
in person, enquiring about the feasibility of a maintenance grant.
He was ignorant of procedure, lacking in guidance and clearly
out of his depth; but these were desperate times. The ostrich had
awakened to its perils. He spoke with several different officers,
each of whom advised him that his application for maintenance
was being made at the wrong time of the academic year; that
the finance committee responsible for deciding the awards had
completed its business agenda for the current academic year and
was no longer sitting; that regardless of the aforementioned he
was under twenty-one years of age and therefore ineligible to
apply; that the responsibility for applying for financial assistance
lay with his parents. That his father had washed his hands of
Johannes's endeavours did not lend much strength to his
bargaining powers; many times Johannes felt like saying to the
officers '*You* tell my father that!' but he would never betray his
father and anyway, he was far too timid a bumpkin to defend his
predicament. Beneath everything – the gaucheness, clumsiness,
ostrich-headedness, paucity of social graces et al., Johannes
possessed an element of character that set him apart from his
fellow being – a deep-seated optimism. No, not the optimism
that bubbles superficially in crowded places, not that superficial
optimism; Johannes was devoid of that acquired facility taught
by far-sighted parents to well-heeled offspring during their early
years. Rather, Johannes's optimism was engendered through

some lonely gene: it enabled him to rely entirely upon himself while ignoring ominous signals – in this case, of financial and social disaster.

So he set off for Swansea College of Art clearly unprepared. He feared a delay in entering until the financial situation was clearer could result in the tenuous reason for his acceptance being removed – and how could he explain that he was but fulfilling an edict to maintain the group dynamic to his parents? Heading as soon as possible for occupation of the offered place in an unprepared state was the least of many evils bearing down on the gamble.

Certainly his father was glad to see the back of him, as it was one less animal demanding succour. But, on the other hand, his father had been too involved in his own social torture to assist with Johannes's great adventure. Eventually with great reluctance his father agreed to pursue the local authority for a maintenance grant – provided he had the time. This was a most unsatisfactory deal but the best Johannes could strike with his irascible and detracted father.

Having no fixed agreement regarding fees and a maintenance grant was just the start of his problems: he had no accommodation booked, nor even anywhere reserved to sleep that night, but hoped the college would assist him in the matter; the autumn term was at an advanced stage, and catch up would be a headache; he had no materials for working at a college of art; worst of all, he had very little money. This was the most inauspicious of starts for such a momentous venture. On the other hand, considering less than two weeks previously the notion had not been on the horizon, Johannes was not doing too badly. His overworked gene of optimism surged as he convinced himself it could have been worse.

Behind the foreground technical worries was the little matter of his pride. Johannes's RAF-induced application fortuitously coincided with a Ministry of Education drive to ensure higher education institutions were fulfilling the contracts of their block grant. For Swansea College of Art this meant, inter alia, the maintenance of agreed quotas on its enrolment lists. For the sake of pride Johannes swept the harsh truth of being an enrolment for nothing other than a statistical requirement out of his mind or, as the vernacular demanded, under a blank sheet of cartridge drawing paper. With the deftness of a chameleon, he had replaced the true line of his acceptance with colourful daydreams.

Thus Johannes began his late-entry studies at Swansea College of Art predicated on two false articles of daydream: that the RAF had helped him due, in their judgement, to his broad talent and unique intellect which would be better developed at a college of art; and that he had gained entry to Swansea College of Art based on his potential and academic achievements. Neither of these delusions had any basis in fact. The whirl of events had gone to the wrong part of his head: the exciting and acceptable parts went to the point of his brain, where they clung, defying any stronger winds of analysis. The rest, in true Johannes Taliesin fashion, were allowed to fall through the lacunae in his judgement. As he had grown up in an environment of dire squalor he found it necessary to resort to daydreams in order to maintain a hold on everyday sanity; but through genetics and physical deprivation insanity was always within range of consummation. Of course, in reality he had more pressing matters to think about. Regardless, his circumstances were far from normal.

In quieter reflective moments when the dust had settled Johannes accommodated his mendacity regarding inspired unofficial acceptance with growing embarrassment. Certainly his Inner Voice of Conscience had never allowed him to bury it. He became strongly aware that altruism is a condition that has no functional residence in Her Majesty's armed forces; that the assistance the RAF Recruitment Office had given Johannes was entirely due to their wishing to preserve unsullied their hard-won reputation for professionalism. The field tests at RAF Uxbridge persuaded them that Johannes possessed a narrow intellect with marginal practical ability, not fortified by an unstable personality. So the persistent applicant to the RAF was kicked gently into the long grass beside the runway. He needed to live with this truth.

From the Swansea College of Art view, the principal had made it clear to Johannes during the interview that the decision to accept him had been guided neither by talent nor potential but by the exigencies of maintaining contractually required group numbers in accordance with criteria governing the recurrent block grant. Johannes's inability to accept this and his numerous other inadequacies, together with a fervid tendency to uphold a pride that had no visible means of support, lay at the genesis of his problems. His life's road was paved with failures, but regardless he was driven by an expansive and unrealistic sense of ambition. Conversely, this ambition depended upon a narrow intellect, which frequently caused the former to end up awry, and the latter indifferent to the consequences.

In order to maintain his ambitious ideals Johannes employed an imagination that, when called upon, could quickly adopt secure perspectives beyond the reality of the moment. His head was filled with a constant conflict where the forces of reality ranged against his appeasing imagination. The former depended upon intellectual superiority fed by a moderate alertness. The latter was supported by a daydreaming facility that frequently proved inadequate to the harsh realities of the objective world. His imagination enjoyed numerical advantage and, given a free rein, would gallop about the boundless wastes of his imagination, daydreaming enemies into abstraction, relying on his objective cerebral government to lapse at the critical moment. A mental war of utter sloppiness waxed and waned through Johannes's early years. The sudden change of ambition from armaments in fighter command at Hornchurch to studying at Swansea College of Art made not the slightest dent in this regime. 'Out of the fire into the frying pan' his father's summation rang.

Mental skirmishes continued to occur with tedious regularity, but Johannes had become inured to their causal embarrassments. As sole companion of the bickering factions of his mind he possessed a surprisingly poor grasp of his mental dichotomy.

For years the inhabitants of his cerebral lands had obtained no better solution than stalemate. But there again, Johannes took for granted that being disliked by everyone he met was the condition of life, just as seeing colours when hearing sounds – everybody experienced the same. This must be life, so Johannes girded his resolution to tough the whole shebang out.

So, armed with inadequate ordnance, Johannes enrolled at Swansea College of Art. Here was the perfect environment of indiscipline and laissez-faire for his self-destruct daydreaming to gain leverage. Conditions abetted hostile engagement and the factions in Johannes's head were seduced into total war. His woolly imagination was caught in flagrante delicto as the forces of reality alighted with alacrity upon his new environment. To be fair he had from time to time made desultory efforts in bridging the gap between the world he perceived and an imagination he preferred, but these renaissances were short lived and did not amount to anything more than futile gestures at kicking a habit.

Johannes found settling into the art education regime was both easy and exciting. Initially he readily made friends, but when they realised that Johannes walked on an eccentric side of the street that marketed the dark shadows of instability, many of them moved their body and soul a sunnier distance away. Regardless of his colleagues' dispositions, Johannes quickly grew to love the art world: it filled his days and nights with swirling images of art students and abstract shapes; colour, tone and form; Classical and modern art; life drawing, pottery and sculpture; debates about wonderful movements that gripped the imagination – Dada, Nihilism, Fauvism, Futurism, post-Futurism along with the experiments being conducted by senior painting students. New ideas like 'designed obsolescence' would grip the studios and corridors in debate, sometimes coming to shouting matches and even blows between the more posy art students. It was all so exciting. Then there was the discovery of the municipal library, a huge blessing in more ways than just the availability of reading matter: a safe house in Johannes's many hours of need which he devoted to reading, reading and yet more reading.

Unfortunately, although he earnestly strove to improve, the general standard of Johannes's practical work was never better than mundane. The general level was occasionally relieved by a spectacular disaster; the only spirits that failed to dampen belonging to Johannes. His tutors were well aware of the euphemism 'group dynamic top-up' inserted by Principal Hancock in the 'for official use only' box on the interview report form, although they endeavoured never to break professional confidences by sharing this information with him. Johannes was however treated according to his statistical infill status, that is, with a deal of kindly help tempered by an askance wariness.

As an undergraduate Johannes's mentality plotted an almost indiscernible compass yaw off the course of steady study into wide stretches of uncharted ocean. Bridging the gap between cold objective curriculum and the warm yield of his imagination became increasingly difficult. He had lost the ability to reconcile the origin of the two elements, and was oblivious to their identity being attached to the same coin. Yet he continued to work prodigiously, enthusiastically, producing mountains of mediocre work, from which hope lingered on that an occasional gem would one day be found.

While residing in a make-believe world of preferment, he nevertheless took his sharp sense of perception for granted. This alone put Johannes ahead of his peers, but the qualities were of little use in a college of art that required practical manifestation of perceptivity, and in any case for Johannes they frequently seemed unsustainable. This proved disadvantageous, for the tutors' expectations that his character should match his sharp perceptive cunning placed additional expectations on his shoulders. Unfortunately his thinking processes were thwarted by unwelcome lacunae, resulting in an inability to process the information his perceptivity reaped. Squaring the two extremes of perceptive sharpness and daydreaming vagueness construed an interesting life.

Johannes transposed an attitude that had developed from his background in rural Wales to the more sophisticated environment of a college of art. This was unfortunate. He hailed from a district that was upland in farming nature, ample in falling precipitation, sparse in population, poor in road network and patchy in services. The few inhabitants walked their neighbours' land willy-nilly, helping themselves to victuals at disposal, each gladly reciprocating. Transposing this collective ownership to the environment of a college of art resulted in Johannes making unwelcome intrusions into studios not on his timetable. He felt free to roam, but few welcomed it.

Hints were beside the point with Johannes, as his upbringing had never utilised inflection as a tool of instruction. As the college of art inhabitants possessed pleasant dispositions by nature, Johannes was never advised that his wanderlust displeased them so: this resulted in their telling everyone about the cause of their irritation except the cause himself. Thus, as Johannes was a newcomer amongst seasoned old-timers, they never informed him of his uncouth habits, so his isolation grew. Frequently the dichotomy facilitated opportunities for chaos, which invariably impinged negatively on Johannes's academic studies. Tutors soon became aware that his verbal cleverness was unmatched by steadiness, while all along his work persisted in showing no great inclination to improve. He continued to confuse quality with quantity.

As his background was one of rural loneliness the art college social life presented many attractions. Soon Johannes was investing more energy in the social life than his impecunious circumstances bade, rather than resolving to return better academic results. His social escapades were often fuelled by scrumpy cider, which left him incapable of most life forces, especially producing artwork.

Notwithstanding Johannes's clumsy fit into the regime of art education, certain tutors possessed the skill to cut through the bumpkin protoplasm. Professor Griff Edwards was blessed with enormous patience allied to an ability to render complicated technicalities understandable to the most simple of minds. One day Johannes was treated to a full morning's private tuition of Griff's legendary perspective tutorials. Johannes was introduced to the relative magic of the eye level; the vanishing and distant points, and the methods employed in drawing the circle in perspective.

The mechanical simplicity of perspective as a tool opened Johannes's eyes to a drawing methodology that hitherto had evaded his best efforts. His coming late to its mechanics added to his sense of renaissance. Overnight Johannes's drawing took on a new line: ill-defined woolly smudges of self-conscious ignorance were replaced by hard lines of mathematical certainty. Johannes discovered afresh the famous perspectives of Canaletto; and the contemporaneous graphics of MC Escher. A period followed during which he produced mountains of perspective drawings, commendable in their accuracy. This was Johannes, all the way down to a line across his index finger: embracing the new enlightenment, the knowledge of perspective afforded a qualified confidence.

Architecture and human anatomy were next in line for the enlightenment treatment. Johannes's facility at drawing anatomical studies of the human skeleton joined the technical brilliance of his perspective studies, whilst his over-enthusiasm for architecture lost him friends, but that mattered not. He would quote pages of the Bannister-Fletcher tome on world architectural history in misguided attempts at impressing girls he fancied like hell. When they ran away gasping for air he naturally assumed most people were unfortunate in not being able to connect with matters of great importance, i.e. those matters beginning to occupy a more serious part of his brain.

These aspects of Johannes's work – anatomical, architectural and life studies, together with perspective – centred around one main platform: drawing. His enthusiasm for the speciality was unparalleled in the institution. But the rest of his work was woefully mediocre; tutors ruefully reflected on the heights of creativity Johannes could reach if his enthusiasm were successfully translated to the rest of his portfolio. It was not only enthusiasm that drove him, but a deep conviction that his work enjoyed pole position in the exemplars of creativity. No one succeeded in skewing Johannes from his mindset that enthusiasm and the production of massive quantities in output were no substitute for the genuine article, but a lingering hope remained with the tutors that one day this avalanche of enthusiasm and production might, just might, come good. But the Quaker work ethic drove Johannes on to wider deserts.

Beyond everything, Johannes experienced the greatest peace of mind when working in the studios specialising in life drawing. Generally, the intermediate course was a dabbler's paradise, where the enthusiast could dip into and taste different disciplines without the necessity for long-lasting conviction. Students were permitted to overstay their dip and taste in an area that gripped their enthusiasm, and so it was with life studies for Johannes.

Professor Ron Cour, the resident sculptor, called upon his great reserves of patience to spend ages demonstrating to Johannes the need for preparation, with careful designing and planning of a project, armatures properly in place, bulking firmly secured and plaster at the right consistency. But lack of patience drove Johannes to work on the final modelling process, having leaped a dozen stages in one. Sculpture was not for Johannes, only life drawing. Underlying all of the failed specialist experiments was Johannes's conviction that success would alight one day like a bird coming back to the ark. This however required mental effort, as the process was mired in simple intuition; how wrong time would prove Johannes to be.

Simultaneously he continued his experiments with scrumpy, all-night discussions and debates. As his reading list was endless, Johannes would quote chunks of Camus, Claire, Cassirer, Corso, Durrell, Kafka, Faulkner, Dylan Thomas, Spengler, Einstein, et al. When his colleagues tired of quotations he would harangue them with readings of his own poetry – work of dubious quality and unfathomable meaning. And so on into a set pattern. Tutors warned him that his forays into existential experiment would one day agglomerate into an uncontrollable disaster. Johannes contrived to fully misunderstand them.

At about this time Johannes began analysing the objects of the drawing process somewhat deeper than the course demanded. His drawing predilection was for linear expression, but as lines did not exist in nature, what was the illusion that invariably conspired to represent the form of reality? While a pure linear circle represented a ball, there were no lines on the sphere that readily presented a means by which the symbol rested in two dimensions, he reasoned. A drawn line representing the curve of a hill was on the one hand a deposit of graphite on cartridge, while simultaneously a figment of the eye and mind representing the notion of a hill. Having walked up and over the hill one could not trample over an imaginary line that had been the curve: having reached the curve, another edge would present itself further off, ad infinitum. These divisions of entity that a line represented an object other than itself or conversely, the is-ness of the line transcending the subject, became the genesis of Johannes's analysis of the concepts of symbolic form that would later surface as a more destructive entity. Meanwhile, on the intermediate course at least, his dogmatically expressed analyses served more as irritants to colleagues and tutors rather than the emergence of a darker persona.

Inexplicably, during Johannes's time on the course, regardless all the ingredients for disaster being ever present, the seemingly inevitable did not materialise. No doubt this was accounted for by the patient forbearance of his tutors, taking everything into account, together with liberal doses of good fortune that seemed to accompany his country bumpkin air when mingling in a world out of synch with all other practical elements, developmental as well as social. The cocktail of forbearance and good fortune had limited reach, however, and extrication from embarrassing situations with no more than wounded self-esteem possessed a diminishing return.

The sole redeeming element of Johannes's bulging portfolio was a collection of superbly executed drawings otherwise lost in over-production of mediocrity. The wiring that differentiated Johannes from the rest was his unswerving self-belief that the successful element eclipsed all other shortcomings. This self-delusion possessed a half-life of certainty that found Johannes on an obtuse bearing regardless it was three sheets to the wind.

3
Life Class

JOHANNES CLATTERED NOISILY through the sprung vanity door into the antique studio for morning session life class, congratulating himself that he had successfully reached his destination. Since before dawn he had been fending off the attendant horrors of a hangover following the previous night's overindulgence in his favourite tipple – scrumpy cider. The factor that won Johannes's favour for the draught rough cider tipple had nothing to do with taste, everything to do with economics – 8d a pint at the Tenby Arms on Walter Road. The sad old addicts smitten with scrumpy shakes in the snug were disconsolate company, but Johannes managed his life on the basis of any port in the impecunious storm that lay siege to the tops of his empty pockets.

Anyway, he had been disturbed since the first stages of tenuous consciousness by the pneumatic drills demolishing the apparatus of his amygdala. When confident the rest of his brain was awake the demolition artists set about his brainstem in order to intercept any messages transmitted to all points south. As soon as this task was complete the drillers cut a crooked hole in the side of his head to elicit escape that the detritus scrumpy leaves in its wake. The old scrumpy shakers wistfully long for the good old days of drilling, as they compare notes and regret the agonies that shaking had beset them. In Johannes's case the drillers were prevented from making an escape by the fortuitous blocking technique of a much-abused organ, which on more sober occasions Johannes affectionately referred to as Brain.

As quickly as the drillers opened a new hole, Brain got in the way. That moment arrived when both Brain and Johannes were praying a divorce from one another.

'*Taking a realistic view of circumstances, Brain is attached and there's no avoiding the pain,*' Inner Voice reminded in trembling tones, '*and serve us right.*'

Every searing pang and throbbing note informed Johannes of Brain's objections to indulging in draught sheep dip. Electrically operated spasms of pain spasmodically darted across as the remaining departments of Brain attempted flight from the cranial drillers.

Unwelcome stirrings in the stomach signified that communications between Brain and gut had not been chemically severed, and new adventures in the lessons of scrumpy overindulgence were beginning. Now both Brain and the rest were uniting in a rebellion against scrumpy-induced self-abuse, and resolved to persist in the lesson for some considerable time: at least for the rest of the day and maybe for the rest of his life.

'Oh God,' Johannes groaned, 'never again.'

'*We always say that, but unfortunately we are so weak we never maintain our resolutions,*' Inner Voice fumbled.

Johannes had collected a drawing board and equipment from his locker. A strong connection existed between hangovers and keys forgotten: the locker door had been subjected to the usual brute force associated with these circumstances. While applying this scientific solution to forgotten keys a thought gallantly squeezed across inflamed Brain regarding the absence of students in the normally busy corridor. It seemed Johannes was a little late; but then it was normal for everyone else to be a little late. However, he was in no fit state to give the matter any further consideration. His head throbbed.

So, Johannes staggered through the sprung vanity door into the life class atelier and curved bumping and wobbling round the privacy screens. He fully expected to see his colleagues engaged in preparation for the morning's sitting, but to his complete surprise, or as complete as it could be under the alcoholically poisoned circumstances, he was confronted by the group sitting around the rostrum in rapt attention. All prime drawing stations had been taken, not with the usual easels and donkeys, but with stools. The donkeys had been cast aside in their manger, the easels neatly stacked Bauhaus-style in the far corner beside the model's changing cubicle. The resident model Sophie was nowhere to be seen.

His noisy entry had been an unmasked interruption: the whole tutor group turned as one to stare at the latecomer. Mr Banshee in Johannes's head clarioned the befallen silence with awful foreboding. Regardless of vomiting twice in the gutter on the way from his bedsit to college and in dire need of sympathy, Johannes was instead subject to righteous staring. It was then he belatedly noticed the lecturer. Instead of the beautiful Sophie posing in one of her Friday morning positions on the rostrum, Professor Bill Price, head of painting department for the undergraduate course stood, garbed in full chocolate brown painting smock. But he was not posing; he was *lecturing*!

Crash! What was the world coming to? Being an intermediate student Johannes had never before experienced a lecture delivered by Professor Price, though college rumour had it that he was very good at delivery. But today was Friday, which meant Sophie, and in Johannes's current precarious state of health he would much sooner cast his cindered eyes over the soothing contours of Sophie's body than those of the head of undergraduate painting. On the other hand, he surely was not in a fit state to produce a sensible drawing. But that was beside the point: what had happened to Sophie?

Johannes's aching head disallowed anything other than superficial thought applied to the matter. Professor Price, frozen in lecture mode on the rostrum, stared along with the rest of the group at the cause of the interruption. They stared as if Johannes were dressed in a clown's outfit. But the cause of their interest was nothing as significant as Coco the Clown; rather, his fellow students were no doubt staring at the strange colours of Johannes's face, the palest of complexions interrupted by the greenest of freckles.

Johannes well knew his face had the knack of performing an elaboration of death mask during times of scrumpy excess. Sadly the faces turned in Johannes's direction were not exuding the sympathy such a death mask worn by someone still alive should normally elicit. Instead, he was greeted by ghostly smiles of satisfied expectation only expressed by those whose secret wishes were at hand, namely, his imminent expiration. This was the gloat of seeing a polemical misfit, rather than one's best friend, fall off a roof. Superimposing their facial arrangements of expectation were the hardly concealed features of disappointment that life had still some little way to go, although the owner of that life had entered the zone of not caring either way.

The assumption that he was only a little late was way off target. Due to an enforced pre-occupation in studying colours in the gutter, he had lost his grip on the normal passage of time. Not owning a timepiece, the exercise of timekeeping was ad hoc on a good day. This was not a good day. For the price of a few pints of scrumpy he could have afforded one at Swansea Market, but as every dedicated art student knew, life was lived through a routine of priorities, and the possession of a timepiece, unless gifted as a Christmas present, was way down the list.

Johannes was *very* late, and Professor Price's lecture had been in session for some considerable time.

'Our *clumsy hung-over interruption is outrageous,*' Inner Voice burst with indignation, taking time off from attending the emergency in the corridors of Brain, *'and it seems it is not only time on which we are losing our grip.'*

Professor Price impatiently tapped his foot on the rostrum boards. Johannes proceeded shakily to a seat, a heavy odour of vomit and scrumpy following him like a faithful dog. Colleagues surreptitiously edging away seemed to increase the ferocity of the professor's scowl. The expected eruption came from the rostrum.

'Hell's teeth, Taliesin, you never do anything by halves!' the professor roared, to the accompaniment of the group's collective snigger.

He and Professor Price had crossed swords soon after Johannes had joined the college, during his wander-into-any-farmland-studio period.

'Can we help you?' the professor had asked of the apparently lost wanderer.

'Er, no thanks, just looking.'

'Who are you?'

'Don't tell him.'

'Johannes Taliesin.'

'Huh! Why did we have to tell him?'

'Are you the late enrolment on the intermediate course?'

'Say no.'

'Yes.'

'Huh!'

The professor painted a look of astonished contempt across his face.

'Huh! We know what that look means.'

'Hmm, we've heard of you, Taliesin. Really! You have no business in this painting special studio, so we respectfully request you leave.'

'So we respectfully request we leave. Huh!' Inner Voice, hiding behind the mask of cranium, was as belligerently inscrutable as

95

always in such situations. Johannes's newfound acquaintance was not enamoured of the look of bumpkin insolence delivered by someone so fresh to the college register. 'Hell's teeth' was the professor's characteristic expletive, sometimes assisted by 'That's another thirteen grey hairs'. But on the wander-into-any-farmland-studio occasion he restricted it to 'Hell's teeth,' which seemed to prefix any comment the head of painting made to Johannes. On one occasion Professor Price entered the large intermediate studio, scouting for talent for one of his beloved painting special courses the following year. A cursory glance in the direction of Johannes's work elicited,

'Hell's teeth, Taliesin, what about the blue?' but not waiting for a reply from someone he had already mentally dismissed, the head of painting department stomped away.

On yet another occasion, when Johannes to every one's surprise and against predictions had reached the second year, Bill Price caught him chatting to a first year girl in an out-of-bounds studio.

'Hell's teeth, Taliesin, what are you doing in here?'

'Chatting up this girl of course, stupid.'

'I'm, er, I'm…'

'You are wasting this student's time as well as your own, Taliesin. This studio is out of bounds to you. You seem unable to grasp the out-of-bounds protocols at this institution. Could you please leave forthwith?'

Johannes was unable to think of the professor without the prefix 'Hell's teeth'; he was unable to think of teeth or hell without a reflex to being admonished by same professor. In the march of time, if Johannes was transgressing some college rule or other, the professor's 'Hell's teeth' prompted him into rectitude. But the war that raged between Johannes Taliesin and Professor Price ignored all references to the Geneva Convention for the treatment of prisoners or late entry country bumpkins.

Professor Bill Price was a flustering but amiable character with an enormous mop of black hair thatching his cranium. He was forever energetically charging hither and thither, regardless an excess of avoirdupois, caring deeply about the education of his charges. When in full flight his chocolate brown painting smock billowed out alarmingly, magnifying his ample form to even larger proportions. Professor Price was a Prix de Rome painting scholar. His draughtsmanship was a superb example to aspiring artists: he drew in long flowing lines with remarkable confidence, and had produced scores of elegant studies as academic references. Johannes admired Price's work but, for many reasons, the admiration was not reciprocated.

Unfortunately the professor disliked the bumpkin upstart Johannes Taliesin. To be fair, he did not dislike Johannes any more than did the rest of the academic staff, but Professor Price was certainly more honest in expressing it. From the start he had identified a knack about Johannes that irritated him to an extreme degree, but he failed to communicate with Johannes an elaboration of the offence. It was clear, though, he found Johannes's backwoods mannerisms, mawkish obduracy and the tendency to dispute anything philosophical quite witheringly unbearable. Johannes however could not take Professor Price's reprimands seriously, for no one's outbursts, admonishments or rages could match the rages of his father. As Johannes had grown up in an eccentric household under siege by permanent dispute, the people at Swansea College of Art by comparison were pleasant ducklings. Johannes was used to his father's temperament being permanently on the rim of extraordinary rage; Professor Price's thrashing at its worst appeared theatrical by comparison. Unfortunately, Johannes never entertained the notion of discussing his background with the tutors: background was something he attempted to bury without trace – a difficult project for Johannes who dragged his background baggage around with him wherever he went.

'*Thank God he's fully clothed on the rostrum,*' Inner Voice noted, '*for ten to one if he had presented himself as the life model of the day we would have vomited again, to be sure.*'

Then, as Johannes was confining his wits and stomach to the same soul, Inner Voice ventured another fusillade,

'*The next vomit will be without doubt all over him; to hell with the college regulation forbidding fraternisation or tampering with the model.*'

Although the headache and hung-over nausea was selfishly demanding Johannes's attention, he was nevertheless all too aware that he had interrupted a lecture in full flow. Endowed with an arrogance that always failed to muster civilised support, it was beyond Johannes's social aptitude to apologise for the interruption. To avoid Professor Price's indignant eye, once at his seat Johannes promptly looked down at the floorboards. In turn the floorboards stared back at him with woody dismay. All the knotholes in the floorboards were watching him, and he began feeling seriously nauseous again. A stony silence pervaded as Bill Price and probably most of his student colleagues awaited an apology, but Johannes's ignorant backwoods obstinacy dug in its heels. He soon convinced himself it was far too late to apologise once he was sitting down –

'*It should have been done upon entering.*' – as the cusp moment for good social behaviour had passed.

Following what seemed an age, with colleagues throwing furtive glances, Professor Price continued talking. He began midway in sentence, the sentence that had been snapped apart by Johannes's rude interruption. It was not what the lecturer was saying that penetrated the haze, but rather his manner of saying it. He stretched each word with righteous emphasis, all the while looking in Johannes's direction. The moment was awful and

Johannes found difficulty in concentrating, for again his rising nausea afflicted the conviction that he was about to throw up over those in his immediate vicinity. He made preparation for a hurried retracing of clattering steps, this time in the direction of the toilet.

Johannes caught Angharad looking at him, and was shocked – regardless his parlous health – to notice pure loathing in the arrangement of her face. He guessed what she was brewing: she could not understand how God could allow such a dishevelled bumpkin drunkard to draw better than she; surely a natural law existed somewhere in Mother Nature's apron pocket that determined distribution of talent commensurate with wealth? How could Mother Nature possibly allow otherwise?

Truth was the majority of the group, excepting Rees Bowen and very few others, resonated with her view. Prissy twits like Angharad had never been hungry, except self-inflicted for the express manifestation of anorexia nervosa, the new fad on the block, a condition that never elicited Johannes's sympathy. Hunger for Johannes was a permanent companion, necessarily tolerated due to circumstances, but never pursued for social games. Superiority in drawing was about the only successful line Johannes enjoyed over his peers, but his arrogance would always spoil the moment.

When it so suited Johannes he quickly forgot that hangovers were the result of undisciplined self-indulgence, that his scarce funds could have been reserved for more pressing needs, that he was wasting precious time that could more usefully be applied to studying during the fleeting years at Swansea College of Art. Johannes's errant ways were needless, but he lacked social self-discipline and the firm guidance that should have been acquired in earlier years. The attitude he heaved around was the result of many contributions agglomerated into an inconsistent superficiality at first appearance, but with an impenetrably complex personality beneath the surface. Of course, Johannes resigned his fate to his low breeding and its consequential impoverishment, but it was too easy an excuse to constantly blame his background as the cause of his weaknesses.

Inner Voice whispered in the still dark night, *'You could easily use your precious time more profitably, and forget about nursing your wounds of history.'*

But the truth remained that Angharad's look of disgust killed him. Beyond his self-inflicted discomfort he would remember the moment. He vowed to stop drinking, at least stop drinking scrumpy, which in practical terms meant stop drinking, as he could not afford any other means of achieving inebriation. Vows to abstention or not: Johannes had inherited a ridiculously low alcohol tolerance; a condition he was fast realising was severely hampering the pleasures of his epicurean tendencies. Hitherto he had assumed his parents' abstemious behaviour related to their Quaker vows, but was now learning the hard way that God can apply vows in a different guise. At the time of the life class Johannes was just beginning to realise that the grandfather of a hangover was the result of a relatively small intake of alcohol; but he had had many previous opportunities to learn the lesson. He resolved to attend to Professor Price.

'... is... to... begin... with... deep... simplicity' the professor drawled, scowling the while at Johannes his interruption. 'When *dedicated* art students arrange for a person to pose naked for their purposes of study, the resultant construct is known as life class.'

'As if we don't know that obvious bit of chatter,' Inner Voice scorned.

But the emphasis on 'dedicated' in conjunction with 'art students' hit the intended target.

'The person posing in such a life class is referred to as the model –'

'As if we didn't –'

'– No protocol determines the gender of the model for life class, male or female; each gender has enjoyed fashionable demand in history, wavering from the extreme with one to the extreme with another, with the third gender in the middle of the fashionable mincemeat –'

'Third gender in the middle of the fashionable mincemeat? What terminology is this?'

A snigger rippled across the faces of the enlightened. Johannes's disposition and last night's scrumpy forbade his seeing anything funny in the obvious.

'– and all the purposes of life study are addressed equally with all genders. If choice is a privilege then the model's gender is the tutor's preference, the students,' or the agency, or the law of unintended consequences. Otherwise the model whatever gender is determined by such circumstances as availability, or the peccadillo of the agency, or tradition, fashion... Of course, all sorts of objects both flora and fauna can be set up as a model for study, from –'

A purposefully intentioned snuffle emanating from the model's changing cubicle distracted Professor Price. So nothing had happened to Sophie; she had been in her cubicle all the time. This was a good sign to Johannes because it meant they would soon be drawing. Sophie's reliability and exceptional modelling qualities placed her services in high demand for both students and academic staff alike. Principal Hancock and Professor Price employed her regularly for professional duties.

The professor scratched his thatch, having lost his line of thought. Obviously Sophie's snuffle was related to something he had said, which in turn must have resonated with a previous conversation of theirs, but Johannes's state of health disallowed any further penetration into its meaning. But the snuffle had so distracted Professor Price that upon resuming the lecture, he set off on a different tack.

'The purposes of life class are threefold,' his live new departure boldly thrust, 'one, to better understand the structure, dynamics and form of the object; two, to develop hand, eye and mind coordination for a better control and command of the processes necessary for externalising notions and ideas of the object in a visual and plastic form; and three, for the production of an image that is required to stand scrutiny as an artefact in its own right regardless of whether its environment is re-configured. In fulfilling the aforementioned objectives, students undertake the study of the model through various two- and three-dimensional media, to better control the eye-brain-hand process as well as master the characteristics of their chosen medium.'

Between the wasteland of Johannes's awful headache and the spectra of his involuntarily exhibited digestive system, the entire scene dominated by his ignorant prejudices, a glimmer of appreciation began to flicker. Conversely, he hoped it would not flicker too much as this would upset the delicate spatial relationship between stomach and toilet.

'This crudely over-simplified introduction to life class,' the lecture continued, 'demonstrates the referential skeletal core-structure to which myriads of differing interpretations, ranging from the whimsical to the serious, are attached. Let us digress for the sake of argument, although I am sure some in our midst would argue without needing digression,' he said, looking straight at Johannes, which brought a burst of fawning chuckles from the group. It was as if Professor Price were throwing down the gauntlet inviting a duel.

'Clothes are worn for two main purposes. A subsidiary purpose eclipses the main one in times of abundance in wealth and security, namely the fashion house fatuousness that would have us believe dozens of purposes exist. But in my world there are two.'

'*He means three. Go on, tell him,*' Inner Voice urged.

Johannes was about to interject when a sudden wave of nausea changed his mind. However, he must have subconsciously signalled some action or other because Professor Price stopped talking and glowered at him.

'Hell's teeth, Taliesin, were you about to interrupt?'

'No,' he replied, regretting his failure to keep the answer shorter.

But the head of painting continued to silently glower, because he knew Johannes Taliesin much, much better, and sought to have the inevitable interruptions from him now and done with. For his part, Johannes wished the professor were somewhere else or, better still, that he himself were somewhere else.

'In my world there are two reasons,' the lecture continued. 'One is to protect the body from alien environments – variations in temperature, dangerous surfaces, solid and gaseous toxins, sharp objects, attack by insects, animals and et cetera.'

The notion of attacks by insects made Johannes wince above his hangover. 'And two, to cover parts of the body that ritual, religion and tradition deem to be the no-show dogma of the era. Thus in certain societies females are disallowed to expose any skin or hair, whereas in others the object is to expose if not all, then as much as possible. At other indulgent periods the exposure of male flesh takes precedence over female flesh, and marked changes in social tensions are reflected in the preferential swing from female to male and back again. It all boils down to Man's hypocrisy, which deems nakedness either forbidden or permissible according to whim and fancy.

'Between the extremes of nakedness and over-covering there exists an ever flexible environment of building and shifting of boundaries, developing and dissolving, but always with an eye on the audience. Whether that audience comprises of, say, paying guests at a theatre, or the Revolutionary Council of some Islamic tyranny, or the sniffy neighbours next door setting themselves up as society's guardians, or the law of the land made by the voted representatives – who will be voted out of office next election unless the upkeep of their hypothetical assumptions regarding control every man and woman yearns to keep over their neighbours – is all immaterial. Because, regardless of changing seasons, changing politics and changing cubicles, clothes come and go.'

Yet another reason unexpectedly hovered for Johannes to regret his shameful entrance and painful torpor: he found Professor Price's lecture interesting even though some of the terms were new to him. He began to feel more insignificant than usual.

'Clubs have always been fashionable,' the lecture continued, 'especially if they are able to exclude the great majority on some pretext or other. Often money alone purchases exclusivity, and members of clubs who have paid dearly to exclude often look down with scorn upon the impecunious masses craving the where with all to purchase entry. Sometimes exclusivity is necessary due to socio-political oppression. In yet other circumstances exclusivity is purchased by the currency of talent and uniqueness, grotesqueness or in-growing brains.'

'*In-growing brains?*'

'But whatever the purpose of the club there will always be a large percentage of society that is, or feels, excluded. Regrettably this has to be the case in our hypocritical society, otherwise everybody would be in the one club, and the raison d'être would have been rendered nought. We cannot have that, can we? Otherwise every Tom, Dick and Harry would barge into our life class any time of the day.'

A ripple ran through the group, with some members again

looking in Johannes's direction. Johannes caught Rees looking with sympathy, and returned a shrug.

'Thus society is riddled with clubs, official and unofficial, highbrow and lowbrow. The members are constantly scrutinising the membership rules, tightening them here and there in order to satisfy their desire to belong to a club that excludes almost 100 per cent of the rest. Groucho Marx said that he did not want to belong to a club that would have him as a member. It is a clever joke, really, because it implicitly scrutinises the hypocrisy of people who, once they are in a club, wish to believe the club is far too exclusive to admit anyone else.

'One such club is life class, the object of which is to bring together a gathering of like-minded souls who, under the pretext of drawing the naked human form, can scrutinise that naked human form of the gender of their choice. I am sure one or two of you were especially disappointed to see me standing here this morning in place of our resident model Sophie. One of your number was so shocked he looked as though he were about to be ill.'

No doubt about it, Johannes's clumsy hung-over entrance had annoyed Professor Price to the nth degree, and rightly so. The lecturer's crude spadework elicited bellows of laughter, and everyone examined the object of mirth for a reaction. Johannes stoically examined the knotholes in the floor and strove to keep the stomach department under control.

'Perhaps if we had apologised for arriving late?' Inner Voice laboured.

It was all very wearing.

'When are we going to start drawing, professor?' Manod asked. This was surprising because Manod's quiet and studious nature never previously contravened the tutor's plans.

'Very soon, Manod, very soon,' replied Professor Price.

'How soon?' Johannes asked, compulsively joining the inquisition regardless of the state of his health.

'Hell's teeth, Taliesin, is very soon not satisfactory to you?'

An uncomfortable shuffle ran through the group. Johannes and Manod exchanged glances.

Apart from the occasional lapse into the liquid world of scrumpy Johannes was thoroughly enjoying year two of the intermediate course. It was a happy time. Before first enrolling he believed – much more importantly, the principal believed – that the meagre dimensions of Johannes's talents had reached a zenith in some previous arcadia, from which they had steadily declined by the time of his interview. Fortunately, through the full-time study of art, and expert attention by the tutors, he was soon experiencing a wonderful enlightenment. It had been the personal tutorial on perspective and its related elements by Professor Griff Edwards that had the lasting effect on Johannes: he took the new-learned tool into every aspect of his studies, especially the life class. His drawing studies improved exponentially and what followed was a complete immersion in, and dedication to, the subject. Life drawing became the prime motivation to his existence and Swansea College of Art the centre of it.

Philosophically, he internalised the power of symbolic forms and the vagaries of imagery to beseech the enemy within. However, his grasp of philosophy was in reality patchy, un-joined up; but this had little effect on controlling his intemperate sorties into debate, regardless the stature of his adversary. Conversely, however, Johannes's perseverance in basic drawing techniques of architecture, anatomical studies and especially direct drawing from the human figure, were helping to overcome much of his initial ineptitude in practical dexterity. But the yawning chasm between a high personal estimation of his abilities and the more realistic certainty held by his tutors was already legendary.

Of the many topics that the study of art embraced, Johannes's favourite by far was life drawing. He preferred life drawing to any of the other modules on the intermediate course; the college policy to employ only female models was another of its great attractions. He loved drawing from the model and would often spend an excessive amount of his free time attending the open access life class studios. Devotion to life drawing, however, had a downside. Although he could draw the human female form very well – and Johannes arrogantly knew it – he was fairly mediocre in other disciplines such as painting, printmaking and three-dimensional design, much to the chagrin of the tutors, who implored him to apply some effort in transferring his life-drawing skills to the other elements of the intermediate course. After all, the purpose of the intermediate course was to provide a general résumé of skills across a wide spectrum of disciplines, and not to specialise in one area alone.

Johannes had erroneously assumed his work was of similar quality across the board, and was reluctant to take his tutors' beseeching seriously. This resulted in a loss of confidence by the staff and a generally sullen reception from most of his peers. Then, in order to put physical manifestation to his mental instability, he would veer north-east into the Tenby Arms and overindulge in a bout of scrumpy guzzling, with the consequent disruption to the following day or longer. Herein lay the reason for Professor Price's impatience with Johannes.

'Of course I shall be concluding very shortly,' the professor said, 'however, as all of you have fallen into the habit of plodding out life studies in the mistaken belief that that is the sole purpose of life class, you have omitted to apply any analytical thought to its relevant infrastructure. Also, you have become accustomed to expect a naked female model, because it is the tradition of the college to employ only females.'

'Are there any other types of nude model,' Inner Voice wondered laconically.

'The more social mores frowns upon the exposure of human flesh, the greater will become the attraction of life class. Some of the world's most untalented posers pretend a talent in life drawing, because society does not allow them to admit with impunity that they enjoy looking at the naked human form. But due to the vagaries of hypocrisy some wonderful paintings and drawings of the human form have been produced as an accidental by-product.

'If you believe the claptrap that artists wish to draw or paint or photograph or film the naked model as pure art-form then it is best to stop participating now,' he declared in more aggressive tones. 'Those who hold a healthy scepticism for such spurious human endeavours are now following me on a journey that should be both interesting and enlightening. Every Friday morning for the following ten weeks we shall look at life class from different angles – educational, artistic, medical, industrial, commercial, fashionable, social, cultural, ethical and sexual. We shall discover what astonishing complexity is developed from a simple beginning. We will analyse both the historical and actual outcomes from the simple instruction, quote, 'produce a drawing of the model'. This simple instruction will develop into statements that evoke inextricably complex socio-psychological reactions.'

Professor Price was talking in a fashion that no member of the group had previously experienced, and a shuffle of unease shivered through the life room.

'Nowhere in the theatre of human activity does the intimacy of having a body come closer to the awareness of being than in life class,' he flourished, in command of both his subject and his subjects.

For Johannes the lecture was now in full swing and, although he still wished to get on with drawing the model, he damned his stupidity in getting drunk the previous night.

'Some will be bold enough,' the lecture continued, 'to dispute the axiom with their own revered awareness of being, such as sex, inebriation and other depths of pleasure.'

In enunciating the word 'inebriation' Professor Price once again turned in Johannes's direction, the action yet again monotonously succeeded in eliciting a snigger from the group. Good heavens! Johannes enjoyed sex far more than scrumpy but, as opposed to women, scrumpy was a compliant accessory to the process. Besides, acquiring a girlfriend in his impecunious circumstances, not to mention his host of antisocial habits, was out of the question. He never admitted to his fellow rough cider shakers, but scrumpy kept him company on the shelf.

Anyway, we miss the point: what does Price mean by depths of pleasure?'

'But examples falling into this category cannot remotely replicate the sustained tension of being that is articulated in the life class. Other pleasures are fleeting, or cause actual harm to the person; but the pleasures and rewards of life study are timeless, and the outcomes can last indefinitely. In life class an unclothed person is scrutinised by one or more fully clothed persons. Generally speaking the naked person must remain motionless, whilst the student is permitted to move around. Absolute stillness is essential for the initial study, and for subsequent sittings of the same pose.'

'What's he getting at?'

'Comparative analyses can then be conducted with a measure of success. Students utter marks on a support, such as graphite on cartridge paper. The emphasis on stillness being essential is demonstrated through the outcome of work from an un-fixed pose, otherwise the marks being uttered to supposedly represent the model would conflate no logical relationship between image and model. Of course, all sorts of variations apply, but it is the purpose of these talks to support the traditional assumptions. Therefore the object of the life class exercise is to construct marks that generate the associative image of the life model.'

'*Huh! We really didn't know that!*' Inner Voice was becoming impatient.

It appeared as though Professor Price was cranking up the pace of his talk, as if he were intending to finish at a predetermined time, but was aware he still had a deal to say. Johannes was longing to get on with some life drawing, as sitting still for such an age was not improving the precarious condition of his stomach.

'Students surrounding the model are at liberty to express whatever images they please, but in such articulation a high percentage of the outcomes would render the commissioning of the model a pointless task. On the other hand, it can be argued that posing a model would stimulate ideas that may well not have come to fruition had the model not been there; thus the commissioning can be construed as being of use, as having added value as an exercise in eye-brain-hand control.'

Johannes's head swirled, for at least two reasons. The lecture floated variously from the obvious into contention and back again to the obvious. He did not know what to make of it; perhaps without the headache and nausea he would have grasped the finer points. His head throbbed obstinately; but he noticed his colleagues in the group becoming fidgety.

The lecture should have been delivered at the beginning of the first year of the course, not at this advanced stage of the second year. But what was Johannes's brain attempting to determine when at best he had made a fool of himself, and at worst had already descended into mindless time-waste? The nausea was probably psychological self-loathing, for he believed all of last night's scrumpy had already departed its host.

'The posing model stimulates the student to produce visual expressions that can be representational or otherwise,' the professor continued, 'the materials used are indifferent to the image whether representational, expressive or abstract. Upon revisiting the image following a suitable time-lapse, associations are stimulated –'

'Oh, we've had enough of this – ask him how long –'

'How long is a suitable time-lapse?' Johannes interrupted.

'A commonly sensible time-lapse,' Professor Price replied, and proceeded with his lecture, '– are stimulated that conjure memories of the production phase. This is partly what I meant by the rewards lasting indefinitely. For outsiders to the club it stimulates a composite of experiences lived, sought and received. The more –'

'Which would be the same for a photograph of a lunar landscape,' Johannes interrupted again. Clearly his hangover had got to his self-discipline, such as it was.

'– photographic-representational the images,' the professor continued, 'the more the viewer's constructive processes are by-passed, and a remembered emotional experience springs to the fore. Effectively the drawn image of the life model is a simple algorithm that invokes the viewer's imaginative pathways into constructing images from a seemingly endless array of memories, a fractal of kaleidoscopic intrusion beyond when cockle robbers came and carried off the medium to a safer studio, some of which could be of the original object of flesh that posed in the life class.'

With both headache and nausea, Johannes was drifting away from the professor's lecture. The cause was not so much the complication but through the incoherent concepts in relation to Johannes's hotchpotch curate's egg of philosophical ideas that he had gleaned from dusty tomes in the municipal library, where he perforce spent most of his weekends due to shortage of funds.

'The more representational or, one could say, pre-digested the image,' the lecture continued, 'the more readily is the mind satisfied with visual image memory the associations so stimulate; to shortcut the process in its divine psychological slipstream of quantum gravity in the environment of the rostrum where success competes vicariously with error for the distinction of parallel reactions and wave-particle duality in abstracting the greatest experience.'

'*We are lost, bloody lost.*'

'What?' Johannes enquired, to the accompaniment of tut-tutting from some of the girls who pretended that they were following the gibberish. A little cough came from Sophie's changing cubicle.

'But here exists a one-way cusp for distinction to conjoin the two-slit trick between the need in expressing plastic symbolic form on the one entanglement and the urge to lust after the model in physical mortal form on the other which, to put it bluntly, is another route to error.'

Another cough, lascivious in tone, came from the changing cubicle.

'Once the cusp has broken it is difficult to retrieve equilibrium from which distinction and error will be competing again on equal terms.'

'*We are lost, lost, and feeling sick,*' Inner Voice was fading.

Johannes was hopelessly lost. The ravages of hangover and his bumpkin incomprehension disallowed another request for elucidation. He was relying on an old trick of hanging on in there hoping an ensuing descriptor would enlighten the theorem, or at least illuminate an avenue along which his ignorance could escape with a reasonable illusion of dignity.

But through the haze of nausea and headache he was still able to focus on the collective biddable dumbness of his colleagues who simply sat there pretending to understand the whole shebang. He could not see how his friend Rees Bowen was able to keep quiet.

'When are we going to draw, Professor?' Manod politely repeated the request.

But the struggle was applying imaginary pressure to Johannes's stomach department, which unrelentingly advised him of its condition. Meanwhile the professor ignored Manod, obviously having placed him in the Johannes category.

'The insertion of the lens is occasioned by the assumption that self is by far more important than art,' the lecture continued.

'Did we pass out and miss something?'

'Pardon?' Johannes interrupted, but the professor ignored him. At least no sound of disapproval came from the group; not even a cough from the cubicle. Johannes strove to grasp a meaning. Either he or Professor Price had taken leave of their senses. Johannes's head began swimming wildly, but he clung on gallantly to avoid having to exit for another bout of vomiting.

'The primordial notion of self is inveigled into image development,' the professor raced on, 'due to a lack of critical self-analysis during the preliminary stages of the set-piece life drawing. Critical self-analysis is occasioned in the appropriate learning environment, which enables an applied spectrum of stimuli by the naked model's lasciviousness, and she knows it, to interface nature with nurture. Life class can be seen as an appropriate learning environment containing stimuli that challenge one's natural inclinations for debauchery.'

Sophie snuffled a private giggle in her cubicle.

'We think this lecture is no longer an educational experience. It is progressively drifting away from the subject of life class… moving towards its socio-psychological implications. We must say

something,' Inner Voice muttered regardless the physical health of its host.

Johannes's jaundiced point of view tangled with the conviction that it was Professor Price, rather than he, who was taking leave of his senses.

'Nothing wrong with social indiscretion,' the professor continued his lecture, 'especially when over-indulging oneself in too much scrumpy cider. Nothing right with it either! But eventually one is deserted by friends and allies alike, regardless of some passing ability in life drawing, or even when discussing the pleasantries of life class.'

Adding to the awful experience his parlous state beset, Johannes could not accept what the professor was saying. This was a blatant provocation, too much for his long-suffering easy-going nature. He had received too many barbed comments from Price; all he had done wrong was to turn up a little late with a hangover. Other students would have taken the day off.

'Other students wouldn't have a hangover,' Inner Voice interjected unhelpfully.

Johannes could stand the comments no more, and could not understand why his fellow students were taking such garble in silence; but their appeasement no longer mattered.

'Oh, come on, Professor Price!' Johannes blurted out, 'your lecture has little to do with the process of life drawing in this life class atelier any more. When can we begin drawing, as Manod has twice requested?'

Johannes's comments had the same effect as lighting a short fuse to a high explosive. Professor Bill Price detonated.

'HELL'S TEETH, JOHANNES TALIESIN!' he raged in dignified posture, 'HOW DARE YOU? WHERE ARE YOUR MANNERS? You are so tiresome! If you had respected punctuality this morning by desisting attention to alcohol last night, your attendance from the start would have given your brain half a chance to grasp the sense of my lecture. As it is you missed the all-important introduction.'

'*Ah! Hence the group compliance.*'

'Hell's teeth, there is such a malodorous ambience of vomit and cider emanating from you it has pervaded the whole of the atelier and is affecting all of us, which I can guarantee was not here before you arrived!' he emphasised the before-you-arrived bit with a stamp of his foot on the rostrum. 'The experience has needlessly added another thirteen grey hairs to my head. Why don't you do us all and yourself a favour by growing up beyond your backwoods ways?'

Good God! Professor Price was cross. This was a body blow to Johannes. Worse, he had lost scent of his own stink. How embarrassing! But instead of growing up and apologising there and then, Johannes did as always in situations such as this: he decided to ignore the advice and once again scrutinised the knotholes in the floorboards.

'*We knew the thirteen grey hairs bit would come into it sooner or later,*' Inner Voice pursued the usual denial trick.

Obviously from the sniggers and mutterings of his colleagues there was tacit support for the professor's words. Instead of facing the consequences of his actions, Taliesin the bumpkin had yet again turned to his very good friend the ostrich.

Then, his voice abruptly reverting to its amiable tones, Professor Price called out in the direction of the changing cubicle,

'We are ready for a pose now, Miss Howells,' he trilled.

Immediately Sophie made noises of arrival amidst the group's clattering about collecting their easels and boards in readiness. Feeling too fragile to draw in his favourite position, i.e. standing at an easel full frontal, Johannes dragged a donkey from its manger and carefully settled down to draw. His head pained, his stomach was churning and his pride was severely damaged.

At last, they were about to draw the model. Johannes hoped the change of operation would have a beneficial effect on his hangover. Sophie stood listening to Professor Price describing the pose he wanted. She wore her usual provocatively short dressing gown, which, due to Johannes's condition, had a deleterious effect upon his self-control. The professor took some time in describing the particular pose he wanted; after all, this was the first of a series of ten.

'Notice how her flimsy bit of filigree dressing gown contrasts with the heavy burka preferred by the other college models?' Inner Voice was attempting to change the subject of his shaming.

'That was a very sensuous talk, Bill,' Sophie whispered loud enough for everyone in the antique atelier to hear.

'It was not intended to be,' he replied in a voice equally intended for everyone to hear.

Sophie giggled as she assumed the pose.

The buzz and clatter subsided and the group settled to work. At last the atelier resembled the atmosphere Johannes so enjoyed, but on this occasion following the outburst his stomach was churning in anguish and he had to fight back the nausea. He concentrated on the task of drawing, striving to forget the embarrassment of public admonishment, hoping co-laterally that his stomach would settle. Sophie had been set in a seated pose, quarter front to Johannes, with her legs crossed at the ankles. She had decided to look straight at Johannes, wearing a Mona Lisa smile. She owned a beautiful body by any standards and had often intimated that she intended departing Swansea for London where models with her attributes could command much higher salaries. But fortunately for the students of Swansea College of Art she never left, due to her boyfriend's commitment to Swansea Rugby Union Club.

Sophie soon realised that, due to Johannes's uncomfortable predicament, her ghostly Mona Lisa smile would skewer him to the spot. No doubt, she had enjoyed Professor Price's outburst, as seemingly did most of the group. Jean Morgan discovered, presumably against her better judgement, that she was working from a donkey that was standing in close proximity to Johannes's. She began edging away, but in so doing crowded the easel next to her.

'Keep still please, Jean, you're as bad as Yoyo here,' said Eifion, who disliked being crowded.

'Well, you try sitting beside this smell, the professor is right,' she hissed.

They were discussing Johannes as if he were not there. Although his head throbbed awfully, it was the stomach department that was giving most cause for concern.

'What are you two printers talking about? Leave me alone with my hangover,' Johannes muttered.

'Oh, shut up, Johannes Taliesin,' she hissed back, 'your puerile interruptions have been as nauseating as ever.'

The word 'nauseating' resonated unfavourably with Johannes's condition. But he resolutely strove to dismiss the word from his thoughts and continued to draw in silence. Professor Price was also silent, moving back and forth behind the crescent, master of his atelier like a latter-day Jean Dominique Ingres. The atmosphere had returned to the usual form expected in life class – pencils and charcoal scraping across cartridge; clicks and rattles of equipment being taken from, and replaced to, the easel shelves; the squeak of an easel's angle being adjusted; the shuffle of a donkey – no one talking.

Normally for Johannes it was a pleasure working in life class, especially when Sophie was posing. Unfortunately, on this particular morning his fragile condition insisted on squeezing between the model and his draughtsmanship. He was experiencing a number of obstacles to a successful drawing: difficulty in fixing the drawing's fundamentals when laying-in the structure, as the proportions persisted in distorting as in a fairground mirror; difficulty in keeping his nausea at bay; and difficulty at keeping sexual thoughts under control, hardly ever previously encountered when drawing the model, which must have been the effects of last night's alcohol.

'This is due to Sophie having fixed us with a peculiar Mona Lisa,' Inner Voice reasoned, *'but it could be the bloody scrumpy.'*

At the best of times Johannes's discipline was limited except when he was seriously involved in producing an acceptable drawing. With the after-effects of alcohol, though, he possessed little discipline in any anatomical department, so immediately began entertaining lustful thoughts that should best be left out of his dysfunctional life.

'Er, perhaps not now,' was the facile advice from his inner being.

It was as if his abused brain felt at liberty to flirt with other impossibilities, as he was failing at the prime task of mapping out the figure. This was bad news; this was Johannes at his weakest. Suddenly the atelier darkened and he began perspiring, his brain having abdicated responsibility for keeping the stomach department in order. He needed fresh air. The hangover, together with Jean's 'nauseating' and his undisciplined fantasies united to trigger a primordial urge deep in the gut, and his stomach obligingly rose to the occasion. Or rather, the remaining contents of his stomach rose to the occasion, although until that moment Johannes had been convinced the remnants had been discarded in the gutter up on Mount Pleasant. The atelier darkened yet more and began swirling. An emergency was upon Johannes.

'Oh God, get out! Get out!'

He started retching as he sat on the donkey, but managed to arrest the first thrust of vomit in his gizzard. Jean recognised the signs and had begun moving away, but before she could progress her travel plans any further Johannes sprang like a cornered jackass, sending her crashing. Devoid of etiquette, he powered into Eifion like a forward before the score line, sending the student and his easel tumbling into the professor, who *just would* be standing there of all places, wouldn't he? Other innocents were sent hither and donkeys thither.

Cutting a swathe of havoc through the life class Johannes charged like a madman for the door. Gasps rang out from the group; Sophie uttered a yelp and reached for her mini dressing; Professor Price, a dishevelled heap under Eifion's easel, squawked 'Hell's tee –' but Johannes had already reached the privacy screen, which as a parting shot he sent crashing. With a flash of the sprung door he was out of the antique atelier and heading in blind panic for the toilets. Blazing blindly down the corridor, crashing through two more sets of sprung doors, swooped down a flight of stairs, sending someone carrying a large folio crashing and, his mouth filling with vomit, Johannes dived into the room of his urgent desire.

To his horror, the one cubicle at the convenience was occupied so, having no time to consider the niceties of it, vomited directly into the urinal. He continued retching and retching until nothing more was left, his head bursting. Bathed in perspiration Johannes was convinced he had finally reached the vestibule to hell.

'God, there's a bloody stink of scrumpy for you,' a voice called from inside the cubicle that Johannes, otherwise preoccupied, had forgotten was occupied.

'If it's scrumpy, odds on it's Yoyo Taliesin puking,' the voice continued.

Johannes did not answer intelligibly. His reply was constituted in the form of more retching, coughing and groaning; he felt too ill to put any other meaning to his noises.

Sounds of haste came from the toilet cubicle; the chain

pulled in further haste, and out came Ken Hendy, wag of the undergraduate painting specials.

'I KNEW IT! I BLOODY KNEW IT!' he roared, 'YOYO BLOODY TALIESIN! Who else would be puking in the urinal at this time of day? God, Taliesin, what a stink of scrumpy! A man can't have a crap in peace these days,' and he hurried out.

With his health embedded in the jaws of hell, Johannes was well beyond caring that he had offended the popularly acclaimed student leader of the painting special cohort. Instead he splashed copious amounts of cold water over his face and worked frantically to tidy himself up. He fought vainly to pull his brain together.

'Shit! We're dying. This time we're dying…'

But it was useless. Having attempted a cursory clean-up of the urinal, he turned his back on it with a 'not-my-job' attitude, worrying more about facing the bigger mess he had left behind in the life class. Johannes's lifestyle and education were at a dismal low. He was in serious trouble and if he didn't consider his position, surely Professor Price would.

'We need to consider matters; we're in a hell of a pickle; we need to consider matters…we need to consider our position…' Inner Voice harped on, and for once Johannes was of a mind to listen to his conscience.

4
Reprimand

T HE REPRIMAND JOHANNES received from Professor Price
the following Monday was expected, humiliating and
very significant. Expected, of course; humiliating, because the
professor, having called Johannes into his office, proceeded to
explain the implications of his outlandishly antisocial behaviour
in a booming voice of sufficient decibel for the whole college to
hear; significant, because prior to his meeting with Johannes,
Professor Price had decided to call in psychiatric assistance.

'Let us begin with basics and proceed both logically and
incrementally,' he boomed in firm satisfaction.

'*Oh God, he's in a magisterial mood. Incrementally, would we
believe.*'

'WHAT?'

'Didn't say anything, Sir.'

'Could have sworn – anyway, you are privileged to be attending
this institution,' the professor advised the whole of Swansea
College of Art, 'through reasons that should be abundantly clear,
you were not accepted to study at this institution on the basis of
talent. If admission had been based upon talent, you would not
have been accepted in the first instance.'

'*We thought we had successfully buried this bit of
information,*' the ostrich in Johannes's head squirmed about in
embarrassment.

'What did you say, Taliesin?'

'Nothing, Sir.'

'Hmm. You are most fortunate on several counts,' he

continued to shout, 'not least the withdrawal of a student immediately prior to your, or more accurately, the Royal Air Force's late application on your behalf; but due also to other staff commitments no one was available to interview you except Principal Hancock. It is well known our principal possesses the patience of Job when dealing with applicants of your lowly calibre.'

Fortunately at this point Professor Price stopped telegraphing intimate details of Johannes's unorthodox entry. He eyed Johannes coldly.

'The implication being no one else would have accepted us, regardless of a shortage of numbers and the bloody group dynamic,' Inner Voice grumbled.

'Precisely Taliesin! Obviously you understand what I am saying,' Professor Price reverted to shouting.

'Informing the whole bloody college with his Swansea Bay foghorn is too much, too sodding much.'

'Less of the backchat, Taliesin!' Professor Price's voice again rose to the heights, 'you are a student at this institution simply because Principal Hancock is statutorily obliged by the Ministry of Education to maintain numbers for each cohort lest the institution takes a reduction in its block grant. As well as that imposition,' he boomed, winding up his anger into the realms of shrill, 'our determination to maintain an entrance quality threshold has unfortunately been countered by a general lowering of standards offered by the secondary sector, result of which has been that the college took no index-linked increase in the block grant during the last financial year. We are caught on the horns of a dilemma, of all botheration!' clearly the professor was taking the opportunity of Johannes's reprimand to give vent to his frustration regarding the institution's financial predicament.

'I shall be frank with you Taliesin. Our dilemma means we

have to suffer the presence of persons like you on our enrolment registers, who are neither artistically nor psychologically disposed to benefiting from a higher education in art and design.'

'*Psychologically? How does he know? Apart from the odd hangover we are enjoying life here,*' Inner Voice whispered.

'Conversely this institution does not benefit from *your* presence. Please regard this as a final warning: if there were to be an advantageous change to the tendering system for the block grant recurrent funding, or fortuitously Swansea College of Art were to benefit from several talented applications for direct entry into next academic session's undergraduate course, the college would send you down forthwith, on two counts: your lack of progress and your antisocial behaviour and, come to think of it, your inability to integrate intellectually during formal lectures.'

'*That's three counts,*' Inner Voice counted.

'That's three counts, Sir,' Johannes ventured, but why he ventured was unclear to him.

'Anyway, as far as I am concerned,' the professor continued, ignoring the correction to his arithmetic, 'this would be good riddance to a problem that has beset us since day one of your enrolment. Good riddance! Do you understand, Taliesin?'

'Yes, Sir,' was Johannes's meek reply, 'but it's three counts,' he repeated.

'THERE YOU GO AGAIN!' Professor Price roared, 'what's WRONG with you?'

Johannes shrugged in what he assumed to be a meaningless way.

'It is easy to concede agreement, but I believe you find it difficult to put application to it. We think you are in dire need of psychological counselling, and we will probably arrange an appointment for you. It is not as if this is a one off. You have raised problems with tiresome regularity. Many of the academic staff would not hesitate to vote in favour of your being sent down,' the professor said with great emphasis on the being sent down part.

'*My God! That bad!*'

'All academic reports I get of you indicate an obdurate recalcitrance that is alarming for one presuming entry to an undergraduate course. Professor Edwards has given much of his own time to assist you in catch-up, and this is how you reward him! Professor Cour believes you are a liability in the sculpture department and Mr Jones does not want you near pottery. Mr Fairley believes you generate arguments for the sake of the polemics, rather than from any intellectual point of view, if you believe. Mr Charlton in printmaking complains that you never clear up your mess; where do you come from, Taliesin – a pigsty?'

'*Spot on, Price, a bloody pigsty.*'

'Yes, Sir, you are quite right – I come from a pigsty,' Johannes blurted.

The professor gagged; his jaw dropped.

'Stop your insolent remarks, for heaven's sake!'

'You asked the question, Sir, I merely furnished you with an answer,' Johannes amazed himself his pluck.

'What sort of answer do you call that?' the professor boomed, his face turning purple.

'*Pinkish-purple, we would say; but perhaps we should ease up on backchat interruptions.*'

'Only one member of staff returns a positive report on you: Dr Fred Janes, reference your life drawing. Only life drawing from all these introductory disciplines! In which case how dare you interrupt a life class of all subjects last Friday in such a disgusting manner?' Professor Price's voice suddenly lost its booming register and elevated into a high squeak. Clearly he had generated an unusual head of anger over Johannes's behaviour, and was showing signs of losing control of it.

124

'*Won't be long before he starts saying hell's teeth,*' Inner Voiced observed.

'Hell's teeth, Taliesin, what do you mean you come from a pigsty?' Professor Price showed a belated realisation of Johannes's contrition.

'Just that, Professor Price, a pigsty.'

The professor promptly dropped the subject of pigs' homes, and proceeded with the reprimand, 'A college of art education should be one of the most enjoyable of post-eighteen experiences. The principle that an institution is established for the sole purpose of education in art is a relatively recent phenomenon.'

'*We knew it!*'

'I *am* enjoying the education here, Sir,' Johannes pleaded.

'Good God, young man, then why don't you act as if you are?'

For no particular reason Johannes had assumed the reprimand would be short and sour. This reprimand was sour but certainly not short, and this one angry member of staff seemed to be settling down for a long haul. Johannes reverted to his usual introspective shell, nervously peering out.

'The pioneering schools for the arts and sciences, which originally addressed the great Victorian fervour for educational enlightenment, envisaged a cohabitation of disciplines,' he squeak-boomed, ensuring anyone else in the establishment not conversant with the pioneering work of the City Fathers would also be enlightened, 'they were inexorably linked to science, manufacturing and commerce and were bound by a set of rules and values designed to hold their students to realistic and achievable goals within a highly competitive environment. I regret the case no longer obtains, otherwise the likes of you would be unable to meet the competition and would be out on your neck, back in the mills or the mines or labouring on the farms to earn your meagre living.

'The fact that the politicians see fit to dictate a numbers game regardless of the deleterious effect it has on the quality of the art institutions is beyond me. Hell's teeth! What effect has this policy on us? The likes of you aiding and abetting our grand decline from the esteemed heights of the past; that is the effect!' Professor Price was venting a head of steam that must have been building up for the whole of the weekend, or perhaps months. But distantly, Johannes discerned another hidden agenda that was equally as tiresome to the head of painting's reprimand.

'Above the entrance to this building you will see a date – 1872,' he continued, 'that was when the City Fathers, like City Fathers similarly throughout the country, set up this institution. Their pioneering energy and far-sighted vision established centres of learning that inspired the populace to strive for greater things. They established educational centres that were a magnet to the populace through their aura of mystique, dedication and high standards, especially peculiar to the institutions of art and science.'

Professor Price was in full flow. Whilst Johannes spent the weekend fretting over his behaviour, the professor had resolved that such behaviour should not be tolerated regardless the government's policy on maintaining group numbers. The reprimand had reached a stage where it was clear to Johannes that his attendance at Swansea College of Art was against the better judgement of the great majority of the academic staff. As he expounded on the hard won advantages for the likes of undeserving souls, Professor Price drilled the message deeper and deeper into Johannes's immaturity. A determined cloud began gathering overhead.

'You seem unaware of the feats undertaken for posterity by the selfless industrial barons of early Victorian times. Without their efforts this country would have a good deal less to offer.

Heavens! We are a grey little country more impressed by our imagination than reality –'

'He's talking about our imagination having no connection with reality.'

'– but it would be a damned sight worse without the path-finding efforts of the unpaid leaders on the municipal councils of yore who cleared the way for the equally inspirational efforts of the industrialists.'

There was no stopping the professor. His voice was so loud the whole college could not avoid being aware of the intricate details of the institution's establishment. Johannes was experiencing a slow death through embarrassment.

'Today the politicians expect to be paid to sit around pontificating on socio-political trivia, introducing little regulations minuscule in their constructive effect but magisterial in their ability to assist our grand decline – pah! Sitting before me this morning is a living example of the current socio-political thoughtlessness, half-baked armchair theories expounded by soapbox cranks.'

It was with no great relief that Johannes realised that he shared the professor's disdain of politicians.

'Don't build up our hopes, sitting before him…'

'An educational experience was cemented to the world of industry and commerce by those far-sighted people. The founding fathers were successful businessmen in their own right, and understood the necessary connection between industry, commerce, education and discipline. Do you hear, Taliesin? DISCIPLINE!' he squeak-roared.

'In those days Members of Parliament were returned through the ballot box on the strength of their public awareness and involvement in these connections. This was no superficial exercise; there were no professional politicians who followed a theoretical agenda of opening the doors to all in order to generate universal progress. Life is still nearer the former and certainly not like the latter. The sooner you adopt a more realistic approach to your education the better it will be for all of us here at Swansea College of Art.

'Not too long ago the boards of trustees of the established schools of art were constituted from the ranks of the professions and they, in consort with the staff and students, proudly upheld and even strengthened the institution's ties with industry and commerce. The learning process was intense, preoccupied, disciplined and focused. The fraternity of the institution ensured a lasting integrity: its achievements and standards were upheld through traditions and rewards that were proudly celebrated.'

Although Professor Price was in rage mode, he seemed intent on offloading several of his hobbyhorses onto the unremarkable shoulders of Johannes Taliesin.

'*It's come to this! Ye gods, we hope he doesn't write a letter to Daddy,*' Inner Voice whispered.

'All of that has changed. Politics has crept stealthily into art education; the genie is out of the bottle. Today the board of trustees is subject to political interference by the Privy Council dictating that we have elected members of the unions and students on the board, of all things. The result is that we have amateurs, politicians who are no better than shrimp-net menders, shelf-packers and idiots like you dictating institutional policy. Lunatics running the asylum!'

'*Uh-oh, we knew it would come back to us. But how could we be on the board of trustees? Ask him, it might detract.*'

'H-How c-could I be on the b-board of trustees, S-sir?'

'*Bloody stutter back – ahem, speech impediment.*'

'Don't interrupt with such absurd questions! And I, after fifteen years of dedicated service to this institution have to witness its consequent decline in the guise of you, Johannes

Taliesin, a group dynamic infill, a statistic to save the block grant of all things, interrupting my lecture with your inane backchat and unsocial disruption!'

Johannes squirmed in his chair. All weekend long he had anticipated a reprimand, but nothing so socially elucidating as this, where his excuses were systematically stripped away, and his failure in grasping the unique opportunity presented to him was laid bare. Johannes's discomfort exceeded last Friday morning's moments by a league.

'Serves us right, that's all we can say, serves us bloody right,' Inner Voice seemed to be siding with the professor, to make matters worse, and gaining strength from the reprimand.

'Arts and sciences!' The professor declared. 'The only science you seemed to have mastered is how to successfully waste your money and time in imbibing alcohol. Shame on you! What do your parents think of you?'

'Oh, God, here we go.'

Johannes squirmed the more, but did not reply immediately, trying to arrange a form of words that would simultaneously say the truth without being disloyal to his parents.

'Tell him the bloody truth!'

'I-I can't tell the whole truth, S-sir, without being dis-disloyal to my parents, that is,' he whispered.

'Well done!'

The remark had no effect on Professor Price, as he must have had a pretty shrewd idea of the rural squalor from which the likes of Johannes hailed. He was aware of the poverty of attitude such deprivation emasculates, the paucity in social ease, the lack of breadth in interpersonal skills, the absence of lateral thinking, the clumsiness in social gatherings, the need to hide behind inebriation; all this and much more. It could be discerned from studying Johannes in isolation; leave alone an abundance of such traits on display in Wales.

'Do you not wish to talk about your parents, Taliesin?'

'N-no, S-sir. I'm embarrassed enough.'

'So you should be embarrassed,' the professor replied, conveniently brushing Johannes's greater implication aside.

'Regardless, you are old enough to manage your own affairs. Look at your scruffy appearance! It lowers the dignity of our institution. Try drinking less, saving your pennies and spending it on your appearance. Try spending more time in the municipal library –'

'I-I do, S-sir!' Johannes interrupted, realising his prime excuse had been deliberately brushed aside, 'Whenever there are no life classes in the evenings I spend time in the library; every Saturday afternoon after morning life class I go to the library, and I have a reader's ticket for special entry on Sundays,' the stutter had vanished.

This stalled the professor's admonition, and threw new light on the message he had hoped was being delivered.

'You spend time in the municipal library, Taliesin?'

'Yes, Sir.'

'With your colleagues of course?' Bill Price fished, aghast.

'Alone.'

'Alone always?'

'Always, Sir. I believe I am one of the very few students who regularly studies at the municipal library,' he blurted.

Professor Price was completely thrown off his stride. He paused, averted his glare from Johannes, and thought for a while. Johannes hardly dared to think that the reprimand was taking a less one-sided turn. After a while the professor levelled a testing question,

'What subjects do you read?'

'Pretty well everything to do with art history, geography, physics, philosophy, psychology... many subjects. I'm also reading current authors,' Johannes was back in his element.

No academic had enquired about his reading. No academic, ever.

'Like?'

'Like Kafka, Koestler, Camus, Corso, Durrell, Faulkner, Dylan Thomas, Gerard Manley Hopkins, John Claire… and others, Sir.'

'Good heavens, Taliesin! What philosophers are you studying?'

'So far I've read Kant, Nietzsche, Russell, Cassirer, Spengler, Hegel.'

'Not in that order, you should say.'

'Not in that order.'

'Quite; and physics, dare I ask?'

'I've read Einstein's Relativity, Planck's black body quanta, Heisenberg's uncertainty principle, Pauli's exclusion principle, Schrödinger's wave-function theories and his cat in a box problem, and bits here and there on particle physics… at the moment I'm reading Ernst Cassirer's *Phenomenology of Knowledge*. That's not science, though; more social science, I think. It's a difficult book.'

'Cassirer?' the professor asked, much more quietly.

'Yes, Sir – part three, *The Concept of Symbolic Form*.'

'Good God!'

'It's difficult, Sir.'

'Didn't know the municipal library stocked Cassirer,' Professor Price muttered.

'It's a recent acquisition, Sir.'

'You mentioned Spengler,' the professor quickly changed the subject from Cassirer, 'what has Spengler written?'

'A famous treaty, *The Decline of the West*, Sir.'

'Good grief! And Faulkner? Faulkner happens to be my current favourite,' the professor added, by way of minding he would be aware of an invented title.

'Oh yes, I like Faulkner, too. I liked *Requiem for a Nun* best, but also *Light in August*, *The Sound and the Fury*, *As I Lay Dying*, *Go Down Moses* and *Intruder in the Dust*.'

Once Johannes had started listing, he decided to mention every Faulkner novel he could remember. There were others, but the tension of the reprimand in Price's office caused his mind to hiccup walkabout.

Professor Price blinked. Then he blinked again. Clearly the realisation that Johannes was reading a fairly broad church of literature and the sciences put an uncomfortable, unsettling, disposition on the reprimand. He had just delivered a reprimand on his favourite theme – the interdependence of art and science. And here this ragamuffin from the backwoods was better read than himself. He had had no idea the country bumpkin before him was so well read. It did not bear thinking about. He sat in silence and continued to blink vacantly.

'Music, Taliesin?' Bill Price asked in a still small voice.

'Blues, Sir.'

'Like?'

'Delta blues singers like Charley Patton, Nehemiah James, Blind Lemon Jefferson, Robert Johnson, Bessie Smith, Peg Leg Howell, Ishman Bracey, Frank Stokes... and many others... there's a book just been published *Blues Fell This Morning* by Paul Oliver and an EP comes with it, very enlightening,' Johannes gushed.

'Good heavens, Taliesin! Extraordinary! Obviously we have not been approaching your idiosyncrasies properly – I doubt if *you* have,' Professor Price eventually burst out. Then he pondered for a moment.

'He's acting.'

'I think we should contact the university psychological counselling service, see what they have to say about you. Carry on with the reading. I now realise the genesis of your polemics.

Good God! But I must say, less drinking for all our sakes, and especially your own.'

He paused. The knowledge that this smelly country bumpkin was better read than himself completely threw Professor Price's mission, took the wind out of his sails, and spoiled his day... how disconcerting!

'I have to agree with Fred Janes, though,' he added, making reparation before some unknown storm were to break, 'you *do* have a definite facility in life drawing. I suggest you attempt to spread that facility a little wider into other disciplines.'

'Yes, Sir. Sorry for my behaviour last Friday.'

'Good God! We apologised.'

'Yes, I should jolly well think so. You can go now. We will contact you.'

Johannes left Professor Price's office still feeling deeply embarrassed.

'It's come to this. Why, we are quite capable of determining our destination; don't need psychiatrists; must keep it quiet.'

He decided not to disclose to his fellow intermediates the impending counselling bit.

5
Washington Drinking Chocolate

BACK IN THE intermediate studio, feeling bruised and confused, Johannes was confronted by Rees Bowen and the others.

'Been with Price?' Rees asked, as if he did not know.

'Mm.'

'What did he have to say?'

'I'm sure all of you heard what he had to say, but I'm not sure what was annoying him the more, political interference in art education or me,' Johannes replied.

'Don't be ridiculous! You are right, we heard him! It's got to be you,' said Gwynfor.

'I agree, got to be you, Yoyo,' said Rees.

'What did he say?'

'Just calling you in, Taliesin, to congratulate you on your remarkable exit from the Antique Room last Friday,' Eifion mimicked Professor Price, 'cutting a swathe like that proves your hidden talents as a forward for Swansea First Fifteen,' Eifion had a talent for mimicry, and his send-up of the professor brought roars of approval from the group. Johannes had earned the ragging; happily it was a convenient smokescreen.

'Come on, Yoyo, what did Price really say? We heard him shouting but the words were lost in translation,' Rees said.

'We talked about the Privy Council,' Johannes said defensively.

'Privy Council?' Rees exploded with disbelief, 'does that mean he's sending you to the board of trustees?'

'No, he's not sending me to the board of trustees. How do you make the connection?' Johannes quickly returned; then, remembering too late that Rees had passed constitutional government at A level, he added, 'No, don't answer that, I realise the connection you're making.'

'I'm sure you didn't talk about the Privy Council with Bill Price,' said Rees. 'He might have mentioned it in passing, passing on to mention the latest instrument that allows political interference from the board of trustees, and I reckon you are somehow connected to that.'

'Good thinking, Watson,' said Johannes, attempting to laugh off the whole affair.

'So?' Rees demanded.

'So I was bollocked good and hard for being such a bloody fool,' Johannes shrugged, 'that I would be kicked out of college if they weren't so desperate to maintain numbers, and all the staff except Dr Fred Janes put in a bad report about me.'

The whole intermediate group was momentarily stunned, and an appropriate silence followed. Johannes's contrition regarding admonishment was something new.

'Come on, Yoyo, what did he really say?' Gwynfor asked, disbelieving Johannes's contrition.

After some thought, Johannes replied, 'I think he was impressed by my reading list.'

'Needn't have told the sods.'

And he immediately regretted mentioning his reading interests.

'Oh, not the reading list trick again, Yoyo. Baffle Price with titles. It's the contents: did he ask you the contents?' Gwynfor cross-questioned.

'No fortunately, but after I mentioned Faulkner my heart jumped when he told me *his* favourite author of the moment was Faulkner.'

'You're a cynic, Yoyo,' said Ingrid, 'what's the point in pretending you don't read those books when we all know you do?'

'Now I've got some wounds to lick,' Johannes giggled, relieved.

Johannes was learning that if he held his breath and nerve long enough, the moment would pass. But its passing did not alleviate his problems.

'Our problems storeroom is chocka-b. Little room for any more. What do people do with them?' Inner Voice niggled.

The moment eventually passed. Work towards the final intermediate course assessments went on as before.

Professor Griff Edwards advised the group that assessments would contribute to a pre-inspection in readiness for a full inspection of the undergraduate courses by Her Majesty's inspectors, specifically detailed by the Ministry of Education regarding the block grant. In his usual affable approach he requested that the intermediate students conduct themselves with decorum appropriate to the occasion of a pre-inspection.

'Perhaps this is what Professor Price was implying the other day,' Johannes surmised.

'Implication or not, Johannes, an inspection is upon us,' Professor Edwards smiled.

The days that followed were hectic. Following a flurry of portfolios and sketchbooks, missing screw-binders and notebooks, everyone amassed their displays for the intermediate assessment and the visits of the external inspectors. Everything was undertaken in a business-like way, and the seriousness of the tutors eventually cascaded down to student level.

It transpired that several students were lacking quantity in the drawing section of their folios: Johannes ample books of drawings were raided in order to alleviate the shortfall. Tutors who had returned disparaging comments about Johannes to

Professor Price were prepared to implement a raid on his folio, while students normally not having the time of day for him were happy to bury their pride by using his work to help them through the intermediate assessments.

'Ironic, really.'

It gave Johannes a clear signal before any results were announced that the internal assessors had passed him, otherwise his folio would not have been raided.

A few days later in the midst of the preparations for the visit by Her Majesty's inspectors Professor Edwards discretely requested Johannes to step outside the studio. That was the hallmark of Professor Edwards, always concerned for the student's sensitivities. Outside, he whispered that a doctor and his assistant from the university were in college to see him. Johannes's heart sank.

'Bloody hell! The Psychological Counselling Service. We hoped Price would have forgotten about it.'

Johannes must have wilted visibly, for Professor Edwards held him firmly on the shoulder.

'Don't worry,' he said in true avuncular spirit. 'You worry too much about things; believe me, everything passes in the goodness of time.'

There was no doubt in Johannes's mind: Professor Griff Edwards was a brick of the first order. But the support did not alleviate a feeling of panic welling up in his gut.

Professor Price had put his office at the disposal of the University Psychological Counselling Service.

An affable middle-aged man and a silent woman not many years older than Johannes met him. They both carried clipboards.

'Shit, bloody clipboards.'

'Ah, Johannes – you don't mind us calling you Johannes, do you?' and, not waiting for a reply, 'Johannes, please come in and take a seat. My name is Dr Tobias Nuttall and this is trainee psychologist Jane Titmarsh. Of course, it goes without saying we are here to help,' he gushed.

'*This is tricky*,' Inner Voice warned.

In line with the normal reaction young women made to Johannes, Jane Titmarsh took an immediate dislike to him and broadcast her contempt in universal body language.

'*She's adopted the normal hate mode with us. Wonder what it is about us that women take an instant dislike to?*' Inner Voice rambled.

Dr Tobias Nuttal was far too experienced to disclose his feelings. His facial expressions were measured and inscrutable. He sat stock still, telegraphing nothing, obviously the result of donkeys' years dealing with bumpkin misfits. Jane Titmarsh, on the other hand, communicated her disdain in upper case. Her immediate statement was to turn her body as far as possible away from Johannes without actually turning her back on him.

'*Look at the way this prat screws her body away from us; and the jib she's pulling! One extra swivel and she'll have her back to us.*'

Jane Titmarsh's face belied her wish to be anywhere on earth but in Professor Price's office interviewing a miscreant art student.

'*Anyway, if we had been good-looking and well dressed, no doubt she would find the ordeal much less taxing*,' Inner Voice growled, as cynical as ever.

Regardless, Johannes had decided that he would do his best to dislike them, for the disliking mode kept panic at bay.

'*Worry mode, then hate mode, but it's tricky*,' Inner Voice meandered.

'We have with us a report from Professor Price –'

'*The professor's written a report! Bloody hell!*' Inner Voice was immediately thrown.

'– who feels you may well benefit from a talk with us. Are you comfortable with that?'

'To be honest I don't believe I need counselling,' Johannes replied, neatly demonstrating that he was not comfortable talking with them.

'Well, as you have been referred to the service by Professor Price, then we should give it go. OK, Johannes?'

'*Say no.*'

'No.'

'Good, thought you would see sense,' said Dr Nuttall, smiling broadly 'in which case we shall begin.'

'*Here we go, the usual pretences. Read about that somewhere in some psychological rubbish. OK, Nuttall. On the other hand, Titmarsh would make a bloody good model for us here. Cracking legs, what we can see of them.*'

'It is pointless being obdurate, Mr Taliesin,' Jane Titmarsh spoke at last, finding it not too difficult to hold a clear handle on what Johannes was fantasising from his eye movements, 'because our methodologies will determine the more your obduracy, the more you reveal about yourself.'

'*On second thoughts, perhaps not a model here after all.*'

'The more I will reveal about one small facet of myself, you mean; perhaps that is the only facet I wish to reveal,' was Johannes's naive riposte.

'*Nice riposte, gets us nowhere,*' Inner Voice, having the usual doubts regarding Johannes holding his nerve.

'But you have revealed so much already,' she snorted.

'*We like the little freckles on her nose.*'

'Yes I know, but only that which I wish you to determine, methodologies or not,' Johannes's reply was the usual unconstructive dogma.

'My, my,' said Dr Nuttall, springing to Jane Titmarsh's defence, 'the report warned us you are aggressively argumentative,

Johannes. Might I make a suggestion: rather than being simply obdurate, let us concentrate on the reasons *why* you feel it necessary to hold an obdurate view. We are not here to pick through the reasons of your admonition by Professor Price, nor the series of altercations you have had with the academics during your studentship here, but what happened long before you came to Swansea College of Art.'

'*Here we go.*'

'We promise Jane will not attack you again,' he said, taking a sidelong look at Jane Titmarsh, 'because you have proven to us that when attacked, you strongly defend yourself, and who can blame you? Mere attack and defence will get none of us anywhere. Surely you have a duty to yourself to find ways of defending your interests without recourse to aggression. Do you not agree with that modus operandi, Mr Taliesin?'

'*Usual Miss Nasty, Mr Nice routine. Say no.*'

'No.'

'Good,' chimed Nuttall, 'and Jane agrees not to be so pointedly personal, don't you Jane?'

'Certainly, Doctor,' the sycophantic actress responded.

'*As we thought, those silly psychological tricks, the hard approach tempered by the soft approach. Like Kafka's Trial,*' Inner Voice calmed.

'It's very clever,' Johannes ventured nervously. 'One of you attacks and the other moderates; I learned about that in Franz Kafka's *The Trial*. Halfway through the interrogation his supporters switch allegiance.'

Dr Nuttall smiled witheringly. 'This is not a trial, Johannes, and regardless we do not believe in switch tactics any more; that method is out of date, even if they still use it in the films.'

Johannes was now not sure of the methods being used but nevertheless realised that he had no option but to co-operate, with caution.

'Don't trust, don't drop your guard for one second, this is getting trickier.'

'What I would like to do is to discuss your history over which perhaps you may not feel impelled to be defensive, that is, your childhood,' Dr Nuttall proceeded tentatively. 'Let us clarify from the start so that there is no argument between you two,' and he nodded in the direction of Jane Titmarsh. Then, following a pause,

'Are there any incidents in your childhood over which you are embarrassed?'

'No, I don't think so,' Johannes cautiously lied.

'Are there any incidents that stand out in your memory?'

'Oh yes, getting lost in a waste field when I was three, Christmases, breaking my arm, passing to grammar school, that sort of thing. All small events in the smaller scheme of things.'

'In the grander scheme of things,' Dr Nuttall corrected, 'I would say in the grander scheme of things.'

'OK, if you say: in the grander scheme of things, but whether the scheme is grand or small it makes no difference,' Johannes replied at his nihilistic best.

'Au contraire, Johannes: major events are often triggered by seemingly trivial incidents. Which grammar school did you attend?'

'Ardwyn Grammar School in Aberystwyth.'

'Did you enjoy your time at Ardwyn?'

'Only the last two years; otherwise I was bullied relentlessly because I was, I was-um,' Johannes stumbled.

'Just say the bloody truth!'

'I was a poorly dressed little runt. That's the best way of putting it.'

'Phew.'

'Were you smaller than the average when at school?' Jane asked in sympathetic tone.

'Much smaller! For several years I was the smallest pupil in the school. Four feet ten and a half inches, five stone four pounds at sixteen and a half; on my school report.'

'Heavens! That is small,' she responded, jerking her head back in surprise.

'Well, you are not small now, Johannes. A bit spare in the rib, as they say, but certainly tall enough,' Dr Nuttall reassured.

'Yes, I grew with a spurt after an accident on my bike,' Johannes replied.

'Why don't they ask us our current height?'

Dr Nuttall moved on to different things.

'I find all this very interesting, Johannes,' he said. 'Tell us about your parents.'

Johannes paused to think. He was very reluctant to describe the reality of his parents. Whenever asked about them he tended to exaggerate certain socially acceptable aspects and airbrush the rest from history. In reality his father was perversely eccentric, but his mother, apart from her synaesthesia, was more or less normal. The parents quarrelled daily. His father's only sibling, Maldwyn, together with their mother, Nain, lived with the family throughout Johannes's childhood. Maldwyn was as eccentric as Johannes's father, but in a completely different way. It was Maldwyn who had encouraged Johannes to pursue art at school.

'They are normal parents,' Johannes said at last.

'I wonder?' Dr Nuttall fished.

'Perfectly normal for the rural part of Cardiganshire from which I hail,' Johannes hedged.

'That's a loaded comment, Johannes, if I may say so,' Dr Nuttall said, quickly alighting on the titbits, 'would you say the people from your rural part of Cardiganshire possess… let me say… idiosyncrasies beyond the norm?'

'Oh, sure.'

'Unorthodox idiosyncrasies?'

'Oh, colossally unorthodox,' Johannes flatly replied.

'My, my, this is interesting,' Jane Titmarsh interrupted the tête-à-tête.

'Are you prepared to describe an incident that would encapsulate your childhood?' Dr Nuttall asked, sensing Johannes's reluctance to talk about his parents.

'Careful, careful: they'll read all sorts of bloody twaddle into whatever we say. These psychologists are twaddle artists.'

'Y-yes,' Johannes said cagily.

'Nothing about the slum, the quarrelling, no running water, no toilet, don't mention the roof leaking in every bedroom. Nothing,' Inner Voice clarioned.

'Good; give vent to your creative talents and give us a scenario,' urged Dr Nuttall.

'I believe I have no creative talents. I'm only good at life drawing, and I read a lot,' Johannes responded, looking directly at Jane Titmarsh for the 'life drawing' bit.

'Yes, we know you are well read, Professor Price's report indicates thus,' Dr Nuttall said.

'Hmm,' Johannes was pleased to hear.

'With regard to creative talents, we are sure you deny yourself just worth,' Dr Nuttall interjected.

'No, what I say is true. The principal and Professor Price have made it clear to me that I was accepted at this college because the Ministry of Education demanded numbers be maintained due to the exigencies of maintaining the block grant, whatever that is,' Johannes confided, convinced the psychologists would have this prime slot of information in the papers on their clipboards.

'You are very frank, Johannes.'

'Only when it suits us,' Inner Voice clambered.

'Only when I have no option,' Johannes's reply was coloured in sour.

'*Go on, we heard the prat, give vent to our creative talents. Nothing to lose. Probably their report is all Price is waiting for to kick us out of here… go on, give vent.*'

'You say give vent to my creative talents. Do you *mean* that?' Johannes hedged again.

'Of course we mean that. Johannes, rest assured we do not say anything we do not mean,' Dr Nuttall emphasised.

'*Like bloody hair oil,*' came Inner Voice's sceptical prattle.

'What did you say, Johannes?'

'Um, nothing.'

'To me it sounded like you said something. Never mind, do go on.'

'OK, here goes. I have thought of an incident that should illustrate the environment of my childhood. I'm sure you will stop me if you don't want it.'

'Please, Johannes, trust us,' Dr Nuttall urged.

'I have always been fascinated by the divergent personalities of my father and his brother, my uncle Maldwyn. I wrote an essay on the subject in the lower sixth. My form master thought it was great and urged me to enter it in the school eisteddfod.'

'My, my! How did the essay fare?'

'Got nowhere, because the adjudicator thought it was fiction.'

'And it wasn't?'

'No, of course not.'

'Go ahead, Johannes, we would be delighted to hear a reconstruction of that essay,' Dr Nuttall enthused.

'Yes, do go ahead,' Jane Titmarsh echoed.

'I'll try to demonstrate the difference.'

'That would be most welcome,' Dr Nuttall flourished.

'No event would better illustrate their differences than the one regarding my asking them for clarification of the DC after Washington,' Johannes trilled, a ground-swell mood change swinging into operation. 'It stands out so significantly in my memory.'

'Careful, don't get sodding carried away again.'

'Good, good,' said Dr Nuttall, not having a clue of the subject of his enthusiasm.

'Good,' Jane Titmarsh echoed, 'we will take notes if you don't mind.'

'It was my uncle who encouraged my interest in art, and every Sunday he would take me up the mountains to draw and paint landscapes. He's now seriously turning to singing. Bass; in fact basso profundo,' Johannes said by way of introduction.

'Excellent. Please, if it in any way illustrates your childhood, then it will serve a purpose,' said Dr Nuttall, hedging his bets.

Johannes had never previously been asked to indulge his memories to a receptive audience. To girls he was keen on chatting up, yes: but they either walked away or fell asleep. Although deeply cautious he had at last the freedom of the stage, Johannes cleared his throat and began to edge obliquely into a scenario.

'Uncle Maldwyn was repairing the netting of the bantam chicken run,' Johannes romped, not caring that notes were being taken of something he was controlling.

'As individuals, of course, both my father and uncle believe they are perfectly normal. We all take them for granted – Mother, older brother Bobby, little sister Francesca, Spot the sheepdog, as well as me.'

'This is enormously interesting, Johannes,' said Dr Nuttall with genuine pleasure, as obviously his experience had quickly identified terrain that Johannes was comfortable ranging upon. Given a sympathetic ear the floodgates should open.

'Could you describe your home, where it is, et cetera?'

'Careful, a trap.'

'Um, yes. It's a farm; well, a smallholding, set in a deep

tree-filled valley in Cardiganshire. The farm has the habit of normalcy, apart from a few leaks, and the river Paith comes into the house and makes itself cosy every time we have heavy rain; the tree blown down onto the barn has stayed there for ever, that sort of thing, quite normal.'

Dr Nuttall and Jane Titmarsh looked at each other. She shrugged and, obviously forgetting her instinctive dislike for Johannes, swung her body part-way back to sitting properly.

'Normal for you Johannes, but not normal for city dwellers,' said Dr Nuttal, 'but please tell us more.'

'Oh, normal for people living in rural Cardiganshire, I mean. As a child having sparse reference in an isolated farmhouse,' Johannes continued edging in at forty-five degrees, 'I assumed everybody in the world was the same. I believed everybody reacted at oblique angles to given circumstances; that it is normal to act with obtuse humour at siege with the world before it recognised one has a point to make.'

'A very obligatory perception, Johannes,' Dr Nuttall mused.

'*Obligatory? What's he mean? Ask.*'

'What does obligatory mean in that context? No, on second thoughts it doesn't matter,' Johannes cut himself off.

'Pertinent. Please go on, Johannes.'

'When I left home to study here I was surrounded for the first time in my life by posing artists whose actions I instinctively *knew* were not real compared to Father and Uncle Maldwyn. I realised the eccentricity of my father and uncle is honest and un-contrived. Although my relatives have a few screws loose the world they inhabit is a *real* world, not the pretentious masquerade of the art world. I would never swap my experiences at the farm. I have grown to realise how mediocre most people are by comparison, even when as artists they are deliberately contriving to be different. Father and Uncle Maldwyn are in a league apart. That's the background I come from.'

'Just previously, you classified them as normal, Johannes.'

'They are perfectly normal, Dr Nuttall. I dislike people deliberately skewing their actions towards the abnormal, contriving to be eccentric.'

'I take it you dislike pretentiousness?'

'Oh yes, that; and phoney-ness, and posing. People are so artificial.'

'All people?'

'Most people.'

'Please continue reminiscing about your childhood, Johannes; I find it most interesting,' Dr Nuttall encouraged.

'So do I,' chimed Jane Titmarsh.

'We fancy her, but she's much too old for us.'

Johannes collected his thoughts. He imagined Professor Price's office had become a small rural enclave at Troed-yr-Henrhiw Farm, where he could express himself without embarrassment. With this simple device in place, he set forth.

'The occasion I am referring to occurred when I was about ten years old. I was exceptionally small for my age, shy and easily intimidated, a miserable little weakling, the dismay of both parents and big brother alike. Nothing has changed in my character as I have grown older, so the shyness disposition is here to stay, much to Father's everlasting disappointment.'

'We are saying too much, falling into the trap.'

Johannes paused in the narrative. 'Am I talking too much?'

'No, not at all,' they both chimed. 'We are fascinated,' added Dr Nuttall, 'please feel free to explain your background in whatever way you see fit.'

'Once when I was very young I overheard Father quoting Ambrose Bierce to Uncle Maldwyn, a descriptor about a woman being mightier than the cannon, for when she poured out of the tops of her stockings she devastated the land. Thenceforward I always thought the same woman had performed a similar act of devastation at our smallholding. Accoutrements dementia, you know, that sort of thing. Since then I have read some of Ambrose Bierce's writing. He's very amusing.'

The psychologists nodded; Jane Titmarsh managed a shuffle.

'Please go on with your narrative, Johannes.'

'We thought, and still think, of the place as a farm and that is good enough for Father, who has no respect for official nametags and abstract authority, unless he were requesting help, when he could cultivate a towering mountain of sycophancy. To exacerbate Father's aura of uniqueness, he intensely dislikes doing things properly. Not that he does things improperly – his Quaker beliefs prevent sorties into illegality and matters contrary to the Almighty. Incidentally, Mother is also a Quaker, from the Friends called Heroes of Conscience.'

'Both your parents Quakers?' Dr Nuttall interrupted, 'Does Professor Price know that your parents are Quakers?'

'He never asked.'

'Hmm. Do go on.'

'More appropriately, as Father is, is, um, as Father engages work with a certain reluctance, he hardly does things at all.'

'Are you saying your father is lazy?'

'No, he's not lazy,' corrected Johannes, 'he just doesn't go out of his way to work, if you understand what I mean.'

'Hmm, perhaps I do,' Dr Nuttall surmised.

'Father has an ample voice and uses it effectively to intimidate everyone within at least a mile. He is tactless in the extreme, which I believe to be absentmindedness mostly, and only a small amount deliberate. Talking to Father elicits either growls or roars, certainly one does not engage in a conversation. He has a short fuse, on a good day, as my big brother describes it.'

'We are being disloyal, too disloyal.'

'Um, apart from this he is not bad at all. He reveres the

Almighty, prays regularly, is scrupulously honest, never steals and never swears. He has an enormous sense of fair play and dislikes bullies intensely, apart from those bullying his runt of a son, which he believes should toughen him up.'

'Did it toughen you up, Johannes?'

'Not a bit. It has only succeeded in cultivating my deep dislike of bullies.'

'Hmm.'

'Uncle Maldwyn, on the other hand, is quite a different personality. He sings conversations, which irritates Father to the point of exasperation. One roars, the other sings, I cannot remember it otherwise. Maldwyn sings in a deep basso profundo voice. He has the strong Taliesin gene that instructs lack of self-belief that has leapt through Father without touching the sides to me. Whilst Father readily erupts into rage at the slightest provocation, Uncle Maldwyn sees the quaint and funny side to everything. If our uncle is not singing, he is giggling.'

Dr Nuttall and Jane Titmarsh looked at each other.

'Would you say you similarly see the quaint and funny side of everything, Johannes?' Dr Nuttall alighted on an opening.

'That you giggle a lot?' Jane Titmarsh added.

'We'd like to make you giggle, if you weren't so much older than us.'

'Er, no on both counts, I suppose; but perhaps, there again…' Johannes stumbled out of the trap.

'Would you perhaps agree that you possess an unorthodox viewpoint of matters?'

'No,' Johannes replied guardedly.

'Really?' Dr Nuttall replied, demonstrably looking at the report sheets to imply that they said differently.

'Well, I don't know; maybe. Perhaps: put it like that,' Johannes fumbled.

'I'm sorry to have interrupted your flow at a time when the

information you were imparting was of great interest, Johannes. Do you think you could get back into the stride?'

'Yes, of course, if you want me to.'

'Yes, certainly; it is all very informative *and* entertaining,' Dr Nuttall flannelled.

'OK, back to the scenario – I could present a different scenario if you wish?' Johannes said, mildly hoping they did not wish for a different one.

'Oh, no, no!' Dr Nuttall quickly responded, 'this scenario that demonstrates from your perspective the difference in character between your father and uncle is most intriguing. Please continue.'

'Just testing, we think.'

But Johannes was unconvinced, so continued, but with caution.

'My brother Bobby warned me regarding our uncle's eccentricity: 'The golden rule is never to ask him questions that require a serious answer,' he would wag a big finger at me, 'unless in dire emergency. Furthermore, regardless of whatever question you ask Uncle Maldwyn, never expect a reply that remotely relates to the question. His answers will smother you in billowing clouds of unrelated facts inextricably bound up with his opinions.' I say these things so the scenario makes sense.'

'Surely,' Dr Nuttall nodded.

Jane Titmarsh looked puzzled.

'On the occasion – am I talking too much?'

'No, no,' Dr Nuttall responded, 'please go on.'

'On the occasion in question Maldwyn is repairing the wire netting of the bantam run. Each morning the bantams are unlocked from their fox-proof chicken shed, and each morning most of them fly into the trees, the yews and laurels. Their brains are very small you see and no amount of lecturing from the family will dissuade them from this silly habit. Whilst up in the trees they lay, and then crow.'

Jane Titmarsh looked at Dr Nuttall. She screwed up her freckly nose.

'Are you inventing this, Johannes?' Dr Nuttall interrupted.

'No, they fly into the trees, honest.'

'No, no! I mean your story that they lay and then crow, surely –'

'I know what you are getting at, the crowing. Yes, many bantam hens crow after laying, and they all copy each other, so after a while the whole run is crowing.'

'And the laying?' Jane Titmarsh asked.

'Yes, they mostly lay their eggs when up the trees.'

'How does the family lecture them?' she asked.

'Er, not a lecture as such; more persuasion to lay in circumstances where the eggs are not broken. They are very small eggs, you know, about the size of a pigeon's egg,' Johannes obfuscated.

'OK, Johannes, sorry we interrupted yet again. Please go on.'

'On this bantam occasion I required help with my homework. Miss Herbert had set a homework essay on the United States. Bobby was with Spot at the Nant-y-Benglog keeps hunting lost sheep; Father was visiting Jones at Waungrug Farm about some slates; Mother was cooking pigswill and was in a pickle. Francesca was too young. So, as the others were unavailable I considered it a sufficiently dire emergency to ask Uncle Maldwyn for help with my homework. Clutching my huge atlas I set off in Maldwyn's direction. He was singing a hymn to a few bantam chickens and himself.

'What does the giant atlas with the little man want today?' he sang.

'I'm writing an essay about the United States of America,' I replied as importantly as possible, indicating the appropriate

151

map on the atlas, 'and there are two capital letters I don't know the meaning of.'

Johannes mimed the holding of an atlas in one hand and pointing with the other. The two psychologists affected deep intrigue.

'FIRE AWAY!' he sang, loud and bass. I remember the bantams that had gathered around his feet scattering.'

Jane Titmarsh jumped at Johannes's bellowing the 'fire away' part.

'What does DC after Washington stand for?' I asked, steadying the atlas and pointing to the culprit 'DC' on the map. Uncle Maldwyn studied the map for what was a very long period of silence for him. Then a look of enormously astonished emptiness flooded across his kindly face. Plainly he didn't have a clue, and the question had hit him like a bolt from the blue. The apparent difficulty of the question pleased me no end. Suddenly, my uncle re-arranged his features to portray knowledgeable authority, as in devoid of any doubt.

'Drinking Chocolate' he sang, nodding his head assertively.

'Drinking Chocolate?' I piped, 'the drinking chocolate Mammy makes for us at bedtime on a Sunday?'

'The very one and the same,' Uncle Maldwyn asserted.

'This is Washington, capital of the United States of America, Uncle Maldwyn. Do you mean Drinking Chocolate after *that* Washington?' I continued to pipe.

'It might not sound quite right to a little man of your stature, but it is one and the same,' my uncle sang, hesitantly, his shuffling feet clearly indicating the right answer was eluding him. Bobby's warning came to mind.'

Jane Titmarsh burst into giggles, and tears rolled down past her freckly nose. Dr Nuttall gently frowned at her.

'Please continue, Johannes, I am most enthralled,' he said.

'*If she goes on like that we'll shag her*,' Inner Voice bragged way beyond Johannes's capabilities.

'I need to know for homework for Miss Herbert,' Johannes proceeded with the narrative.

'Yes, you said,' replied Uncle Maldwyn, 'in which case Drinking Chocolate has to be the right answer.'

'Maldwyn's singing lacked conviction; by now I was sure he was wrong.

'I'm sure Miss Herbert won't agree with Drinking Chocolate,' I nagged.

'I am absolutely sure Miss Herbert will not agree with Drinking Chocolate,' Uncle Maldwyn sang in return, as by now he was embarking upon one of his obfuscating ploys, 'she will be so cross her face will look like a brown paper bag that has been repeatedly dragged across a ploughed field by a highly strung pit pony let out for its fortnight's holiday.'

'His singing became happier, which made my heart sink, because I knew this was in the direction of confidence.

'Daddy says that,' I rejoined, being easily led off the subject.

'WHAT? Your father says Miss Herbert will not agree?' my uncle's deep singing voice rose to a cracked tenor of amazement in mock surprise, 'I was unaware he knew Miss Herbert!'

'No,' I replied, having been caught on the obfuscating line, 'he says it about Hannah Tŷ Cornel and the brown paper bag bit.'

'Oh, everybody says that about Hannah Tŷ Cornel,' Maldwyn dismissed, returning his voice to the bass baritone, 'your father and I witnessed it as young boys at Gwaryfelin Farm.'

'I was confused as to what they had witnessed at Gwaryfelin Farm, but to compound the obfuscation, my uncle sang on,

'Evan is seven years older than I,' as if this was the correct age for witnessing brown paper bags being dragged across ploughed fields by holidaying pit ponies at Gwaryfelin Farm. And then,

'I should advise you there is a copyright on it,' he threatened in dark operatic tones, but happy I was no longer harrying him on the subject of Drinking Chocolate, 'because I was the first to see the incident at Gwaryfelin Farm'.

'Daddy says Gwarfelin Farm was so steep it had no fields,' I added, now securely sidetracked by a technique my uncle had honed to a fine art on gullible little people like me. As Bobby had warned, our uncle employed the method in place of correct answers.

'How would your father know?' Maldwyn asked, 'He is much too old, and anyway we left the farm before he was old enough to leave.'

'We had journeyed into the land of illogic on the keel of an aria, but my uncle wore such a dignified look of conviction that I seriously considered I had missed something of importance a few exchanges back. His dancing word-games were close enough to logic to make sense, like a jigsaw physically fitting but with its face wrong.'

'A jigsaw physically fitting but with its face wrong,' echoed Jane Titmarsh.

'Wonderful,' added Dr Nuttall, 'we must remember that descriptor. Go on, Johannes, this makes wonderful listening.'

'You mean much too young, I think, perhaps, Uncle?' I timidly ventured.

'How could that be? Your father is seven years older than me! Your mathematics needs attention – tell Miss Herbert to forget about essays on the USA and concentrate on teaching you algorithms instead,' he was now singing backstage, out of sight.

'Alga rhythms?' I squeaked, 'What are alga rhythms, Uncle Maldwyn?'

'Did you hear me say alga rhythms? Surely not! Never heard of such things. Why should I advise on a subject I have never heard of?' he sang in accentuated surprise, 'What you should have heard me say, but obviously the listening department of your little brain was not attentive enough due to worrying too much about next Sunday's drinking chocolate and, may I add, too much debating with uncles, was logarithms. Tell Miss Herbert to concentrate on logarithms.'

'Logarithms?' I piped, ignoring the debating hint, 'I'm sure you mean subtraction, Uncle Maldwyn, which we learned last week. I know about subtraction,' I prattled on, foolishly competing out of my depth in my uncle's successful game of obfuscation.'

All the while Dr Nuttall and Jane Titmarsh wrote copiously on their clipboard notepads. Johannes wondered whether the notes were destined as a report to Professor Price. He paused.

'Do you wish I continue?'

'Of course!' they chimed simultaneously.

Jane made a little shuffling gesture that took her deeper into the chair as if settling down for an enjoyable listen. Dr Nuttall continued in his posture, inscrutably frozen that only a hundred years' experience could enable.

Johannes collected his thoughts.

'Subtraction, contraction, abstraction, merrily, merrily,' Maldwyn sang, happy now that he was back in the driving seat. 'But don't be silly, how could your father be too young if I am seven years younger than he? How can you subtract his greater age from my lesser one? I have decided: Washington Drinking Chocolate it is,' and he returned abruptly to his job and hymns, signalling his boredom with the subject.

'Which left me no better off as regards my homework, and wondering the connection between drinking chocolate and Washington in the world of Maldwyn's imagination. Madness in Uncle Maldwyn's method was more than scratching bantam hens. I believed in my little way that madness ran through our family like the cow slurry through the farmyard, touching everything it sticks to. Yet Maldwyn's method for drinking chocolate failed me.'

'Aha, Johannes! You declared earlier that your parents were normal. How could madness run through the Taliesin family yet still manifest normality?' Dr Nuttall levelled.

'Isn't he a clever smartass,' Inner Voice grumped.

'Yes, perfectly normal,' Johannes bluffed.

Dr Nuttall stared witheringly, the mask of inscrutability slightly skewed. Jane Titmarsh stared admiringly. A dichotomy was forming in the interrogation phalanx.

'They don't agree about something, but we must be on our guard.'

'If you have any more to say, please carry on,' said Dr Nuttall.

'I'm sure Johannes has much more to say, Dr Nuttall,' Jane Titmarsh encouraged.

'As I staggered back to the house with the huge atlas, I heard Father returning from his trip to Jones Waungrug, his Austin 7 buzzing up the lane that wound higgledy-piggledy through the pine trees to our farm. I was undecided whether Father's arrival at that moment was fortuitous in availing me homework assistance, or perhaps otherwise.

'Whenever I interrupted Father, regardless of what he was doing, whether it was feeding the pigs or napping in an armchair, he would roar at me to 'Go away and play!' loudly – he has always talked loudly – regardless of my question or story to tell. Even if we were sitting around the table enjoying Mother's cawl he would talk loudly. Loudly!'

Johannes had roared the 'Go away and play' bit as loud as his voice would permit, at which point Jane Titmarsh jumped inches off her chair.

'My, my,' she said, 'does your father really talk like that?'

'Louder than that. He often talks in upper case, but we call that shouting. Unfortunately my voice is not big enough to convey the exact volume,' replied Johannes, 'but I'll try.'

'In that case we have to be grateful for small voices,' Jane joked and all three laughed.

'Do carry on, Johannes,' Dr Nuttall smiled, his ameliorative mood having returned.

Johannes collected his thoughts.

'Sometimes, pausing just long enough to listen, he would emit monosyllabic grunts and a 'Rarswyd fawr' or two.

'What does 'rarswyd fawr' mean, Johannes?' Dr Nuttall interrupted.

'Large shivers,' Johannes replied matter of fact, 'Father had worked conscientiously to develop his remoteness, having lengthier conversations with inanimate objects like spanners and wheelbarrows than his children. His conversations with the animals lasted ages.

'Anyway, the Austin 7 clattered to a stop, belching steam from its radiator and pouring rusty water from some unknown source between the front wheels. Father had expressed his mood of the day by thrashing the car; this was a clear sign now was not the time to ask questions about homework. Before he climbed out I could hear his voice high in distemper, promising the car the most hideous damage involving acetylene blow-torching and strange mechanical dysfunction I did not understand. Father was in one of his rages.

'Clearly this was no time to verify my uncle's dubious Washington Drinking Chocolate. Yet there again, my Inner Voice, which on several occasions had succeeded in getting me into the most amazing trouble, was encouraging me.

'Take the bull by the horns and have a go,' my Inner Voice urged. I have an Inner Voice, you see, which talks to me all the time.'

'An inner voice, Johannes; hmm, very interesting,' said Dr Nuttall.

'Inner Voice, with capitals, because he's a proper noun,' said Johannes.

'At last I'm beginning to understand some parts of Professor Price's report,' said Dr Nuttall, 'please go on, Johannes.'

'No time was convenient to ask Father anything, but the present circumstance had a special ring of hopelessness about it. I wavered, feeling it was best to wait for Bobby to return from Nant-y-Benglog. But my tragic inability to assess the proper intensity of circumstances allowed me to proceed with the homework question. There again, perhaps an intelligent question from his 10-year-old son might, just might, offset his mood, so my cautious judgement was brushed aside by hastiness.

'Dad!' I blurted.

'Perhaps not now, after all,' Inner Voice dithered second thoughts on the matter.'

'Incidentally,' said Johannes, changing the tone of his voice, 'Inner Voice always talks in a small voice in *italics*.'

'Always in italics?' Dr Nuttall asked.

'Always in italics.'

'Thank you, Johannes. We will note accordingly. Please proceed.'

'Father ignored me.

'Cythrel car! Overheat would you?' Father roared in deep conversation with the car.'

'Cythrel, Johannes?'

'Vixen.'

'Can I ask a question, Dad?'

'This was easily my worst move of the day so far. Father turned and glared at me with the most ferocious of faces. Obviously, he had matters on his mind, but I realised too late and being thus committed I gallantly battled on. But intrepidity meant nothing to my father when he was in one of his rages.

'WHAT?' He roared in upper case. Whenever Father is in a rage he always uses upper case, as I said. On this day his temper was upper case. Upper-upper case. His roar startled the pigs into squealing, and it shook me so rigid that I forgot the question.

'WHAT IS IT THIS TIME?'

'Perhaps we should not be quite so theatrical, lest these two think...'

'Um, I, um... er...' But I had completely forgotten the question, regardless the heavy atlas bearing down on my little arms.

'GET ON WITH IT!' Father began stamping. The farmyard mud splattered everywhere. This was a sure sign one either got on with it or got out of his way.

'Er... um... Uncle Maldwyn says the DC after Washington in my atlas here stands for Washington Drinking Chocolate...' my voice trailed away as I realised I was telling a tale on my uncle, rather than courageously asking my irate father his unequivocal view on the DC matter in question. Am I talking too much?'

'No, no! Don't ask again. I'll tell you when you are talking too much. Please proceed with the scenario, Johannes,' Dr Nuttall assured.

'SO?' Father asked, and spinning on his heel walked away.

'So is it Drinking Chocolate?' I asked, clambering after him through the mud, atlas flapping.

'If your uncle believes DC on the map stands for Drinking Chocolate, then why should I dispute his wisdom?'

'This answer lacked the customarily arrogant certitude I had grown to expect of my father; by now he was several paces away and disappearing towards the farm workshop. I squelched through the mud after him, holding the atlas high above the mud splash line.

'Is it?' I asked plaintively, giving the subject one last shot.

'Father stopped and swivelled round. His face was very red. Obviously he did not perceive my tenacity in the same light as I did. He glared down at me yet again.

'Go and play!'

"But, Dad, this is homework I have to do for Miss Herbert.'

'Then go and ask your mother.'

'I did and she didn't have time because she's in a pickle.'

'Why don't we give up?' Inner Voice pondered.

'RARSWYD FAWR!' Father roared, 'can't you see the car is playing up? I'm behind with the pigs, Jones Waungrug doesn't want the slates after all, your mother is in a pickle, and YOU are asking me about drinking chocolate out here of all places. What's wrong with you today? And before long, mark my words, IT'S GOING TO RAIN AGAIN!'

'His voice rose and echoed from the farm buildings and the spruce tree stand, from the high field behind them, and the woods up the valley. At this he turned again and sloshed through the mud to the workshop, which strengthened my suspicions regarding Drinking Chocolate. Incidentally, at that time I always thought of drinking chocolate as Drinking Chocolate the proper name, you know, with capitals, because I had no alternative. Only Bobby and Francesca were left. I doubted Francesca would have the answer, as she was only five.

'I could see Bobby coming down from the Nant-y-Benglog hills. Spot was running all over the place, which meant they had not found the lost sheep. I stood forlornly in the farmyard mud, waiting for them to arrive.

'Upon arriving, Spot wanted to read the atlas as usual. Ignoring formalities, I dived straight into the subject.

'Bobby, Uncle Maldwyn says the DC after Washington here on this map stands for Drinking Chocolate; what do you think?'

'Where is Uncle Maldwyn?' Bobby asked in dismissive tone.

'Mending the bantam netting. What do you think?'

'Where is Daddy?'

'In the workshop; the Austin 7 is playing up. What do you think?'

'Where is Mammy?' Bobby asked, moving towards the outhouse and showing signs of irritation.

'In the boiler house and she's in a pickle. Bobby, what do you think DC stands for?'

'Listen, where is Francesca?'

'In her roo –'

'Go and ask her,' he dismissed.

'Bobby, be sensible. What do you think the DC stands for?' I asked for the umpteenth time, following him to the outhouse. I ran the risk of being smacked telling my big brother to be sensible.

'Listen brat, we couldn't find the sheep. The fencing has gone over for yards at a time; we'll lose the whole flock next. This place is going to the dogs.'

'Spot barked in agreement. I was getting nowhere.

'Oh, no one is of any help,' I whinged.

'Bobby levelled on me. 'I don't care what the DC on your map stands for – that's it, I've just thought of it – DC stands for Washington Don't Care. Seems as good as Washington Drinking Chocolate to me. And do you know what else I think? I think God created sheep to test our faith in him, that's what I think.'

'Father arrived from the workshop.

'Did you find the sheep?"

'No,' Bobby replied sheepishly.

'Then Father turned on me.

'DC stands for District of Columbia, and don't ask me why.'

The proximity of Father's roar attracted Maldwyn from the bantam run and Mother from the boiler house. Her face was blackened and eyes red.

'How's the pigswill cooking?'

'I got into a pickle with the boiler: it backfired and soot rolled down the chimney into it,' Mother said, promptly bursting into tears.

'I noticed the tears left white lines down her face giving her a comical make-up.

Francesca arrived, sleepy-headed, and bleated that she was hungry.

'Shoes, Francesca,' said Mother, forgetting her tears, 'don't walk out here without shoes on, sweetheart.'

'I can't find them. Do you know where they are?' she asked.

'Where you left them, sweetheart,' said Mother.

'How's the bantam run coming on?' Father asked of Maldwyn and, without waiting for a reply, 'What's this drinking chocolate nonsense you've been telling this one?' Nodding in my direction, 'Don't encourage him with any more nonsense, he's stupid enough as it is."

'*Careful with the self-flagellation,*' Inner Voice sensibly tempered, but Johannes was too deeply involved in the theatricals to heed his inner caution. He raced on,

'In one swoop the truth had come out that I had blabbed on my uncle. I squirmed, Spot barked with pleasure, as the gathering of people had now assumed the proportion of a flock, and rounding us up was in order.

'Suddenly, Father cracked.

'RARSWYD HOLY MACKEREL FAWR!' he roared at the top of his large voice, 'There's sooty swill for the pigs, Jones Waungrug doesn't want the slates after all the fuss he made, the Austin 7 is finished, Bobby can't find the lost sheep, all my brother does is encourage this idiot to believe more word fantasies instead of repairing the bantam run, the little one will get pneumonia without shoes and, mark my words, IT'S GOING TO RAIN ANY MINUTE!' in capitals.

'Father's long list of woes sounded very funny from my childish perspective. I promptly burst into giggles.

'AARGH!' Father roared in capitals.'

Suddenly, Jane Titmarsh could take no more of Johannes's loud theatricals, so she reverted to her side saddle mode of using the chair, the while squirming and fidgeting uncontrollably. Her face had become excitingly flushed, as if she were partaking in an activity of dubious clinical ambition, the while demonstrably avoiding Johannes's gaze. Meanwhile, Dr Nuttall was contending with his own problem: one side of his face developed a pronounced twitch, while the other side stoically retained its inscrutable countenance.

'Perhaps we've gone too extreme with them, but must say Nuttall is demonstrating a remarkable feat of dual facial management.'

'Sh-shall I finish off, Dr Nuttall?'

'Um, that sounds like a good idea, Johannes,' Dr Nuttall's stoical side replied.

'OK... bursting into giggles during moments of strife had its genesis in these times of meagre and struggle. The tendency has remained with me since, guaranteed to let me down at awkward moments, like now for instance,' said Johannes, promptly bursting into giggles. Clearly, staging the scenario had been as much a strain for Johannes as his audience.

'Ah!' said Dr Nuttall's stoical side, while the twitch gathered in magnitude.

'Finish off, that twitch looks dangerous. And get a grip on our bloody giggling,' Inner Voice urged.

But Johannes's giggling insisted on taking its natural course. After some embarrassing seconds, during which time Dr Nuttall and Jane Titmarsh continued fighting their own demons, Johannes regained his composure.

'Thank you, Johannes, we most certainly got more than we had expected and have learned more this morning than the whole of last week at the Sunset Club for Derelict Landladies,' Dr Nuttall's voice quavered, 'um, what are your responses, Miss Titmarsh?'

'I have to say I found Johannes's unexpected theatre amusing at first, but I am afraid it went out of control after a while, which greatly alarms me.'

Johannes could not understand, as the latter part of his scenario had been just as controlled as the beginning.

'The latter part had been no different to the beginning,' Johannes defended.

'I, um, tend to agree with you, Johannes,' Dr Nuttall responded, 'but I also sympathise with Miss Titmarsh. Most of the sketch was alarming and I have to say I have not interviewed anyone with – how can I put it – unorthodox imagination. Perhaps it would be better for all of us to leave it there for the time being, and we will compile a report for Professor Price in due course. But I feel bound to make one more comment: I have never had to call so much on all the skills of my profession in order to control my alarm.'

'I asked you several times!' Johannes burst defensively, his eyes glued to the twitching half-face.

'I confess this is true, Johannes. Thank you, that will be all for now.'

As Johannes left the office, Dr Nuttall and Jane Titmarsh sat rooted to their chairs staring blankly into silence.

'*Do you know,*' Inner Voice growled, '*we have the distinct impression those two nutters could do with the services of the University Psychological Counselling Service themselves before nosing into our life.*'

'What was that you said, Johannes?' Dr Nuttall snapped.

'Um, nothing, didn't realise I had spoken.'

'Good day to you, Johannes.'

'*Bloody...*'

6
Painting Special

F OLLOWING THE INTERMEDIATE course assessment results, Johannes was advised of the external moderators' remarking upon the imbalance of his folio in favour of drawing. This was remarkable, considering this was *after* his folio had been relieved of many drawings in the raids. But for Johannes the tomb raiding exercise indicated an irrefutable logic: long before the results were published it was obvious that he had passed.

The reveille boosted Johannes's self-belief in regard to his drawing skills in particular and capability in general. But Johannes's inability to avoid an impulsive decision based on his narrow skill, which he determined to see as broad, and his dithering indecisiveness over obvious facts, sent him in a south-easterly direction down a strange lane.

Traditionally, the last three weeks of session on the intermediate course were given over to trial periods on the specialist undergraduate courses of choice. Without hesitation Johannes chose painting special, and resolutely closed off all other choices. The logic was simple: painting special was dominated by life studies, the only discipline in which he felt comfortably competitive, as the course followed a path of the Old Masters in studies of the figure and composition. This entailed working in oils on canvas, graphite on parchment and etching on copper plate. Subject matter was based on the human figure and creative imagination.

But the painting module on the course was a huge problem, because although no one was aware of it, Johannes's synaesthesia confused his way of mastering the objectivity of colour. All the tutors were aware that Johannes was hopelessly dysfunctional in colour use, that something was drastically wrong, but no one could identify the cause. Johannes compensated by drawing with the brush, rather than the more orthodox use of the brush for applying fields of colour. This had driven such purists as head of painting Professor Bill Price quite apoplectic and, when Johannes chose painting special for undergraduate studies, Price had a bad day at the office.

'Hell's teeth, Taliesin! Are you sure you know what you are taking on? I would have thought graphic illustration, preferably black and white illustrative graphics, would be better suited to your drawing abilities.'

'No, Sir; graphic illustration does not work from the figure as painting special does,' was Johannes's sensible if perhaps adamant reply.

'I have to say the prospect of your graduating from an undergraduate study in painting special can best be described as vanishingly small.'

'Oh, good,' was Johannes's buoyantly sarcastic reply.

'Hell's teeth! What's good about vanishingly small, Taliesin?'

'At least you don't put my chances at zero, Professor.'

'Your optimism is a phenomenon apart. Good heavens, young man, in the world of degree assessment, vanishingly small and zero pretty well enjoy the same nihilistic point.'

'Yes, Sir.'

'And do you know what is a point in physics, Taliesin?'

'Yes, Sir.'

'Well, what is it?' the professor demanded.

'In physics a point is a position with no dimension, Sir, but a point of nihilism is a condition in psychology where retraction is a function of the possible,' Johannes replied.

'Good God! Regardless, take heed, Taliesin,' the professor

snorted, 'whilst we agree with Dr Janes you have a measure of ability in life drawing, the painting special course demands you major in *painting* the figure, and I have no faith your painting skills can embrace that challenge,' Price was indeed being reasonable.

But Johannes dug in, believing he had come thus far by sheer doggedness, and would therefore continue along the successful path. After all, was he not a group dynamic infill in whom no one except Fred Janes had any faith? Painting special it had to be, as life drawing was the only skill in which he had confidence.

'Even your life drawing is merely descriptive and demonstrates no powers of creativity at all!' Bill Price began to harangue, as his reasonable attitude was making no headway with Johannes, 'I'm sure your lack of creativity would not be identified in illustrative graphics. Besides, painting special demands single-minded fitness for purpose, which the Psychological Counselling Service reminds me is not altogether your companion.'

'Did you hear that? The bloody Psychological Counselling Service!' Inner Voice must surely have been asleep until that moment.

Bringing the University Psychological Counselling Service into the debate was a significant error on Professor Price's behalf.

'What did they suggest *is* my companion, Professor Price?'

'They did not suggest anything! It was from the general ambience of their report that I was taking your lack of fitness for purpose,' the professor responded irritably.

'May I see the report?'

'Certainly not! It is a confidential report to me about one of our students who is giving cause for concern.'

'Perhaps if I were to see the report I could make amends for what seems to be causing academic staff disaffection with me.'

'Whilst I agree with you the academic staff have disaffection for you, it is college policy not to disclose the contents of confidential reports, and that's the end of the matter,' Professor Price responded curtly.

'That's it; our decision is buttoned up.'

But Johannes had scored a moral point, and Professor Price's demeanour could not conceal his unhappiness at constructing his own checkmate, especially with Johannes Taliesin.

Bringing the Psychological Counselling Service's report into the debate together with the implication that painting special was a creative cut above illustrative graphics drove Johannes resolutely against the latter and towards the impossible former. So, to the professor's utter dismay along with all of the other tutors except Dr Alfred Janes, who were associated with what was regarded as the flagship of Swansea College of Art, Johannes Taliesin enrolled on the elite undergraduate painting special course. This decision came at a crucial juncture in the institution's history.

At that moment in the academic cycle, enrolment numbers to the college of art and quality assessment outcomes were both being rigorously monitored by the Ministry of Education. At stake was the college's eligibility to continue provision of undergraduate courses. But Johannes was unaware of the greater bureaucratic machinery afoot. From his perspective he believed academic resistance and obduracy were of a personal nature. Johannes had always confused doggedness with stubbornness, so persisted in his intent towards the impossible. After all, his options were limited and, although most academics realised this, they did not wish to be seen to be conceding to Johannes's obtuse choice of specialist undergraduate study on the college's flagship course.

But of course Johannes was not alone in denial: for different reasons the whole of the academic body of staff was in collective denial. Art education was at the cusp of change. The reservoir of largesse that faithfully supported the old elitist art education centres was drying up. The traditional means of financing through a combination of municipal and private funding was increasingly subject to political interference, which resulted in a contagion of government inspectors spreading like an unwelcome rash across the face of the country's art and design provision.

Reviews were under way that would soon bring into existence a statutory requirement that colleges of art maintain numbers through a new granting realism that demanded value for money and more public accountability. Public accountability! The very thought stuck in the craw of dyed-in-the-wool traditionalist art academics. What was the country coming to? Obviously these reviews were undertaken as political expedients, a sop to voters, and had nothing whatever to do with quality of outcomes and value for money: so the thinking went in the groves of academe.

Regardless of the obduracy of academia, the allocation of recurrent block grant funding would in future be subject to a strict formula, rather than the customary method of simple demand via local council lobbying. The academics were plunged into deep shock and, although making a brave and valiant effort to man the barricades, they nevertheless gave vent to their frustrations on such quota infilling miscreants as Johannes Taliesin.

Although the new funding apparatus being proposed departed appreciably from the chronic institutional overspend that had hitherto been met unquestioningly by the municipal councils, the early 1960s funding mechanism still had a long way to go before it could be termed as an efficient and unequivocal tool: art colleges were still miles adrift of the clinical accountability of industry and commerce, and even *that* was sloppy compared to many international competitors. But the sacred cow status enjoyed by art and design was being challenged, and all the horrified academics seemed capable of doing was to run around like headless chickens.

All of this was too far in the background for Johannes, the typical unwitting pawn on the periphery of unsavoury bureaucratic scenes. It was beyond his comprehension, and he remained oblivious to the greater political war being waged. Unless students sought out the information individually they would never be advised on the politics of financial administration, except in the case of better housekeeping.

Johannes's friend Rees Bowen was conversant in such matters. But Johannes soon lost his grasp of the technicalities when discussing the ins and outs of recurrent funding with him, 'I'm sure all this business of reviews and inspections doesn't really affect us,' Johannes said confidently.

'Don't be so sure: you are ill served by your tenuous grasp, Yoyo,' was Rees's reply.

'How does it affect us then, Rees?'

'In many ways! For a start we might find a reduction in our consumable materials allowance. This would hurt you more than me because, whilst you are wholly dependent on handouts, I'm in a position to purchase much, if not all, of what I require. But a reduction in college funding for apparatus and equipment would affect us all.'

'What's the difference?'

'God, for one who spends so much time in the municipal library, you are extraordinarily dim about higher education funding,' Rees retorted.

'Yes, you are right. So, what's the difference?'

'Cartridge paper, acid, copper plates, printing inks and suchlike given for use in the studios are known as consumables. Apparatus and equipment includes items like easels, donkeys, furniture, printing presses and the like. You must think all these grow on trees, Yoyo.'

'Don't they?' replied Johannes, 'No, only joking, and I get what you are saying, Rees. Except in my case there are no trees, no trees that I can shake, that is; I beg and scrounge wherever.'

'Honestly, Yoyo, I don't know what to make of you these days. You seem to have blinded yourself to the realities around us. No wonder you wind old Pricey up. The college supplies a hell of a lot of things that you use for free!'

'Hmm.'

Regardless Rees's updating on consumables, and with all the events transacting, the academic staff had no option but to accept Johannes on the undergraduate painting special course. They were caught on the sharp points of a painful dilemma: due to no overall improvement in Swansea College of Art enrolment returns, Johannes's status as a statistical remedy to Ministry of Education quotas pertained. On the other point, his low quality outcome would be detrimental to the college in the event his work was reviewed during an inspection.

Johannes was the beneficiary of a situation that the complacent academics failed to see coming some years previously, which a period of astute marketing would have remedied. To be sure, however, if the college had enjoyed a fortuitous upturn in quality student enrolments, Johannes would never have been enrolled or even so, would have been unceremoniously dumped following the fracas in the life class. He chose to thrust all of this background debate beyond his little world; it was maintained as background equally by most academics, whose perspectives centred on presenting an image to the next official inspection that all was fine on board the sinking ship called Swansea College of Art.

Within the confines of the staff's narrow perspective it was important to preserve the status quo. What this really amounted to for Johannes was that they did not wish him to join a small elite group of talented painters, talented that is within the parameters of their curriculum and the nod of gurus in the claustrophobic crucible of Swansea College of Art. Painting was seen as the sexiest discipline in the college; consequently it would guarantee to attract disproportionate attention from visiting inspectors. In this conflict in a teacup it never occurred to the academics that the inspectors may well have already derogated the college's status by examining its statistical track record of poor enrolments and previous shaky outcomes.

'Be warned, Taliesin; painting special attracts the attention of inspectors like flies around a gluepot,' was Professor Price's dig at Johannes on the subject. But his incredulity knew now bounds, 'Who would believe it?' he despaired, 'A late entry numbers infill devoid of any skill enrolling on the painting special course! Hell's teeth! Now I have witnessed the blessed lot!'

'But I am probably the best read of all the students on the painting special course, Professor Price,' Johannes gambled.

'Oh, I'll grant you that, Taliesin; but the inspectors look for practical realities, not literate abstracts. The only reason I would point an inspector in your direction would be if he had an interest in Faulkner.'

'Or Camus, Kafka, Durrell, Cassirer, Oliver, Einstein, et al., Professor.'

Through his childhood circumstances of meagre and struggle Johannes had long since perfected the art of head burying and, not only oblivious to the broader perspective of the college's fate vis-à-vis national change, he was even blind to the parochial message being paraded at the bottom of the teacup. No one could hold a candle to the perfection of Johannes's blinkered mindset.

Ken Hendy had by now moved to the final undergraduate year of painting special and, due to his undisputed charisma and undoubted talent in painting, was the natural leader of the group. Upon learning that Johannes had joined them he once again lost his jovial presence of mind, the previous occasion being not one to dwell on. The senior painting specials held a council of crisis in the etching room studio.

'Johannes Puking Taliesin joining painting special?' Ken Hendy exploded, 'Jesus Christ, that's the end of us as a centre of excellence in painting. No, second thoughts, that's the end of Swansea College of Art. What's Price doing, allowing it? Taliesin the puke artist shall not ruin painting special, not if I can help it.'

So it was that the un-elected student leader of the painting special group went in search of Johannes Taliesin. On discovering Johannes in the Antique Studio cutting hardboard to A1 size with a borrowed saw, he immediately attacked.

'What are you doing, Taliesin, cutting hardboard in the Antique Studio? Has it occurred to you this studio is only for painting and drawing the model, not cutting hardboard.'

'Yes, I know,' Johannes replied.

Having by this stage out-faced the psychologists and the formidable opposition of Professor Price, Johannes's skills in obduracy were maturing fast alongside his drawing talents. Lectures from students, even charismatic students like Ken Hendy, left him ice cold.

'If you know, then why do you do it, for heaven's sake?'

'I don't do it for heaven's sake: I do it for my sake,' Johannes replied.

'You know what I mean!' Ken shouted, quickly losing his rag.

'Of course I know what you mean, and you should know I know what you mean. The workshops are locked because the workshop staff have already gone on holiday. Even if I could retrieve a key to the workshops, they are out of bounds unsupervised. If I don't prepare these boards now I will have no other opportunity because tomorrow I start night-shift in a bakery,' Johannes retorted.

'What do you mean, night-shift in a bakery?' Ken asked.

'I mean night-shift in a bakery, which I have to do for the whole of the bloody holiday because I don't get a grant like most people.'

'Johannes, you swore!' exclaimed Ken Hendy, attempting to deflect from the embarrassing turn of information his intervention had procured.

'Yes, I bloody swore! And no doubt I'll bloody swear again as it's a pleasant way of relieving my frustrations with such a lot of one-eyed selfish people around me!'

'Good God, Johannes! I didn't know you had it in you; puking, yes; but swearing is another matter,' Ken responded.

'I haven't got it in me,' Johannes replied tartly, 'that's the bloody problem, I haven't.'

'What I came about was the odd idea that you believe you are up to the standard required for the painting special course,' Ken Hendy fought back.

'Well, I am up to the standard. I've argued Price to a standstill on the matter, so if necessary I'm quite prepared to argue you to a standstill as well. Anyway, since when were you the designated quality adjudicator for the course?' Johannes was becoming uncharacteristically heated.

'It seems some of us have to in order to maintain standards,' Ken shouted.

'You have no authority, moral or academic, and you know it, so will you please leave me alone? I don't have much time as I start night-shift in a bakery tomorrow night.'

'Clearly the shy backwoods Johannes Taliesin is becoming increasingly reactionary and bloody-minded. We shall have to keep our fingers out of his trough!' whereupon Ken Hendy retreated from the Antique Studio. From that moment he never intentionally spoke to Johannes again, which meant many of his acolytes were also struck dumb.

'Phew! We didn't know we had it in us!' Inner Voice crowed.

Notwithstanding the immense noise of discouragement from academic staff and colleagues alike, the lack of support no longer impacted on Johannes.

'Lack of support doesn't mean a bloody thing to us anymore, they can all go and piss into the wind.'

Following the long vacation of night-shift baking, a pale and even slimmer Johannes settled down on the painting special course. Around him his suntanned colleagues boasted their wonderful international holidays, hiking in the Swiss Alps, diving off to Minorca, sailing their father's yacht around the Mediterranean, borrowing Mummy's car and driving down to the toe of Italy. All Johannes could contribute to the conversation were tales of tedious times peeling off hot bread from steam pipe ovens throughout every night, and snatches of interrupted sleep during the daytime. When asked about his holidays he would remark without elaboration that he had not had a holiday, but at least had earned some money.

However, during the holiday period, in the few hours remaining in the late afternoon of each day between sleep and work, Johannes began drawing ethereal landscapes and writing abstract poetry. This work marked a psychological shift in his disposition: a change to a darker character that on his return both the staff and his colleagues could not help but notice. So much tough physical work, and so many unsavoury incidents at college in the past three months impressed Johannes to build a socio-psychological hermitage about him. It was at this time that the legacy of bakery night-shift work caused his sleeping requirements to take an abnormal turn, i.e. henceforward he got by with short power naps, day or night.

175

Concomitant with Johannes's constant problem regarding lack of creativity and generally low skill level he was systematically building up a folio of untoward events. At the time of entering the painting special course he had blotted his copybook big time through the excruciatingly embarrassing event in life class, the subsequent reprimand from Professor Price, followed by a deeply humiliating counselling session with the University Psychological Counselling Service. These related issues lost Johannes the little kudos he had had. Regardless, he was actually enjoying the painting special course, and continued to be an eager visitor to the Swansea Municipal Library.

The life-drawing module was his saviour, but he struggled courageously to express figure colour-work, the result of the synaesthesia battle going on in his head.

Unsurprisingly, Johannes discovered an immensely satisfying sympathy to etching, but never fully mastered the problem of volte-face printing, which did not prevent his production of etching prints in enormous quantities, although not many could be classified as passable.

His compositional paintings were rendered on hardboard, the poor man's answer to canvas. Johannes could not afford real oil paint from real tubes of oil paint. His oil paints were constituted from tempera powders mixed with raw linseed oil. This produced a syrup-like texture in the oil paint that rendered it almost impossible to apply in naturally flowing brush-strokes. Once applied to the hardboard, the goo had an affinity with gravity like no other natural stuff containing mass, remorselessly travelling downward over the painting as dervish lava, producing grotesque imagery on its way. Too often Johannes viewed the end product with humour, but tutors viewed it with dismay and frustration; certainly humour never intervened in their judgements.

So Johannes compensated for all the drawbacks of weakness

in painting, composition in oils and, to a lesser degree, etching, by concentrating on straightforward drawing of the figure. His implements were usually cartridge paper and pencil. Occasionally he ventured into charcoal, thick stick graphite, conté crayon or pastilles, but the medium of first and last resort was a hard black graphite pencil that yielded a flinty line, as opposed to the thick oily graphite pencils many students preferred. Johannes was happiest when the cartridge paper resisted the pull of the graphite, so drawing became a hard masculine action: this gave him better control of linear work.

He drew the nude figure from all angles in all poses in varieties of lighting and settings. He was a fixture in the Antique Studio life classes, regardless of which discreet cohort had been timetabled for its use. The college of art boasted other life study studios besides the Antique Studio and, faithfully, Johannes could be found working in them also. His favourite model for drawing studies was Sophie, not only as she possessed superb classical form, but she was also an excellent model at holding a pose and re-taking that pose after a break, no matter how long the interval.

His excess of life drawing study paid dividends, but had a deleterious effect on the other modules of the painting special course. Johannes stoically refused to let the discrepancy of work balance in his folio bother him; he optimistically believed examiners and inspectors alike would be wowed by the abundance of quality life drawings presented. Consequently, the painting tutors – Professor Price particularly – despaired of his ever getting to grips with the task of oil painting.

Many people engaged in talking *about* Johannes Taliesin, but few talked *to* him. No doubt, there was much to talk about. Visually, he was an indecorous sight. His attire was in a serious state of ruin. His trousers – his only trousers – the drainpipe fashion, displayed many examples of his unskilled hand stitching masquerading as repair patchwork. He had discovered a source of patches: discarded off-cuts collected in a large recycling bin in the fashion department. Instead of brazenly walking into the studio, he inveigled fashion students to supply the patches on the basis they were to be used as paint rags. In their innocence the girls had donated the materials believing they were to be used in the furtherance of Johannes's art, but at a later date one of the girls recognised the rags attached to his drainpipe trousers walking down the Endless Corridor.

'You know those paint rags we gave Yoyo Taliesin last week?'

'Yes, what about them?'

'I've just seen them walking down Endless Corridor!'

'What? How?'

'Attached to his trousers, would you believe?'

'No!'

'Attached to his drainpipes! On my mother's grave!'

'I've always said, he's a strange one. Last paint rag I'll give him, too embarrassing.'

'Oh, I don't know; perhaps next time we'll give him highly colourful ones and wait to see where he attaches them!'

And the second year fashion cohort burst into squealing laughter.

Johannes's sartorial shortcomings were colour-matched more by the creeping stealth of general over-use and ill repair, rather than by design. His sweater, originally a neat fitting number his mother had knitted six or so years ago had assumed the sloppy variety. Now it was only partly there: ragged at elbow, neck, cuff; the only area enjoying a questionable form of integrity was the front, which was preserved by cascades of linseed oil, oil paint, fixative, coffee, scrumpy. Each variety of natural preservative vied for attention according to the propensity of the individual viewer to be disgusted.

Over the lot he wore a once-black-but-now-faded-grey

duffle coat, worn both winter and summer, which conveniently hid other sartorial deficiencies. Beneath the sweater – his fellow students could but guess, as following a line of non-washing Neanderthals established by his paternal grandfather and re-enforced by his father, he avoided the gruesome task of contact with water, so avoided peeling below the sloppy sweater layer.

It was impossible to define the colour of Johannes's suede boots. The suede itself, long since surrendered to over-wear, had become an all-weather shine. In a similar gesture of despair the heels had departed the company of the soles, leaving ankle-hugging shines. The soles sported gaping holes that were daily stopped with cardboard mustered from the cardboard off-cut depository outside the graphics department. Water effortlessly flowed inward on rainy days, readily returning the way it had entered when he reached a dry environment. These faithful remnants were the only footwear Johannes possessed. The aroma from his feet combined stale Danish Blue with pig dung, although even the best-trained olfactory detectives experienced difficulty in differentiating between the finer divisions of the thick odour that emanated from the foot department.

'Taliesin, pardon my asking, but do you ever wash your feet?' painting tutor-cum-painter George Fairley ventured.

'Frequently, Mr Fairley.'

'The odour emanating from the region of your feet belies an obvious infrequency,' he articulated in his strong Edinburgh accent.

'I can assure you, Mr Fairley, my feet get a washing every time it rains.'

'I guessed so. We seem to be suffering the current drought in more ways than one, would you not agree, Taliesin?'

'Yes, Sir, back home in Cardiganshire the fields are parched.'

The state of Johannes's personal welfare gave the college philanthropists cause for concern. He was seriously malnourished and suffered a medical classification of being 'chronically underweight'. Fortunately his art student status exempted him from the unwanted attentions of institutional medical people and affiliated busybodies. For some time he had avoided registering with a general practitioner, as his name was still on the lists of the family one back home. His state of health had long since been a matter of public concern, primarily on account of other healthier students contracting maladies by having been in disease-jumping proximity to Johannes.

'Have you visited your doctor recently, Yoyo?'

'Oh, don't you start as well, Rees.'

'Obviously I'm not the only one concerned about your health.'

'You are the only one concerned about my health, Rees. The others want me to visit a doctor in case I have a contagious disease.'

'Skeletal people like you contract less contagions than do fatties.'

'That's greatly comforting, Rees.'

The main cause of Johannes's graveyard condition was a dire lack of funds, but doubtless with his undisciplined dietary habits and his extremist tendencies had he been financially comfortable he would have been as fat as a hippopotamus in less time than it takes to say,

'Two helping of fish and chips, please, on the same plate.'

But it was not to be: he suffered permanent hunger, except when working night shift in the bakery, but then the extra calorific intake was easily defeated by the sheer heat and labour.

Although Johannes would have preferred a friendly ingratiation with his fellow students, he possessed an enormous handicap to better public relations – his personality. It took him some considerable time to realise the superficiality of people in the art world; that no matter what he did or said, people disliked him on account of his physical and animal appearance, of his prickly here and there personality and his capricious moods of indifference. In upholding his peasant innocence he readily produced a disarming grin, stimulated partly as a defence procedure and partly due a repetitive nervous spasm, which proved unimaginably irritating to those occupying the same studio. The grin was dominated by a gap in his front teeth, the result of a rag stunt involving breaking into the local gaol that fortunately did not go according to plan.

'Hi, uncle, we've come to fetch you!'

'Uh-oh! Below, Dyfnallt, there's a bloody prison warden.'

'Below, for God's sake!'

'Nice human pyramid, boys.'

'There's a warden, on *our* side of the wall! Pass it up!'

'Are you coming in or going out, boys?' the warden asked,

'Uncle, we've – what? Oh, shi –'

'Chri – watch where you're – shit!'

'Sorry, Mr Warden, just a rag stunt.'

'Bugger, I've lost a tooth.'

'Uh-oh, Yoyo's lost a tooth. Mind, it was rotten, hanging in there.'

'Let me see – you've lost two by the look of it, Yoyo – no, only joking, one will do!'

'I'll have to report this to your vice-chancellor,' the warden threatened, refusing to accept their game was but a rag stunt. It became another blot on Johannes's file, along with his gappy grin. A visit to a dentist was far too traumatic an ordeal for Johannes to even contemplate, as no doubt when repairing the gap the dentist would be attracted to the challenge the remainder of his set presented.

Some wisps of downy red beard hung about his weak chin, framed by the usual acne that rampaged across a thin, extremely pale, face; the rest of his face was dotted with greenish freckles, ad hoc. Atop this unprepossessing visage was a self-barbered patchy thatch of un-groomed bright ginger hair, matted and long at the rear due to prolonged neglect and being out of scissor reach. He held a slight suspicion that being the owner of ginger hair registered a disadvantage in the ranks of superficial humanity, but had no scientific evidence to support his suspicions.

The genesis of the suspicions was due to his father's cautionary prefixes: 'Just because you are ginger blah blah…' or 'You have to resist prejudices against your ginger colouring because blah blah…' Over the years these insensitively sown seeds grew to become Giant Californian Redwoods that defied axe and psychologist. It would take years yet before Johannes realised his father's genius lay in the deft planting of a seed that would take root following a supposed throwaway remark.

Temperamentally Johannes was certifiably edgy, at the most even of times. Apart from the rare outburst of nervous chatter he normally manifested long periods of morose introspection, much to the relief of the painting special group. In fairness to Johannes, his conversational regime was dictated by his fellow students' disinclination to congregate close enough to enable the mechanics of talking to function, on account of his distressing body odours, augmented by his other antisocial tendency – argumentativeness, closely allied to a compulsive giggle disorder. Johannes was better read than most, if not all, of his fellow painting specials. His reservoir of information was a handicap, though, due in the main to his immaturity in despatching colleagues who had the temerity to argue on matters of book-based fact.

Johannes was devoid of rage, much to his father's chagrin but his mother's delight. As compensation he had a good line in irritability, such as with drawing and painting materials, which of course possessed a life of their own, and generally with people nosing too close to his affairs. He reserved his greatest contempt for his drawing hand, which went AWOL all too often, especially following his brain's close encounter with the alcohol vehicle scrumpy.

Johannes housed many psychological and physiological disorders. One, known as sound-colour synaesthesia, was a distinct handicap to the process of learning; another was the work ethic. As his father had successfully kept the work ethic at a healthy arm's length, it must have been his mother who imbued him the handicap. It was difficult to ascertain which of the two inheritances was the greater handicap. His work ethic ensured the over-production of mountains of artwork, which quality was almost wholly mediocre: unfortunately Johannes had long ago muddled quality with quantity in an inextricable tangle.

The second inheritance of synaesthesia – colour-hearing syndrome – presented problems of a much more fundamentally incurable nature. Due to a genetic cerebral wiring unorthodoxy words assumed viability and priority through the colour they triggered before their meaning was grasped, which led to misunderstandings of monumental stature. In his paintings, Johannes's colour use represented both the visual and audio worlds, which led to endless misinterpretation. The result was visual and verbal chaos, neither one thing nor the other, and although Johannes was striving for lucidity throughout, neither he nor his mentors were aware of the underlying cause of his dysfunctional colour intrusion on perception.

To compound the live new departure, numbers also possessed colours: some number colours being more prominent than others. For example, the prominent colour that five assumed was of a higher value than six's colour, with many similar instances all the way to infinity. Hence Johannes would often take the value of a number from its colour. Ten was numerically superior to eleven, which might account for his always being short of cash. The syndrome synaesthesia, taken together with his battle between objectivity and daydreaming imagination, afforded an interesting life.

It was not long after Johannes commenced the painting special course that the academic staff associated with that course became convinced his painting and colour works were awful, to the great despair of everyone. Generally his work was mimetic and reactionary, of a struggling classical style, anchored in the work of the French neoclassicists with flourishes of Impressionism, but unfortunately without the substructure. His synaesthesia guaranteed sporadic swerves into abstraction, which lacked the follow-up, was clearly out of context, and invariably ruined the struggling mimetic classical theme. Thematically his work was taking on an increasingly dark nature.

The main obstacle to Johannes's development, apart from an obvious lack of talent, was his conviction that he was an artist of the first rank: he obstinately refused to accept otherwise, much to the frustration of his tutors and irritation of his contemporaries. Trouble was, due to his deep-seated insecurity, Johannes would not be told, regardless how obvious his errors.

'Stand back from the easel, Taliesin, let me see your painting. Hmm… hm… structure lost in too many focal points, don't you agree?' Professor Price said on one particular occasion.

'Um.'

'Re-classify the underlying fundamental, if you don't agree.'

'Seems alright to me, Sir.'

'Good Lord, Taliesin! You can't even compose properly. Like this… and this… and here. There! Can you not see the structure was all out?' as the Professor ably demonstrated with a few charcoal lines across the painting.

Meanwhile his colleagues had ceased working on their own paintings to stand around gawping in thrall at the entertainment that always ensued when Professor Price and Johannes tangled in discussion.

'Yes, Sir, you may be right.'

'Stop obfuscating, for heaven's sake! There's no may be about it! I *am* right! Anyway, what is your subject matter?' he demanded.

'It sort of began as a view of work in the Aluminium Wire and Cable Company on Jersey Marine, but I had other inspirational notions after I had started.'

'Of what?'

'Of Dante's *Inferno*,' Johannes replied, knowingly hesitant.

'Hence the structure has become lost,' Professor Price was unforgiving, 'what are you superimposing on the composition?'

'I'm reading this book on time dilation and compression,' Johannes responded enthusiastically, 'reviewed distantly history seems to be compressed, so all events crush upon each other; but in the present – real time, that is – it is spread out with ample space between events. It's the same when one thinks back on one's own life: one doesn't think of the gaps or the spaces, just the events.'

Professor Price stared at Johannes and blinked theatrically.

'I must confess I'm not too sure what you are talking about, young man. Besides, why are you superimposing these ideas on top of a composition of the Aluminium Wire and Cable Company and Dante's *Inferno*?' the enquiry was quite reasonable, but it appeared the logic was beyond Johannes.

There followed a typical Taliesin delay in delivering a reply.

'*Shit,*' Inner Voice interjected, '*Pricey has got a point. We must admit it.*'

'Well, perhaps.'

'WHAT?' the professor exploded.

The audience was greatly entertained.

'*Go on, admit it, before he blows up into bits of avoirdupois all over the bloody Antique Studio.*'

'I believe it's one and the same thing, Professor Price.'

185

'Hell's teeth, Taliesin, is your mentality descending into something worse!' the professor roared, 'too much reading and not enough practical painting!'

Whereupon he stormed out of the Antique Studio, a move obviously designed to preserve his own health.

'And what are you pygmies staring at?' Johannes growled at his colleagues.

Such was Johannes's stand-off relationship with the head of painting, which surely possessed the impetus to cascade down to other academic staff responsible for input to the painting special course.

Johannes's written work, as with his practical painting, was produced on a voluminous scale with scant regard for meaning. What was committed to the written word was mostly unstructured, fold-in, stream-of-consciousness stuff, heavily influenced by his reading of Joyce, Faulkner, the nature poets, Camus and Kafka, the lot interspersed with irrelevant passages of quantum physics and cosmology. His synaesthesia guaranteed beautiful colour schemes within the sentences that were regrettably meaningless to everyone, except the author. He would gush readings of his work at anyone prepared to stand still in his vicinity, but mostly they glazed over. No one at Swansea College of Art could profess the slightest empathy with Johannes Taliesin's literary creations.

Patterns of his inflated delusion meandered their well-exercised pathways, and no one had a clue whence he derived the engine that drove his grandiose notions of artistic infallibility, poetic transcendentalism and literary flourish. Considering the meagre and struggle of his rural background this was unusual stuff, and the author was being labelled by his contemporaries as strange, distant, out of touch. To all intents and purposes Johannes engaged a state of deep psychological denial whenever his peer group were audacious enough to be judgemental.

'If forced to return a normal acceptance mode, we think the balance of our mind could be in serious jeopardy,' Inner Voice's galactic truth cascaded.

His irredeemable character glitch lay in a seamlessly selective amnesia. Unwelcome matters of fact obtruding on his daydream world or detracting from his postulated self-delusion would be peremptorily wiped from his memory with a codicil banning return.

Having failed to register with a general practitioner since enrolling at the college of art, Johannes had assumed that he could reserve, or if needs be agglomerate, a list of afflictions as they presented themselves, for a one-off flying visit to the family practitioner back home, if he could afford the fare, that is.

One such visit was necessary during his first year on painting special, due to a nasty little rash on his penis that refused to depart following what Johannes had assumed to be a night of too much scrumpy-induced blindness with a girl of ill repute. It was of little comfort to Johannes that, due to the excesses of scrumpy and, more likely, morbid complexes of inadequacy, he had failed abysmally to fulfil his side of the bargain. Apart from the psychological trauma of panic-induced impotence, the occasion in question saw his inebriation obstructing a proper definition of reality, whereby the girl of ill repute had taken one whiff of his body odours and was off into the night.

Be that as may, instead of prescribing Johannes the required medication and done with, the horrified family practitioner delivered a lecture on the sexual behaviour and moral decline of young people in Wales. Johannes felt he had mistaken his doctor's surgery for the anteroom of the local Pentecostal Adventists: his embarrassment knew no bounds.

'Did you not wear a sheath?' Doctor was aghast.

'Er, no, Doctor.'

'What?'

'Why doesn't he get on with the prescription and done with?'

'No.'

'Did it not occur to you the girl might get pregnant?'

'I withdrew, I think.'

'You THINK! Are you no more sure than that?' Doctor exploded.

'*They'll hear him in the bloody waiting room,*' Inner Voice was laden with worries.

'I had been drinking scrumpy, so I was a little bit, um, a bit…'

'Are you saying you were drunk?'

'*Oh, God,*' Inner Voice groaned.

'A little bit, Doctor.'

'How drunk? Were you just merry? Or would you say you were not in full control of your behaviour? How drunk would you say you were?'

'*Don't tell him! He'll raise his bloody voice again.*'

'Blotto, Doctor, if you must know.'

'*Oh God! What did we have to tell the nosey bugger the truth for?*' Inner Voice was aghast.

'This is getting worse! Are you aware of the other risks attached to unprotected sex?'

'Um, that's… that's why I'm um, why I'm here, Doctor.'

'Apart from the risk of the girl's pregnancy, there is also a health risk. Really, morals are getting very loose these days. I thought we had re-established firm morals after the war, but it appears morals are as loose as ever in certain sections of society. I blame rock 'n' roll.'

'*Nothing to do with music.*'

'What?'

'Didn't say anything, Doctor.'

'Thought for a moment… it so happens this Practice is participating in a survey regarding the morals of young people in Wales. Does everyone behave like you at Swansea College of Art?'

'*Watch it, a trap,*' Inner Voice rang the warning bell.

'I think you could say that the majority of the college and I live separate existences, Doctor.'

'*Good answer.*'

'Surely not!' Doctor exclaimed.

'Surely yes, so I don't know, Doctor. Anyway, I don't ask them and if I did they wouldn't tell me; I would get a ragging for mounting a moral crusade.'

'*Good answer, rub the moral bit in.*'

'Why on earth should your fellow students give you a ragging for taking a moral stance, for heaven's sake?' the doctor was into everything.

'*Uh-oh.*'

'Because...' Johannes stuttered, 'because they wouldn't expect me of all people to launch into a moral crusade.'

'That tells me everything I need to know about your attitude, Johannes Taliesin. Is your father aware of your behaviour?'

'*Oh, buggeration! Perhaps not such good answers. Sod it.*'

'No, Doctor, and I hope he remains unaware.'

'Of course he shall remain unaware. But if I were not bound by Hippocratic protocols I would make it my duty to inform him,' Doctor snapped. Then, after a pause, he added, 'How is your father? Haven't seen him in years.'

'He is as always, thank you, Doctor; but I also have hardly seen my father in years.'

The lecture ended and Doctor set about examining the article in question. Rather, he did not touch Johannes for fear the rash would jump.

'Let me see... hmm... pull back the foreskin... hmm... put it away!'

'Well, Doctor?'

'That is not venereal… all my experience tells me that is probably due to a general malaise caused by unhealthy living, to a run-down condition and your infrequent use of a bath. That's another thing,' Doctor wound up his anger once again, 'young people in Wales DON'T WASH any more!'

'I washed before I came –'

'Shut it! Don't bring him back onto the venereal thing… lack of washing, good reason.'

'Your panic is a false alarm. That rash is not venereal in origin. And if you MUST indulge in extra-marital coition WEAR A CONDOM!' Doctor roared his lesson to the waiting room and the street beyond. Then he calmed his voice, and asked,

'What's your diet like?'

'OK, I think, Doctor,' Johannes was feeling a good deal more cheerful.

'Do you eat fresh fruit regularly?'

'Um –'

'Tell him the truth, it won't harm.'

'Er, no, Doctor.'

'Thought so. Fresh vegetables?'

'No.'

'Proteins – meat, fish, poultry?'

'Now and again when I can afford it,' Johannes now felt sufficiently relaxed not to hedge.

'AFFORD IT? GOOD HEAVENS! Of your own admission you DRINK!' Again the parley of listeners in the waiting room was furnished with up-to-date details of the consultation, 'If you converted some of your alcohol money into fresh fruit and vegetables, you would not be here wasting my time,' Doctor was once again raising his voice, this time lecturing beyond the waiting room, perhaps the whole of Aberystwyth.

'Oh, good God! Let's get out of here,' Inner Voice had had enough.

'I will write a letter of introduction to the venereal clinic in Bronglais Hospital if it puts your mind at rest. Here is a prescription for the rash,' and he scribbled a prescription.

When Doctor began to write the letter of introduction, Johannes interrupted.

'Thank you, Doctor, but I am pleased to take your word for it.'

As he hastily left Doctor's consulting room, Johannes tried to slip out un-noticed; some hope: all the waiting patients turned to look at him as one.

'We bet at least five of these will know our parents, damn gossips.'

The family practitioner had metamorphosed into a latter-day Pentecostal what-is-Wales-coming-to tub-thumper who ordered Johannes to live a more sensible and abstemious lifestyle by eating nutritious food, take plenty of exercise, have early nights, resist the demon drink, avoid women: the usual Victorian hogwash that delivered nought except onanism. Good heavens! Of course his father was unaware of the little malady, but as a precaution Johannes decided never to visit his family practitioner again.

The painting special students were in their painting atelier tackling a challenging subject colloquially known as compositional design, the same compositional design that Johannes used as a tool to express his newly acquired notions of time dilation and compression a few weeks earlier.

Most students found their solutions evolved systematically: the overall design of their paintings looked so natural that their work had the appearance of having flowed effortlessly through countless processes of development toward perfection without a brushstroke straying into the wrong place. Johannes constituted the remainder of the group: those who needed to work harder to eventually deliver a lesser achievement.

He experienced no problems with structural design – formal elements, focal points, tonal dynamics, balance, tension and so on, so long as his unrestricted imagination did not obtrude. For him it was an elusive colour ambiguity that caused his colour schemes to go AWOL. Problem was Johannes nor anyone else for that matter had realised he was blessed with a colour-hearing condition.

Professor Price burst into the atelier. Glancing around fleetingly, he made a beeline for Johannes. Following more than the lion's share of trials and tribulations Johannes had adopted the circumstantial feeling of being constantly hunted, so Price heading in his direction had the effect of plunging his spirits.

'*Shit! What is it this time?*' Inner Voice was quick to identify a look of non-conviviality zigzagged across the professor's face.

'Taliesin,' the intrusion announced with a large voice, 'could you come with me, please?'

'Is it a lengthy departure, Professor Price?' Johannes asked in a deliberately casual manner.

'I cannot discuss it here. Please look sharp.'

'Just wondered if I needed to wash my brushes.'

'Oh, I see. Yes, you had better swill your brushes, but hurry up, please.'

Outside in the corridor, Bill Price explained in the same voluminous voice,

'You will recall we set up an appointment for you to see the University Psychological Counselling Service?' he boomed to Johannes in particular and Swansea in general.

Johannes's heart sank.

'*Shit! We thought that was over and done with.*'

'As you probably know we uphold a college policy not to disclose the contents of reports of that nature that we have commissioned,' he continued.

Johannes thought frantically.

'*What's he getting at?*' Inner Voice sifted for answers, '*We know the University Psychological Counselling Service sent a report about us, but we weren't given a copy, and –*'

'You mentioned the report before, but I never saw it, Professor.'

'No one said you had, Taliesin,' the professor raised his voice yet further in order that the whole of south Wales could be kept informed of Johannes's progress with the University Psychological Counselling Service, 'it is just that we find ourselves in the difficult position of having to transgress our policy rules in order to satisfy the demands of the University Psychological Counselling Service whereby they wish their client to be made aware of the report's contents. Do you understand?'

'Yes,' he answered in a small voice.

'We have had a bit of a debate with them over this matter, but they have insisted you should be made aware of the report's contents,' the professor was by now engaging a de rigueur irascibility.

'Oh.'

'The psychologists are here at the moment, in my office. Are you prepared to meet with them?'

'*Say no.*'

'Do I have an option?'

'Yes.'

'In that case, yes,' Johannes said, not knowing the response.

'Good heavens, young man, don't you realise this sets a precedent in transgressing college policy on confidentiality?'

'*We didn't set up the bloody meeting with those loonies in the first place. Obviously Price doesn't want us to see the psychologists or perhaps he doesn't want us to learn the report's contents,*' Inner Voice scratched around for meaning, '*but we wonder why he doesn't want us to meet them?*'

'Yes, but if they are already here, then they are here to see me,' Johannes realised his logic could have been construed as insolent.

'*Hmm, just about insolent enough.*'

'Hell's teeth, Taliesin!' the professor could no longer disguise his anxiety, 'they paid *us* the visit to discuss our college policy. As we adamantly refused to transgress college protocols regarding disclosure they subsequently requested audience with you. Be clear: in the first place they did not come to see you.'

'*In which case, we'll bloody well see them.*'

A few students began loitering in the vicinity of the discussion ostensibly for reasons of examining the corridor's current exhibition. Their loitering succeeded in goading Johannes's mood from embarrassment to indiscretion.

'Adds up to the same thing, as I see it, Professor Price.'

'Insolence! I throw you to the wolves: in you go!' and with a swish of his hand Price directed Johannes towards his office.

As he walked down the corridor to meet the psychologists, he was gladdened to hear the professor having a go at the eavesdroppers,

'And what are you lot of busybodies loitering around here for? The work pertinent to your module is much further up the corridor!' he bellowed.

'Come in,' Dr Nuttall's voice called.

Johannes entered the office.

'Hello again, Johannes,' Dr Nuttall breezed, 'as you can see Jane Titmarsh is with me as before.'

Jane Titmarsh nodded acknowledgement.

'Please, Johannes, sit down. Thank you for coming at short notice. Our original intention was to see Professor Price only –'

'Huh!'

'But we encountered certain interpretative difficulties regarding disclosure protocols so felt it opportune to see you direct. Are you in agreement with having a short discussion, Johannes?'

'*Say no.*'

'No,' Johannes surprised himself by obeying his miscreant conscience.

'Come, come, Johannes! We are here because we have been fighting your cause; surely you will grant us a few minutes in return.'

This last had the desired effect of obliging Johannes to feel sufficiently humble to concede the ground.

'*We don't want to know what's in the report,*' Inner Voice niggled.

'I'm not sure if I really want to know what is in your report,' Johannes was speaking honestly, for which not only were the psychologists surprised. Reasonably, Johannes was feeling particularly sore. A few minutes ago he had been contentedly grappling with colour schemes in the peace and quiet of the painting atelier, since when he had been harangued by Price and subjected to the usual public humiliation, and was now face to face with the psychologists whom he had hoped not ever to see again.

'*And God only knows what Price has been trying to suppress,*' Inner Voice suggested.

'We will be brief, Johannes. OK?' Dr Nuttall ventured, as Jane Titmarsh was watching him with a mixed expression of sorrow and contempt.

'*Sweetie Pie's face is a strange picture!*'

'OK,' replied Johannes, his recalcitrance palpable.

'Good,' said Dr Nuttall, 'I will get on with what I want to say, and will not mince my words.'

'*Shit! Here we go again.*'

'Frankly, Johannes Taliesin, we don't know what to make of you. We have had reports from your tutors on the intermediate course in art and crafts, and have seen the report from the Royal Air Force. We have also had the privilege of reading the report written by Principal Hancock on the occasion of your late application interview to this institution, a subsidiary report submitted by Professor Price concerning your behaviour during a life study class, which precipitated our being called in and finally a breakdown of the sectional marks for your intermediate course assessment.'

'So?'

'Beg your pardon, Johannes,' Dr Nuttall quizzed.

'Didn't say anything.'

'We thought you did,' Dr Nuttall replied, glancing quickly in Jane Titmarsh's direction, who reciprocated by nodding acknowledgement.

Dr Nuttall paused, and both psychologists stared in silence at Johannes.

'We've slogged our vacation away doing sweaty nightshift in a bakery just to finance this sort of treatment! Bloody shit!'

'Well?' Johannes posed, insolence welling up.

'Well, for a start, Johannes, we believe your attitude is a grand cover for many matters you do not care to discuss.'

'So?'

'So, are you prepared to discuss matters in an open and trusting dialogue with us?'

'I don't know.'

'That is precisely the point, Johannes: you really don't know. You don't know why you act out of synch with your fellows –'

'We thought we worked in perfect accord with other people: we mostly ignore them.'

'Beg pardon, Johannes?'

'I didn't say anything.'

'Could have sworn you interrupted yet again. Did you hear Johannes say something, Miss Titmarsh?'

'Yes. I believe Johannes said something like 'the perfect accord of ignoring people' or some such phrase.'

Johannes looked scathingly at her.

'If she were alone with us in our bedsit we would give her a bloody good shag,' Inner Voice whispered the boast as a precaution.

'And to continue, you don't know the effect your actions have on your fellow beings; and thirdly, you most probably don't know the dimensions of the issues you are burying.'

'That's it. Try not to say any more.'

'The common thread through all of the reports identifies your inability to fit in with others, whether socially, academically or as a member of a team.'

'That team thing is the bloody RAF,' Inner Voice whispered.

'What is your response to that, Johannes?' Dr Nuttall asked.

Johannes shrugged.

'Your intermediate course assessment marks are quite extraordinary. You obtained average marks for every module except life study, in which you gained 100 per cent, with an overwritten comment by the external examiner, quote, 'the most exquisite life study talent I have witnessed at this level' unquote. How come your work is so, how shall I say, unbalanced, Johannes?'

Johannes shrugged.

'Do you realise your life study is as good as the external examiner commented?' Jane Titmarsh ventured.

'Oh, better than that!' Johannes said, breaking his silence and bursting into giggles.

The psychologists looked on with scornful dismay.

'Please, no more giggling, Johannes,' Dr Nuttall pleaded, obviously remembering.

'OK,' Johannes grunted.

'And Professor Price, contrary to what you think, has a good deal of time for you,' continued Dr Nuttall, 'in one passage of his report he says, quote, 'by far the best read student currently attending this college; would that he could translate some of his enormous literary knowledge into practical craftwork; his life study and eclectic reading stand alone' unquote. What is your response to that, Johannes?'

'I'm aware Professor Price is frustrated with me, but I do my best, you know.'

'Hmm. Let us get to the crunch, Johannes,' said Dr Nuttall, 'we believe you possess a psychological disposition that determines unawareness that your normal countenance can erupt into extreme behaviour without external provocation. The last time we met, you unequivocally proved the transformation of behaviour from normal to extreme without any external prompting. It upset Miss Titmarsh to an extreme degree.'

'*Upset half of your face as well, we remember,*' Inner Voice snapped in a whisper.

'We are professionally concerned that the contents of our report have been withheld due to the college policy of non-disclosure of confidentialities. This does not help you. In fact, we are concerned to the point where we believe it would benefit you to be seen by us again.'

'*Shit.*'

'If you agree we will subject you to colour-sound tests, because many of the reports identify problems you have with colour. We do not intend intruding in the normal tuition of colour management – that is college of art terrain – but rather in colour perception. We know it is not colour-blindness because you have passed your Ishihari tests perfectly. Rather, we believe you suffer from a condition that has been recently identified at Bristol University as synaesthesia, or chromothesia, whereby the patient –'

'*We're a bloody patient now!*'

'– experiences colours when hearing sounds. Our profession is just freshly aware of this condition. Does this resonate with you? Do you recognise what I am talking about?'

'Oh, colours when hearing sounds… of course I do; I presume most people experience colours when hearing sounds, don't they?'

Dr Nuttall and Jane Titmarsh gaped at each other, then burst into whoops of joy.

'Oh God, now what?'

'We've got one of the answers!' whooped Dr Nuttall, 'No, most people certainly do not experience colour when hearing sound, Johannes.'

'How frequently do you experience colour when hearing sounds?' Miss Titmarsh enquired.

'Oh, I see colours when hearing words, names, shouting, doors banging and so on, and when reading numbers, days, months,' Johannes recited, 'Thought most people experienced the same to a degree. Jane is cadmium yellow, by the way.'

'Good heavens,' Dr Nuttall exclaimed, 'the name Jane, I take it?'

'Yes. You are dark chocolate brown with tinges of alizarin crimson.'

'Good heavens,' Jane Titmarsh exclaimed.

'Heaven, five, November, Wednesday are almost the same colour as Jane, but I'm sure there is no other connection,' Johannes said flatly.

'Amazing! Synaesthesia is very rare. We believe true cases are about one in three thousand. It creates much stress for the sufferers, especially in their early years. We will make quick progress from here on, although we have to be sober enough to advise that we think you are hiding other intractable problems as well.'

'Hmm,' Johannes sniffed.

'Would you be prepared to undergo some clinically controlled tests? Yours is the first case we have encountered!'

'Hmm,' Johannes again sniffed, 'explains why I'm having problems with colour. Is it curable?'

'We don't know, Johannes, but we'll have a go.'

'How exciting!' Jane Titmarsh gushed.

We could sh –' Inner Voice stifled.

'Um, didn't say anything,' Johannes blurted, 'but I've always been conscious of seeing colours when hearing sounds.'

The painting special students were all anticipating Johannes's return. The majority would not have lowered their dignity to ask him, relying of course on Rees to put the right questions.

'Why has Price got it in for you so much, Yoyo?' Rees bluntly enquired.

'Because I'm such a threat to him,' Johannes replied, while looking at the rows of blank female faces looking in his direction. The reply had the intended effect of obliging them to get on with their own business. Rees immediately cottoned on.

'In what way are you a threat to him, Yoyo?'

'I have a condition that he's frightened of contracting.'

'Dear me,' said Rees, shaking his head and playing the scene perfectly, 'are you going to disclose the nature of this condition?'

'Synaesthesia.'

'What?'

'Synaesthesia. It's what yokels in rural Cardiganshire inherit due to generations of inbreeding,' Johannes replied flatly.

'Sounds serious, Yoyo.'

'It is serious, Rees. There's probably no future for me in art.'

'That's enough!' Rees choked, 'now tell us what the real problem is.'

'Synaesthesia, I told you,' Johannes replied.

'OK, seriously, what is this synaesthesia thing?'

'Apparently a colour-hearing malady that I had presumed everybody more or less possesses, but the shrinks tell me I'm one in three thousand.'

'You're not joking this time?'

'I have not been joking all along.'

All Johannes's fellow students had unconsciously resumed their staring.

'Manod is dark Prussian blue, Pauline is purplish-brown, Jean is fawn, number six is bluish-silver, nine is the same colour as Pauline, Sophie is pale cerulean, August is pinkish-wine, Wednesday is the same colour as five which is the same colour as Jane, ten is numerically more than eleven and so on all the way up to insanity,' Johannes flourished, 'only thing is I thought everybody experienced life in this mode, that's why I never mentioned it. Anyway, let that be an end to it and leave me alone in my unorthodox insanity.'

'You're kidding us, Yoyo,' Jean could not help but erupt, 'Sophie is blonde, how can she be that colour you think?'

'OK, I'm kidding, and the shrinks are making it up, and Sophie is blonde and Price –'

At the striking of the sound 'Price' he walked into the studio. His glare denoted he had surely heard Johannes uttering his name.

'Of course, it only happens to us, God orchestrating the timing and all that,' Inner Voice cursed.

'Could you please get on with your work, Taliesin, and try not interrupting everyone else's concentration,' the professor growled.

7

Consummation of Number 2 Above With Ease

I T BEGAN SO unexpectedly.

Sophie Howells, Johannes's favourite resident life model among the several models at the college, spent most of her contracted hours working with the painting special course. Due to her outstanding qualities as a model the academic staff including Principal Hancock would avail themselves of her services. The principal had produced several admirable oil studies of Sophie, one of which Johannes inadvertently ruined by his clumsiness on the day of his admission interview.

Sophie was an artist's dream, being anatomically symmetrical. She replicated the best examples of the nude in classical studies, possessing a figure of rare perfection with a superb bone structure that accorded with the best anatomical luminaries. Her muscle tone was always in exemplary order, which greatly assisted learning in the classical mode of life study, while the consistency of her skin tone was greatly appreciated by painters, staff and student alike. Her attractive features and natural blonde hair placed her in great demand as a photographic model. Sophie was worth the drawing effort and, as aptly put by painting-tutor George Little,

'If you cannot produce a worthwhile study from model Sophie Howells, then forget about life study as an option.'

Sophie occupied a permanent apartment in Johannes's fantasies. But apart from being intimidated by her magnificent attributes, Johannes's social, physical and pecuniary inadequacies determined she would remain only in an apartment of his dreams. Another major deterrent to Johannes transacting fantasy to reality was the giant muscle-bound rugby-playing gorilla Sophie exhibited as boyfriend, whose readily adopted responsibility was to guard her beautiful body with gorilla-like propriety.

Gorilla nursed a particular dislike for callow art students, whose envious daily task was to produce nude studies of his girlfriend. He characteristically growled whenever painting special students accidentally strayed into his part of the rainforest, and was constantly alert to the slightest incident that would give him just cause for putting them beyond hospital. He served as a signal deterrent to any besotted art student entertaining fantasies of bedroom mazurka with Sophie. A deterrent of minor relevance considering the ever-ready prime weapon of physical re-alignment was a college rule that strictly forbade students fraternising with college models.

Soon after taking up studies at Swansea College of Art, Johannes was surprised to discover the relatively small number of fellow flag bearers of truly bumpkin class. This dearth was due to lack of money in the lower rural classes; also, historically art colleges attracting their numbers from urban middle classes, with a bias towards females, exactly as the RAF staff sergeant had tendered in his sales pitch.

For the perverse thrill of it, well-heeled female art students would play chase-but-never-be-caught games with bumpkin detritus washed up from Ruritania. On rare blue moon occasions Johannes would find himself in demand as the bumpkin-for-the-night stooge. The games lasted as long as it took the well-heeled girls to become bored with Johannes lecturing them on Cassirer, Einstein or whatever line he was reading at the time, which state of attention usually arrived before the end of the first drink.

Art college rumour had it Sophie played similar games for the sheer wickedness of it. Details would be discussed and savoured by whispering gaggles of callow young swags from the order of those not yet bitten. In spite of her attractive physical endowments and charming personality, the resident model of choice possessed a vein of evil that ran obliquely through the gold. At times her ploys aspired to a level of fine art, manifest from the perspective of the hapless art student as the malicious tendency to play pussycat and defenceless mouse with socially maladroit bumpkins. Once her point had been proven she would express her boredom by despatching the unwitting fool with a swift praying mantis flick. The icing on her cake would be to complain to her gorilla boyfriend that the hapless bumpkin had molested her, whereupon Gorilla would ensure the offender would spend an unplanned holiday in Swansea Infirmary. So far Johannes had escaped any re-arrangement of his anatomy due in the main to Sophie's olfactory senses strongly objecting to his malodorous proximity. But it has to be recorded Johannes's main preservation order was his instinctive fear of gorillas.

The defining event that determined Johannes's long-term descent into Hades would take a precipitous dive began quite unexpectedly. Sophie, normally enjoying the distance the life room afforded between her and Johannes, decided to break her own taboos. In so doing, she must have implemented tremendous will to override her senses in gaining closer proximity to Johannes's scent. Certainly, all logical reasons evaded Johannes's later analyses.

She set a simple trap, having long since recognised the need to articulate a sophisticated trap for Johannes would be unnecessary. Due to his overriding weakness for all women, Sophie coming top of his all women list, Johannes did not persist with the instinctive defensive reaction an occasion of this sort should have triggered. Disregarding his fear of gorillas, together with other malfunctions that he was all too aware of, Johannes the malodorous bumpkin readily fell into the trap. The event itself was simple and straightforward, but for Johannes the associated ramifications grew in their dominating complexity as time went on.

Late one winter's evening, Sophie was posing for a life drawing class in Life Room 3, which was situated at the darker zone of Endless Corridor. No member of the academic staff came near on such late night life-drawing sessions: it would have been quite unusual if an academic had been present at all in the entire building. The absence of academics had become common knowledge, so a habit developed among the undedicated students, of which the college of art was generously endowed, to quietly slide away before the end of session.

Eventually on this particular evening Johannes was the last in attendance, oblivious to his solitude, studiously drawing the model. From her vantage point on the rostrum Sophie had observed the gradual leakage of undedicated students, until just one was left – Johannes. This situation was not unusual, as Johannes was almost invariably the last student drawing in Life Room 3 during a late night session.

Once they were alone, Sophie decided to embark on a little flirting. It quickly became apparent that for her flirting meant getting to the point without too much preliminary wordplay rubbish. Johannes, oblivious to the plan being laid four metres across the studio, was contentedly grappling with the usual elements that accompany life drawing – anatomical proportion, the dynamics of the figure, tonal consistency, linear descriptors, overall design, et al. – matters that embalmed the tranquil arcadia of classical life study. Suddenly, the beautiful introspective tranquillity of his life was shattered.

Sophie broke her pose and, without garbing herself in dressing gown, crossed the studio floor in Johannes's direction.

Johannes was floored, but automatically continued the task of observation that good life class demanded. At close up range Johannes noticed her flushed complexion and wet lips. She was breathing heavily, as if it had been a long walk across the studio floor. He noticed horripilation on her breasts and nipples: previously Sophie had never been close enough while naked for him to observe this phenomenon.

'Do you get a hard on when you see me naked like this?' she purred.

'*Sodding shitting gulp!*' Inner Voice gagged.

Johannes automatically leapt into denial mode. As he often worked scenarios of this delectable extreme into his daydreams he was able to cope manfully with them, being his own inventions. Obviously this was another of his daydreams, albeit an extraordinarily vivid one, so his denial determined to continue drawing, perhaps a little more nonchalantly than normal. But as Sophie came closer the daydream insisted on possessing a material form and Johannes's referential marks cut across his carefully crafted work. She delivered her naked body tight up to his easel; standing so close he smelled her sweet perspiration, the quintessence of aphrodisiac to a country bumpkin. Johannes had never experienced anything like this before.

'*Please God! Please say this is not happening,*' Inner Voice trembled all over its brain.

That was the moment when reality crashed home and Johannes, flustered beyond control, checked the entrance, the vacant studio, hither, thither and back to the entrance again. He began counting backwards.

'*Count backwards, for God's sake!*' Inner Voice scrambled.

'*Seventeen…*

Engrossed in our studies we had not realised we were alone with the model.

Sixteen…

We have never been addressed in such manner before, leave alone by the beautiful Sophie Howells.

Sixteen... um...' Inner Voice flustered.

'*Um... Thirteen...*

Did she say hard on?

Eight... Oh, our God!' Inner Voice gulped.

'*Ten... she used crude language...*

Sex, um six... did she say hard on?'

Johannes lost control of his backwards-counting decoy, so his mind dutifully followed. His heart pounded painfully; he blushed everywhere but stoically drew doodle marks over life drawing, ruining the whole evening's work.

'*Did she say hard on?'* Inner Voice gasped.

'*Seventeen – did she say hard on?'* the skill of consecutive counting had gone.

Then belatedly Inner Voice regained composure, and screamed a warning,

'*We are not hearing this! It truly can't be happening. Ignore her; remember the gorilla lurking in the trees outside in Alexandra Road. Run away now while the going is good. Bugger our drawing board and things, run!'*

Regrettably, Johannes's testosterone overrode Inner Voice's good advice and, applying granny knots to the responsive processes, attempted to answer Sophie's question. His dry tongue had an idle time waiting for orders.

At the flicker of an eyelash Sophie recognised her prey had turned to almond oil.

But the almond oil frantically drew on, looking beyond Sophie at the non-existent pose on the empty rostrum, scared a non-existent member of staff should walk in, terrified Gorilla should swing out of the lighting fixtures, knowing all the while if caught in delecto flagrante Sophie would have blurted, 'He dragged me over to his easel, I was fighting for my honour, thank God you arrived before –' But Sophie simply said,

'The pose has walked over to you, Johannes.'

'*Shit.*'

'Yes,' he said, still drawing, looking at the empty space.

'The pose is standing beside you, Johannes.'

'*We know.*'

'Y-yes,' he trembled.

'You haven't answered my question, Johannes,' Sophie said and, taking a firm grip in the area where she assumed his genitals should be, added, 'let's see if the answer to my question has practical manifestations.'

Johannes instinctively pulled back, but the vice-like grip on his genitals forbade too great a backwards lurch, owing to the discomfort the action elicited. Simultaneously, he took another glance in the direction of the modesty curtain that screened the door in the event Taliesin's Law of Cussedness would invoke the appearance of an academic or anyone for that matter at this late hour. His embarrassment became a guiding beacon to all country bumpkins drowning in their own bumpkin-ness.

'*This is our pumpkinisation, she has a vice-like grip on the source of our testosterone,*' Inner Voice strained.

'Hmmm,' Sophie muttered with the tone of a family practitioner on discovering things not to be as robust as expected with the patient, 'perhaps you need a drink or two. Let me buy you a drink; I know you poverty-stricken painters are penniless most of the time,' whereupon she released her grip.

'Thank you,' Johannes breathed, more in relief that his testicles were allowed to resume their natural orientation than response to her generous offer of a drink.

'The pleasure will be mine, I can assure you,' she said, 'don't worry if you have no money, I've got plenty.'

Lack of money was of permanent concern for Johannes,

but at that moment money was not the subject that occupied prime position in his mind's panic department. Two other more fundamental concerns dominated his thoughts, with a drink being bought for him and lack of money to reciprocate the gesture being very low on his list of concerns.

'*Don't go for a drink with her! It's obvious what she wants, and we are bound to fail,*' Inner Voice frantically warned with regard to the first fundamental concern, '*and then there's the small consideration of gorillas,*' with regard to the second.

'Just give me a moment to put boring things like clothes on,' she breezed comfortably, 'and I'll see you downstairs' whereupon she disappeared to her changing cubicle.

'Great,' Johannes lied.

'*Shit,*' Inner Voice despaired.

Sophie did not wait for excuses or a refusal. She knew. The stupid grin on his face signalled all she needed to know, and probably she could *hear* Johannes's heart pounding like a jackhammer.

'*For God's sake don't go for a drink with her! What if Gorilla catches us?*'

Inner Voice squeaked the warning. But as with all sexual addictions the testosterone department was glued shut to warnings as his genitals had clogged the free passage of reason.

'*Oh God, what if Gorilla catches us?*' Inner Voice persisted in bringing Gorilla into the scenario.

'*No, second thoughts, the worst scenario is we fail yet again; worse even than death by Gorilla.*'

True, failure was Johannes's biggest concern: worse, much worse, than death. But the prospect of an exciting sexual event following all that explicitness was so irresistible he shut out thinking of the consequences. Not just yet, anyway. *And* there was a free pint in the offing. Perhaps he would make his escape later, after the pint. Internally he was in turmoil. Here was a salutary example of Johannes embarking on an enterprise with a woman with the full knowledge that if he became too excited – which invariably occurred – he would not be able to perform. He *always* got too excited, and he *always* failed to perform. He was already too excited just thinking about it.

'*If we have to go through with this, try to calm down. Don't let her see all this shaking and hear our rotten teeth chattering,*' Inner Voice resigned to conciliation.

Johannes threw his implements and the ruined drawing into his locker. He was in a dream, and in a flash was on his way downstairs, struggling to control the shakes.

'*Control our bloody shakes, for God's sake. Think of leave-alone alternatives, escape clauses, weighing the consequences, and a thousand others*' Inner Voice ran through the well-worn mantra that possessed the only certainty that it gathered add-ons each time it failed. Upon the mantra having no material effect on Johannes's mental turmoil, Inner Voice had returned to the alternative objective.

'*She's not down yet. Run now, while we've still got life in us!*'

But Johannes did not run: he stood there shaking from the cold and other causes in the winter's night, his mind a delirium of anticipation, fear and excitement.

'*It's obviously a trap. Keep an eye out for Gorilla. After all, what would beautiful Sophie want with a scruffy bumpkin like us? She could have half of Swansea with a click of her fingers,*' Inner Voice was back in warning mode, becoming more animated by the minute. '*She's a Messalina, full of intrigue; it's all a game with her, she'll play with us, then watch with pleasure as Gorilla puts us to the sword. God! Our feet are cold! Run now, while there's still a chance of escape, it will warm up our feet as well.*'

But still Johannes did not run. Instead he stood waiting, shivering from the cold and shaking with excitement. While waiting at the entrance to the college on the dark, cold Alexandra

Road, he got to wondering what use was knowing the difference between shivering and shaking. No clear difference emerged. All that possessed the point of his brain was the exciting panic that Beautiful Body was going to buy him a drink, with the promise of something else as well... It was of little assistance to the process of thinking that at the time the point of Johannes's brain had developed a penis-shaped droop.

Sophie joined him, and they caught a South Wales Transport bus to Uplands, the same Uplands where Dylan Thomas was born and grew up, but there for Johannes the connection ended. Sophie paid for the tickets and Johannes earnestly thanked her for rescuing him from exposure to the winter cold by paying for access to the warm fold of the bus. After nervously checking, Johannes was relieved the bus carried few passengers, none of whom were students of the college of art. He even checked the driver. His mind continued to dart about.

'*Try saying something interesting, positive.*'

'Did you know the engines in these double-decker buses are 6,500ccs?' he blurted.

'No, I didn't,' Sophie replied, gazing through the windows, her mind on other things.

'And they are fitted with special gearboxes for Swansea because it is so hilly,' he gabbled on.

'No, I didn't know that either,' she said, her eyes glazing over as she was still thinking of other things.

'*Perhaps not that subject. For heaven's sake, talk about something that will interest her.*'

Johannes had never mastered the art of outwardly manifesting the objectivity that his inner thoughts suggested. More often than not he suffered under the delusion that his inner conscience was an alien to be manfully disregarded. The occasion of Sophie's invitation for a beer as a means to nether procurements did not have the slightest effect on this mental set piece. On the bus to Uplands the gap between imagination and objectivity was as wide as ever.

'I gained permission to paint on site at AWCO – the Aluminium Wire and Cable Company – on Jersey Marine a few weeks ago. You wouldn't believe how dangerous it is on the factory floor,' Johannes was earnestly trying to impress.

'Oh, I would,' Sophie responded casually, 'I know the owner; he showed me around one Saturday afternoon when Garin was playing away at Cardiff.'

'Two downers in one bloody sentence. Sod it.'

'Mr Trumpett-Hardon?'

'Yes, Trev,' she replied.

'Mr Fairley negotiated my entry permit with him.'

'He's quite a man – Trev, I mean, is quite a man; pity his spare time is limited by a wife and two brats,' she continued in casual mode –

'Shit.'

– the while gazing dreamily out of the window.

'Bloody Trumpett-Hardon, would we believe! She's been everywhere; we're out of our league. Jump off the bus now, don't wait for it to stop.'

Inner Voice, not missing the opportunity to nag the obvious, became desperate.

'Do something dramatic, commit suicide, jump off the bus. The headlines would read well for us: "Brilliant Art Student Murdered on Walter Road – thrown off bus by escaped gorilla from Swansea Zoo; leaves a legacy of master paintings; whole of Wales mourns loss." No, perhaps not the whole of Wales, and a legacy of second-rate drawings would be more accurate. No, on second thoughts: "Art Student Throws Himself off Bus; Cause of Suicide Unknown." No again, perhaps "Cause of Suicide Remained on Bus Fully Aware of the Power of Not Wearing Her Underwear in Public." No! We don't mean that either, damn it, just jump off the bloody bus!'

Following his short sojourn in suicide territory, Johannes re-engaged his meagre hand.

'The other night in The Kings Noel Philpot said he would take me up in his plane.'

'He must have been drunk, he only takes girls up in his plane,' Sophie responded absentmindedly.

'Has he taken you up?'

'Oh! Many times. He puts it on autopilot; Noel said that if I played my cards right he would teach me how to fly the thing. I took him up on it.'

'Have you been learning how to fly his plane?' Johannes asked incredulously.

'Oh yes, but I have to pay for every lesson with my body.'

'Jump now.'

'Rarswyd!' Johannes gasped.

'What?'

'Oh, I said rarswyd: it means shivers.'

'What are you shivering for, Yoyo? It's quite warm on this bus.'

'Tell her it's a bloody expletive.'

'It's just an expletive used in rural Wales,' Johannes shuffled.

'Leave it in rural Wales, Yoyo. Anyway, one day I'll fly away from all this and live in a castle with its own airstrip, where toyboys will be air-stacked in circles waiting to land and pay homage to me, or something like that...' she trailed off.

Johannes's hitherto fervent imagination went blank and Inner Voice's reality sighed.

The bus stopped at Uplands Square; they disembarked and Sophie headed straight for the tavern that shared its name with the district. On entering she made a beeline for the bar, to Johannes's mixed surprise and relief, for he had assumed she was a cocktail lounge person. His relief was temporary. Several regulars were sitting at the bar who, upon recognising

Sophie, allowed their faces to take on a variety of lascivious slants.

'Hi, boys!'

'Evenin' sweetheart, where 'ave you been these few days?'

'Working my clothes off.'

A roar of approval was followed by beer glasses licked and stools jigged. Johannes laughed with them but underneath his edginess surged increasingly brittle. Many concerns returned to fill the blank that was his mind, only one of which he could reconcile with some degree of sanity.

Occupying pole position on the raft of his slippery slope was the prospect of Sophie's Gorilla happening upon them and despatching him in a one-sided bar-room brawl. If through good fortune Gorilla were elsewhere, the main hurdle of excitement that possessed unmoveable certainty would be, in the cast-iron likelihood of his being invited back to her flat, Johannes's inevitable failure to service Sophie's sexual needs. A third unappetising scenario was for the bar-huggers to start splashing money around, whereupon he would be exposed for what he was, an impecunious dupe.

Far down the list was his devising conversational matter that could match the eloquent bar-room frippery, at which he had always been inept. Lower still he worried about entertaining Sophie long enough to steer the point of her brain away from her devouring urge for instantaneous sexual gratification. Somewhere at the bottom of his list of concerns was a matter that could facilitate his expulsion, i.e. the college commandment uttering 'thou shall not fraternize with models', but fear of breaking this rule was surely eclipsed by the other more pressing scenarios of denouement.

'We never know, perhaps if someone volunteered to buy her over, it would be the best thing for our salvation,' Inner Voice chirped.

But this sensible optimism was overruled by Johannes's

excited imagination of two unknowns, i.e. sex with Sophie followed by death by Gorilla. Instead of addressing these grave threats seriously in his hour of need, his mind continued to buzz nonsense.

Sophie bought a pint of Brain's Bitter for Johannes and a triple vodka for herself. Thanking her earnestly he compulsively gulped half of it between bar and seat. This amazed Sophie but, perfect model to the end, she retained her poise, aware that it was she who was the centre of attention. Whilst the bar-huggers stared lustfully at Sophie, Johannes in turn attracted glances of disbelief.

'They're not amazed we've managed to pull someone so gorgeous; they're amazed that someone so gorgeous is towing a scruffy skunk like us,' Inner Voice's put-downs were unrelenting.

'Where did you find this one, sweetheart?' one of the bar-huggers jerked a thumb in Johannes's direction.

'He's a painting special student at the art college, been drawing me in the nude this evening,' she replied.

'Oh God, no! Shut up, we'll die.'

'Does he do you justice, sweetheart?'

'Oh, he knows how to use his pencil, boys,' and Sophie winked broadly.

Johannes darted across to a quiet little table as far from the bar as possible.

'Now then,' Sophie said loudly, in a tone implying a previous conversation was about to be continued, 'how far had our conversation got in Life Room 3?'

Johannes cringed.

'You worried about that shower at the bar or something?' she laughed, 'I'll talk sex talk quieter if you are embarrassed.'

'Yes, please,' Johannes sighed the request with relief.

'Yes please what? Sex talk or quieter?' she asked.

Johannes was out of his league, out of his depth, out of the little heaven of his drawing world, over the lip of his smelly little world and clean into Hell.

'*We should run out now,*' said Inner Voice, '*We'll be mocked for it, but respected in fifty years' time.*'

'We were discussing Ernst Cassirer's *Phenomenology of Knowledge*,' Johannes blurted, ignoring his better sense.

'*Prat.*'

'What?' she demanded, frowning in her idiosyncratic way.

'I'm reading book III at the moment *the concept of symbolic form*,' he uttered in flat monotone.

'What?' she demanded again, this time wrinkling her nose.

'*The concept of symbolic form*,' he clockworked.

'Good Lord, Johannes Taliesin, who cares about the concept of symbolic form? Come on, drink up, let's go back to my apartment and talk about a different symbolic form, a much more important concept. Come on, it's just up the road.'

'Apartment?' he asked feebly.

'Yes, apartment. What did you think I had?'

Sophie stood up and, not waiting for a reply, hurled the triple vodka down her beautiful throat in a single gulp. Turning to the gawping bar-huggers she threw them another big wink,

'Good night, boys!' she said, pushing out through the door.

A roar of gladding guffaws hailed her farewell. Johannes had not finished sipping what was left of his drink after the initial gobbled onslaught, but quickly reverted to the original mode and polished it off.

'Good night,' he said, which elicited a deal of mastering guffaws, but with different tones. The visit to the bar room had metamorphosed in the space of a hiccup into another of Johannes's mini-hells.

But of course a much worse hell was his way heading. He had reached the point of no return and the noose was tightening around his wretched neck. Earlier he could easily have made a bolt for it, down Walter Road, up Mount Pleasant and back to his unheated bedsit… but he could never again have held up his head. Sophie would have crowed all over Swansea that Johannes had chickened. Worse, he had chickened with embellishments that would surely have elicited a command to Gorilla to put him out of his misery. Turmoil had settled in his head for the night; he could no longer rely on fire escapes. The forces of objectivity were invading the turbulent meadows of his imagination and, for all the practice he had had in daydreaming, there was no escaping this monstrous tsunami.

Beneath the surface of his attempted insouciance Johannes hated himself the many aspects of his physical inadequacies. He hated it all. His lack of money had its genesis in a slummy upbringing of dire rural poverty, from which start he was always playing catch-up. With it came a concomitant lack of self-confidence, a programme of failure and unrelenting poverty, constant denial. His lack of confidence disallowed him to admit the obvious, hence his constant imbroglio on the edge of both society's and sanity's ideals. Of course, just above this quagmire was the superficial veneer of a clown presuming confidence and oozing braggadocio.

'*Too bloody late now, we should have cut and run earlier,*' Inner Voice resigned, '*We've brought this on ourselves. Get on with it and see what happens; we never know. We'll never succeed until we succeed.*'

Johannes's mind danced on the points of a trident: excitement, fear and dread. Excited that his sexual fantasies were about to become real; fear that Priapus would abandon his drooping ship at the crucial moment of need, which so far had been an unfailing occurrence during similar circumstances. The excitement and fear were inserted under a perspective of dread: when, according to a pre-arranged plan Gorilla inevitably arrives at the scene, Johannes the stooge would be despatched in an end with horror.

'*Perhaps it would be better to plead for horror without end... um, no... an end with horror it will have to be,*' Inner Voice gibbered.

Sophie wasted no time. She rushed into her apartment, Johannes gingerly following. He had had no idea, imagining Sophie lived in a crummy bedsit similar to his, which image vanished at the sight of her luxurious apartment. Its splendour surprised and intimidated him. All on a model's pay!

'*How quickly our bit whatever it was of confidence evaporates.*'

'Nice apartment.'

'Hmm,' she said absentmindedly.

But Johannes barely had time to sit down before she got to the point.

'This is what I mean by talking about something more important,' she said, whereupon without a do-you-want-a-drink or a by your leave, she began undressing.

The routine was performed in a glint, and a wisp later she was purring naked on a sheepskin rug at Johannes's feet.

'The naked state is how you see me most of the time, so that is what I'll be now. Let's see how good you are with your anatomical pencil!' and her purring turned to a gurgling of anticipation. The challenge was upon him. All the vacillating had systematically reduced his options, leaving just one.

Sophie was indeed unbelievably beautiful. Johannes could feel the warmth emanating from her naked body; following the Life Room 3 experience this was the second time he had been so close to it. But this time it was different: this was challenging his fantasies to realise a different action.

Johannes's heart was hammering. He wished this were a dream in which, standing manfully to attention, he serviced Sophie in such astonishing animal fashion that her howls of ecstasy were heard all over Uplands, and the experience changed her so radically that she immediately abandoned her career as a model, taking up instead the worship of a mysterious religion that used his prancing member as a figurehead.

Alternatively, he wished this were a dream from which he could wake up, because he was already failing at the first task of controlling his sexual excitement. Unfortunately this was his fantasy come to reality and there was no escaping Sophie inviting him to do his manful best.

'*Please God,*' Inner Voice grovelled, '*Please help us to…*'

God had long since thought through the mechanics of human copulation and, although his attention was somewhat distracted by a war raging across most of the planet when Johannes's ingredients were in the mixing pot, The Great Alchemist had nevertheless remembered to include the components necessary for the successful achievement of the process. It was now Johannes's responsibility to turn into three dimensions what God had supplied in the flat-pack. Unfortunately Johannes was unable to master the instructions properly, and the components were destined to remain more or less at the flat-pack stage.

'*Oh God!*' Inner Voice whimpered.

'Wh – what about Gor… Gor…?'

'Garin, you mean?'

'Y-yes.'

'Oh, he's away on a rugby club trip. Come on, Johannes, show us your manhood!'

'*SHIT! The moment of truth has arrived.*'

The moment of truth had indeed arrived. Johannes's burden in life was an over-developed sexual attraction to women that had no backup in personality, physical aptitude, money, social training, social dignity, practical aptitude, intellectual maturity and many more of the usual things that go into building a young man's character. His case was hopeless. Nevertheless, he loved women so much that his thin veil of arrogance would assert itself, disguising the deficiencies for just long enough, at least for self-delusion, just long enough... If on the rare occasion Johannes enjoyed a close encounter with a woman's body, he lost control of his own. He should have overcome the confounded hindrance half a dozen years ago: dwelling on his failure to do so had never helped, and certainly did not help at the moment.

His lack of confidence would lead to worshipping the most stupid of women who provided the remotest of an opportunity. He would flatter and trill at their inane chatter, so long as it was rewarded with the chance of getting closer to their bodies at the end of his ordeal. But almost invariably Johannes's complaint conspired to ensure it was the unfortunate woman who suffered the real ordeal.

In traversing life's patchwork eiderdown of sexual encounters, even Johannes at his clumsiest was occasionally successful in getting into close proximity with women's bodies. Unfortunately, though, his encounters had invariably been disasters of the first order. He had never attained the 'wham bam thank you ma'am' achievement that his imagination claimed or, worse, his contemporaries bragged. The deep embarrassment would linger with him long after the event. To compound his embarrassment, Johannes's compulsive nature contrived to do nothing by halves: his disasters were towering edifices of un-conjugal humiliation; irredeemable concatenations parodying uselessness that slid down slimy holes into his private hell. To compound the humiliation, his failures were of course shared by the unfortunate woman of the moment, who never deserved to share his malady.

When confronted by circumstances such as the instance presented by the delectable Sophie, Johannes's track record was no other than hideous. A display of disquieting contradictions conflated in the great absence erroneously assuming to masquerade as Johannes's mind.

'Sexual encounters manifest our worst weaknesses. They bring to the droop the psychological pickle of our mentality; they display on a dinner plate our frailty and weaknesses. We are pretentious and filled with make-believe charades, the pickle we're in. Our lust causes compulsions; weakness causes our obsessions. There are fears and phobias, our on-off schizophrenia. Our lust causes aspirations to magic up sexual fantasies... constant war between daydreaming and objectivity navigating us into a pickle like this – perhaps we could jump out of the window,' his Inner Voice of reason concluded exiting the window, regardless the apartment's first floor orientation, the only possible let-out left to avoid the burden of impending failure.

Sophie reclining naked on the sheepskin rug in her warm apartment perfectly fulfilled Johannes's nether-most sexual fantasy. But the fantasy manifested as real flesh by Sophie was easily overridden by his collapsing confidence initiated by fears of failure and inadequacy. The armies of imagination were fleeing the scene of battle in their droves, tails hanging forlornly between their legs.

The naked Sophie waited expectantly, burning for sexual gratification, unaware that Johannes's manhood was with the army deserting the battlefield. The most beautiful woman in Swansea College of Art, delectable territory forbidden to students, was unwittingly projecting Johannes once again into his private hell.

Of course, Johannes believed all the way to heaven that women were God's cleverest invention. His encounters with them, however, did not remotely reflect the value of his belief in this wondrous quantum of natural engineering. Usually his luckless women were unaware of the nightmare of uncontrollable excitement wracking his soul, as he maintained a convincing facade of smoke and mirrors, until the chimera exploded almost invariable prematurely, before their very bodies. Encounters arranged into one of the following categories:

1. Following a fleeting all-thumb fumble dumb, the while having lost control due to convulsions of shivering excitement, foreplay out of the question, Johannes would prematurely ejaculate long before achieving erection, fortunately or unfortunately, according to the immediate circumstances of his environment, while still fully clothed.

2. If on the rare occasion Johannes managed to reach the state of undress without falling victim to number 1 above, the moment his naked body touched the woman's naked body he would experience a parabolic arc of uncontrollable ecstasy throughout every fibre of his being, which would immediately trigger an ejaculation with no regard to the important detail of having first achieved erection.

3. If ever managing to reach a state of undress and simultaneously avoiding the catastrophes of numbers 1 and 2 above before achieving erection, Johannes's trembling frame would nevertheless succumb to the excitement listed in numbers 1 and 2 above, by ejaculating within a nanosecond of commencing penetration. These occasions, however, were so rare that they became the yardstick by which Johannes could claim a limited measure of success.

4. On the one occasion alone did Johannes manage to avoid ejaculation during the stages listed at 1 to 3 inc., above. With both naked bodily contact and penetration actually achieved, although from the female's perspective of limited nature in both quantity and quality, the excitement caused Johannes's heart to go seriously ballistic, whereupon he

exhibited what could best be described as a spasm akin to rigor mortis, before passing out. Upon regaining consciousness he discovered he had already been fully re-clothed by his worried hostess, and was being urged to drink tea with lashings of sugar. His hostess, convinced the attack had been epileptic rather than orgasmic, earnestly suggested that for the sake of his health he refrain from such recreational activities in future.

As if Johannes's miserable track record with women, and his flaunting the rule forbidding fraternising with art college models were not sufficient to drive him insane,

'Yes, a third problem haunts us because we haven't jumped out of the window yet: it's the horrendously unique Sword of Damocles in the form of Gorilla. We seem to have forgotten his abundant destructive energy needs the battleground of at least two games of rugby a week in order to bring his testosterone levels down to those of mere mortals. Yes, he may be away on a rugby club trip but any one of at least a thousand events could conspire to bring him back here in one bound... come on, the window solution.'

As Johannes's inadequacies placed him well below the level of mere mortals any confrontation with Gorilla put a rather hopeless prognosis on survival. Gorilla was much larger, fitter, stronger and infinitely more aggressive than Johannes and would not hesitate to resort to death by dropkick as a means of despatching his girlfriend's suitor. Both disclosure and death were inevitable given the nature of the beautiful creature writhing on the rug before him.

Weighing up all the disparate matters confronting him, Johannes's urge to attempt copulation was still far greater than his fear of the consequences of excitement-related impotence, expulsion from college, death. Fortified by a sex drive quite disproportionate to the capacity of its owner to achieve fulfilment, and never having been in this circumstance before although fantasising it at least a million times a week, and with the clear understanding that an erection, if ever he were to achieve one, has neither conscience nor care for the well-being of the appendage body, Johannes abandoned all further considerations.

'What about venereal disease? We haven't considered VD yet!' Inner Voice tried a final deflating throw of the dice.

But as sexual delirium does not give a damn for physical inadequacy, expulsion, disease or death, he flung care, clothes and Quaker guilt aside.

His thin, naked body hung over her like a desert corncrake. Who cares? This was a thousand Christmases rolled into one. Sophie was irresistible and Johannes had never ever experienced such promise before.

With the panache and sangfroid of a man-about town who had successfully performed the act of sexual intercourse countless times previously, Johannes launched himself at her, landing on her beautiful body with a fleshy crunch. She let out a gasp. The impact had winded her, but Johannes was beyond caring, or perhaps it did not occur to him to care. With his heart pounding ridiculously in its little cage, he sallied forth regardless and, parting her beautiful thighs, performed number 2 above with consummate ease.

'Is that it?'

Johannes was shaking, limp and wet, everywhere.

'Er, sorry.'

'God, they are right, you *are* a little squirt,' she muttered contemptuously, pushing him aside, 'and you smell something else; I'm disgusted with myself for not resisting your pestering advances.'

Following a short pause in her flow of disappointment she added the afterthought,

'And I'm winded,' and she shot off to the bathroom.

Johannes hurriedly dressed and let himself out. His caution was electric high in case Gorilla was lying in wait ready to pounce.

Once on the street he made haste to put distance between him and Sophie's apartment, his sense of shame and embarrassment groping around in the slimy darkness of Hades, far beyond description.

'We warned us! We brought this on ourselves! Our sense of shame is far beyond description.'

Hotfooting it back to his bedsit, Johannes's mind was a parley of panics. He attempted to shut the debacle out of his mind, but the magnitude of his denouement rendered the ostrich routine impotent. Inner Voice nagged relentlessly,

'Now we're in a bloody mess! Jesus Christmas, what a bloody mess! And who are they she referred to? And talk about pestering advances! We've been set up, our God! Set up!'

Surfacing through the maelstrom, regardless of his sexual inadequacy, the matter of his impending death now assumed priority on his lengthening agenda of urgencies although, if he lived long enough, he was aware the shame would return to haunt him. But concerns of pride and embarrassment were relegated for the time being: his untimely death would deal with such matters. Johannes's embarrassment could not match the horror of impending death, perched at pole position on the point of his witless mind. How on earth would he convince Gorilla it was Sophie who made all the advances before the fatal blow struck? Would Gorilla wait for him to explain? Never! Besides, his explanation would sound unbelievable, given the subject matter of her attention was such a smelly wimp. In hind-thought 'I'm disgusted with myself for not resisting your pestering advances' guaranteed Gorilla would be informed.

'It no longer bears thinking about. We brought it on ourselves.'

His brain wisely elected to stall, go blank. An armistice between the advancing forces of objectivity and the defenceless shambles of imagination was called, but it lasted about the distance of two lampposts. He decided to attempt the ostrich technique once again, it having been proved advantageous for albeit lesser issues on previous occasions. Forgetting death by thug, which would be justifiable, Johannes applied a cursory tilt at amnesia. He pointed his brain at the softer problems: embarrassment, loss of pride, laughing stock, smelly socks, going insane.

'Stop! This is too much! We must simply concentrate on death.'

Fathoming the depth of a conspiracy was far beyond his means this dank miserable night, but his conspiracy obsession worked at it. Surprisingly, Johannes had enjoyed a measure of successful denial on previous occasions of Total Embarrassment, admittedly after pondering the subject day and night for at least a week.

'We are quite good at fathoming conspiracies, we get it from Daddy.'

Johannes had the determination to work obsessively,

'On the other hand, we don't get our idiot tendency from Daddy. Idiot, the warning signs and all that! Besides, whoever was it who informed Sophie that we were a little squirt?'

Trouble was the description fitted Johannes's miserable dimensions perfectly, and made consideration of the matter all the more embarrassing. Wracking his brain, he made tenuous connections, but embarrassment persisted in overwhelming rational thought.

'Idiot… idiot… idiot.'

At first Johannes suspected Ceredwyn, a girl from Neath now attending York University. She was a wonderful character and a Communist.

'*What point in trawling the entrails, the damage is done. Forget it. What an idiot we are!*'

Johannes had succeeded to the attempt stage of the copulation circus with her only after revealing his father was a Communist. He clinched the deal by relating the snippet that his father christened their Large White breeding sow Voroshilov in memory of a favourite general and Communist Party member. Ceredwyn was won over by the embellishment that Voroshilov was converted to communism through his father's horse whispering expertise. It was a little disconcerting that Ceredwyn voiced a preference for his father, but Johannes proceeded shakily to his inevitable denouement.

'Don't worry, bach, *that* was a new experience for me,' she said, laughing like a Red Army choir, 'I never knew that could happen without the little thing erecting first.'

Anyway, her Communist father knew Joseph Herman, he of the 'fundamentally I very kind man, I no believe in kicking dead horse' about Impressionism. Joseph Herman was one of Johannes's painter heroes, despite the disparaging comments about Impressionism, a movement Johannes appreciated. No, definitely, Ceredwyn was as sure as the Volga Boatman: she wouldn't blab.

Many other faces and names blurred the screen, but more often than not, getting as far as chatting a girl into bed meant Johannes was also on the slippery slope to Brahms. The more he pondered connections the more he unveiled denial and consequently the more his paranoia developed. Soon connections became abundantly obvious, so he hastily ceased thinking of them, as the memories made his scalp crawl with embarrassment.

'*Fancy forgetting obvious connections, idiot, idiot, idiot.*'

Now that he had put a prudent distance between himself and Sophie's apartment the hotfooting slowed to a trot: down

Walter Road, left at The Tenby of scrumpy significance, and straight up the steepest hill in Swansea the whole width cobbled, with railings running up the centre. Although gaining altitude Johannes paradoxically felt his life sinking to new depths, into an abyss marked humiliation.

Realistically all the tittle-tattle about his bedroom denouements was academic. The realisation of what he had done, worse, leaving his mark in failing to have done, came back with a thump. There was no concealing it: he was in the anteroom to hell.

'It's whom they tell, and how they tell it.'

As if Johannes was unaware. All the darkened windows of Mount Pleasant were watching him.

'God! We've just realised! The smell from our sweaty socks will hang inside her apartment forever, tincture of dead cheese. That's an obvious giveaway, Gorilla will recognise our stink with a twitch of one large flaring nostril, perfect excuse for legitimate execution.'

Johannes tried not to think about it, but…

'Isn't it ironic – when we want to fill Sophie's cavity, we can't. When we don't want to fill the apartment with essence of sweaty sock, we can. Did God invent that little paradox? Probably, during tea break on the third day:

'Here's your tea, sweetheart. What are you thinking about?' Mrs God asked.

'Well, my dear, I was trying to think of a little paradox that would infuriate sentient beings all over my universe for aeons to come.'

'Now don't overdo things, dear; there are another three days left to be completed yet, and don't forget you promised to include my joke about artists.'

'Yes, sweetheart, I deem one joke to be enough; it is a paradox I am divining this time.'

Inner Voice prattled on, the irony of his thoughts losing…

'God has a profound sense of humour, which we fail to see at our peril. God must be laughing himself silly at our predicament, proving the paradox creation works.'

Johannes crabbed upwards, his untied belt trailing behind him on the cobbled slope. This was no way to treat a hand-me-down belt given by his Uncle Maldwyn for passing, albeit *just* passing, his A level art. So he quickly reined it in and belatedly tied it, having neither noticed nor cared that his trousers had been hanging loose. For one so emaciated a belt of some sort was an essential item and, in normal circumstances, he would have checked at least three times that the object was fulfilling its function before venturing out. But these were not normal circumstances and to make matters worse it began to rain.

'What were Sophie's sinister motivations? Cannot be sexual desire with such smelly impecunious losers like us! Withered and smelly losers! This is pure misery, let's get home to our crummy bedsit.'

At that moment, determining Sophie's motivation evaded the point of his brain that, like everything else attached to his ineffectual person, hung innocuously. Perhaps she was simply demonstrating for herself the enormous power her beautiful body possessed, another way of saying 'get lost, little squirt'.

'But she could have done that with any one of a number of more eligible males around her. No, we just happened to be there when the fancy took her, just happened to be in the wrong place at the wrong time. What a mess! Now the icing on Sophie's cake will be to test her boyfriend's loyalty, and his dedication to her by reducing the population by one. It's beyond possibility that Gorilla would believe our side of the story. No hope. His predilection will be to believe the most tenuous of reasons, whereupon conducting legitimate assassination to subsequently receive society's praise for protecting his girlfriend's honour. Jesus, is there any escape from this?'

Inner Voice's whinging was relentless.

The rain appropriately accelerated into the usual Swansea downpour, its onset perfectly timed by a conspiracy of Nature to coincide with Johannes's nadir of self-disgust. The swelling rivulets down the hill squelched through portholes in the masochistic apparatus that remained as boots. But Johannes was past caring.

8
Johannes Paints Sophie

'*S*OPHIE DOESN'T SEEM *to have reported it to Gorilla*' Inner Voice dared whisper as Johannes timorously surveyed the townscape on his way to college, '*Inexplicable, really, as we can't deny her libido must have been frustrated to... to... whatever happens to libido when bumpkins fail to satisfy it, which would have justified the biggest blab across Swansea. Proceed with caution, utmost-utmost caution.*'

Not taking the non-appearance of gorillas allied to Sophie's assumed compassionate silence for anything other than a fortunate breakdown in the gossiping habits of humanity, Johannes continued to tiptoe around Swansea during his unexpected stay of execution. His cautionary defences were raised beyond eyebrow level. Before embarking on any journey he nervously checked the townscape was clear of animals, scanning from windows before departing buildings, peering around corners for the all clear before venturing around them, seeking out sanctuary in the municipal library's reading room, a zone he felt confident gorillas were disinclined to frequent, and generally acting at an electric level of tension.

'*Maybe perhaps we're getting a bit obsessed,*' Inner Voice had the temerity to observe.

As the first day passed and, to his astonishment, he was still in one piece Johannes began to believe in miracles; his state of nervous delirium calmed to a level of merely hyper-wrought.

After two days of mouse-and-catting with every shadow that resembled a giant prop forward, Johannes was way off food, while his nervous condition had severed any permanent contractual compliance with what little sleep he took since the bakery night work. Tensions were now residing in a lack of resolution, even though he feared one. A profound sense of hopelessness descended around him, eroding what remnants remained of his mental stability.

'Surely there will be a conclusion at some point? Doesn't bear thinking about.

We suppose we could go on like this for the rest of our short natural... won't complete our studies... death might be an acceptable alternative, so long as it is not Gorilla choosing the mode of despatch...'

Instead of enjoying his three to four hours sleep, Johannes now sat in the corner of his bedsit throughout the night repeatedly drawing stages of the death throes of his little wizened pot plant that would have appreciated some water, daylight, fresh air... His drawings were assuming a darker ambience, with hard black lines menacing the pale withered leaves, Debuffet-style. Many were scoured out, drawn, redrawn and overdrawn, scratched through to the board. Passages in the drawings more resembled moth displays as a result of nervous over-working. The first day of a basic level psychology course would have been sufficient to enable a student's analysis of Johannes's drawings as revealing something dark and foreboding, deeply unstable, alongside a straightforward preoccupation with death.

All this had not gone unnoticed by staff and students at the college. Seeking help from the University Psychological Counselling Service was out of the question.

'Imagine it! Explaining consummation of number 2 with ease to the two psychologists. How would Jane Titmarsh have coped with such graphics? She would have wet her knickers, and not with urine,' Inner Voice was becoming flippantly coarse as the waiting game went on.

He weighed the consequences of confronting Principal Hancock with the problem.

But the principal could well have been furnished with details detrimental to the truth by this stage, having been informed during a professional nude study session with the very Sophie, epicentre of Johannes's nightmare.

'*Whatever should we think of confiding with the principal for? Forget it! Commit suicide now before it's too late to commit suicide. They won't let us commit suicide in asylum, straightjacket and all th –*'

So Johannes decided he had no option but to continue the superficial pretence that nothing was amiss. It was this pretence when everyone could see he was adrift from reality that made him a choice case to be wondered at, a cut above his peers in eccentricity, an exceptional individual with obtuse ways of dealing with life's tests.

He regularly placed the incidents of his life into the wrong perspective: trivia were magnified out of proportion; life-threatening events trivialised, while if possible both were hidden from public scrutiny. His unorthodox methods of dealing with crises had long since left his peers despairing of rendering assistance. Most of his fellow students had adopted the attitude whereby they let him get on with his problems, while watching from askance the spectacle of a fellow student disintegrating before their eyes.

Precise day counting had long since lost its purpose for Johannes. But the crunch inevitably arose when the painting specials were preparing for life class in the Antique Studio with Sophie as the model. Those around could not help but notice Johannes's changed appearance. His normally dishevelled condition, to which every one was inured, had taken a turn towards the rabid. Rees felt obliged to broach the subject, and sidled Johannes into a corner of the Antique Studio.

'Yoyo, you might live under the illusion that ordinary persons are unable to discern any deterioration in your general dishevelment,' Rees whispered in jocular sarcasm, 'but as you know I am exceptional at spotting the difference between general dishevelment and the onset of insanity,' he paused a while for the effect to sink in, 'so I am impelled to ask what is the matter with you these days?'

'*Deny everything,*' came the Inner command.

'Nothing,' came the hissed verbal.

To discuss the matter with his fellow students flapping their ears and especially with Sophie in earshot in her changing cubicle was very far down on Johannes's agenda for recantation. Rees disregarded the nothing reply, immediately sensing his friend was in real trouble.

'Aw, come on, Yoyo! Don't give me that nothing rubbish!' Rees burst his whispered frustration, 'you've been shaking like a leaf for some days, your work has taken a nosedive and the Yoyo odours are stronger than ever – which I didn't think was possible. Got to be something wrong; what is it?'

'Nothing,' came the obdurate reply, 'just an attack of nervous debility I've suffered from since lightning struck the farmhouse and set it alight – didn't I tell you?'

Rees stifled a giggle.

'No, you didn't tell me the cock and bull story about nervous debility caused by lightning striking your farmhouse. Your nervous debility is a fixture, we all know that, but come on, Yoyo, what's the real reason for the splurge?'

'Oh, leave off Rees, please,' Johannes grimaced.

'That bad, huh?'

'Yeah, that bad.'

'Come on, you can tell your mate Bowen about it.'

'And if I tell my mate Bowen, ten to one my mate Bowen will tell his mate Michelle, and three minutes after that the whole bloody fashion department will know, then the whole bloody college, then Swansea. I'll be the laughing sto – no, forget it, best left unspoken,' Johannes listed sotto voce.

'God, this sounds bad,' said Rees, lowering his voice yet further, 'you in trouble with the police?'

'No.'

'Landlady?'

'Always in trouble with that old scroat.'

'KGB?'

'Wish it were that simple.'

'A woman?'

'Rees, will you please leave off?' Johannes protested.

'Aha! It's woman trouble. Who is she? Do I know her?' Rees was on to it.

'Rees, I'm absolutely, positively not going to disclose the identity,' said Johannes.

'That's the end of the conversation, then?'

'That's the end of the conversation. Thanks for your concern,' replied Johannes.

'Do you need any help?' asked Rees, ignoring the rebuff.

'I might need your help' Johannes wavered.

'Financial? She bribing you? Oh, no! She's pregnant! My God, Yoyo, you're in *deep* trouble.'

'No, no, no and yes, in that order. That's the end of it; now please leave off,' Johannes was visibly shaking.

Johannes's state alarmed Rees. He knew from experience that Johannes was devoid of rage, so the protestations were to no avail. Rees was about to wage a counter-attack when the interrogation ended by George Little entering the Antique Studio.

George Little could not see the point of Johannes's attendance at the college of art. While the latter made a small degree of effort to alleviate the tutor's distaste, George Little displayed his hostility to Johannes if not in open court then certainly in grimace and nuance. Rees cast a glance at Johannes signalling that the interrogation was only temporarily interrupted. Tutor Little set the life drawing class to work.

Once Sophie had been set in the pose the usual scramble for advantageous angles ensued. Under normal circumstances Johannes would have been in the forefront of such undignified manoeuvring, thrusting his easel here and there like a fencer lunging at their opponent. But on this day Johannes was uncharacteristically hesitant and hung back, to the extent where it became apparent to his painting special colleagues that all was certainly not right. The reason soon made itself obvious, even to the most dim-witted of observers: Johannes was avoiding an angle that necessitated eye contact with Sophie. This was most unusual, for he was notorious for choosing the most full frontal and facially exposed angle as possible. But this day he chose a view from the far horn of the crescent around the podium that presented a bland back-view of Sophie, which only merit lay in guaranteeing nil eye contact.

Sophie Howells was aware of Johannes's feeble manoeuvrings. She attracted George Little's attention, spuriously explaining that the angle of lighting was harsh on her eyes on this occasion and could she alter the angle of the pose, please? As the tutors were disposed to keeping their chief model happy, George Little being no exception, he agreed the lighting might be bright, so allowed her to skew around to a shadier angle. The sighs from some members of the group who had already chosen an angle that suited them were lost on Johannes for, to his horror, Sophie turned directly in line with his gaze. Looking straight at Johannes, she arranged her features in a latter-day form of Mona Lisa.

Once again the group settled down. Except Johannes who, shaking in a maelstrom of confrontation, huffily heaved his easel to the opposite horn of the crescent, accompanied by much muttering and clattering. The bare boards and high ceiling echoed in the otherwise silent studio as others had already settled, accentuating the scuffle and clatter of Johannes on his journey seeking a lost world. On the way he passed the already settled Rees Bowen.

'Hell's teeth, Taliesin!' he good-naturedly mocked a Price admonition, 'for goodness' sake, settle down.'

Johannes uttered a low growl of disjoint. Nearly ten minutes had elapsed since the start of the session and he had yet to draw a line.

Johannes set about making amends, this time with studies of the new back angle view. With vigorous actions of pencil and rubber he scribbled, scraped and stumbled until an indefinite smudge had flooded across his parchment. From the start it was never going to be a life study, even as a drawing in the abstract it was without structure and going nowhere. Johannes's only area of competence was reduced to the machinations of a nightmare.

George Little worked his tutoring way round the crescent until he reached the last station. He could not have been unaware of the noises of industry coming from Johannes's direction, but upon arrival was confronted by a mess that possessed no representational history. Mr Little had the reputation for being a fair but thorough tutor.

'Not going according to plan, Taliesin?'

'Hm,' Johannes croaked.

'Fact is, did you have a plan?'

'Hm.'

Johannes *did* have a plan, which was to keep away from Sophie's Mona Lisa gaze and, more generally, stay alive; but George Little knew nothing of the private turmoil.

'Obviously not,' he said, 'I suggest you move around to your usual position, say forty-five degrees left, where the angle is more challenging to your competence. Perhaps we might see something other than a disaster from you.'

'Hmff,' came a strangulated croak.

Upon hearing the tutor's instruction Sophie uttered a little giggle of pleasure. Forty-five degrees left was the last position Johannes wished to take up. On no account could he look Sophie in the eye, especially as he had already attracted adverse attention by twice avoiding his favourite angle. His colleagues in the painting special group suspected something afoot, and were anticipating a Johannes spectacle. But his next move astonished them, while at the same time insulting George Little. In a gesture that confirmed his descent into Hades was well advanced, Johannes walked out of the life class.

Some while later Rees caught up with Johannes in the loft – the students' retreat – sitting alone, face in hands; shaking.

'Hi, Yoyo! Thought you'd be here,' Rees affected conviviality.

'Mm,' Johannes mumbled, after a long silence.

'You OK? What came over you? Am I allowed to ask?'

Johannes's reply was a long time coming.

'Mm.'

'Articulate, except I cannot discern if it was a yes or a no.'

Another long silence; Johannes slowly lowered his hands from his face, revealing a flake white visage with peculiar vermilion blotches, from which peered his bleary eyes. He was perspiring profusely.

'No.'

'I'm still in the dark,' Rees affected a good-humoured laugh.

'I'm not feeling OK,' Johannes responded.

'Thought so. You look anything but OK. Have you got a fever?' Rees asked, but continued without waiting a reply, 'to the inexperienced, one would define your big production in the life class as a silly antic. To the experienced, I would say you were avoiding eye contact with Sophie. To the medically experienced I would imagine they would diagnose a case of advanced –'

'So, Mr Holmes, what about it?'

'So, persistence against recalcitrance, or maybe obduracy; can't quite identify the appropriate word that describes the malady inflicting our old sport Taliesin these days,' Rees responded, 'my guess is your problem can be narrowed down to the life model Sophie,' he paused, 'am I right? But I can't work out your condition.'

'Shit! Why don't you leave off, Bowen?' Johannes uttered in a tone meaning capitulation.

'Yoyo, you swore,' gasped Rees and, addressing a ghostly audience in the empty loft, repeated, 'Yoyo T Swore! A Quaker who visits the Friends Meeting House at least three times a week swore!'

'God knows all about my swearing. I regularly swear inwardly,' Johannes seemed at pains to explain his swearing was not new, at least not new to God.

Rees's attempt at reducing Johannes's tension was well placed, but hardly moved the mood.

'This means it *must* be serious.'

'Mm, of course it's bloody serious.'

'You always fantasised about her – we all do! No, I tell a lie: I fantasised about her until I met Shelley. Did you try to take your dreams a bit further than the fantasy threshold?'

This last hit Johannes hard.

'Listen Rees, let the subject drop, please. I'm fed up with everything at the moment.'

'Guess you are not going to tell me about it?' Rees nagged.

'You guess right. Not a word to Michelle, now.'

'Well, in my view, Johannes,' Rees had lost his characteristically good humour, 'you seem always to do things arse over tip. Why can't you do things normally? Anyway, my advice is you should apologise to George, although knowing you, you'll probably do the opposite.'

'OK, OK; I'll apologise to him when I see him,' Johannes promised.

'Don't wait until you see him. Go to the staff common room and apologise to him straight. Get it over and done with,' Rees ordered.

'Mm,' Johannes replied, confirming his lack of conviction.

They were joined by a gaggle of commercial graphics students, popping up one at a time into the loft through the trap door leading from the spiral stairs. Their buzz of excitement was a welcome diversion as Rees was getting too near to the reality of Johannes's predicament.

'Must be lunch time,' said Rees.

Any diversion was welcome at that moment, including the roof falling in, or the loft crashing down to the corridor floor far below. Johannes was in a bad way. He wanted to be a million miles away, but was trapped by his weaknesses; and his undergraduate commitments, lack of income and no spare cash translated into folly. His wriggle room was unbearably narrow, claustrophobic.

'Hi Rees, Yoyo. What gives?'

'Everything!' said Rees optimistically.

'Nothing,' said Johannes, beyond the threshold for disguising his frame of mind.

'What are you lot so happy about?' asked Rees.

'Oh, we were just talking about a new Delta blues album Don Williams has got,' replied a graphic illustration student name of Dyfnallt.

'It's got Peg Leg Howell on it,' Janet Llewellyn gushed enthusiastically.

Janet gushing about blues wrenched Johannes from his wallow.

'Who else?' Johannes asked.

'Ishman Bracey, Peetie Wheatstraw, Charlie Patton, can't remember most of them; only heard it once,' came back.

'Charlie Patton! Crumbs, he's the greatest,' Johannes reacted, leaning heavily on his smattering of Delta blues knowledge.

'He's playing it on the graphics gramophone now,' said Dyfnallt, 'gobble our sandwiches and we're back there.'

'What are we waiting for!' said Johannes, disappearing through the trapdoor, temporarily forgetting his troubles. 'You coming Rees?'

'Sure, I'll pick up Shelly, she hates blues.'

But the moment passed. After listening to some of his favourite blues singers, the blues got Johannes and he was plunged once again into a pall of sour humour. He avoided George Little, as apologising for his unnecessary bad behaviour was completely out of reach of his wavering sanity. Johannes alone realised how seriously unstable his thinking had become. Others, even Rees, believed he had simply become a little more extreme than usual.

'*Maybe perhaps we have become a little wobbly, not much, but we think it's got something to do with servicing failures, gorillas, beautiful models, life –,*' Inner Voice was rambling. But it was bad news for Johannes.

Gwynfor had procured two tickets for Wales against England at Cardiff Arms Park the coming Saturday.

'Everyone's doing something else, so I suppose I'll have to offer you the spare ticket,' was his laconic introduction of the subject to Johannes.

'Great, but I'm broke.'

'I'm offering it free.'

'Thanks a million.'

'We'll have to hitch.'

'What's new?'

'Early start. Jersey Marine, seven-ish,' said Gwynfor.

And that was it.

'We are Gwynfor's last offer as everyone is doing something else,' Inner Voice summed up the reality of his popularity.

The following morning proved to be another ordeal for Johannes. He blanked his mind and sailed into the storm. Occupancy of the Antique Studio was given over exclusively to the small, some would say intimate, but in Johannes's current frame of mind, claustrophobic, painting special group. The routine project of life painting, the core of the painting special course, was a mixed blessing for Johannes.

Under normal circumstances he loved working in the life room, but his painting manifested the usual synaesthesia-based illogical discrepancies that so far he had not been able to overcome although, according to the painting special tutors, there were signs of mechanical success since the psychologists had discovered the problem. Eifion suggested his work looked more like 'painting by numbers', which possessed more than a streak of truth. Even Professor Price grudgingly conceded that Johannes's technical painting facility was showing some sort of improvement, though the creative aspect was still on compass yaw, always ending up in the studio next door. Unfortunately, following the incident any quality achieved had vanished into a black hole.

'It's The Incident in caps from now on.'

Johannes's current Sophie obsession, augmented by fear of confrontation at any moment with Gorilla, galvanised his increasing mental unsteadiness. Either of these matters ensured the nightmare would not go away. From every perspective the life painting session abounded with disadvantages. Johannes's guilt hung in foreboding clouds that shrouded the drapes of the Antique Studio, the students' drawing stations and the model's changing cubicle. Mists of apprehension billowed from every corner and niche of the atelier.

Under normal circumstances Johannes would have been delighted that Sophie was the timetabled model for the painting project, and with a spring in his heart he would have tackled the project with alacrity. As Johannes saw it, the advantage a small group presented was the opportunity for him to choose an easel station that avoided eye contact with Sophie. The project tutor was Professor Price; George Little must surely have furnished details of Johannes's bad behaviour not only to Professor Price, but the whole of the senior common room.

'The webs are getting more tangled by the hour! Let's get out of here! We could jump ship to Patagonia,' Inner Voice clearly rattled in his head above the noise of preparation.

But Johannes had performed the getting out of here trick once, so a second time would have to be a complete vanishing act.

'Perhaps not Patagonia just yet – Wales are playing England on Saturday.'

But Johannes no longer had faith in his conscience. He prepared the palette and brushes, brought a primed hardboard canvas from his locker, set up an easel and awaited the pose being set in order that he could take evasive action. He did not have to wait long. To his dismay Price, having wheeled the podium back from its normal crescent line, set Sophie in a standing pose facing ninety degrees to the crescent base. Obviously, this set-up was a conspiracy following yesterday's debacle with George Little. Price was testing Johannes from the start.

'Sod it! Placing her there, deliberate!' Inner Voice sprang, *'Tell the bugger we don't want a standing pose.'*

Johannes reviewed the situation with increasing dismay.

'Go on, tell him.'

He considered the alternatives. Very few sensible ones presented themselves.

'*Go on, tell the bugger.*'

'Er… could we have a different pose please, professor?'

'Why ever for, Taliesin?' the professor asked.

'What's up, Yoyo? You like standing poses. Leave it,' Rees spoke gently.

'Um, for a change perhaps,' Johannes niggled, ignoring Rees's advice.

'A change to what, Taliesin?'

'This *is* a change, Johannes Taliesin,' Ingrid Svikeris interposed, 'we have too many seated poses.'

'You prefer the standing pose because it's simpler,' Johannes retorted, which happened not to be true.

Johannes was under colossal pressure, but Ingrid and the rest of the group were not to know. Of course, Rees had an inkling. The others came to Ingrid's defence.

'We're happy with a standing pose!' they chimed variously.

Sophie smiled.

'*We can always walk out… again.*'

Support for the standing pose, from Ingrid et al., caused Johannes to relent. He shrugged. Full-frontal standing pose it was to be. Sophie arranged her face to form her Mona Lisa smirk once again, purpose of which was lost on everybody except Johannes and perhaps Rees. There was nothing for it but to tough it out.

'*Here we go. This is hell. We know we won't succeed in toughing it out!*'

To confirm the pose fix, Bill Price chalked a reference around Sophie's feet and at each corner of the podium.

But Professor Price had other matters on his mind.

'The pose will be repeated for four sessions,' he announced. 'Principal Hancock wishes we pass on an important message to you. Her Majesty's chief inspector Charlton and his team are due here three weeks from today as the second part of the national inspection of all art and design undergraduate provision in order to sustain or re-classify our degree-awarding status. I cannot stress enough how important this inspection is to Swansea College of Art. The government is hell-bent on reducing the number of degree-awarding art colleges in the country and, for a number of reasons which I do not intend to discuss today, Swansea College of Art is vulnerable. Principal Hancock jolly well expects the painting special group to produce something of worth for the chief inspector to see on his rounds.'

'*If Hancock let's him through the door, that is.*'

'What was that, Taliesin?'

'Didn't think I'd said anything, Professor Price.'

'Muttering under your breath! If you have anything to say, Taliesin, speak up!'

'*Go on, tell the bugger what we thought we didn't say*' Inner Voice whispered.

'It's well known the principal is disinclined to welcome Her Majesty's inspectors to the college, Professor Price, and on that basis I thought it very unlikely Chief Inspector Charlton and his team will actually materialise,' Johannes uttered, not sure whether he had thought his thoughts, or spoken his thoughts.

Professor Price gasped; some students sighed in theatrical scorn.

'*Uh-oh! We must have spoken them.*'

'Knew you had muttered something out of line!' the professor snapped, 'Principal Hancock, for all his good intentions to keep Swansea College of Art an inspector-free zone, has no choice in the matter. The chief inspector has a government mandate to enter this college when and as he pleases. I suggest, Taliesin, that you concentrate your efforts more on your work and less on the politics of management. Heaven forbid if you were ever to aspire to management –'

A burst of tittering interrupted the professor's flow.

'– Regardless of your imagination, you must endeavour to produce your best, understand?'

'We'll give these shits what for, mocking us. Say no,' Inner Voice whispered.

'Yes, Sir.'

In addition to striking her usual pose, Sophie decided on this occasion to arrange a lascivious smirk of triumphal proportions. Johannes strove to ignore this new departure in triumphal provocation and settled down as best he could; his mind was in turmoil. Yesterday's debacle with George Little –

'For which we are yet to apologise.'

– Added to his feelings of conspiracies, whisperings of inadequacy and being hunted by gorillas. He had become a pastiche of skulking around corners, looking in mirrors, darting around like a frightened rabbit. His general studies had become disastrous; arguing with Price whether a chief inspector would arrive or not neither proved nor improved a thing.

'Perhaps we're losing our mind.'

Johannes had long since forgotten to count his blessings, for which however he no longer cared a damn. Here in the Antique Studio Sophie stood in the flesh reminding him of his monumental inadequacy. Currently the greatest of his problems was the need to produce a full-length study of his fixation in oils, of all nightmares. That the chief inspector and his team would then examine it exacerbated the pressure. The college's eligibility to retain its degree-awarding status was a bridge too far for Johannes in his present state.

Normally, having set a pose Professor Price would have left the atelier during the early stages of a project. But on this day he lingered back, pensively, no doubt concerned about the impending inspection. The painting special group had taken his words seriously, and were already busily mapping-out the figure in earnest. Through scraping of charcoal, the rumble of 6B pencils on cotton duck or the brushing on of a wash, one way and another, the industry of life study in oils was under way.

The group's canvases displayed a variety of preparation methods. Rees's top quality canvas was stretched tautly by means of corner expander wedges; Ingrid had persuaded her boyfriend, Ken Hendy, to stretch her canvas for her, which he had done superbly with brute force and stapling gun; Jerry utilised a mixture of stretching techniques. All other canvases were purchased ready-stretched, except Johannes's pathetic hardboard, which presenting a non-viscous surface aided in its betrayal by a grotesque convex warp.

'We are competing with this well-heeled shower – we bet gorillas can't paint – lauding their ready-stretched canvases about the place – look at our pathetic piece, not even grade A hardboard,' Inner Voice's huffing was on a deteriorating slope.

The hardboard 'canvas' was heavily primed in rose madder. An advantage hardboard brought was in the cheaper material enabling scraping off recently applied paint easier; the disadvantages were snobbish dislike for anything other than pure canvas and a tendency for the oil paint, if loaded too heavily, to slough. This latter concern evaded Johannes on account that he rarely had sufficient paint with which to overload the hardboard; furthermore, his paintings regardless of material support never attained a quality that demanded public acclamation.

After a while, satisfied that the painting special group were setting about the work which would deliver the goods in readiness for HMI Charlton's visit, Professor Price left the atelier. From the moment invigilation ceased, matters for Johannes took a distinct turn for the worse. The praying mantis set about the psychological decapitation of her victim through enactment of perfect theatre. The smile she threw in Johannes's direction possessed such groaning lasciviousness that it tipped his last resolve into the waste paint jar. Her subtle facial gestures placed his weaknesses on a plinth for all to observe. The moment pierced a waver in his weak psychological character that made it impossible to face Sophie down. The distraction was enormous and quickly undermined his drawing rhythm.

As a remedy Johannes decided to commence painting before the mapping-out was complete.

'*What are we doing? We are bypassing the only stage at which we are competent,*' Inner Voice squeaked the warning, '*what are we doing? What are we doing?*'

But Johannes battled on regardless of his inner misgivings. This was entirely the wrong decision, as he found his tendency to draw with the brush conflicted with the preliminary blocking-in of large areas. In a gathering fluster, he began mixing the pigments from raw directly on the board.

'*We know the mixing process should be undertaken on the bloody palette, but then cockle robbers come and steal the pigment off our warped hardboard, and Strait is the Gate no doubt, Tuscany Flowers – what the hell are we doing?*'

He did not care what he was doing. The colours became dirty. Representation of the figure began curdling in amorphous non-representational shapes as the imagery of the standing pose slipped away from his brush, slipped out of the hardboard grasp.

'*Vatican Cellars,*' Inner Voice garbled, trying the old detraction gamble.

His grappling with demons was both external and internal. Fortunately the model's first rest period broke the chain. As standing poses were more demanding than the otherwise, models were allowed more frequent rests. Sophie walked around looking at each painting, omitting to wear her dressing gown.

This was mildly frowned upon by the academics; upon realising such display they would command 'gown on, please'.

Obviously Sophie had calculated Professor Price would not return as soon, so tiptoed around the easels naked. The provocation was blatant and aimed at her victim. When passing Johannes's station she puckered and lingered: he stared ahead at his painting. She lingered longer.

'*It's that warmth again! We are going Eyeless in Gaza, perhaps –*'

Rees gave Johannes a sympathetic glance. The display over, Sophie disappeared into the model's cubicle. Clearly from the stunned silence his colleagues twigged something was up. Johannes, hating every second of it, was ready to explode with embarrassment. He walked out into the Endless Corridor seeking consolation.

At the commencement of the next session following the short break, Johannes determined to rectify the glaring errors –

'*We blame the brush. Come on, brush, get a sodding grip* '

– in proportion his brush had wantonly uttered.

'*Bugger the brush! Abandoned on the stair –*'

So he decided to paint with a palette knife, as its hard-edge precision gave him much needed reassurance. The knife however demanded greater quantities of paint so he busied himself mixing powder white with boiled linseed syrup, and prepared other warring pigments from his tubes. The manufacture was out of kilter with the quiet atmosphere of life class.

Lashings of oil paint created senseless mountains of farmyard slurry across his palette and, with the aid of a spade he soon set about layering it onto the board. But although Johannes was applying thick layers of oil paint, the imagery was not conforming to a representation of the standing model. He impatiently applied corrections over the slabs of fresh paint already in place. Johannes was disintegrating.

'The Snows of Kilimanjaro, if we please, or even the origins of corruption –'

Sophie shook her breasts, almost imperceptibly, dim and rhythmic, to the accompanied titters of the more secure students. Her banal action, however, was designed to call down anything but humour in Johannes, who co-operated with Sophie's theatre by not seeing the joke. She repeated the offence, ever so gently, the while nailing him with her Mona Lisa.

'Could you please keep still!' Johannes's intolerance exploded, which was met by giggling whispers from the others, as the rest of her body was professionally stock-still.

'We're losing the dog's sodding bollocks –'

Clouds descended, trapping sight of diminishing escape returns. Heavy overloaded paint began vomiting down his canvas board. Shapes whose intention was representing the figure, smeared and distorted into vague nettles and wasps. Sophie's mouth grew large and cavernous, moist and sucking, her tongue licking across the atelier, smothering Johannes's canvas board, and sucking at his head. He gasped for breath.

'Think of other things – the concept of symbolic forms – the simplest and surest way to demonstrate the significance of the universal symbolic function for the formation of theoretical consciousness would be to turn to the highest and most abstract achievements of pure theory – what the hell are we thinking?'

Shaking his head vigorously, Johannes momentarily regained stability. He studied his painting as best he could in the circumstances. What a mess! What a bloody mess!

'The painting is perfect! We are the mess! The painting is the message –'

He began rectifying the sloughing, but the more the correction the more Sophie avalanched down the picture, distorting into horrific shapes of gnome and goblin, limbs askew and heaving on a sheepskin rug. He corrected more hastily; paint dripped from the canvas board onto easel and floor. The figure assumed an unfamiliar form, gaunt in apparition, hollow in search, frightening in image, naked in threat and taunt.

'We were glad when they said unto us, better an end with horror than horror without end –'

Johannes had been losing control of his painting for several minutes, but now he was unsure of the awful mess, as the painting had taken control of him. Palette strokes loomed away across the atelier, enlarging while they flew. Sophie the medieval monster simultaneously registered at several points of the life room, each beckoning to Johannes to join her – here, on the ceiling, here in the paint store; no, everywhere in her cubicle, beckoning for him to join her, gargoyles at the ready.

'Not in the cubicle!' Johannes yelled out.

His fellow students gave fright at the shout. Rees's look of concern for his friend was wracked with astonishment.

'This is bloody torture! Let's get out of these cellars! For in the theory the connection stands out in full brightness and clarity. We find that all theoretical determination –'

'This is bloody torture!' he shouted, 'Let's get out of these cellars, for in theory the connection stands out in full brightness and clarity –'

His colleagues looked on in alarm. Scraping the avalanche no longer affected the image on his board. The oil paint crept up the palette knife, over his hand, travelled his arm and was now attacking his perspiring face.

'We can't take much more of this, we can't take much more of this, we can't – why didn't she like Cassirer's phenomenology of knowledge?'

Sophie continued to smile at Johannes – she smiled from the podium, she smiled from the grotesque mess on his canvas board, the gargoyles in the ceiling smiled. Her mouth spoke from the glutinous mass of his painting, 'come and join me in this beautiful slurry, come and screw me here; no, no, NO! Not another little squirt, but a proper screw, as only a gorilla can screw. Come here, snivelling wretch,' he heard her call from the ceiling, 'and make amends for your pathetic display; if you don't, I'll tell everybody you can't do it. This is your last chance.'

'My God! She's going to tell Gorilla. We can't take –'

'Come here now,' Johannes heard Sophie calling again, back in his painting again, 'I know you can't do it when I'm lying down… here's your opportunity to make amends and take me standing up. Come on, little squirt!'

'She knows we're a little squirt. Ignore her voice! Oh, let's die!'

Johannes strove to eradicate the delusions from his mind: dwelling on the twin prongs of his guilt and failure served no purpose. Satan's cooking instrument disguised as a palette knife, every symptom her map. The Antique Studio began to swirl, the spotlights dimmed. Sophie was in the middle, writhing on an oily sheepskin. His fellow students had gathered around, goading him to have another go.

'We –'

The studio rocked, the floor tilted and heaved up as a grassy field. Tall grass everywhere, sloping down to the door. Deep in the realm of human indignity nestles a smutty little prayer many self-deluding pygmies believed in.

'Requiem for a Nun, we –'

Johannes was alone in the middle of a hay field, bathed in glorious sunshine. Grasshoppers chirped and skylarks sang. Everything about the scene was summer and peaceful. But the fleeting paradise turned quickly to hell as Sophie stepped off the podium naked and, entering the field, walked through the hay towards him, provocatively exhibiting her beautiful form, the new development exuded an erotic dimension. Unable to resist the soft temptation of skin and pubic hair, the tallest grasses ejaculated over her belly and thighs: Sophie's eyes rolled in the pleasure Johannes had been unable to fulfil.

'That's how it is done, useless little squirt; watch and learn a lesson!' she writhed.

Spreading her arms and thighs, she slipped evermore through the tall wetting grasses, drinking the canvas to full stretch. The eyes had intercourse with the shapes.

'Machiavelli perhaps, or Schiller – the eyes have intercourse with the shapes.'

Finding Sophie's exhibition of naked indulgence both provocative and enticing, Johannes willed the dream to last forever.

'Too late! We know that's the origin of corrupting an error –'

Too late, the error committed, the spell was broken by participation in a dream combining with a futile attempt at controlling it. Johannes was never able to control it.

'We couldn't control it in a month of Sundays, we –'

The dream was turning; Sophie's flesh, peeling away from the bones, fell amongst the hay. Bleached bones, maintaining their angular skeletal form, unassumingly walked on through the atelier. Turning towards Johannes, Sophie's grinning skull displayed wide mysterious eye sockets. As the skeleton walked on, so the dark eye sockets stared at Johannes: all the knotholes in the atelier floor were watching him, all the knotholes in the atelier floor were watching him, all the –

'This is hell, this is hell on top of something –' Inner Voice stumbled.

The dream turned again: the moaning skeleton changed her perspective, now coming from dead flesh rotting in the hay. Again the perspective changed, the hay began to moan; Sophie's skeleton walked on, walked on through. With intensifying moaning, but of course it came neither from skeleton, flesh or hay: it was Johannes moaning.

'This is hell, this is hell on top of something!' Johannes cried out.

Rees Bowen, seeing his friend in obvious distress, threw down his brushes, dashed round to Johannes's paint-strewn station.

'Yoyo, take a break,' he hissed an attempt at discretion.

'Leave me alone, I'm OK, the gorilla died in the hay,' Johannes moaned, his mind hovering somewhere not in the atelier.

He did not recognise his friend, unaware of his mess, unaware Rees was attempting a rescue.

'No, you're not OK, Yoyo; take a break,' Rees hissed.

'Leave me alone, Sophie, I should have listened to my conscience,' came Johannes's reply, still not recognising Rees, 'I did not pester you, it was you who pestered me, pestering, the shallow turnpikes drift asunder, leave me alone!'

'What should we be saying, what –'

The painting special group, transfixed, edged away uncomfortably.

Rees shrugged his shoulders, stood back, alarmed, 'Yoyo, for heaven's sake, get a grip,' he shouted.

'We heard her – telling us to get a grip of all things –'

Janet Jones, not so discreet, let fly, 'Good heavens, Johannes Taliesin, whatever it is that is troubling you, we don't want to share it,' Janet Jones let fly, 'listen to Rees, take a break and get out of here. Just get out!'

'Cool it, Janet. Can't you see he's not well?' Rees interjected.

'Bitch!' Johannes shouted, 'Bitch, bitch, fucking bitch!'

It was not clear to whom he was directing his calling, Janet or Sophie. His head was down, examining the knotholes.

It was obvious to all in the atelier the centre of Johannes's angst must be Sophie. All eyes looked from Sophie to Johannes and back. Unbelievably, Sophie continued to pose, seemingly unmoved by Johannes's breakdown. She was at the summit of her achievement, her face flushing with excitement, her body swaying with pleasure, her libido experiencing gratification at last. Rees, having no influence on his friend, moved away.

For Johannes the certainty was at hand he had arrived in hell. During an idle moment Cain struck a red bell, the admission of another soul. Nothing in his charter required actions of deliberate construction, leave alone an act that zoned perilously with Adventism. Consciously contributing to machinations of insanity implied miscalculation, mischief on dangerous ground.

'We heard her tolling a red bell, we heard.'

Again Cain struck the red bell: red noise everywhere, a rookery of noise, crows shod in galloping hooves. Motets in the wires, rain on the panes, red crows painted on the sky, cantatas of red noise, noise everywhere. A deserved pound of flesh in the hay; Cain was playing idle mischief with Johannes's lost mentality.

Standing the grey face could see sawn cut block grey, her fingers as tree roots marching to sanctuary: and through the sieve when grief seemed new the sprouting seedlings gathered.

'We were glad when he said unto us, come into the house of the Lord.'

But twisted beaks could not part, purred her life from its symbolic feel, buried youth in fleecy clothes, shagged to ribbons in the olive groves, tended the image in her coke-bucket mind.

'Perhaps not,' Inner Voice retracted.

The trees marched, a rebellion of wood. All the knotholes in the floor were watching.

Johannes knelt on his haunches; holding his hands in his head, oil paint smearing face and hair, he looked across in searing despair; all the knotholes could do was stare. His colleague students ceased working, moved in collective alarm.

'Stand up, we're making a spectacle of ourselves; we think erect is good, crumpled bad –'

'Johannes Taliesin, poet painter, who was alive for years before he was born!' Johannes yelled out.

'He's gone mad!' Janet Jones cried, 'Bonkers out of his head; do something somebody!'

Standing up, Johannes unscrewed the butterfly retainer, wrenched the board from the easel: paint dripped onto the floor.

'Back on the easel, put it back on the easel…'

'I have a theory,' said a new voice, the voice of an angel perhaps, 'albeit a wild theory: I wonder if he is properly dead?'

'We are becoming senile, maybe an end with horror, put the bloody hardboard back on the easel.'

'That contradicts the college regulations,' replied a second angel perhaps, 'dead and he would not be here being chased by animals; alive, and he's here. Unhappily he's alive and here, but insane.'

'But it often occurs with chickens,' the first angel perhaps persisted.

'We don't get this: now they think we are a chicken,' Inner Voice reckoned plaintively.

Deranged, too much debate in his painting, he charged across the atelier floor with the painted board high, insanity a-mock. Sophie's Mona Lisa smirk rapidly turned to a look of horror. Giving her no time to take evasive action Johannes brought the paint-laden weapon down on her body. Paint sloughing across her face, breasts and belly, she slithered screaming out of the Antique Studio, a painted nude shrieking hysterically down Endless Corridor. Sophie Howells had at last lost her sophistication. Johannes's colleagues like a crowd taken aback by the suddenness of attack, shouted orders to everyone and to no one in particular. Johannes had not only lost his cool: he was clean out of it.

'NOW we've gone senile! What a bloody mess! What did we

do THAT for? We were in a mess before, but this really improves matters... now we're in a bloody mess... Requiem for a Nun in Vatican Cellars.'

'Yoyo! What in God's name? Yoyo!' Rees called.

'Requiem for a Nun in Vatican Cellars,' Johannes was frothing gibberish.

He had gone mad.

9

The Clothes Clapped Their Hands With Glee

'Yoyo, *THERE YOU* are,' Rees Bowen walked over from the lockers. 'Hell! That was a show yesterday. What came over you? Where did you go? People were looking for you.'

'Nothing.'

'Nothing, you say! Yoyo, what a mess! There's talk Sophie is going to sue you. Shelley tells me gossip has it she had a job getting the paint off her tits. Where did you disappear? I followed after you, but you'd gone. Have you seen Price? He was wild, looking everywhere. Asked me how to get to Rhondda Street. Were you there?'

'Yes, I saw him. I've got to go to the principal, that's why I'm here. Not worried about seeing the principal, I expected as much,' Johannes replied with an artificial calm. 'Have you seen Garin around? It's bloody Garin I've got to avoid.'

'No, but I'm sure he will be looking for you. God! Price was wild yesterday. You don't do things by halves, Yoyo. I've never seen anyone crash his canvas over a model before, except in the movies, van Gogh and all that.'

'Van Gogh never crashed his canvas over a model,' Johannes said, matter of fact, 'and anyway mine isn't a canvas; but I can understand Price was wild. He was wild when he came to see me. I counted the Hells Teeth expletives – actually, I lost count at around thirty,' Johannes said, and gave a little nervous giggle.

'Johannes,' Rees measured, using the label Johannes for his friend only when matters were deadly serious, 'Johannes, it's not a giggling matter, if you don't mind my saying: this is serious.'

'Do you think we don't know that?'

'Nothing I can't handle, Rees.'

'Aw come on, Johannes, attacking a member of staff – the model is staff whether you like it or not – is an offence payable by expulsion. Do you realise that?'

Students passing down Endless Corridor gawped silently. No doubt Johannes was the talk of the college. They must have been thinking,

'There's Johannes Taliesin, painting special, who went mad yesterday in the Antique Studio and poured paint over Sophie Howells the model. Worse than that mad artist who cut his ear off, van whatshisname.'

Others whispered in awe,

'So *that's* the one who attacked the model with a tube of paint – doesn't look as if he's got it in him.'

While pretty little fashion girls rolled their eyes as if,

'Using the model as a paintbrush! What's the college of art coming to?'

'They say there was a fight and he was stopped just in time from throwing the model through the window.'

'No!'

'Yes, on my mother's – the window was closed, they say.'

Ken Hendy passed by glaring as he gave Johannes a wide berth.

'We bet some of his glint of fame has been dulled. Next time he'll have to ride two bicycles down the corridor at the same time,' Inner Voice was back to the perfect we-are-rational-but-it's-too-sodding-late mode.

'No. They won't expel me, they can't afford losing the numbers at this juncture in the inspection round.'

'Listen to him! They will, Yoyo. It'll demonstrate to HMI Charlton and his shower an example of resolute management.'

'Shit! Didn't think of resolute management; not in this place, at least.'

'No, they won't, Rees,' Johannes countered. 'Anyway, we'll see what the principal has to say.'

'Yes, they will.'

'He'll say you are out, Yoyo.'

'Shit! What a bloody mess.'

'I've got a good excuse full of mitigating circumstances,' Johannes invented.

'No, we haven't.'

'What mitigating circumstances, for Heaven's sake?' Rees was getting exasperated.

'Can't say until I see the Prink.'

'When do you see him?'

'Twelve.'

'Hell's teeth, Yoyo,' said Rees, emulating Professor Price's exasperation, 'how can you be so calm about the mess you're in?'

'We're not calm.'

'I'm not calm, it's just I've got no choice to be otherwise, Rees, and stop sounding like Price, had enough of him last night, in front of the sodding neighbours as well.'

'Never a truer word, you've got no choice. What's this big thing between you and Sophie, anyway?'

'Yoyo, what happened to you yesterday?' Manod came by, conveniently interrupting.

'Nothing, Manod.'

'You've gone loopy,' Manod chuckled, 'no, correction: you've always been loopy; now you've gone completely round the bend,' and he laughed the more.

'Wrong conjugation, Manod; you must have been absent from school when they taught conjugation,' Johannes hissed.

'No need to get personal, Yoyo.'

Michelle joined the throng, casually linking arms with Rees.

'Yoyo, I always suspected there was something wrong with you,' she blurted.

Johannes winced, 'Mind I don't do the same to you one day when Rees is not looking,' he threatened.

'Promises, Yoyo,' Rees joked, grinning broadly at Michelle, 'that should be worth watching!'

'Huh!' retorted Michelle, and gave Rees an affectionate kick.

'What are you going to do until twelve?' Rees enquired.

'Library,' Johannes answered curtly.

'If Garin comes after you, give Manod and me a call,' said Rees. Manod nodded.

'If I survive long enough to call,' replied Johannes, shaking, 'but at the moment it's good to know I've got bodyguards I can rely on.'

'Gosh,' Michelle squeaked, 'is Garin after you? How exciting! It's true, then, Sophie Howells must have done something really naughty to you to cause you to attack her with a painting.'

'Shelley, go to your classes; this is man's stuff,' Rees rebuked, unlinking arms.

'Oh sure,' Michelle tossed back, 'man's stuff pouring paint over naked ladies.'

'Don't forget, call,' said Rees.

'And if you don't call, we'll still know, by the howls of pain as Garin pulls your arms off,' Manod giggled helpfully, as Johannes slunk off to the library.

But Johannes did not read. He was irremediably banqueted in a predicament of his own concoction. His conscience could not make a bigger production of it: all parts of the lesson had been learnt, rampaging through the groves of cerebral departments in certain delight that the end was at hand. Certainly his predicament was serious enough to consider the sacred tomorrows for which he had grown accustomed to having an inalienable right were about to be exculpated. He had never been in such trouble, and he reflected how easily the conscience abandons ship without the slightest acknowledgement of being part of the whole cerebral shebang. In fact, his conscience was weighing its options with a remarkable air of disloyalty.

'Now we're in a bloody pickle,' Inner Voice continued the persistent ring.

Long before Johannes was knee high to Spot the sheepdog his parents had impressed upon his endemically weak character that embarking upon a chant ad nauseam with regard to his failure, incompetence or stupidity was good for the soul.

'Now we're in a bloody pickle.'

The memory of such endless chanting needed to be bleached; bleached of the incident or, failing that, smeared across humanity's tut-tutting for the full realisation of embarrassment. Best of all, repeated until such time he felt sufficiently humiliated to commit an act of self-destruction.

'That's an idea.'

Regardless, whichever event occurred the soonest, it would still not appease God's wrath, his parents had impressed upon him.

'Now we're in a bloody pickle. Can't begin to think of a way out of it –'

Not that his parents articulated such capital ultimatums linguistically: parental communications were neatly condensed into either a fixed glare accompanied by a growl from his father or a head-hanging sulk by his mother, each symbolic vessel carrying more than sufficient information to furnish a full shelf of parables, metaphors and miracles, as both of them had long since given up. Miraculously, the understanding had been communicated by way of a process no more sophisticated than a series of monosyllabic grunts combined with facial expressions. Despite the lack of a preordained agenda the training programmes cohered logically to impinge on his immature mind. Even when too remote to divine, the entity of impossibility was alive and well, existing happily in his elliptical thought patterns.

'Must think of a way out of this mess; what a bloody pickle –'

Normally Johannes's prime objective in the event of a glitch would be to engage denial, a strategy with a reasonable record of success in previous predicaments.

Unfortunately, contrary to his normal modus operandi, the dense fog on this occasion involved other people, which made realisation of a denial strategy somewhat complicated, unwieldy.

Johannes set off up Endless Corridor to keep the twelve o'clock appointment with Principal Hancock. His only defence lay in the previous day's breakdown being the inevitable outcome of mounting tensions.

'Tensions following our deeply embarrassing denouement of what little remained of our manhood, and our subsequent terror of annihilation at the claws of a gorilla,' Inner Voice summed up, having abdicated all responsibility for the fracas.

The tipping point had been a silly little smirk from Sophie who was justifiably enjoying her venereal superiority, but apart from oil paint on the floor, the easel, Johannes's head and a good proportion of Sophie's bare body, everything else was trapped in Johannes's rampant imagination.

He surveyed his predicament. The Endless Corridor was its normal buzz of student activity: foundation students, raw and eager, carrying bundles of work; fashion designers trailing cut-out garments; sculptors lugging armatures. Paintings, photographs, portraits, pictures and pots perambulated with their proud owners. Students smiled happily or smirked admonishingly according to their knowledge or otherwise of Johannes's madness.

'*Look at them! Look at our bloody pickle,*' Inner Voice whinged, '*everything seems to go right for everyone else, but nothing goes right for us.*'

Johannes had never been in such trouble. An inability to control his own urges or satisfy those of a libidinous Sophie Howells provoked scores of imaginary conspiracy theories, which his brittle psyche was unable to handle.

'*Resulting in an unwarranted attack on her during life pose,*' Inner Voice was belatedly coming to terms, '*what a bloody mess –*'

In brief due course this incurred the towering wrath of head of painting Professor Price – who was never even-tempered with Johannes – resulting in a rendezvous with Principal Hancock. No doubt the whole affair would most certainly lead to an unplanned exit from the college of art.

'*What a confounded bloody infernal mess, which means we have to go back to Aberystwyth to live and we'll no doubt bump into the bloody family doctor in Peacocks of all places and he'll ask us in a loud booming voice if our bloody venereal decease has cleared up. What a bloody mess.*'

Concurrent with the drama of his stupid theatre playing its act through to an ignominious end, he needed to avoid a certain type of animal as a matter of life and death. Fortunately Rees and Manod had pledged their bodyguard stuff, but they could well be ten miles away when his arms were being ripped off. All this should not have occluded his better judgement on a clear day.

'*All because we failed to deliver a simple shag,*' Inner Voice held the high ground in articulating smart conversation.

Johannes's failure to deliver was too much for his inexplicably inflated ego to bear, while taking leave of his better judgement was certainly not a clear day's intention.

'*What a bloody bloody bloody mess –*'

Approaching the principal's office, Johannes recognised the perilous predicament of all small independent institutions of art nationally. Their economy of scale was too insignificant to maintain provision without government subsidy, the new methodology dispensing with those wasteful formats. Swansea College of Art was no exception. He was not empowered to change the articles of the new Act.

'I was glad when God said unto me...' he muttered to the Endless Corridor.

Then, gathering the dignity his status demanded, he set about the unenviable task of advising the principal of the steps needed to avoid certain –

'*Oh God!*' something went deep within Inner Voice.

'Hi Yoyo, is it true?'

'*What is he talking about? Say the truth.*'

'Yes, it's bad news, I'm afraid: the college is doomed.'

Endless Corridor passed by languidly. He took to examining its details – fresh magnolia distemper, the picture rail overloaded in readiness for the all-important inspection – one of his life drawings occupying a prominent position, new chandelier chains scintillating in the bright lights. Johannes was not to be fooled by the superficiality of it all. New fittings, indeed! The lick of paint had not reached roy cant spel.

His task was to go directly to the origins of the college's decline. How would the academic staff react? Most likely in the normal way – calling crisis meetings with the unions, marches with the aid of rent-a-misfit, demands that the government do something about it. Not a lot at the moment, nor in the future for that matter: academics are like that; shaking the money tree simply inculcates a dependency culture in the next generation of students.

'KW Hancock, ARCA, Prix de Rome' and above it 'PRINCIPAL,' was proudly declared in old gold Baskerville font on Windsor blue. The lettering possessed an impression of notes in Latin by Gibbon for a George III commission.

'Two hoots to the tittle-tattle,' Inner Voice in courageous frame, *'and stop being so bloody sorry for these people.'*

Regardless of loin-girding by the Inner Department, Johannes timidly tapped on the door, and promptly scooted to the waiting-to-see-the-principal-bench opposite, his inspectorial fantasies primer washed beneath. Crowds passed by.

'Hi Yoyo, waiting to see the principal?' a passing sadist asked the obvious question of one sitting on *that* bench of all benches.

'No,' Johannes replied, impassively.

'The rumour must be wrong, then?'

'Depends on the rumour, stupid,' Johannes snapped.

'Uh-oh, have fun! See you down the King's tonight,' amends being made by Sadist.

'Probably not, I have reports to write.'

'We're going down the King's anyway.'

'Min.'

A distant call of a buzzard soaring high above the pines, but as it was Swansea College of Art it had obviously emanated from the general squeak-easy rabble. Johannes began wondering about an onomatopoeic uttered by a sufferer of Tourette's Syndrome, a malady he had read about when hiding from the world in general. His hyperactive mental state jumped about, alighting on this and crashing on that, but mostly describing a neat figure eight. Having decided the call had not come from the principal, he continued to attend to the full advocacy of the Endless Corridor.

'*It's obvious we're going to be kicked out, dishonourably discharged... what do we tell everyone? God! The embarrassment... we can't go back to Aberystwyth, that's for sure, too many doctors. Try the RAF again: Hello Sergeant Handlebar, remember us? Thanks for leaving the option open for us to join fighter command at Hornchurch: we decided the RAF is by far the better platform from which we can develop our potential. This time we'll gain entry and pass with flying colours and fly over Swansea and strafe the bloody College of Art, and we'll nuke the Uplands, and you are right, there's a hell of a lot of pretty women in the place.*'

'COME IN!'

Principal Hancock's voice sounded above Endless Corridor's hubbub, and even soared above Johannes's reflections on meagre struggle and gaining his pilot's licence at Hornchurch. The call jolted him from his reminiscing; this time he was sure the call was a command emanating from beyond the Windsor blue door. He leapt up and entered.

'*What do we say in our defence? Now's a fine time to start worrying about defence! We could say a clandestine banditry back home is threatening our family with murder if they don't up the protection payments of shallots...*'

The principal's office-atelier was held in a hush of luxury. At first glance, it appeared no one was in, and Johannes assumed he had walked into the wrong room. His state of mind was causing difficulty in thinking clearly; but he was sure the principal had called and was somewhere hidden behind a vaulted buttress or a languid screen.

'*Oh, God,*' Inner Voice whimpered, '*at all costs we need to maintain the charade.*'

The atelier's spacious elegance displayed the discrete mixture of business and leisure characterising the exclusive artistic styles of the decadent 1930s that had been carried over to post-war art institutions. Johannes had not visited the principal since his interview and the fateful cork catastrophe. The atelier had been extensively refurbished and his paintings-in-progress were now housed out of Taliesin-harm's way behind elegant screens. Obviously the Taliesin debacle had taught the principal that his paintings were too valuable to be endangered at the altar of clumsiness by members of the Disgwylfa Fawr tribe of cardboard cut outs from Cardiganshire.

Principal Hancock, a painter of superbly refined stature, stoically avoided an air of decadence. Paradoxically, his new office arrangement displayed all the arrogance of finery, the result of pre-inspection advice on affecting a cosmopolitan image, or so Johannes assumed from the perspective of his infinite amazement. The atelier harked back to the ostentation of early empire, with artefacts drawn from influences and impressions, from the classical right up to the present. Here was an office-atelier abundantly furnished with pieces of oaken accoutrement appropriate to chief executive management at a metropolitan centre of art education. The floor was luxuriantly carpeted in rich Wilton patterns of burgundy and mahogany. Johannes's sole-less boots sank comfortably into the warm pile, a treat to the parts of his feet normally making contact with cold stone. He looked about nervously, waiting.

Ahead stood the principal's large desk, which was familiar to Johannes from the day of interview, inlaid with dark viridian leather; but now the whole piece was finely polished. A matching leather swivel chair with inlays of ox blood stood beside at an angle, and another chair of similar coloured leather was drawn up rather close to the former. Two cups and saucers of fine Swansea porcelain containing the remains of tea sat on a silver tray, together with sugar bowl and milk jug all of the same set that Johannes recalled seeing in a glass case at the Glynn Vivian. Drinking tea from such valuable objects was the stuff of dreams.

'*No doubt a pre-inspection visit.*'

As the principal did not appear to be in his office-atelier Johannes, alighting on the slightest excuse to escape the inevitable, turned to leave.

'Be with you in a moment,' the unmistakable voice of the principal called out.

Johannes's eyes darted about nervously. The principal's voice had emanated from behind Victorian screens of elaborate fabric, which function must be to section off the painting from the business front, pure Parisian atelier-style. Johannes's throat was dry with tension.

Glancing about again, his eyes twitched nervously from elegant object to sumptuous piece. The whole room was a feast of displays, which paradoxically calmed yet intimidated him. Johannes was familiar with the original oils that decorated the walls, having seen them on numerous other occasions hanging in the Glynn Vivian. A painting by Evan Walters of his sick mother in bed, Ceri Richards's cathedral under the sea, Fred Janes's portrait of the poet Vernon Watkins and a landscape by Herman Shapiro, *I Gaze across the Distant Hills*. To his extreme right Johannes noticed two glass cabinets containing displays of Swansea porcelain, components of which tea set were on the grand desk.

Again studying the desk that at first appearance seemed strictly reserved for the purpose of business, Johannes was surprised to note that the principal still maintained his collection of different pencils, quills, graphite sticks and other drawing accoutrements standing in blown glass goblets. Three beautiful watercolour brushes of Russian squirrel set in Chinese bamboo lay alongside the goblets. Strange, thought Johannes, for Principal Hancock was not a watercolour artist. Then an unusual instrument caught his eye: an airbrushing pen that had the appearance of having been recently used. This was stranger still for a traditional oil painter of the classical mode to be using an airbrush. What would the principal use an airbrush for? A gold bladed letter opener with a handle of beautiful cut crystal glass resembling an ancient sash cutlass lay for decorative purposes next to a collection of glistening writing instruments. Evidence of administrative paper work was limited. The whole exuded a style of relaxed academia, which conspired to seize Johannes by the dry throat and exaggerate his useless predicament, his meagre and struggle. His heart was racing, and nothing in his power could calm it.

Beyond rich curtains of dark plum hanging from sparkling brass rods above the large windows Johannes could see across the roof of the Glynn Vivian to the terraces of higgledy-piggledy houses climbing beyond. High up on Mayhill clothes hanging on windy clotheslines clapped their hands with glee at the theatre of Johannes's plight.

Principal Hancock began talking in low confidential tones. From the form of words Johannes construed a model must be behind the screens with the principal.

'God! He's got someone with him!' Inner Voice shrieked.

The principal used only Sophie as his model. The shock of realisation was too hard to bear: here behind the screens was the *very* person who had caused Johannes's earlier outburst in the Antique Room.

'Oh, our God! He's got that bloody Sophie with him! We can't believe our fucking luck these days!'

Transfixed at the spot through intimidation and inferiority, his whole being froze. Imagine it –

'About to be admonished or worse in the presence of our bloody victim,' Inner Voice could but bleat pathetically.

All the bickering inadequacies of his life failed to plumb the hell gathering about him. He began inventing scenarios in hell where each vile torture took the form of animated entities ripping arms off before inventing worse tortures... conjugate the verb to torture.

'*Our God!*' Inner Voice bleated, '*ten to one she knows we are here!*'

The idea hardly bore thinking about. Johannes's tension became electric.

'*That's the bloody tête-à-tête tea for two, ten to one; assistant from the pre- inspection team, our ass!*'

It could not get worse.

This was the moment Johannes began believing in the power of hexing, his last station of sanity. His father had all along believed in the power of hex but Johannes, in his naivety and goldfish existence, had dismissed the notion. He now joined the ranks of hexers and, to get the thing to work first time, strove mentally to utilise the power on Sophie, the principal, Price and the luxurious atelier-office, all simultaneously.

'*Why stop at these four?*' Inner Voice chirped gleefully, '*Go the whole hog and hex the bloody lot, except –*'

'No, hold the pose; I'll finish this passage.'

Principal Hancock's voice from the other side of the screens interrupted Johannes's hexing plans. Then,

'Who is it? What is your business?' he called absentmindedly, as one does when concentrating on the process of painting.

'Taliesin, Sir.'

As the cause of his predicament was also behind the screens, Johannes chose to forego furnishing the principal with information regarding the second question. A long silence followed.

'Which Taliesin?' the principal asked. Obviously he was so engrossed in the life painting he was applying only half of his brain to the presence of a visitor the other side of the screens. The principal's amnesia gave Johannes a glimmer of hope.

'I believe there is only one Taliesin in the college of art, Sir. Me.'

Another silence.

'Take a short break, Miss Howells,' the principal murmured, this time not absentmindedly.

'Aha! That confirms it! We bloody well knew Sophie was behind the screens!' Inner Voice squeaked.

A burst of energy erupted with sounds of brushes being vigorously sluiced in a turpentine bath, together with the scuffling and scraping of necessary cleaning up. The sounds were familiar to Johannes for, as a painting special student, he had to perform the brush cleaning ritual on a regular basis. Although sharing the experience of brush cleaning with the principal, one significant difference separated them: Johannes was floundering in a miasma of uncoordinated colour schemes, clumsily applied pigment, constituted powder oil paints, cheap hog-hair brushes, etc., while the principal was a superb painter whose brushwork was set on exemplary draughtsmanship. The brush swilling operation seemed interminable.

'No doubt he's demonstrating the proper treatment of brushes; we would be surprised if he left them to stiffen like we do at times. Mind, we don't have Scandinavian turpentine spirit like he has. We are fortunate even to have ordinary industrial white spirit on a good day,' nagged Inner Voice, *'Come to think of it, at times we don't have paint – except yesterday when we had too much of the bloody stuff.'*

At last the demonstration stopped.

'I shall be back shortly,' the principal said quietly but with firm optimism.

The screens wobbled delicately and Principal Hancock emerged. He wore a scowl and a Windsor blue painting smock splattered with flesh-coloured oil paint, the while wiping his hands methodically on a paint rag, which material Johannes noticed was far superior to many of the pieces performing patch duties on his trousers. A paint-splattered smock and paint rag seemed wholly incongruous in such a refined environment.

Principal Hancock unambiguously communicated his tetchiness at having his atelier work disturbed, which sin the college rumour had placed fairly high on the cardinal crime list for proper indictment. However, this was of minor concern to Johannes, all things considered, as he had been despatched to the principal by Professor Price without regard to anyone's convenience. The principal's scowl turned into a glare, which in turn metamorphosed into horror.

'Oh, so YOU are Taliesin! Damned inconsiderate!' thundered the normally softly spoken principal, as no doubt memories came flooding back of a disastrous incident during Johannes's interview all that time ago. How could Johannes forget? Through his clumsiness he had damaged one of the principal's beautiful paintings-in-progress of the nude model – as luck would have it the very same model behind the screens at this very same moment. But Johannes's clumsiness had matured to unassailable Olympian heights since those first groping bumpkin days, as his present predicament stood good testimony. However, one of his apprehensions had already been realised – the principal had unfortunately recalled the disastrous interview.

'*Oh God,*' Inner Voice groaned, as many clever replies flashed like lightning across the voids of Johannes's lacunae. He was undecided as to how to deal with the unusual circumstance.

Years ago he had been far too timid an unkempt runt to retort sharply to a principal. For the time being he held a check. Besides, this principal was renowned for his superb draughtsmanship. After all, there were rules; even in dire circumstances Johannes would not demean someone of such superior talent. Instead, Johannes affected politeness. But good manners were of minor importance in the perspective of his turmoil.

'Yes, Principal Hancock.'

'You know why you are here?' the principal spoke loudly and clearly, enunciating the words with a cut crystal accent.

'The idiot.'

'Rather, do you realise why I am here, Principal Hancock?' Johannes Taliesin replied calmly.

Principal Hancock's face began taking on the composure of purple-endowed apoplexy, which under the circumstances added to Johannes's alarm.

This was the moment Johannes had been dreading. Confronting the reason for his predicament was reconciled to the moment of hell's suspension. Did a last idea spring forth that could afford him wriggle room? Johannes thought of the 'and with one bound Eric was free' doing the rounds in his repertoire of escape clauses; but a successful direction to the bound, or perhaps the excuses to evince the direction, evaded him. In the midst of the confrontation the need to suppress a giggle was upon him, of all things.

'Oh dear, that awful feeling is coming back again! Oh dear! Oh dear! As I Lay Dying,' Inner Voice was no support, a gibbering void at the onset of another attack.

Johannes had to fight back the hysteria. His mind began buzzing with pointless thoughts/evasions/denials, the dire circumstances of his early years causing gross reactions in later life, the Welsh mafia demanding more protection payment of shallots and similar such panicking paraphernalia that rendered him beyond straight thinking. He had to fight back the giggles as well as hysteria.

'Scientific evaluation of lost cretins concluded unequivocally that hysteria and giggling are two sides of the same coin,' Inner Voice was departing the scene.

The principal sat down in the leather swivel chair at his desk, indicating to Johannes with an authoritative flick of the hand that the other chair be moved to the opposite side of the desk. Having done so Johannes sat down, hoping he had no wet paint or allied detritus from the Antique Studio attached to the patches attached to his trousers.

'*He wants to savour our smell to compare it with that bloody model.*'

'Well?' the principal asked.

'*We don't blame him or anyone for wanting our smell the inverse ratio of –*'

Johannes stared blankly, shaking horribly.

'Well?' the principal repeated.

'*She's listening for any word we say! What about saying –*' but Inner Voice clammed at the moment of need.

Johannes was attempting to formulate the most satisfactory route through his nightmare. Thoughts of wending his way through a treacherous bog on a dark stormy night without a hurricane lamp came as a welcome alternative. A propos now any alternative would be welcome.

Finding a form of words to explain his behaviour that would satisfactorily meet the principal's view, which no doubt had already been communicated to him by both Price and the model, without confessing too much embarrassing detail whilst simultaneously avoiding incurring the wrath of the eavesdropping Sophie if he strayed too far from the truth was an exacting challenge. No doubt the scheming Messalina had retold the details of Johannes's venereal disaster at her apartment two weeks previously by elevating the incident to a straightforward Rape of the Sabines. Her cock and bull story had already joined the lexicon of detrimental sagas Johannes was required to confess in a Kafka kangaroo court. What a bloody mess –

'*Perhaps if we were to throw ourselves through the window?*' at last a sensible suggestion from Inner Voice, but fortunately or otherwise Johannes could not recall advice regarding a suicide gene running in the family.

'We are a prat: left with the only option of suicide, we think; but we could run away and jump ship at Swansea docks: Taid had done it successfully, runs in the family. Just a thought of second from last resort.'

However, notwithstanding family traits and the time constraint at his disposal, Johannes began giving flight serious thought as a means of realistic escape. No, the sill was too high off the floor; besides, chances are he would not land on his feet in the street forty feet below; an idiotic idea, but under the circumstances worth considering as a second from last resort.

'What if we exposed our smelly feet? The principal would possibly crash to the floor in a swoon, Sophie would possibly run out from behind the screens in the nude to investigate the rumpus, and whilst everyone was preoccupied we could possibly make our escape in one bound.'

This was the best idea so far, especially the getaway part. But of course it was another futile plan: the odour possessed sufficient strength to have seeped out from the remnants of his boots beforehand, and all those within a hundred yards would have long since become acclimatised to its toxicity.

'Well?' the principal asked yet again, but Johannes was far from hearing him.

It was at that moment Johannes wondered why Sophie had failed to recognise the odour the moment he made his entry into the principal's office/atelier, thus identifying the intruder for her eminent employer. There again, she probably had done so; obviously a sub-plot existed that evaded analysis. After all, the office/atelier hung with the aroma of Scandinavian turpentine spirit, rich linseed oil and Old Holland oil paints, all edged by a hint of furniture polish: discernable to those used to the aroma of such substances. Not to lose out in the race to rock bottom Inner Voice made an abrupt change of tack.

'*That accent is no more Royal College of Art than Price's is,*' came the prattle.

This was serious. Yesterday's bout of insanity was certainly re-establishing itself. Consideration of an accent as logic integral to coping with the problem that beset him was so off beam, so veered north-east of his predicament that Johannes realised that he had again lost his grip on the reality of the circumstance. If these were the best defences his inner thoughts could conjure then he was once again in dire trouble.

In what by now was a gathering panic, Johannes struggled to point his brain through the fuzzy darkness of bells clanging, machines humming and panic rattling in the halls of his hysteria. But all he succeeded in achieving was to slip further away from the light, the meagre reality he recollected being the nature of his plight. High up on Mayhill the clothes continued clapping, an action that had now lost its visual poetry and had instead become devouring.

'*Don't worry,*' Inner Voice surrendered, '*this is another nightmare; our worst nightmare so far, admittedly. But we'll wake up laughing presently and realise all this has been nothing but a bad dream in closets too far and the pigs need feeding –*'

Johannes's inner conscience invariably took time off from reality during moments of hazard, leaving him stranded for cohesive thoughts or even words, and right now he was striving to hold some semblance of order in the disordered un-joined up departments of his mind. At all costs he must fight against a repeat of yesterday's insanity. Meanwhile the principal was strumming his fingers on the desk.

'I am waiting, Taliesin. Do you know why you are here?' the principal's voice rang determination to elicit a confession.

Johannes's mind curved back to the reality of his predicament.

Of course he knew all too well the reason he had been despatched by Price to the principal. He was also aware that the cause of it all, from his perspective at least, was sitting behind the screens, probably with no clothes on. Of course he knew.

'Of course we fucking-well know.'

But against his better intentions his mind was gathering in turmoil: he imagined he could hear Sophie masturbating on the chaise longue, for a chaise longue it surely was, as he could hear the apparatus jiggling and squeaking rhythmically. Obviously, Sophie was hugely enjoying every second of his discomfort; the idea had delivered her of several orgasms already.

Johannes shook the image out of his head and, continuing to avoid eye contact with the principal, nervously glanced around the office-atelier.

'Can we see that? Her jiggling about is making the screens move towards us!'

Johannes imagined he saw the screens moving bodily towards him, but another shake of his head sent them scurrying back to their station. Monumentally unsettling, his denial standoff was tearing rifts in the fabric of his reality.

'The pictures are rattling… principal seems oblivious! Uh-oh, here we go again, fuck it!'

Next the walls bulged and wobbled, and the Speer, Richards, Janes and Shapiro paintings rattled perilously on their wires. As the carpet zoomed up towards him, so it as quickly shot back down again. This unnerving departure from the reliability of the building was sufficient a crisis to cause Johannes to look the principal in the eye for the first time.

'What is making the floor and walls move?' he asked of the principal, struggling to keep his voice just a shade below the panic line.

'Taliesin, stop talking nonsense! Answer the question, please explain why you have been sent to me.'

'The walls – look there, the paintings are shaking.'

A snuffle came from beyond the security of the screens, its author conversant with Johannes's departures from reality. Principal Hancock examined the shaking wretch before him with a mixture of exasperation and concern.

'Please stop obfuscating, Taliesin, and let us resolve the purpose of your visit,' the principal said with an air of patience administered only by one of great responsibility.

'I'm not obfuscating, Sir; I cannot understand how you are not aware we are in an earth tremor, or something similar,' came Johannes's earnest reply.

The snuffle grew into a giggle, causing the principal to glance in irritation in the direction of the screens. From his expression it was obvious that what he had assumed to be a straightforward reprimand was not progressing as such. Johannes, edging about for escape mechanisms, imitated the principal, and also glanced in the direction of the screens, at which moment a new development caught his eye from further over to the left. A wide door stood ajar, revealing another room adjacent to the principal's atelier. Its decor was similar to the principal's office/atelier, with refined furniture and sumptuous carpet, emanating an atmosphere reminiscent of Jean Dominique Ingres's atelier.

'Obviously we've gone bloody ins – how could we have missed it? It's to do with – how did we miss such an obvious extension, how – ?'

Someone whom Johannes could not recognise was painting an elaborate neoclassical composition on a large canvas supported by an old-fashioned boat easel; the remainder of the view was obscured from his madness.

'This calls for investigation, private ateliers disallowed by rules of engagement according to – um, according to the Ministry of Education,' Inner Voice squeaked.

Johannes's mental state obliged a reaction. He sprang up and scooted across to investigate the newly discovered atelier. It did not occur to him to beg leave of the principal, or to answer the question hovering at hand.

'Do you know there is someone working in the atelier next door?' he asked with all concern. Curiously the principal did not reply.

'This is out of hand. Why does the principal not reply? Conspiracy is deeper than we suspected, must put in our report –'

Johannes peered into his new discovery, but in so doing his attention was taken by a sudden violent wobbling of the corner screens.

'Look out! They're about to ' Inner Voice squeaked.

'Look, Mr Hancock, the screens are about to fall over –'

The principal seemed to pay no attention, and was still strumming his fingers and looking in the direction of the chair Johannes had vacated.

'Bloody fool isn't listening to us.'

Inevitably, the vigorous wobbling caused the screens to crash over, revealing Sophie reclining naked on a chaise longue. She was holding her pose but, as Johannes had guessed, was masturbating furiously. Upon being exposed and seeing Johannes staring at her she hastily grasped her gown to cover up. Meanwhile the principal continued sitting at his desk, unmoved by the commotion.

'Why is the principal indifferent to all these goings on?'

'Would you please return to your seat, Taliesin?'

'Did you witness that, Mr Hancock?' Sophie shrieked in horror, 'There you are, proof if you needed it! Now he's attacking me in front of you. Please protect me from his vile intentions, Mr Hancock!'

'I – I –,' Johannes fumbled, 'I didn't touch the screens.'

'Oh, for heaven's sake!' the principal burst with exasperation, reaching for his ornate telephone.

'I – I – she invited me – I lost my sense of decorum… I was unable to… for many reasons… I am Johannes Taliesin, creep of the rural squaddies… I – I performed… she called me a –'

'*Which we bloody well are!*'

'You should be aware I have been avoiding… um… dodging behind trees and lamp posts, around every corner, looking through every window… for two weeks… I haven't slept for two weeks for fear of gorillas.'

'*Let's exaggerate it a bit; say seven bloody years,*' Inner Voice goaded.

'Correction, I mean I haven't slept for seven bloody years,' Johannes gabbled.

'See? He was gabbling like this when he raped me! And to think I am carrying his child, the child of a lunatic,' Sophie squirmed in horror, '*do* something, principal!'

'*God! We got her pregnant! Time has arrived to throw ourselves through the window! Chief Inspector Charlton is not going to like this at all!*'

'Taliesin!' the principal called, 'return to your seat this instant!'

But the principal's command meant nothing to Johannes.

'Watch him, Mr Hancock, there's no telling what he'll do next. Keep that letter-opener away from him. God, he smells something else!'

'Obviously, as you refuse to offer any explanation in regard to your conduct, together with your current behaviour,' Principal Hancock said in despairing tone, 'I regret to say am obliged to take a position.'

'*Who is he talking to?*'

'Your unacceptable behaviour in physically assaulting a member of staff,' the principal continued, 'plus a catalogue of transgressions that have been tabled by head of painting department Professor Price, including this insolent recalcitrance to explaining your behaviour force me to the regrettable conclusion I have no alternative but to suspend you from Swansea College of Art forthwith.'

The red noise in Johannes's head drowned out the principal's words. He hoped he had been unable to hear the judgement.

'Ignore the old fool; we didn't hear that judgement. We have more important matters to deal with, like falling screens and models masturbating.'

'My decision is subject to endorsement or otherwise by the disciplinary sub-committee of the board of trustees,' the principal spoke automatically, 'drawn up under instrument 13 dotty 5 brackets e close brackets of the Instrument and Articles of Government, brackets amended 1958 close brackets. Any appeal must be submitted in writing to the chairman of the disciplinary sub-committee of the trustees within three days of today's date.'

'He's leave of his bloody taken, senses he's leave –'

'Do you understand the consequences of this decision, Taliesin?'

'Consequences?'

'Consequences of what decision, Mr Hancock?'

'Let us be in no doubt,' Principal Hancock said very determinedly, 'the consequences of your unacceptable behaviour are that you are suspended forthwith and, following our reports, it is highly likely the disciplinary sub-committee will sustain my decision.'

'He's playing with words, trying to draw us into an argument, he's –' Inner Voice squeaked loudly.

'No, regrettably I am not playing with words, Taliesin, and trying to invoke an argument is beneath the seriousness of this occasion. Collect your belongings and report to my secretary when she will give you your notice of suspension in writing,' Principal Hancock's voice was very grave. Suspending students was a rare occurrence at Swansea College of Art; now was not a particularly expedient time to reduce yet further the already depleted enrolment totals. Sophie had disappeared from sight.

'*Phle's lala to gorilla hunting me Sophie glitch glitch raped us instead,*' Inner Voice went.

'Yes, yes. From this moment your personal life is no longer the college's responsibility,' the principal said curtly.

'*Oh, horror! We can't… Must telephone a Kr –*'

'It's a bloody conspiracy, I can't, I don't, I won't, I can't –'

Johannes had lost control of Sophie's position. His mind was noisy. All the tensions, worries and obsessions that he had bottled up exploded forth with a vengeance. His head buzzed horribly as if a food-mixer were stirring his brain.

'*The window solut –*' Inner Voice squeaked lucidly.

Unable to face the predicament any more he quickly darted across to the large window. Principal Hancock, taken by surprise at the sudden action, swivelled in his chair. High up on Mayhill the clothes were amazed at Johannes's performance by clapping more energetically. While making a desperate attempt to climb the sill, the pain in his head exploded. Everything went blank.

10
Frameshop

A FTER GOD HAD administered the flying ointment Johannes hovered majestically out of reach. Everything around him floated; colours disintegrated and mingled, mixed on the board. He could climb onto the windowsill easily enough. It was only forty feet to the street below, but suppose he didn't land on his feet?

'Bugger it! We'll only be killed, so what? We don't have to worry about gorillas any more, or filling in forms, pregnant models, saving face, lack of money, patching our trousers. Look! The clothes on Mayhill are urging us on to greater feats of ridiculous theatre…'

'Taliesin, for goodness' sake, get down!' he heard the principal call.

'He's given me syphilis and I'm carrying his baby; with his genes ten to one the baby will be born a cretin, what I've been through for the sake of art! My flat belly was a unique selling point in my business; now it's swelling out of all proportion to the selling point; and my tits still sting from that industrial chemical he uses to mix his second rate powder paints.'

'Calm down, Miss Howells, it cannot be as bad as all that; even Taliesin does not use industrial chemicals to mix his oil paints, I have told you before. And you,' the principal called toward the window, 'would you please slip down off that sloping windowsill! I cannot understand how you can maintain a grip on it,' he heard the principal say.

'It's because God covered us in flying ointment, foolish principal; but we admire the way you are coping with the minor crisis in your

284

atelier, considering a major governmental inspection of the college commences this morning.'

'Get him out of your atelier, Mr Hancock,' Sophie Howells was winding up to the required hysteria, 'hand him over to the police for repainting parts of me by spectral assault; all that cheap vermilion tint he uses for skin tones, like Munch on a bad day.'

'Calm down, Miss Howells, Munch never had a bad day,' the principal reassured, then added, 'even in his dotage.'

'Do something,' she shrieked, 'I've already got one baby with hair all over it, even on the soles of its feet; now there's a cretin on the way.'

'Calm down, Miss Howells, it seems Taliesin's hysteria is contagious.'

'It's bad enough hiding the hairy one in the pantry when I come to work,' she screeched, 'now I'll have to hide another one in there and it's not big enough, what with the bales of hay and the feeding trough,' Johannes heard Sophie's hysterical blabbering, 'Quick, call the police before he escapes through the window frame!'

'Could you please ask Cornelius to step into my office, some matter of urgency,' he heard the principal speak, clearly not addressing Sophie, 'and ask Fred Janes to pop in as well.'

'What does he want Cornelius for?'

'Get down, Taliesin, I'm sure your incompetence will interfere with a clean break of the neck,' he heard the principal forecast.

'What does he want Fred Janes for? At least Fred Janes believes we can draw.'

'Go on, jump, you syphilitic scrumpy sot! Good riddance to a useless squirt of feral paint,' he heard Sophie goading.

'Feral paint? Surely we should have heard feral squirt. She showered for three solid hours after our denouement, much longer than it took her to remove our vermilion tint. Fortunately for her

Gorilla came home and saved her from slipping down the plug hole.'

'The object is to talk him down onto *this* side of the window frame, Miss Howells, not the direction you advise and by the way, please replace your dressing gown as I'm expecting visitors.'

Johannes's inability to match Sophie's seductress qualities led to the inevitable happening.

Soon the vitality of the imagery skewed beyond Johannes's reckoning as the voices faded. He began to assume more the position of a deferential spectator than a miscreant statistical add-on that fulfilled a group dynamic, who had become the subject of expulsion. Renouncing all objectivity, capitulating to his fantasies and successfully detaching his mind, he was able to see a body climb the window frame; for now the sheer wonder of the imagery far exceeded the mundane presbytery of his capacity. Assuming the unassailability of achievement as the definitive procedure of certainty, Johannes simultaneously took leave of both Mr Hancock's office/atelier and his senses: the body climbed through the window, grabbing his floating mind, tugging it along as a balloon on cotton. At that time, penetrating the window frame seemed a logical act of consummation. But the simple venture brought with it many unforeseen circumstances that began contradicting his plans for escape.

'Miss Sparrow, could you please summon an ambulance as a matter of great urg –' a distant voice sounded through the fog of capitulation.

Up and through the frame, overpowering fumes of oils and medium, turpentine and linseed, moving figures, passing faces. More figures peering down, modelled in pure oils by palette knife alone. Old Holland palette fields, more mellow than Bob Ross, quickly moved about as if in some private panic of their own. Sophie stood over and smiled, her dressing gown covered in Lukas vermilion tint. Cornelius glowered, brandishing a one-legged parrot; Professor Price grimaced, tugging at his teeth; Sophie Howells paraded nude, displaying a perfectly flat belly covered in cream; Principal Hancock as Franz Hals's character from *The Laughing Cavalier* scowled by. Strange faces, not previously painted, completed the circle. Things not from the Antique Studio walked backwards up the wall.

Johannes launched himself street-ward, prosaically noting in passing the verso of his canvas was much more refined as the side he normally lived in, clearly a side belonging to a more perspicacious audience. Some angles of his condition were not as attractive as those first encountered. Landing on a soft fleshy carpet of titanium white skin, he bounced a smear that palette knifed the floor of his painting. Johannes attempted to break loose, but sticking and multiplying with ferocious embrace, its consuming brushstrokes attached all the stronger.

Having launched his body through the window, Johannes became an artefact in an ethereal maquette, prematurely ejaculating over the soft fleshy carpet, simultaneously doing justice to number 2 above. Glancing back, nothing was left of the window, even the building, or the fence into the waste field: they had disappeared. His ethereal brainwave had begun in ejaculations and brushstrokes, for the painting was not the desirable object she had appeared to be from the perspective of the life class. Alas the frame of entry, high up there, dissolved seamlessly into layers of inaccessible altitude and oil paint, cementing his entrapment to wilfulness and guilt. Inevitably he became entangled in the crude symbolism of his maladroit palette-knifed strokes.

Johannes Taliesin was trapped in his painting of Sophie. Against his better panic the painting embraced him incrementally, her arms warm and soft as freshly mixed oil paint, simultaneously electric yet smooth. Once united, she refused to let him go. He had confused desire with love, being quickly overwhelmed by the transient ecstasy of failure, ignoring Inner Voice's warnings to,

'Escape, fool! Withdraw while we have the option.'

Disregarding illogical assumption, Johannes had been reluctant to hold back from a physical climax all the way up to the heaven of his fantasies: proceeding with a voracious lust that had no physical means of support, he landed on his feet. Violation possesses no compassion for the victim; in a sway of ecstasy he had abandoned all thoughts of a dignified withdrawal once the pain in his head had ceased. The principal was right all along: incompetence had interfered with a clean break of the neck.

Lost in the landscaped expanses of *Nude Study Number 69*, Johannes disguised his folly beside large palette knife scrapings, the while effecting the employment of logic to elicit an escape. But morning brought the stale smell of Quaker guilt; and worse, for he was trapped inside her. In a cowardly new world of two-dimensional images and barely a grasp at being, time's arrow fled the scene. Embraced in the oil of his painting, he contemplated the grand predicament of his own making. The tyrant gifted a universe of no people owns everything of nothing. Johannes, wandering freely inside *Nude Study Number 69*, unassumingly fails to locate the return frame to his studio of mahogany shadows.

'Why didn't we think of doing this sooner? This is so peaceful. It's Gorilla free, Sophie free, principal free – why didn't we do it sooner?'

The press and buzz of people had gone. Languidly casting around for a frame of immense insignificance and no longer holding any desire for hysteria, Johannes set off on the trail to the Frameshop he knew must be there.

'The press and buzz of people have gone,' Inner Voice stated the obvious.

Yes, he knew. Presently, not many perspectives down the distant point forty-fifth street which he could not remember painting, he discovered colour-work on a glass door. It held his attention long enough, as escaping cockle robbers claimed, for a measurement of the usual oil-paint-on-glass affair for which brushwork is difficult to control. Managing the dream to his satisfaction, Johannes desired it lead him to the frame. Brushstrokes projected incongruously, more contradicting the whole than contributing to unity. Individual hog hair bristle strokes grooved the paint. These had previously pretended in the Antique Studio, marks sliding and swerving in uncontrolled manner where the brush failed to define a form, caused equally by the glossy surface of glass support as allowed by incompetence of hand on the heaving mound of grass. Nebulous shapes formed on the glass and resonated with the pervasive atmosphere of uncertainty and endlessness. Details failed conspicuously, but a difference in scale threatened the perspective of Johannes's attention. In comparison to the claustrophobic clutches of *Nude Painting Number 69*, the glass door painting within the painting was tangible and comforting.

Who had painted these clumsy details? Although the characteristic colour scheme belied the work of the elusive Laughing Cavalier, he was far too proficient a painter to be satisfied with the crudities of this oil on glass. Stretching before Johannes were the dark Sargasso knolls of paintwork as guardians of a mountain keep. Closer examination revealed a handle painted on the other side – how could he have missed it at first glance? Images were appearing as he watched, verso work still in progress, wetly, finishing touches being applied transfixed Johannes as the picture organised itself into larger swathes. But the technician responsible for such growth appreciation was invisible. A self-painting door that, as with all passages of the painted world since Johannes's leap to freedom, embraced a tangible appearance once he had recognised its existence; expressed possessiveness, once he had penetrated her.

'*Impossible,*' Inner Voice croaked.

'Impossible,' Johannes exclaimed loudly, and looked around hesitantly lest he were overheard talking to himself inside his painting. He half expected Laughing Cavalier to open the door to Swansea College of Art, demanding an explanation.

'Oh, it's you!' he heard Laughing Cavalier roar, 'It's that recurring nightmare Johannes Taliesin! What may I ask is impossible? Besides, why haven't you finished that depressingly awful painting of Miss Howells you were engineering?'

'I believe I was attempting to finish the painting when the model suddenly leaped from the rostrum and spread herself over it, ruining my hard work,' Johannes countered in defence, unable to bring himself to give the model a name.

'That is not her version of the episode, I caution you,' Laughing Cavalier intoned in words, 'her version expressly submits the word hard never entered into it.'

'Was it you painting a handle onto the glass door?' Johannes asked, exercising his will to change the subject, a prerogative of dream ownership.

'Don't be ridiculous!' Laughing Cavalier scorned, exercising his will to be evasive.

'The glass entrance door to the arcade?' Johannes persisted, unperturbed by the evasion.

'Do you realise illicit copulation with one's painting is a grave offence in the codes of spectral rape atoned only by climbing through a high window, any high window will do, and leaping to one's death?' Laughing Cavalier entangled the procrastination.

But the ghost of Johannes the artist readily grasped the opportunity for justification.

'I have not copulated with my painting!' he protested his innocence, 'I have not even copulated with the model, leave alone copulating with a painting of her. But, upon reflection, I would have unhesitatingly proceeded if the machinery had functioned as God intended.'

'Your physical inadequacy delivered you a great fortune down here below street level, mark my words, as no cretins will be born,' Laughing Cavalier intoned the judgement.

'Wait until I get back to Troed-yr-Henrhiw, I'll ask my father to travel down to Swansea to have a word or two with you,' Johannes threatened.

'You *are* in Troed-yr-Henrhiw, you fool,' Laughing Cavalier replied, 'and I am protected from wordsmith fathers by a moat full of angry gorillas who never mastered the art of swimming. Besides, don't forget to paint the hinges properly lest they fail in the function God intended, else the door to the arcade and its Frameshop will remain forever closed to your search.'

'How did you know I was looking for a Frameshop?' Johannes caught.

'Thank Goodness you didn't paint a revolving door, otherwise you would revolve for ever in your painted indecision,' said Laughing Cavalier, roaring with laughter at his own joke's manufacture, or perhaps he was secretly enjoying the alternate joke of Johannes's failure to satisfy the firmament's lust. The occasion of Laughing Cavalier actually laughing took Johannes by surprise, as he had never previously witnessed such an event either inside or beyond his dream.

'Perhaps he didn't know we were looking for a Frameshop; he just guessed, because everyone presenting themselves at the glass door is searching for the Frameshop, perhaps.'

As no response was forthcoming to the Frameshop reference, it went by seemingly unchallenged in Johannes's new land of clouding cuckoos, as Laughing Cavalier washed into the background of faded colours.

'Get on with it!' Inner Voice's patience snapped, *'now*

that the handle has been painted for you by whomsoever, stop procrastinating and turn the confounded thing.'

Although the handle was a two-dimensional affair painted on the other side, Johannes made a clumsy grab at the shiny glass surface, the while checking up and down the street that such a ridiculous manoeuvre was not being observed: fortunately forty-fifth street remained a still life Canaletto painting. No sooner had he returned his attention to the problem than the glass door lurched open, revealing a shopping arcade cobbling away at a pace from the street where Swansea College of Art passed by the entrance with no noticeable attachments. Laughing Cavalier was nowhere to be seen, his absence fully expected in this painted cloud of cuckoos.

Johannes entered the arcade. The sprung glass door slammed shut behind him, its painted handle sheering off in the slam to become a scattering of coloured red dust on cobbled floor. An important message was written in dust between the cobbles, but Johannes failed to read it due to his entrancement by the scene before him.

Many shops of old-fashioned form scattered up the arcade, displaying various titles. 'Ye Olde Tea Shoppe', 'Cloisters', 'Beneath the Gilded Willow Groves the Curlews Sing', 'The Bored Room', 'The Model and her Elders', and so on in dream quality. But no people! Although he found each shop to be captivatingly unique, a general ambience of mystery hung through the arcade's perspective of accentuated foreshortening all the way to the vanishing point, deserted and eerily silent, devoid of shoppers and window-gazers. Distantly, ever so distantly, the delicate strains of harp strings being plucked floated and faded, but Johannes could not identify its source. Otherwise silence prevailed, failing to cast a shadow.

The arcade's atmosphere, with its dense oils, turpentine spirit, thinners, raw linseed oil, accelerator and retarding medium, was heavier than the painted street, denoting Johannes had penetrated deeper into the belly of *Nude Painting Number 69* than ever he had done in the other world. Cobbles, inconsistent in form and nature, reached across the arcade: here printed, there scumbled, distantly palette knifed; the whole having been painted with a brisk deliverance, on which the drying agents had been overdone.

Johannes walked on down, past book 'Ye Olde Reede', haberdashery 'For Ten Pins', pen 'Mr Quilpepper', paper 'Papyriformats' and establishments of similar ilk that infused a deep sense of atavism and security. Decorated in burnt umber, rotting gold, hessian colours, cobweb and clover, the lot genuflected to a Windsor blue base of pragmatic familiarity that must have been fading for a thousand years. The whole seemed right in its cerebral composure, perfectly imagined for the purpose of dream. Landscapes, townscapes and thumbnail sketches disconcertingly broke through the superimposed facades. Waves of a raging ocean obtruded in the midst of net-curtained domesticity and textile factors, the incongruity of a panhandled galleon becalmed in a fine sable westerly zephyr, the painting's intellectual hygiene having broken the plimsoll line to haywire. A crucifixion of the sea allowed daughters of the wind to swing keys at their hips. The incongruous arches of 'The Shivering Money Tree' beckoned.

But lo! Opposite 'The Shivering Money Tree' was the frame shop he had been seeking! Above its leaning eaves read, 'Ye Oldest Frameshoppe' decorated in old gold on Windsor blue. Beneath the swinging title, an advertisement: 'Frames Found and Factored for Ladies, Gentlemen, Commoners and Dead Men Airbrushed'. Johannes was sure he did not subscribe to the first and fourth categories, but deciding on which of gentlemen or commoners was relevant paralysed his already drying mind. As no one was present in the arcade to assist in a judgement, he decided the matter should be fixed to possess little importance.

Large windowpanes on 'Ye Oldest Frameshoppe' held dimpled indentations that afforded distorted views of the interior. Johannes could discern sufficient of the Frameshop's contents to give encouragement that his search was courting success. He opened the elaborate fleur-de-lis-decorated door and entered. The action triggered a mechanism that sent a bell clanging loudly to startle him. The mighty noise threw his colour-sound palaver into witnessing clouds of scarlet billowing about the shop's interior, colouring everything bright scarlet in the door's vicinity. The red noise was one of the brightest Johannes had ever seen, momentarily blinding his ears. Obviously the proprietor must be deaf.

Fortunately the red noise quickly dispersed to the periphery of the Frameshop, readily fading into numerous frames on display, bouncing amongst their algebra, trickling to silence in their geometry. The obscured view through the dimpled windows had not enabled justice to the amazing stock of frames on display. Every category, format, function, texture, pattern and weight abounded. Frames of specific helical function, as those gyrating around ornate leaf-shaped mirrors snuggled in higgledy-piggledy piles with antique gilded numbers of B-flat pizzicato; organic art nouveau danced curvilinear frames around self-centred mirrors; multicoloured outfits masquerading as many-angled structures vied for geometric attention; a peacock prance marshalled alongside cascades of different scaled displays. Row upon row threaded out from the pulsating Frameshop wings; the walls hanging from floor to ceiling with bundles of inchoate representations no doubt factored for the constituencies of gentlemen. Garish new articles cavorted with disintegrating antiques, youth brushing against senility, satisfying the need of the commoners' reference to the slogan.

'*Where are the frames for dead men airbrushed?*' Inner Voice squeaked a whisper.

The cluttered pile upon pile was reminiscent of a warehouse set aside for specialist patronage. But here no nodal meeting point existed, with points of sale everywhere and nowhere, a frame lover's delight. Then a narrow gangway weaving between the piles towards the rear of the shop made its presence known. Aromas of wood, paint and varnish pervaded. Two pale light sources entangled their desultory lights across the picture.

'*Perhaps the frames for dead men are sitting in the spaces between the frames,*' Inner Voice proffered languidly.

All surfaces – floor, walls and frames – were crudely finished in clumsy brushstroke and hesitant palette knife that professed difficulty in explanation. Large gaps pierced the Frameshop's walls, through which new incongruities shone from beyond: passages of paintwork, detailed sketches of nudes, partly painted landscapes that boasted incompatible perspectives, and seascapes fading on the horizon, taking 'avast there, ye laggardly pompolions' with them.

Many of the frames were poorly mitred; few held a right angle with pride. Wet paint glistened through in the feeble light. Some frames had been completely airbrushed off the scene, remaining only as outlines against the background of painted frames.

'*Aha!*' Inner Voice alighted, '*the frames for dead men airbrushed.*'

While the living left no trace, the airbrushed frames left dark shadows, criss-crossing the angles of other lighter subjects; Johannes checked: solid objects left no shadows.

'*We are not casting a shadow!*' Inner Voice squeaked a shudder.

The whole scene was disconcertingly flimsy, almost nebulous; an unsure dust circle set for the palette's stage. Johannes shivered.

'Where are we? What in God's name are we doing in this place? Perhaps it is not a place!'

Nothing explained itself, as patterns of objects playing games with the worldview of their shapes identify themselves. Suddenly Johannes felt beset by his dreams.

Of course, the frame Johannes sought was old right-angled section, rectangular, sturdy, painted white with sash affairs either side set in the verticals. It might be glazed or, heaven forbid, the glass might be broken.

'If the glass were broken surely we would be adorned with cuts,' Inner Voice reasoned.

He examined his arms and hands: much paraphernalia abounded of the unwashed parts, but no cuts. He was reassured in his search for the frame. Judging from the abundance of frames on display, Johannes felt confident that his search was over.

Beset by the clumsiness of brushstroke and mitre Johannes was confronted by the objective mediocrity of his artistry: the sloppy draughtsmanship with its concomitant paint sloppily applied. He failed to identify anything of admirable standard. He had smugly assumed that his artistry was of unquestionable, even unassailable, quality. But, having penetrated his work to the heart, every passage was embarrassing in the extreme: previously he saw in his paintings only that which he had desired to see.

Delusion mesmerises the drive that is capable of making amends: witnessing the many mistakes in measurement, in the mitring angles, in slap-dash scantiness, omissions, unfinished passages, lack of revision, illogical colour schemes – cast him irrefutably into self-doubting his artistic proficiency that perhaps had never really existed.

'No wonder Price was always irritated with us... um, why are we thinking past tense? Is always irritated...'

In his new predicament, out of the fire into the frying pan,

Johannes had no choice but to accept the truth he had always denied in the place from which he had recently escaped.

As Johannes was taking stock of the Frameshop's contents, a pitter-pattering of leather slippers on palette knife painted floor drew his attention. There, from an Aladdin's cave of glistening intaglio and sparkling beads in the darkly airbrushed shadows emerged a young woman, cautiously pattering forward. Her movements were heavily mannered; her out-of-perspective feet pitter-pattered daintily. Johannes gasped a small surprise: a person at last!

The young woman's face was dominated by enormous dark eyes, disproportionate to the head; so large were the eyes that they left little room on her upper face for other features. The tiniest of noses balanced above a full succulent mouth, from which a tongue repeatedly ventured out to moisten the enlarged varnished lips. The remarkable face was adorned by a few palette strokes of shining black hair, with a touch of golden scintillation, almost lost in palette knife edge. Here adorning the Frameshop was an exaggerated Sumerian sun-worshipper, direct from Erech. Whether her face was the result of his poor draughtsmanship, brushes too large, or perhaps a subliminal influence from the time he studied the ancient civilisations of Sumeria and Elam, he was unable to judge. The article before him was Gudea's daughter, pattering amidst the frames of a Lagash temple, come back to life in his *Nude Painting Number 69*, living in his escape route.

She was surely a beautiful princess. Parts of her were discernibly finished in cheesecloth shirt and terracotta cardigan, but the rest of the body save for the slippers was airbrushed away, trailing to a background haze where her legs dissolved into Frameshop, unblended colours and frames, in turn becoming an unfinished landscape of olive groves beyond. The glass painted door incident melted into insignificance against this motley of colossal beauty and incongruous brushwork. Nothing collaborated in the figure. Johannes was once again ashamed of his workmanship: the unfinished state of her beauty resonated with the general sloppiness of his technique. In the background landscape the disproportionate trees picked up their roots and marched a rebellion of wood, metamorphosing to a rebellion of wooden frames containing poorly mitred corners.

'Can I help you?'

She spoke, a purring gentle velvet voice, wafting him deeper into the shimmering haze, on royal roads to nowhere gaze, as she writes her truths on the water's face, in the solitude of Pasargadae. Her kitten call came from rushes, from the swish of sable hair brushes, kissing the eyes of sightless bands, through Ahura Mazda's stroking hands, courting the advocates of lonely fires, perfuming the obelisks their awful desires; an irresistible force of religious intrigue, where sitting astride the rhythmic droves, was shagged to ribbons in the olive groves. Johannes's dream lost him in fantasy.

'Can I help you?' she purred again, 'a red noise from the front stirred me.'

Johannes, dreaming of forget-me-not blue ribbons in the olive groves, contrived not to hear her. The sound of her purr slipped by in a whisper of powder blue, trailing away amongst the frames, beyond his shoulder, rebating off the mitres, forming eddies of forget-me-not haze in every corner. Entranced by the Delft blue haze as a Chinese reduction firing, Johannes's blue mind airbrushed dust between the displays. The blue brought recollections of *The Blue Wind of Plynlimon*, which Johannes had painted at Troed-yr-Henrhiw some years in the future.

Instead of explaining his purpose Johannes could but stare with amazement at the apparition. She was magical: sounds transforming to colours more readily than his synaesthetic colour-sound sensations. The object of his search seemed irrelevant in this hall of atavistic female form; her sounds turned to colours. He guarded against raising his voice lest the whole Frameshop fill with polychromatic distraction. Her huge eyes mesmerised him.

'Wh-who are you?' he stammered.

'The proprietor. Can I help you?' she waited, purring patiently.

At which the apparition blinked enormously, slowly, much as a cat when contemplating a distant object with feline curiosity combined with contentment. Johannes had never before been confronted by a Sumerian votive figure that could move and close its eyes. Normally transfixed on the sun, these huge orbs instead blinked and stared at Johannes.

'*We don't like this, let's get out of here,*' Inner Voice, true to Johannes's overwrought amygdala, perceived danger with this strange but beautiful encounter.

But another department drew him as the cat by curiosity to this animated painting and, besides, he felt sure the frame he sought was at hand.

'I'm looking for a frame,' he said at last.

She looked at him, her stationary eyes mesmerising him. Then, following what seemed to Johannes to be an interminable pause, the huge eyes blinked again.

'Come to the right place,' she said, licking her lips full.

'It's a special frame.'

'All frames are special,' she purred, 'what is particularly special about the special frame you seek?'

'It's a window frame, large, of the Victorian sash variety, which uncannily disappeared when I arrived in my painting, and God knows what dimensions it assumed after the accident.'

The votive figure continued staring at Johannes in tranquil harmony. He experienced difficulty in looking at her, for she displayed an incoherent mixture of exquisite beauty and crass blunder. His craft of crude brushwork mocked. Why had he left her unfinished? Why had he used brushes inappropriate to the task? Her legs were skipped away to background landscape, an afterthought of airbrush, drybrush and carelessness with hog bristle, ill chosen for purpose, ill met with drying oils, unfinished and scumbled, trailing into frames and unfinished landscapes beyond.

'By accident you must mean your big production of throwing yourself through the window,' she said in monotone purr.

'How do you know?' he asked, squirming.

'We saw you,' she replied.

'You *saw* me?' Johannes spluttered.

'*Who is the we?*'

'Yes, we saw you,' she continued in her flat monotone purr, 'but others,' she corrected, 'say you didn't jump.'

'*We thought as much: suicide genes don't jump in our family,*' Inner Voice contradicted earlier window advice.

Unforeseen consequences of his escape were mounting. Any resistance Johannes had to the painting's seductions weakened further; the need to return became confused with events in his painting.

'*This is worse than before our escape,*' Inner Voice was losing its languid air, to be replaced by the harbingers of pessimism. Johannes saw himself mount Pegasus the winged whore escorted by her four apocalyptic servants crudely painted as angels. But these were life drawings he had produced on the same canvas on which Frameshop was supported, showing through patchily from beyond the darkest night, beyond the doubt of hemlock, flying free to a new nirvana, flattered in a giddy whirl: the red noise of war, famine on black, death on the airbrushed pale; all followed by righteous white.

'*We must ask her who is the we she refers to.*'

'Who is the we you refer to?' Johannes asked, confused, mission lost.

'The other characters and me of course,' she replied, 'but surely you should be more curious as to how we saw you.'

'This should be interesting.'

'Er, yes, you are right. How did you see me?' he corrected.

'We were all here as usual, and saw you jump through the window. Can't understand you did not sustain any broken bones and cuts. Could be due to your incompetence.'

'I landed on my feet, as planned.'

'I was asked to say that by the others. To me it's immaterial how we were able to see you,' she purred as in mission accomplished.

'Aw, bollocks to this, let's get out of here.'

Johannes glanced back through the fish-eye dimples into the arcade, hoping to see Troed-yr-Henrhiw, or some other reference of sanity. But the arcade, the higgledy-piggledy shops and deep atmospheric perspective were still there, just as they were a few moments before. Fool was he in his pleasurable riding, committing a venture at the height of his bloom, mocked by the prophets of doom. On the Mount of Olives he had oiled her lusting. Fool was he to be flattered by her embraces, through his poverty of morals, poverty of attitudes.

'Anyway,' he said, wrenching his thoughts from wistful flagellation, 'the frame is Victorian window-sized, so big,' and he drew a vertical rectangle in the air.

'What measurement would that be?'

'I would say about 320 by 230 centimetres – I'm guessing – plain moulding, rebated for single glazing, painted white. It possessed a semi-circle above, which was immaterial to the incident.'

The proprietor continued to stare, occasionally blinking her colossal eyes, computing the figures. In the silence Johannes was able to contemplate his predicament more thoroughly. The young woman had made the most of the fate his clumsy brush had bequeathed. Gallantly, she acted as if the crudities and anomalies were of no consequence. Whence had the fortitude originated? Certainly not from his paintbrush, nor the Old Holland and Bob Ross paints, or others on the palette at the time. Nor from his thoughts as he painted *Cloud Cuckoo Land*, notwithstanding the obvious non-transferability. He could not recall ever designing-in fortitude.

Seeing her standing in linseed elegance, mascara complicit with make-believe was the saddest picture in the world. After all his years as an artist, Johannes had never realised one could recreate handicap by proxy through crude brushwork.

'It must have been a very special frame to become distorted as you leapt through it,' she eventually replied, 'however, I only deal in imperial. You painted me during that epoch.'

'*Shit! This gets more complicated by the minute,*' Inner Voice despaired.

'That long ago? I don't have the slightest recollection working on a painting of a Frameshop, or painting you, leave alone a pre-metric date when I was supposedly painting this arcade. Damn the metric,' Johannes responded in frustration, for his readiness to embrace metric might transpire to cause his perpetual entrapment.

Then another thought, 'If you were resting on the rose madder ground of another painting, and I thought metric when working on it, then perhaps you should be familiar with the metric system.'

'I'm not familiar with the metric system. Anyway, rose madder is an effective screen for measurement thoughts – you of all people should know that,' she replied.

'Not even seeing me practice my jumping and landing technique?' he asked.

'Measuring systems are interchangeable for jumping and landing techniques; anyway, imperial is my method of measuring,' she purred, adroitly avoiding further scrutiny of her observing techniques, 'convert the figures into imperial and I'll see if I can help you.'

'Mathematics was never my strong point; it took years to get my mind around metric, but as needs must I'll have a go,' said Johannes whereupon, displaying outward signs of strife as he churned the mental arithmetic, he tackled the conversion problem.

'Hmm,' he said at last, 'let me see... ten foot tall by six foot nine inches – ish.'

'Ish is not accurate enough,' she replied, ahead of her enigmatic smile. As she uttered the ish, forget-me-not blue wisped out of her mouth and floated about the frames. Again the unrealistic captivation, the same temperamental fragility that had occasioned Johannes's blunders throughout his natural state was at work.

'There's no denying it, we are doomed through our weaknesses, bloody doomed.'

Unfortunately another development began edging into the frame: due to his lack of self-control the proprietor was becoming the object of Johannes's desire.

'We need to take a firm grip on this situation. Perhaps the application of a little strength of character would be in order. Bugger the doomed part.'

As if she was endowed with power over him, the young woman compounded Johannes's predicament by spinning out her time; after all, as an inanimate image of oil paint on a rose madder ground, she was empowered by eternity.

'OK,' said Johannes, losing faith with the past by falling through time, elevating history around him, 'perhaps you could trace the frame by title.'

Clearly, his ineptitude so laboured by Principal Hancock had conspired a series of circumstances to deliver him of the Frameshop.

'Window frames don't have titles,' she purred the correction.

'I know that, stupid! How about *Untitled* window frame?' his impatience transgressed the dream's protocols.

'Yes, *Untitled* has come in recently.'

'Good. Was it signed?'

'Don't know,' she replied, 'but the agent said it was by Obscure Welsh Artist.'

'Acting impatient gets us somewhere at last –'

'Did the agent mention any name?'

'I've just told you – Obscure Welsh Artist.'

'Yes, I know; but did he give a name to the obscure Welsh artist?'

'I told you twice: Obscure Welsh Artist is his name,' she repeated monotonously.

'Damn this bloody obfuscation!'

'If I decide to be an obscure Welsh artist I will be one, without push needed to inveigle a jump,' Johannes muttered, 'may I see it, please?'

'Obscure Welsh Artist, all proper names; you should know that: Mr O. W. Artist.'

'Oh God! Regardless of all proper names, may I see it? If I saw it, probably my questions would be answered.'

The young woman repeated her routine of wide-eyed staring, interrupted only by the occasional flutter of her large eyelids.

'Intriguing,' she said.

'God! Are we getting nowhere, and irritated!'

Inwardly Johannes had long since lost patience. Obviously impatience was a malady of his new historical dimension as it assumed its outward manifestation.

'I'm sure it's not intriguing; it's more like irritating!' he burst out uncharacteristically.

'All this is beyond my extruded intellect,' she went on in monotone, 'how does seeing it answer your questions if ish is not accurate enough?'

'We are beside ourselves with frustration,' Inner Voice availed, *'but reason tells us we shouldn't be.'*

'Clearly this is conjugating the verb to frustrate,' Johannes declared in hopeless fashion.

Pigeons were coming home to roost. The dispersed logic to his request –

'Indeed, the illogical quest in the first instance.'

– reminded Johannes of games he played with friends when he desired peace and quiet, for they quickly made excuses and left. The proprietor of Frameshop had perchance recorded one such game on the vinyl of her rose madder ground, for where else could she have gained the intellect for such mental convolutions? But her allusion to extruded intellect took Johannes off-guard. His frustration was compounded by the timelessness; he had to fight back the urge to run amuck amongst the crudely painted frames. The application of certain patience should help undo the wrongs of his false start. Nonetheless, Johannes was indescribably frustrated; so frustrated that he lost his grasp on the illogical predicament that he had allowed to develop around him following the great escape.

Johannes decided to look for the frame himself. Without a word of courtesy to the proprietor, he began a frantic search among the hundreds of frames on display. Picking his way through them, another anomaly attendant on Johannes's predicament presented itself. The Frameshop and all its frames were it seemed still in the process of being painted. Frames whirled into view, oils glistening wet, familiar scents of Old Holland drifting by.

'Hey! These frames are appearing as I watch – look there, one has just been over-painted with rose madder – and now immediately it's being repainted old gold!'

As he spoke, Johannes turned to the proprietor and was no longer surprised to discover her legs were being re-painted; remarkably, they no longer trailed into the background. Buckles appeared on her slippers, a general sharpness was applied to her edges, and a sense of completion matched the whole.

'Well, that explains a lot!' exclaimed Johannes, 'Up until this moment I believed it was I who had painted you.'

She waited for her lips to be painted into a rearranged smile before replying.

'You did, partly,' the new smiling mouth said, 'but only partly. Laughing Cavalier is finishing the job because he especially hates sloppy workmanship and half-done jobs.'

'Oh no! Not Laughing Cavalier again!'

'He used to especially dislike me when I was a student long, long ago,' added Johannes, 'I might have known he would be painting away in the background. I cannot escape from my painting; neither can I escape from Laughing Cavalier.'

'You *are* the artist who painted us bedraggled higgledy-piggledy half finished, but not *the* artist,' the proprietor said.

'I now know I am *the* artist.'

'No. *The* artist is Laughing Cavalier,' the proprietor replied.

'Don't stand for that! Argue with the bitch! After all, you are the artist and she is only two-dimensional.'

'As Laughing Cavalier is painting amends, is it asking too much for him to paint the frame I seek?' Johannes asked, looking about in the hope Laughing Cavalier could hear and thus oblige.

'He has just washed it out with rose madder ground,' she said, smiling.

'WHY? What purpose does that serve?'

'Laughing Cavalier wishes to keep you as a prisoner in the painting. He believes it is safer for artist's models and the maintenance of cordial relationships with gorillas if you remain suffocating in your painting.'

'Damn him! I'm getting out of this mad shop! I'll find another means of exit.'

'Laughing Cavalier said you wouldn't find another means of exit,' she threatened.

'When did you discuss me with Laughing Cavalier? What is this conspiracy?'

She blinked hugely, and shook her head slowly and sadly.

'You of all people should know I have witnessed all your movements after you painted me in parts. I am here because I was there at the time, which of course is here all along. You painted me virtually as I am, but to my eternal gratitude Laughing Cavalier is painting reality in place of your ambiguity.'

'Obviously I didn't paint any sense in you, or this Frameshop, if that is what you are implying by ambiguity,' Johannes muttered.

'One cannot paint sense into a Frameshop, but Laughing Cavalier is painting the sense into me you omitted with your sloppy ambiguity. You painted me on top of landscapes already here. I was painted fully grown, although some characters enjoy the privilege of growing up on the tip of a sable brush,' she smiled, 'but parts of me were missing. You over-washed a landscape *Two Views of a Different Field* with the usual rose madder ground before painting my friends and me on top of it.'

Johannes struggled in vain with the convoluted imagery. This was not a dream. He could not recall painting her, or even *Cloud Cuckoo Land* on top of *Two Views of a Different Field*, only, as it happens, *Nude Painting Number 69*.

'Besides,' Inner Voice reminded, '*Two Views of a Different Field is on display in Troed-yr-Henrhiw*.'

'Yes, but it is true I used rose madder ground to prime the canvases.'

'Beg pardon?' the proprietor said.

'Sorry, I was thinking with someone else,' Johannes said quickly, 'but *Two Views of a Different Field* is in my studio at Troed-yr-Henrhiw.'

At this prompt the proprietor looked into a particular frame that had been standing on display alongside.

'I can see back a long way. I see two figures: a middle-aged gentleman not dissimilar to Laughing Cavalier in features and a beautiful blonde Sybarite, repairing the damage you inflicted when you went insane. Some of the attendant staff agree with the clothes on Mayhill that it was a symbolic set piece. But we characters know it had nothing to do with a staged act, more to do with your escape into insanity from an insufferable predicament based on your inability to deliver sexual gratification and your fear of gorillas.'

'It is not my studio you are looking at through that frame,' Johannes said brusquely, 'stop dithering and find my studio at Troed-yr-Henrhiw.'

'If you wish, you can climb through the frame and return to the predicament whence you came,' she suggested.

'What would be the point of doing that?'

'You could unwind your insanity.'

'What nonsense! Anyway, that happened a long, long time ago,' said Johannes witheringly, 'I don't know what purpose it would serve; or if it is necessary any more to face the genesis of my change of mind.'

'Have a go, because if you don't, here is where you will remain in limbo forever. Take care when negotiating the membrane,' the proprietor said with advocatory authority.

'I've got it now!' Johannes exclaimed, 'Having escaped

from one unholy mess in my life, it's better to avoid a similar predicament in the first place than having to escape from it.'

'Something like that; but go on,' replied the proprietor, still unsure of the transformation.

'The idiot still thinks we are a student escaping persecution. We will leave through the door we entered.'

'But I no longer wish to jump from one predicament into a previous one,' Johannes replied.

'Go on,' she goaded.

'You still believe I am a student having stumbled into my own painting. Nothing of the sort!' declared a reinvigorating Johannes, 'I remember the mess, but it no longer holds my attention. It is the mess of my lack of painting skill trailing down through history that horrifies me, the mess of drawing errors. Mistakes in painted passages, in subject matter, in choice of characters, in painted mitres off the forty-five, everything! Yet in those days believing my work was perfect, I smeared my satisfaction like gravy over a stale cake.'

'What an amazing speech we are delivering to the two-dimensional daughter of Gudea!'

'Coming into this Frameshop opened a door on an historical perspective. I am steadied with resolve: the wall of ingratitude that confronts me is immaterial. Your attitude implies ingratitude for being painted into existence, which I wholly understand. Look at you, you poor wretch, riven with mistakes and ambiguities.'

'We were programmed to blame you,' the proprietor replied, 'who else can we blame other than you for the errors in your creation? Laughing Cavalier has attempted to make amends. While he felt nothing but disgust for your shoddy workmanship he felt compassion for us. Personally, I feel sorry for myself.'

'I feel sorry for you, too.'

'You feel compelled to create, we were painted to be ungracious by compulsion,' she said.

'I have grown old and angry, and the bilge swindlers worked hard to wreak a form of compassion from me,' Johannes rejoined, 'not only are there errors in my techniques, but errors in my judgement as well. I have never been able to create as much as a blade of grass.'

'Wow! We are impressing ourselves.'

'If you didn't create characters like me, then nothing exists to be ungrateful,' she persisted.

'Obviously one of your flaws is incorrigibility. I am incapable of creating anything, leave alone characters,' said Johannes.

'One dark winter night Laughing Cavalier arranged a soiree for us,' the proprietor confided, changing tack, 'during the party he called us to gather around him. He advised us that humans were unable to see what we were doing because observation would immediately de-materialise us.'

'Why did Laughing Cavalier want to say that of all things? I'm observing you now, but you are not disappearing,' said Johannes.

'He warned us a cautionary tale concerning the huge potential stored in tubes of oil paint awaiting the moment to be released as characters,' she continued, 'and that we should be aware of the colossal amount of ingratitude embedded in the pigment awaiting release; we were enthralled,' whereupon she paused to lick her huge mouth wet, 'Laughing Cavalier said we were naive to believe anyone would be grateful for being squeezed out of tubes. What is your view? Do you believe characters are ungrateful for being squeezed from tubes?' she smiled a mixture of hemlock and urban haze with forget-me-not blue pouring from wet lips.

'Obviously, Laughing Cavalier took advantage of a captive

audience, a clumsy attempt at seducing painted characters,' Johannes responded dismissively, 'he predicated false scenarios based upon unsubstantiated initial conditions. Besides, why am I bothering to psychoanalyse the actions of two-dimensional images? Silly! Next I'll be explaining the portents of illusory psychology or some other delusion. I no longer dwell in the realm of animals and am anxious to leave this conundrum as quickly as possible. But I must say, I am sorry my lack of skill has left you in such an incomplete condition.'

Realising he would not find an escape frame in the Frameshop, Johannes turned to leave.

'Um – before you go!' the proprietor called, so anxious to detain Johannes in the Frameshop that she took the conversation round in circles, 'I feel bound to say that some of my friends were damaged when you went insane – I mean, changed your mind and Laughing Cavalier is unsure of the progeny of your characters, so cannot make good the initial conditions.'

'I don't care; I'm going back,' came Johannes's blunt reply, as he moved towards the exit.

'No, please don't go,' the proprietor called, 'you are a fascinating entity in three dimensions, even more three-dimensional than Laughing Cavalier; I am just beginning to understand you.'

'Regardless,' Johannes was quite unimpressed, 'conversations go round in circles in this Frameshop; I must get back.'

'In that case,' she said, throwing one last chance to despair, 'before you go I must show you my body.'

'Show me your body? Here, in the Frameshop? What if someone comes in?' Johannes said, being so easily diverted from other intentions when a woman – even a two-dimensional woman – makes such an offer.

Without answering, the young woman began peeling off her cardigan and shirt. She executed the process with practised deftness, as if undressing were a regular part of her work in the Frameshop. Beneath the shirt – nothing! Nothing!

'Nothing! God help us!'

Johannes was taken aback: he had not painted a body. All that could be seen in the space of her body were the displayed frames in the background. This was no ordinary strip show. With the shirt gone nothing remained save her head and hands. Crudely painted slacks – one leg of which Laughing Cavalier had partially corrected, the other lost amongst the frames – floated in dissolute relation to her head. Nothing else remained; an illusion where hitherto clothes had implied her body by the usual chicanery of paint. Nothing remained save blue haze, frames and passages of *Two Views of a Different Field.*

'God help us! We must have jumped straight into hell,' Inner Voice gasped.

Johannes was surprised and disappointed. Surprised by empty space yet simultaneously disappointed by the lack of female body, regardless the pretensions. As the proprietor moved, so the frames beyond gently undulated. Otherwise, nothing remained.

'It's the stuff of dreams we have so often read about, except –'

The reality was closer to mystery, and demanded a logical clarification.

'All these images are beyond our world of logic, occupying a parallel universe or some such clever thing like that; we will wake up in a minute,' Inner Voice reassured.

'I cannot believe you did that,' Johannes said, taking a check on his astonishment.

'I didn't,' she replied, 'you did.'

'Yes, yes,' he checked, 'I must have painted you straight onto *Two Views of a Different Field* without preparing the canvas with primer. What is the point of painting a body in order to paint clothes on top of it, especially when there is no intention of displaying the body?'

'When you painted me on top of *Two Views of a Different Field* you positioned my naked body against the wet grass in the different field. It was the most exciting sexual experience I have ever had,' said the young proprietor, 'I wanted you to prime me out with rose madder and do it again and again; each time I would have been ready for another climax,' and her huge eyes in the detached head swooned in memory of the unintended debauchment.

'*We are... we are bloody speechless!*'

Johannes was as usual speechless, and had quite forgotten his intention to leave. Then, as he was adjusting, frames displayed on the sidewall mitred to become a door, not previously on display. The new door creaked open and through it walked Laughing Cavalier, the one and the same who complained at Swansea College of Art by the arcade's entrance. He held the bundle of paintbrushes in his left hand, from each of which dripped variations in blue: Prussian, French ultramarine, cerulean, cobalt, so on; it did not seem to matter that oil paint dripped onto the floor inside *Nude Painting Number 69*. Several thick sticks of charcoal protruded from a top pocket on the left of his painting smock. They had been interfering with his face for some time for his greying goatee was pitch black on the charcoal side. Likewise the left side of his mustachio; his nostril and aquiline nose were still being drawn in charcoal. As he walked, they drew; as they drew, Laughing Cavalier endeavoured to ignore them by maintaining a nonchalant air of detachment.

'*This is typical,*' groaned Inner Voice, '*when the dream gets interesting we either wake up or are disturbed by some bugger like this!*'

Laughing Cavalier's charcoal features scowled ferociously at Johannes.

'You again!' he raised his voice, 'I thought I had seen the last of you at the painted gate,' and turning to the proprietor said,

'Please replace your shirt, Miss Ulanova, I have advised you on several occasions not to display your nothing in public. It is most distressing seeing frames where you should have been painted.'

As he raged, the charcoal continued to draw his face into darker lines of anger.

'It was a painted glass door, not a gate,' Johannes corrected.

'Did he persuade you to take off your shirt, Miss Ulanova?' asked Laughing Cavalier, ignoring Johannes's correction.

'Yes, he has been taking advantage of me,' she said, 'you arrived in the nick of time.'

'God knows what he would have done if he had succeeded in getting your slacks off,' Laughing Cavalier growled.

'Here we go again! We distantly remember a model accusing us of tampering with her. What is it with these women – except of course this is not a woman.'

'There's nothing there except an undulation,' Johannes protested the inappropriate detail.

'Why did you relent, Miss Ulanova?'

'He was very persistent; paintbrushes everywhere.'

'But you knew he hadn't painted your body,' reasoned Laughing Cavalier.

'I was about to leave, and she volunteered,' said Johannes.

'Telling him would have sufficed, Miss Ulanova.'

Meanwhile the charcoal continued drawing furiously, presenting a plausible explanation for Laughing Cavalier's irritability. As he came to a standstill, the conjugal charcoal ceased its drawing exercise. But the stationary Laughing Cavalier had now contrived to position himself in the narrow walkway between Johannes and the exit, and the scheme of irritation transferred to Johannes.

'*How irritating, how astronomically charcoaly irritating,*' whinged Inner Voice, '*of all places this recurrent headache chooses to stand he has to be between us and the exit. Damn him!*'

'I have been busy painting amends,' Laughing Cavalier's charcoal drawing said to Miss Ulanova.

'Yes, I noticed,' replied Miss Ulanova, 'and a superb job you have done on my buckle; I am sure it will assist in improving the Frameshop's trade. But might I suggest, Mr Cavalier, that you beware the charcoal, whose vigorous drawing is making it difficult to discern your pleasant smile from a charcoal sketch on coarse cartridge.'

'Thank you for your timely advice, Miss Ulanova, you are an artist's dream,' at which point Laughing Cavalier turned to Johannes and, switching his features from charcoaled conviviality to lines of scoured disdain he roared at Johannes,

'You have a lot to answer for!' as dust from the charcoal shrouded his face.

'Mr Cavalier is right,' agreed Miss Ulanova, her voice muffled behind the shirt she was replacing, 'you have a lot to answer for because you are the artist who omitted to paint my body.'

'*Here we go again, the bloody –*'

'Emboldened yet more,' Johannes suggested, intrigued by the theatre.

'It is not only your sloppy omissions!' snapped Laughing Cavalier.

'It appears you know it was I who painted her, this Frameshop, the arcade, *Nude Painting Number 69* on top of *Two Views of a Different Field*, the lot.'

'Of course I know that,' replied Laughing Cavalier, 'we all know that.'

'Of course he knows that,' echoed Miss Ulanova.

'But I cannot recall painting you,' Johannes addressed Laughing Cavalier.

'You didn't,' interjected Miss Ulanova, her shirt back in place, 'he painted himself with ease.'

'Paint by numbers,' Johannes antagonised.

'Consummation of number 2 above with ease,' Inner Voice remembered.

'You did not paint me,' said Laughing Cavalier darkly, 'and as much as I regret contradicting my friend's faith in me, I did not paint myself, either. My existence in this painting is entirely due to your undisciplined thoughts trawling the depths of your memory when you were working on *Two Views of a Different Field*. It is known in the profession as spontaneous virtual parallax, and in other renowned establishments people have earned doctorates in assessing the impact of such phenomena on the intrinsic aura of history of painting and the characters therein.'

'Ivan Stravinsky Stravar.'

'What if a painting does not contain any characters therein?' Johannes pondered.

'There you go again, interrupting before hearing the full explanation,' Laughing Cavalier fretted. 'To continue: the scholars are not awarded doctorates. But that is beside the point: the point is you would not know about natural interactions between thought and complex quantum entanglement in pigments, as you were hard pressed even to grasp the basic fundamentals of the Temple of Khonsu at foundation level, leave alone quantum mechanics.'

'How do you know?'

'Mr Cavalier knows these things,' Miss Ulanova interjected yet again.

'Look at the slap-dash rubbish you have the infamy to call drawing! Look at Miss Ulanova: look at her blouse, one sleeve

316

longer than the other! You have a lot to answer for!' Laughing Cavalier had so worked on his anger that a strange mixture of froth and charcoal effused from his mouth, adding a porridge bulk to his goatee.

'My, my,' remarked Johannes. 'I experience difficulty in separating memory from reality when such atavism is dredged from history. I am ready to leave this madhouse this very second. Please stand aside.'

'The awkward cuss, standing in front of the exit,' Inner Voice grumbled.

'I was obliged to maintain the group numbers imposed by the butchers, bakers and candlestick makers – pompous elected pumpkins, clueless when it came to the ethos of true art education, smearing scraps of populist art smothered in cork dust across the boardroom table as if they were Leonardo da Vinci incarnate,' Laughing Cavalier glowered, 'look where pandering to their foolish hobbyhorses got me – enrolling you of all people. The grand decline of Swansea College of Art was ably abetted by your Machiavellian subterfuge masquerading as a painting special candidate.'

'Thank God we are not the only target for Laughing Cavalier's bilious attack, but it's hard to believe.'

'After you changed your mind,' Laughing Cavalier continued, 'God knows what possessed you to continue your studies in art at a mental institution. They must have been constrained for numbers in their rehabilitation dabble classes, as were we for the group dynamic, but obviously their standards were lower, or you forged your testimonials.'

'Forged our testimonials? What's the prat on about? We were not good enough to forge testimonials, too inept. Anyway, how could one forge testimonials in a mental institution?'

'At least we went down saluting the flag of quality,' Laughing Cavalier growled.

'A better quality of death, saluting values,' Johannes interrupted Laughing Cavalier's flow.

'A bit of sarcasm should get his charcoal frothed up again. We find this stuff exuding from his mouthpiece to be quite nauseating.'

'Now you have the gall to invade your painting,' Laughing Cavalier continued, not acknowledging Johannes's comment, 'and parade as if you are the creator of all. Your uncontrolled imagination has trapped me in this confounded mediocrity. Fortunately your memory of Swansea College of Art must be limited, otherwise I would be an entrapped character in all of your scrappy paintings and drawings, busily amending your incompetence.'

'Why are you not entrapped in other students' work?'

'The affront of it! What a stupid question!'

'The affront of it! What a stupid question!' Miss Ulanova echoed.

Laughing Cavalier's anger mounted yet again; the charcoal sticks jiggled excitedly and his brushes dribbled in consort onto painted floor, frames and shoes. A painting entitled *Variation in Blue* within *Nude Painting Number 69* was gathering apace, no doubt to fetch a tidy sum by the clueless chatterers.

Laughing Cavalier's strident criticisms stimulated too many malfeasant memories for Johannes's comfort, but threw no light regarding the mannequin Ulanova. The effigy of his old principal was indeed the last character Johannes wished to meet in this embarrassing predicament. To encounter him in a less successful painting made entrapment all the more nightmarish. He assumed a leap through the window would end all his troubles; instead the action resulted in a recurring loop of events that painted an image of insanity.

'You, and a model name of Sophie Howells, must recur in many of my paintings,' Johannes suggested.

'Don't be foolish,' Laughing Cavalier gasped, 'we know you did not come about your predicament as the result of unfortunate timing, we know you had choice all along. You fell for it due to the low threshold of your self-discipline, lusting after an opportunity for self-gratification. I suggest you search your conscience a little more objectively than you have hitherto done.'

'I know all about interactions between thought and the quantum entanglement of pigments,' Johannes retorted, 'what defeats me is the ability of inanimate two-dimensional images to communicate without continuing entanglement in the nightmare mode.'

'I wouldn't know,' replied Laughing Cavalier, 'I am the principal of a college of art, not a quantum physicist.'

'Principal of a college of art, not a quantum physicist,' Miss Ulanova echoed.

'A moment ago you were declaring with authority the mechanics of your appearance in my painting, and my certain ignorance in such matters. Step aside and allow me depart this nightmare; it is not worth submitting that Miss Doppelgänger Ulanova delayed me until your arrival by an invisible strip tease. I believe you two are in league with some greater machine the likes of which I cannot fathom. Step aside, I say, otherwise I shall physically throw you aside.'

'That's telling him, but we bet he won't step aside, so we'll have to throw the prat aside.'

'I came here to rescue Miss Ulanova,' Laughing Cavalier justified and turning to the proprietor said, 'Come with me Miss Ulanova and I will paint in a proper body,' and, turning to Johannes, added, 'when recalling history I suggest you be a little more truthful with events. You constructed the most terrible lies about my model.'

'Terrible lies about my model,' purred Miss Ulanova.

'*Your* model? Since when was the proprietor – Miss Ulanova – your model?' Johannes's question missed construction points everywhere, but everywhere.

'*Pretend to be more angry,*' goaded Inner Voice, '*after all, we created all this. Ahem,*' Inner voice realised, '*come on, we didn't construct lies.*'

'And by the way, I didn't construct lies about Miss Ulanova.'

'In your painting you make out the jury found you not guilty of those perverse acts against her,' Laughing Cavalier levelled.

'Perverse acts against her,' the echo purred.

'And you contrived an acquittal, Oswald Spengler indeed!' Laughing Cavalier shouted.

'Spengler? What *are* you talking about? Step aside, I say.'

'The mental torture you inflicted upon her, to what purpose? So much for *The Decline of the West*, what distortion.'

'*He's off his charcoaled head.*'

'So much for *The Decline of the West*, what distortion,' came Miss Ulanova's echo.

'*They're both off their heads, one charcoal, the other oil,*' Inner Voice corrected.

'You are both effigies with limited programming,' said Johannes, 'off your heads.'

Unrelated accusations triangulated as Laughing Cavalier harped on,

'The poor girl was so mesmerised by your assault on her intellect that she readily succumbed to your sexual advances,' his narrow line of attack was unrelenting, 'she will probably never recover.'

'She will probably never recover – er, won't I?' mewed Miss Ulanova.

'*Way beyond us, but we don't care.*'

'I neither know nor care what you are talking about,' Johannes protested.

But Laughing Cavalier was in full flow and certainly believed he at last knew what he was talking about.

'She refuses to model these days, and is a day patient at Cefn Coed Hospital for cerebrally infirm paintings,' Laughing Cavalier continued, 'she can no longer look in the direction of the setting sun, as it reminds her of that traumatic Spengler experience. It is entirely your fault.'

'I thought Sophie was your model.'

'Who?'

'Yes, who?' came the Ulanova echo.

'Sophie Howells.'

'Oh! Sophie Howells. That was decades ago, Taliesin; I suggest as you fall through time, take a look at your clock occasionally.'

'That's it, out of my way, you silly old bugger,' Johannes had had enough of the verbal chicanery, 'regardless your case of mistaken identity, if Miss Ulanova were to model for you she would not be there, you would be painting space except for her head. Your accusations are all nonsense, and if we were not in *Nude Painting Number 69* I would sue you forthwith.'

'The space apart from my head,' purred Miss Ulanova, 'and my hands – don't forget my hands.'

'What *are* you talking about?' asked Laughing Cavalier, unsure whom he was addressing.

'That I said nothing of the Spengler kind is immaterial to the outcome of this predicament,' Johannes wagered, 'as it would not have mattered if I had assaulted her non-existent intellect with *Atonement* or *Requiem for a Nun* or *The Wave Function* for all it seems to mean.'

'McEwan, Faulkner, Schröedinger,' snorted Laughing Cavalier, 'all those years ago.'

'You die before *Atonement*, Mr Cavalier,' Miss Ulanova whimpered.

'Huh? How are we all talking in the future?'

'You annoy me so much,' Laughing Cavalier droned on, the while ignoring Miss Ulanova's slip, 'confusing epochs of reality with entanglement.'

'Oh, at last the whole thing dawns on me,' Johannes gasped, 'we are all in a quantum entanglement transaction – how stupid of me, it's clear to me now, why didn't I think of it before?'

'What?' Laughing Cavalier demanded.

'What?' Miss Ulanova echoed.

'Let me explain,' said Johannes, 'The entanglement is all in the m –'

A crashing tsunami of rose madder emulsion roared across the ceiling and down the rear wall of Frameshop, obliterating all before it. Laughing Cavalier, instinctively recognising the danger, charged past Johannes like a bull in a fr –. Abandoning his dripping paintbrushes and scattering the display frames hither and thither, he made a lunge for Miss Ulanova. Firmly gripping her shirtsleeves he dragged her unceremoniously towards the sanctuary of the side doorframe.

'Here we go again!' whooped Miss Ulanova.

Another massive rose madder tsunami brushstroke washed across the Frameshop, now dangerously close to Johannes. He watched in horror as large swathes of frames were obliterated.

'Oh joy! Oh ecstasy,' Miss Ulanova gurgled in a coarse voice, 'another opportunity to copulate with paintings past!'

'For God's sake, pull yourself together, Miss Ulanova, there is no time to waste, our lives are in danger; let's get away from here, quick!' cried Laughing Cavalier, tugging at her limp form, recognising the peril he and Miss Ulanova were in. Speed was of the greatest urgency. But it was already too late, for Miss Ulanova was smearing across the painted surfaces in votive ecstasy.

Laughing Cavalier desperately tugged her submissive form to the side door, as waves of rose madder emulsion thundered towards them, washing on relentlessly. Uttering a last shriek of ecstasy, Miss Ulanova disappeared beneath its rapacious currents. Laughing Cavalier was next to go, thrashing around hopelessly for his already submerged model.

It all happened in seconds, just long enough for Johannes to recognise the horror of what was happening, to realise his own life was in danger. He shot a glance behind him: to be trapped under the massive coat of rose madder opacity meant certain death! Outside, the arcade was still intact. He dived for the Frameshop door and, tugging it open, was greeted by the clanging red noise adding to the roar of the rose madder tsunami. Johannes's attention slipped off its priority. He pondered the door's dilemma: to abandon its duty in announcing arrivals and departures, as a priming tsunami was about to destroy it? Or be sucked into its death?

'FOR GOD'S SAKE! It's now or never: sort our bloody priorities out! GET THE HELL OUT OF HERE!' Inner Voice screamed.

Johannes snapped into action; as rose madder primer reared up for a final deathly brushstroke, he gathered his wits and shot out into the arcade. He had escaped the turmoil in Frameshop, but the tsunami still crashed towards him. Racing across the arcade, Johannes headed for 'The Shivering Money Tree' opposite. Urgently seeking a place of refuge – a matter of life or death – he crashed through its door and landed in a reception hall.

11

The Shivering Money Tree

'MY! YOU'RE IN a hurry!'

'Getting out of this weather, Miss Brown,' Johannes responded.

'Dreadful stuff, Principal; roll on summer I say,' the receptionist replied.

'The politicians bang on about global warming, yet the weather appears to be getting progressively colder, or is it my imagination?'

'Not your imagination, Sir, it's definitely colder today than it was yesterday.'

'The politicians use it as an excuse to lever more money out of our pockets,' the principal growled.

'Yes, Sir; if you say,' Miss Brown looked quizzically at the principal as he walked on through the reception hall.

'Wonder what caused the extreme heat during Roman times? They cannot blame fossil fuels and cars for that,' he called back to her.

'Central heating, Sir,' she replied, but otherwise had lost the thread of the conversation.

Johannes set off for his office.

'Morning, Mr Taliesin.'

'Good morning!'

He skipped up a flight of stairs and into an anteroom. Three doors leading off: 'Johannes Taliesin; Principal', 'Susan Harefeld; Principal's Personal Assistant' and the third door, originally labelled 'Meeting Room' where every Tom, Dick and Harry could hold a gathering, now boasts since Johannes took up the post of principal at Nehemiah Institute of Art and Design 'Boardroom' in gold lettering: one small act of many Johannes had undertaken to distance management from the proletariat. Next to the boardroom entrance a vestibule led off: today it housed many overcoats on its hangers. Susan Harefeld's door was ajar.

'Good morning, Mr Taliesin.'

'Good morning, Susan.'

'Weather to your liking?'

'Oh, sure! This late blanket of snow took me by surprise, must admit,' Johannes replied, 'I notice many coats; many people here so early on such a dreadful morning. Am I late or something?'

'No, you are not late. How did you find the roads?'

'Reasonably clear, thank goodness. The snow button on my car doesn't seem to help me – must be the way I drive, can't be the BMW,' Johannes shuddered.

'My husband has a similar car: he swears by the traction function,' Susan smiled.

'Hmm… a snow button assisting traction… hmm. If they were to make it front wheel drive there would be no need for all that paraphernalia,' Johannes dismissed.

'Must ask my husband what you are doing wrong,' Susan joked.

'I've never come to terms with the demise of the horse-drawn carriage!'

'Some farmers still use them on market day,' Susan was quick to acquiesce.

'For show only, back at the ranch they have their Mercs ticking over in the barn,' was Johannes's smiling response, 'but it's as well there's snow about,' Johannes said, returned to the subject at hand, 'I have to watch my speed these days, damn speed cameras everywhere camouflaged as lamp posts or posing as trees; the

Chilterns are littered with them, pretext for generating more governmental revenue.'

'Speed cameras on trees! Yes, Mr Taliesin, can't say I've seen any,' Susan replied sagely.

'You don't have to look out for them as your car is incapable of reaching a velocity equal to the speed limit.'

'I can but agree with you, Principal,' and they laughed heartily.

Johannes Taliesin enjoyed a good informal but business-like relationship with his PA. He had appointed her from the general secretary pool soon after taking up the post at Nehemiah. His predecessor managed with a part-time secretary only, regardless the burgeoning bureaucratic demands of Whitehall since incorporation following the Education Reform Act. Fortunately, Susan had learnt the essentials of administration as a general secretary. Johannes believed the convoluted funding and tick-box audit systems that the government had imposed on higher education were designed to constrain, not liberate, and he had set about introducing an awareness programme.

Susan Harefeld's main professional call was to maintain strictest confidentiality with Principal Taliesin's office: an aspect of title she was quite able to cope with due to her many years' experience. She also coped well with the principal's occasional irascibility, his fearless approach to hard work and long hours, and his obliquely eccentric worldview.

But Susan, along with many others at Nehemiah, could not understand Johannes's declared opposition to the national culture of unquestioning tolerance of art its whim, fancy and self-indulgent foibles. The principal gave short shrift to anyone not sharing his mission that art should play a more functional, and less decorative, role in society. His ideology had sent the Nehemiah academics into deep protectionist shock; it stimulated much plotting and knife sharpening, which unsurprisingly was the usual pass-time in art college common rooms, i.e. the local pub. If the hate flavour of the month had not been the introduction of a more realistic twenty-first-century curriculum, it would have been any of many reactionary causes quivering for attention on the ready-to-use shelf. Johannes Taliesin held no illusions regarding the myth of reactionaries masquerading as cutting-edge post-modernism, or post-multicultural social statement, or post-Twitter spontaneity or whatever the Luddite chatterers labelled it. After all, from the academics' perspective, it was in their interest to maintain the status quo.

'Let's see what Mr Postman has brought me today; any Whitehall directives?'

'Yes, one big one; the usual batch of industrial tribunal update cases which I have placed in the LBW tray, lots of blah-blah stuff that I have redirected to the appropriate offices; and this e-mail from the funding council marked urgent,' she said, reaching over.

'They put 'Urgent' on every directive these days, ever since the Russell Group began ignoring them,' Johannes quipped.

'The other innocuous mail is on your desk,' she said.

'Thanks.'

Johannes skip-read the printed e-mails as he disappeared into his office. It was a confidential attachment to an enlarged document sent under separate cover.

'I've found the catch,' Johannes said absentmindedly.

'Would you like a coffee before you start?' Susan called.

'Do we have a full complement?'

'Seems so, apart from Arnold Leathwate, still in hospital.'

'Poor Arnold, must pay him a visit this evening. As members of the board have battled through the blizzard I won't keep them waiting any longer. Must just glance at the confidential PC and check the VR before I start. Coffee at official coffee break, unless I flag, when my faithful St Bernard will scoot off to get me one.'

Johannes checked through the electronically collected messages.

Susan came out into the anteroom in readiness, and called through the open door of Johannes's office,

'Your papers are at your place, Mr Taliesin. Clerk has delivered minutes of the last meeting.'

'Hmm. No doubt someone will complain about late delivery, can't blame Clerk, though. Can't blame complainers, either. Anything else?'

'Yes. Jennifer in reproduction has copied the funding council document and I've tabled it.'

'Good girl,' said Johannes, his mind on other things, 'this e-mail – 'Variations to the Funding Methodology,' hmm... suspicious bells already clanging in my head...'

'Yes,' Susan said, compliantly.

'Bugger them! The funding council no doubt wants to smuggle something through under cover of undue haste,' Johannes cursed.

'Everything else is there, Mr Taliesin,' she said, not endorsing his rant.

'Good. Thank you, Susan, you are a PA in a million.'

They entered the boardroom. An immediate hush fell.

'When a group of people fall silent immediately one enters a room, guaranteed they have been talking negative stuff about us,' Inner Voice substantiated Johannes's deep cynicism of human nature.

'Morning ladies and gentlemen,' the principal chirped outwardly.

'Morning,' came a chorus.

'Wetting their knickers at the notion of promulgating the art and craft movement a hundred years out of date,' Inner Voice growled.

Johannes Taliesin took his seat at the head of the boardroom table. He quickly flicked through the funding council document, which gave fuller background to the e-mail attachment. Identifying the paragraph that gave notice of intention to review the subject-base principle of guaranteed funding, Johannes muttered, sotto voce, 'Aha! Flesh on the bones of the catch.'

'Found something interesting, Chairman?' the clerk to the academic board, sitting next him, had observed.

'Only the funding council's flavour of this month,' came the quiet reply.

Those sitting nearest waggled their ears.

He tapped the table, signalling a call to start the meeting.

At other times in the privacy of his office Johannes had intimated to his vice-principal,

'My views regarding constitutional committees like the academic board and the board of governors sit on a paradox. On the one hand, I treat such committees as sanctuary when difficult decisions have to be made through majority vote and presumably under the cloak of anonymity. Contrarily, if a decision leads to institutional problems the next committee of authority, the board of governors, automatically blames the chairman of the promulgating committee, blowing to pieces so-called collective responsibility of the democratic process. Such is the Privy Council's pretext at democracy, and the hypocrisy of human nature for which I nurse a highly developed sense of antagonism generously spread with pessimism.'

'Cynicism, I would call it, Principal.'

'OK, pessimistic cynicism, if you must. Anyway, this invidious position of the ex-officio chairman of the board is a malaise of the British managerial system, borne of a too-liberal approach to safeguarding the weak and incompetent, while propagating the myth of democracy.'

'Yes, Principal,' his VP would respond good naturedly, 'you have descended upon us from another age, Ghengis Khan's

Mongolia comes to mind, or perhaps some similar mysterious land on the planet Zog.'

'Somewhat harsh, I think, but I would not expect you to respond otherwise. The myth in democracy is a misguided belief that incompetence and negligence in the workforce is always the fault of the chief executive, whose summary demise, the assumption goes, will immediately restore the hoi polloi's soundness of reason and reliability. Forcing the captain to walk the plank perpetuates the myth that the workforce is a truthful upstanding pillar of society, my wretched Aunt Hannah's haemorrhoids! But one cannot blame the ordinary member of staff: it is the Privy Council systems that are at fault: the hoi polloi are merely exploiting the council's deliberate weaknesses, albeit in their eternal ignorance.'

'Those must be some haemorrhoids, Principal!' VP ventured, 'but as you know, I hold other views.'

'Yes, gravitating to centralisation camouflaged by interminable committee work that describes majestic figures of eight, interspersed by the occasional declaration of appeasement to the proletariat. You know, I intensely disagree with the appeasement approach, but sometimes due to historical baggage concessions have to be made that conflict with logic. In a people-intensive industry like education there is no avoiding the tendrils of Buggins' turn, old-boy networks, buddy clubs and all the other paraphernalia of overindulged entities.'

'Ouch!'

'Don't forget the important decisions taken by the academics at their daily meetings with the junior common room at the local hostelry,' Principal Taliesin in full flow, 'I believe the constituted structure is a great disincentive to the junior ranks striving for better achievement, as they are made all too aware that their laziness, sloppiness, incompetence and dishonesty will always be hidden behind the British institutionalised process of blaming the chief executive for their errant ways, while praising the hoi polloi for any institutional reform. Bloody cockeyed socialism! When industrialists want the institution to undertake a major supportive project,' Johannes continued the sermon to his vice-principal, 'they first visit the chief executive. But when those same individuals want anecdotal ammunition to use against the institution they visit junior staff, as if looking at the institution through the bottom of a beer glass gives greater insight into its workings than the worldview held of necessity by the chief executive.'

'Ouch again, Principal!'

'It is this press-based negative mentality that I most dislike about the national institutionalised systems of governance. One cannot blame the ordinary member of staff, though: their ignorance simply fills a vacuum.'

The vice-principal reeled from the onslaught, although he was becoming acclimatised to the principal's outbursts.

'It is now 9 o'clock so we'll get started,' Chairman announced crisply, 'if we get a move on we should be out by 10 o'clock tonight.'

False groans good-naturedly chorused. Like Johannes, some members of the academic board disliked meetings; unfortunately others, mostly elected members, relished them because it was a legitimate instrument for avoiding studio and lecturing duties.

'More like out by coffee break.'

'Apologies for absence?'

'Arnold Leathwate.'

'Arnold Leathwate. Clerk, Please send a 'get well' letter on behalf of the board to Arnold Leathwate.'

'Agreed.'

'Item 1: minutes of the last meeting. I understand they have just been tabled. Could the clerk please advise the board the reasons for their late delivery?'

'I beg the board accept my apologies, Mr Chairman,' Clerk to the board tripped out his bullet-proof reason, 'The reason for late delivery of the minutes lies in my time being consumed in aggregating the throughput figures for the whole college brought forward by two weeks at very short notice by the funding council.'

'Yes, I am aware of the pressures being brought on the institutions by the funding council box creators, more of which later. Apologies accepted?'

'Accepted, but may we have a few minutes to peruse them, Mr Chairman?'

'Surely.'

Johannes paused a while as members shuffled through the minutes of the last meeting. To the staff of Nehemiah Institute Johannes Taliesin was an enigma. In the goldfish bowl that was art education the academics were heavily weighted towards people-watchers. With an enigmatic chief executive abroad the pursuance of minutiae, however trivial, was tantalising. But Johannes never disclosed his affiliations; he upheld his privacy with inscrutable discipline, and always maintained an aloof personal standoff. He regretted confiding his ideologies with the VP because before he learned better he had discovered a slanted interpretation was being cascaded down to the junior common room via the local hostelry, pillow and all other points of contact on the nine-o-nine to nowhere.

Johannes held strong prejudices against the self-serving political establishment, sloppy national institutions, bad government and burgeoning bureaucracies. His bête noire was the masquerade that Whitehall governed the country, when it was palpably obvious that the politicians had no say in the matter, as the un-elected bureaucrats of Brussels had taken over control of the little over-populated island off the west coast of Greater Europa.

He snapped out of his dyspepsia.

'Do I take it the minutes are a true record of business undertaken at the last meeting?'

'Agreed,' members chorused.

Item 2: matters arising. Any matters arising not already listed on the agenda?'

Johannes glanced around the table. He was met by silence.

'I take it there are no matters arising.'

'Move Item 3. Refectory turnover. This is the main item on the agenda. It is a very vexing issue. In the two years plus I have had the privilege of managing the institute this matter has been tabled on five separate occasions, not including affiliated matters arising. Clearly, fellow members of the board, we have been going round in circles.

'The reason we have been going round in circles is obvious: the only sensible decision to be made is the very onerous one of closure, and we have been desperately hoping a more favourable solution will emerge from the interminable discussions we have had on the matter. But I am afraid this might well be wishful thinking on my behalf. So today we have to agree on a strategy, as the funding council audit is now demanding resolution by 31 December.'

'Firstly, I call on head of finance Mr Bulbright to speak.'

'Thank you, Mr Chairman. I have tabled a detailed breakdown of the figures, labelled 3A – does everyone have a copy? As members of the board are aware we have been concerned for some time about the falling patronage of our refectory. Our surveys show this is not to do with the choice of menu or quality of cuisine, but rather a trend towards the growing popularity of local hostelries, to the detriment of the institute's refectory turnover. At the last meeting of the academic board I was commissioned to compile figures that reflect throughput over a three-year period up to the present.

The figures in the Appendix to 3A do not present encouraging news, Mr Chairman. Put bluntly, the refectory is operating at an overall loss of approximately £450,000 per annum. The on-costs are compounding at 18.5 per cent per annum and to make matters worse, the investment needed to update the area far exceeds its capital worth. The number of full-time equivalent staff employed at the refectory is twenty-three at an average salary per f.t.e of £23,700 plus of course the 18.5 per cent on-costs to the corporation. This returns an overall annual wage bill of £549,000.

'£549,000, Mr Chairman,' Mr Bulbright repeated, 'the figure does not include administrative backup, maintenance of apparatus and equipment, services, insurance and et cetera. The cost of utilities, adjusting for inflation, comes out at approximately £300,000. Turnover for the period 6 April last year to 5 April this year was just over £487,000 giving a deficit of £450,000 in round terms. Of course, we shall undertake a much more detailed survey before the December audit, no doubt in my estimation the result of which will most probably return a more negative outcome.'

'Thank you, Head of Finance,' said Chairman, 'clearly we do not need rocket science to adjudge this haemorrhaging of institutional funds is unsustainable. It appears our options have been systematically squeezed by succeeding contingencies until we are left with just one. Before I spell out the details, I will throw the discussion open.'

'*Here goes! The same old mantras about to be trotted out,*' Inner Voice groaned.

An animated discussion ensued: the usual committee-based answers to all problems of this nature poured forth: proposals variously demanding either more money from government or from the institution's contingency fund, a standing committee be set up to visit other institutions, purpose of which would be to examine their refectories with a view to gleaning the secret of profitability.

'Mr Chairman, with respect, all of these proposals have already been tabled on previous occasions,' Mr Bulbright was weary of the old fatuous proposals, 'and yet I have to manage the finances of a utility that is drawing funds from other viable functions in the institution. How long can this go on? Mr Chairman, if I may: when this item arose last year the academic board requested senior managers take the refectory campaign to their respective staffs and students to encourage more patronage of the refectory at lunchtime and evening.'

'Yes,' Chairman responded, 'and I'm sure you are not the only member who recalls that proposal, Mr Bulbright.'

Some members of the board winced, but Chairman Taliesin allowed the meeting to flow.

'Not only has the proposal not been embraced, Mr Chairman, but circumstances oblige me to accuse my colleague senior managers of indifference to the consequences, as they themselves have been seen leading the way to the local hostelries at lunchtime.'

Chairman Taliesin slapped the table with his hand, a marker of the moment.

'I believe it is referred to in all key analyses of industrial decline as mismanagement by bad example!' Head of Finance continued, 'some of those senior managers are sitting around this table today. They have the gall to demand more funding from the institute's contingency fund. Mr Chairman, their hypocrisy beggars belief!'

Members of the board had not witnessed head of finance so animated. His accusations stunned members into silence, which Chairman allowed be sustained.

'Obviously,' Chairman spoke at last, 'an air of 'not my problem' pervades this institution. How can Nehemiah possibly survive in a competitive market if the culture of the workforce is one of responsibility abrogation?'

Chairman waited for responses.

'Some of us have been trying, Chairman, but the odds are stacked against success.' Representative for fashion and textiles said, 'yet others of us have been desperately cobbling together old machinery due to the lack of additional funding, when £450,000 of our money goes down the drain each year. I propose we close the refectory forthwith and stop the haemorrhage before we are all pulled into the black hole.'

'There will be an increase in deficit as we have to pay redundancy awards,' Mr Bulbright warned, 'but that option is economically more acceptable than the present situation.'

'Better an end with horror than horror without end. I believe Schiller wrote,' Chairman said, neatly bringing the refectory closure round to becoming a given, having allowed the dreaded proposal to emanate from the floor, 'this is a grave matter. Many members of our staff will lose their jobs through the fault of circumstances beyond their control. Therefore, before we agree on the inevitable proposal, let us run through the options one last time, for a multitude of reasons. I will list the proposals from today's discussion and from the minutes of previous meetings. Some of them will appear futile.'

Chairman paused before delivering the *coup de grâce*.

'Notwithstanding Finance Officer Bulbright's figures need finalising, I believe from this and previous meetings the sharpest pencil will not make an appreciable difference to the £450,000 annual deficit. Bearing the aforesaid in mind, the following are pie-in-the-sky proposals drawn from previous meetings of this board. One, to lobby the education authority for top-up; two, demands for more institutional contingency money to bail out the refectory; three, the funding council be approached to bail out our refectory debts; four, a sub-committee be set up to determine the secrets of viability enjoyed by refectories at other institutions.

'These points can be given short shrift,' Chairman continued, 'taken in the order I have given them: one, obviously atavism is alive and well and thriving at Nehemiah Institute. Some of our current students were not born when Parliament began debating the Green Paper 'Meeting the Challenge', which led to incorporation of the higher education institutions, effectively ending local education authority responsibility to the higher education sector. Two, contingency funds are drawn from the income of every faculty and department, which is subject to audit, both internal and external. Financial rules of this academic board, the board of governors and the funding council disallow expenditure on non-viable projects, with the caveat of short-term exigencies, and even then a memorandum of elucidation has to be tabled before the board of governors. Three, the funding council does not finance functions ultra vires to their strict formulas. Four, expensive away-day jollies for the usual sub-committee worthies will return with glaringly obvious findings: that refectories in other institutions enjoy patronage from staff and student bodies, thus rendering them viable. Case for support closed,' Chairman Taliesin shared Mr Bulbright's indignation.

'Might I remind members of the academic board of the directive laid down by the funding council's funding methodology: 'to increase income the institutions are free to recruit more students within the provision of the overall net.' In which case, is the academic board prepared to table a motion that the institution needs to recruit more students?' Chairman asked.

'We would if it did not contradict the Delaney ratios,' came the response from the board.

'Updated edicts render the Delaney formula defunct. The

funding council's funding methodology threw Delaney out of the window twenty years ago. Where have you people been?' Chairman Taliesin responded. 'So I repeat my question: do we have a proposal that the institution recruits more students in order to meet the refectory's insolvency?'

The silence that followed was the usual method members of the academic board utilised to deal simultaneously with saving face and engaging denial.

'On the basis of our predicament, Mr Chairman,' Head of Finance said, 'we have no alternative but to face reality. I therefore propose this board recommends to the board of governors that the refectory be closed without further delay.'

'Proposal seconded,' said the fashion and textiles representative.

'The proposal is,' chairman cleared his throat, 'This academic board recommends to the board of governors that, with regard to the figures supplied by the monitoring survey undertaken by Finance Office Services, the refectory be closed without further delay. All those in favour?'

Hands were elevated, some reluctantly, hesitantly; others with alacrity.

'Thank you,' said Chairman, 'motion carried. Consequently, I will need to table this proposal at the next meeting of the board of governors. I'm sure they will produce innovative suggestions: that I should look again at the college contingency fund; that I should approach the funding council for more money; that I should examine refectory policies at other institutions. All the air-head proposals tabled repeatedly by this academic board will once again be thrown at me by the elected butchers, bakers and candlestick makers of the board of governors.'

'Silence meeting our outburst against outdated assumptions regarding HE funding to be expected. Guaranteed our insult will

be delivered to the butchers, bakers and candlestick makers by the usual tongue-waggers,' Inner Voice vented cynicism.

Chairman concluded with a scathing attack on the dependency culture of art and design education, 'The refectory need not have arrived at this predicament,' he stated the obvious, 'if the problem had been addressed in good time, with appropriate strategies for recovery, and with 100 per cent commitment from the body politic. But this problem has gone the way of all similar disasters at art institutions: how can we expect inmates marinated in a culture that encourages self-indulgence with regard to studio expression to behave as responsible business heads when it comes to maintaining the fabric of the corporation? The money tree so many became adept at shaking before incorporation is now bare and shivers in the cold light of market reality.'

Members of the academic board mostly sat in silence.

It was moments such as these when Johannes Taliesin gave vent to the many years of deprivation, meagre and struggle he personally witnessed as a child, teenager and student, while all around him well-heeled colleagues looked down their noses at the demeaning process of striving a little harder to generate an institution's income. Johannes's preparedness to face up to funding realities was out of synch with their indulged lifestyles. He was angry with both the general and the specific.

'Rightly or wrongly, we believe these well-heeled slugs don't have the foggiest clue how mind numbing and psychologically belittling real poverty can be. Look at them – expecting someone else to pay for their indulgence. Everyone doling out orders, no one prepared to take them.'

'Move next item,' Chairman said crisply, 'Item 4: The Denaro Enigma, whatever that is supposed to convey. Who is to speak to the Denaro Enigma...?'

Later that day the VP called by Johannes's office.

'Main item went easily enough; I thought we would have had more opposition.'

'It's easy enough to close an operation down if there are no representatives of the agenda's item on the board, and as long as the real profligacy goes untouched.'

'Real profligacy, Principal?'

'The waste of public money that masquerades as education in some of the faculties in this institution.'

'Which would those be?'

'I'm sorry, Vice-Principal; if you are unable to discern the difference between departments that contribute the merely desirable to society and those that effect an essential construct, then who am I to take a hand in your enlightenment? I would consider the meeting to have been a success if we had seriously thrashed out a solution that brought financial viability to the refectory by involving all of the faculties, the staff and students of the institution, in a constructive manner. But we took the soft option: we closed the refectory. God help us in art education, our culture is a hundred years out of date.'

'Sometimes I wonder where you came from, Principal.'

'I don't wonder, I know; but to be fair to you I do not wish to burden you with the knowledge.'

A few days later Principal Taliesin was invited to attend a pre-preview of the Fine Art Degree Show. He was in the middle of preparing paperwork for the board of governors while fending off academic staff-instigated deputations from the refectory. Johannes was in a deeply angry frame of mind, and the act of inviting him to a pre-preview did everything to trigger his suspicions and nothing to alleviate his mood.

The show was customarily held in the generous acres of the Fine Art studios, temporarily converted into a gallery. Space occupancy ratios had long since been confounded, all for the wrong reasons. As the principal entered the studios he noticed a higher level of giggling and mastering than is normally exhibited by the anarchic staff.

'Beware, this shower is up to something.'

His defences automatically rose.

The usual array of exhibits confronted the visitor, displaying ingeniously arranged segments of society's castaway flotsam coupled with an affected jetsam indifference whether the exhibitor were awarded a first class hons or the exhibit was unceremoniously dumped in a waste bin. No one at Fine Art Nehemiah feared the latter, as each student had slavishly emulated either a resident or visiting guru before whose shrine they had genuflected their daily ablutions. Proper or improper cultivation of the guru was the fine art of fine art studentship.

Systematically over the years the incumbents in fine art – academics, visiting gurus, examiners, part-time tutors and students – had turned an education that had been a joy into a serious political tool for establishment hate. If comments critical to this anti-establishment regime were uttered by Joe Public tax-payer, predetermined defences would be whisked off the shelf and machine-gunned at the offending party. The principal – any principal – had long since been elected as the icy face of the enemy, and was a sitting duck in the year-round shooting season.

On this day Principal Taliesin was escorted by a group of unusually polite fine art undergraduates. Johannes was politely inveigled and maliciously coerced to follow a predetermined tunnel through various structures that he failed to recognise as art.

'If this stuff is up-to-date, then by God, we are aeons out of date.'

The gap in lack of recognition Johannes put down to various deprecatory maladies as premature aging, being too long removed from the coal face, too many late hours spent in critical management combat where the forces of the dependency culture met the forces of Mammon, among other allied viruses. Regardless of attempts at comprehending the playgroup games, the principal was always, would always, be wrong.

While crawling through the artefact tunnel constructed of straw bales, Johannes strove for a solution to the puzzle to what had changed with his personal cutting-edge painting before becoming a principal to the pumpkinisation of his work after the appointment, but his thoughts were peremptorily curtailed as he unintentionally placed his hand in a dollop of fresh cow-shit. The trivial act of defacing the principal's dignity was greeted by howls of laughter from the tutors and hyena echoes from their students. The head of fine art was in the audience: big error.

'Don't lose our cool, for God's sake,' Inner Voice urged, *'concentrate on an inconsequential detail, such as separating the sheep from the goats. They have delivered unto us a golden opportunity.'*

It was natural, given the embarrassment of having fallen for such a mediocre set-up, Principal Taliesin's thoughts should fleetingly turn to the nagging question as to the purpose of art colleges. Admittedly, he was very much part of the established order of art and design education, which put added emphasis to the embarrassment. The historical impasse demanded serious analysis of a so-called vocation that could only contribute cow-shit out of context. No doubt the perpetrator would be awarded a first class with honours for an outstanding artefact of social statement.

Principal Taliesin experienced a vivid recall. As a painting special undergraduate at Swansea College of Art he had asked of the famous painter Joseph Herman, who was paying the college a visit,

'Do you like the work of the French Impressionists?' Johannes had chirped.

'Fundamentally I am a kind man,' Joseph Herman replied in his heavy Polish accent, 'I do not kick dead horses.'

'Perhaps our subconscious is drawing parallels with the inanity of Nehemiah fine art students, or the Joseph Herman aphorism transcending the feeble-mindedness of fine art undergraduates, or would the Glynn Vivian have ever allowed cow-shit through its hallowed portals? Perhaps not, especially in the last of these recalled hypothetical atavisms.'

Perhaps many artists, having been caught by a similarly inane jape, would have lashed out in fury at the nearest person, be they male or female, staff or student. A flurry of cow-shit and blooded noses would have brought the sorry absurd state of art education into perspective and many would have awakened from their daydream. A touch of thuggish behaviour by the demeaned principal would have injected the much-needed shock of reality into the whole affair. On the other hand, there would not have been one senior manager in the whole institution who would have broken their chains of political correctness to declare the principal had been humiliated by a dollop of cow-shit and was justified in acting like a deranged bull.

If Principal Taliesin had performed the natural scenario of his impulse he would have been suspended by the chairman of the board of governors, article 10.9 of the Articles of Government would have been invoked, all the pompous and ceremonially virtuous butchers, bakers and candlestick pygmies of the board would have pontificated until their underpants were akin to the dollop, whereupon the said principal would have been blackballed. The press, more pygmies driving on the motorway to the land of hypocrisy, having ascertained the miscreant's identity, would have similarly wet their knickers with the pleasure of a field day in an exhibition of tub-thumping disingenuous virtuousness accompanied by a breathtaking degree of cant.

The student's 'work of art' would have assumed overnight

fame, would have been purred over by the liberal establishment, whose sense of survival knows no limits to vacuity, and would have become a shrine of social virtue on BBC Newsnight. Not that cow-shit art has any intrinsic value apart from being manure, but rather from the sense of occasion and ethos the tarot would demand unearned largesse be thrown at it, and the BBC can always be relied upon to support anything anti-establishment. Good money would be thrown into the abyss, atavism the opium of dreamers. The spectres shudder, and no one cares a damn. The Privy Council's hidden agenda of control flows on in subtle forms, giving powers to the butchers, bakers and candlesticks to exercise their political but superficial prejudices.

As time passed, the ethos of art and design would change the reality into myth, by elevating the cow-shit artefact and its authors onto the folk hero rostrum, simultaneously lowering the dignity of the principal to a shade that enabled the cow-shit to eclipse all of his brave deeds in art college management when rescuing its incidental trivialities. Institutional survival has no place on the scale of magnitude compared to cow-shit art. After all, one must always maintain a sense of balance and perspective. So much for hypocritical buffoonery; art has no values, just the flexible values of a tart.

'*Keep calm. Think about delightful asides like roasting the head of fine art in warm hydrochloric acid,*' Inner Voice tempered.

Principal Taliesin called out one word, modelling himself on Professor Price of long ago,

'Water!'

And, knowing what was meant, two tutors dashed to fetch a bowl of water, whilst the rest, staff and students alike, stood about sheepishly.

'*Now there's a thought to make us laugh,*' Inner Voice mused, '*sheep playing around with cow shit.*'

Having washed his hands, swilled his wristwatch and cufflink and attempted a cursory clean of the left wrist shirt cuff he called out, obviously enjoying the role as the offended party,

'Telephone!' and, after a pause, he glared at the staff and growled, 'sheep playing around with cow shit.'

Having dialled through to his personal assistant, the principal ordered in loud voice so no one was in doubt,

'Call a senior management team meeting in my office for 8.00 a.m. tomorrow; three-line whip; thank you, Mrs Harefeld.'

Whereupon Principal Taliesin walked out, accompanied by his dignity, which he had just managed to retain, recalling the superb role model for retention of dignity in the face of outrageous misfortune Principal Hancock had displayed all those years ago at Swansea College of Art. Although Principal Taliesin superficially expressed his lack of amusement, inwardly he was delighted a circumstance that he had long been awaiting had at last occasioned.

'*Got them. Maybe herein lies the germ of an alternative proposal for the refectory we could place before the board of butchers, bakers and candlesticks.*'

Johannes was quick to notice a change of display had been undertaken in the boardroom: student work from the Department of Painting had replaced Department of Graphics work. The paintings were superbly framed and had been sympathetically selected considering the venue, i.e. no cow shit.

'*Perhaps we should not be so hard on them after all,*' Inner Voice wavered, but then dived into an abrupt change of mood, '*bugger it, no one ever sympathised with us when we were a miscreant student, except Griff Edwards and Fred Janes. Perhaps we should temper that respective percentage.*'

'Ah, *do* come in, ladies and gentlemen,' the principal spoke softly, 'I trust you all had an easy journey this morning?'

The senior managers were unusually subdued.

'I acknowledge the change of boardroom exhibition: thank

you for the effort, but that is not to say I didn't enjoy the graphics. To business – I'm sure you are aware of the reason I have called this unscheduled meeting at such short notice.'

The senior managers muttered their awareness in various noises. Truth was some faculties were being penalised for the irresponsible behaviour of others. Some had discarded the cloying mantle of tradition and had staggered a certain distance towards the gain line, but even so were hopelessly outmanoeuvred in catch-up gamesmanship. Those were the areas where there had been a measurable effort to renew. Others were unfortunately embedded in the historical ethos of art colleges, of which they were well pleased, and all the imploring for a live new departure not only meant nothing but was obdurately positioned to remain meaningless. Only harsh action would avail.

Through the years of meagre and struggle Johannes had of necessity learned the black art of opportunism. The embarrassing cow-shit incident had presented him with the perfect excuse to implement a change of culture that he had for some considerable time intended, that is, as soon as the opportune conditions arose. If nothing else, the doltish cow-shit incident proved academics were not thinking too deeply into the consequences of their actions, otherwise Principal Taliesin would not have been so conveniently gifted with the tool he sought.

As the senior management team had accepted collective responsibility for the college's cultural direction, admittedly with some diffidence, they were contractually obliged to foreswear their private romantics in favour of institutional good health. Leading the chief executive into a trap within a playgroup pile of straw bales and cow shit bent the moment of unreality impossibly, out of which only one outcome was feasible.

'Yesterday we witnessed Nehemiah Institute of Art at the nadir of its collective delusion as a participant in our society of flexible values,' the principal began, 'even though society at large has already lowered the barriers to inestimably deprecating levels: we cannot for a moment defend the edict that values are too high for mediocre participation these days. That tutors, visiting gurus and course leaders et al. snub the belief they are educating our young people seriously begs the question – but are they aware of their objectives? Please feel free to interrupt me.'

As no interruption was forthcoming, he continued, 'I am obliged to acknowledge that tutors and students in fine art were yesterday pleasurably rewarded their assiduous planning. But what an acknowledgement! The look of blissful achievement on their faces as I emerged from the straw bale tunnel splattered with cow shit tells you all you need to know about the sorry state of fine art today. The tutors had successfully inveigled their dummies into an intellectual dead end; out of date by well over a hundred years, Alfred Jarry and his Parisian shit flingers and all that.

'Incidentally, I cursed myself for not having recognised the tell-tale signs of conspiracy – goodness knows I have been at the uncomfortable end of conspiracies on sufficient occasions to have learnt to read the signs; I recall the buffoon from the photography department with his camcorder trained on my every move, followed by his perspicacious editing and cutting in order the presentation made the principal out to be a nervous cretin, much to the enjoyment of our goats and sheep. Yesterday the huddle forming a shape of conspiracy, 100 per cent turnout of painting and sculpture tutors – that only happens when free alcohol is being handed out. I should have read the signs, but must confess I had one or two unwelcome duties needing attention.

'It appears the aim of the project was simply to embarrass the principal. But to choose to mount this prank so soon after the academic board voted to terminate the contracts of dozens of employees at the refectory can best be described as bad timing,' Principal Taliesin paused, 'Bad timing!' he roared, 'Clearly, asking academic staff to take an institute-wide view, leave alone a national view, is hoping for too much. Even academic senior managers are myopic, choosing to limit their horizons to individual subjects. The adage silk purse from sow's ear springs to mind.'

'I beg your pardon, Principal, what exactly do you mean by that?' the head of painting at last erupted.

'I mean you are paid far more than you are worth. I mean you assume a position in academia that flatters your contribution. In the groves of your academe, at the end of every vista, I see nothing but the gallows. If you want a fight, let's have one,' the Principal challenged; he was indeed in the mood for a brawl. For their part the senior managers, not knowing the principal's background let alone his stable, were stunned by his aggressive language. The challenge went unreciprocated: prudence advised they ride the storm more or less in silence.

'Unfortunately,' Johannes continued, 'this leaves the perpetrators defenceless in the face of current accusations in Parliament by Her Majesty's loyal opposition that art education contributes to the country's already filthy environment. That it aids and abets the national culture of detritus by setting up undergraduate study courses in graffiti, rubbish dump sculpture, elephant dung painting, to which is now added Nehemiah Institute of Art contributing a submission to a fine art degree show of bales of straw and cow shit. And they call it art! What an outrage! The bit is between the teeth of the opportunist elected members and the feral press.'

It was hard talk, but with a basis in current political thinking. The senior management team expressed a shuffle of discomfort.

'Get to the crunch, Principal,' one called.

'We'll get to the crunch, sooner than you are prepared.'

'When ministers accuse me of participating in the sector's collective descent into a mindless realm of bagged ferrets I cannot deny it. We have lost sight of our purpose in art education. Worse, we cannot defend that which we pompously refer to as education. For me the saddest indictment is that we have turned our mediocre activities entirely inward, like those ferrets in a bag. But to exacerbate our ignominy we fight blindly inside an ivory tower whose walls are lined with mirrors, basking in our own reflections, neither seeing nor being seen by the outside world. We have long since lost sight of the greater public, nay the taxpayer, whom we ostensibly serve.

'Once upon an ancient time art institutions were built as institutions of science and art for which the purpose was abjectly appropriate: industry and commerce enjoyed a symbiotic relationship with art and science. But that has gone, gone. In fact, I am a hypocrite preaching thus, because when I enjoyed my art education all those years ago, I also was imbued with the belief that I could do what the hell I liked and damn the public, much as is today's ethos of irresponsibility.

'But since Royal Assent of the Education Reform Act, responsibility rests squarely with the institutions rather than the overseeing authorities. That is the difference between then and now. We must start acting responsibly – educationally, financially, strategically. We are an art institution situated in a city that for nearly one and a half centuries has supported its lone HE art establishment. We have no rivals, nor are we likely to have any in the foreseeable future. By enjoying independence we alone must uphold the values of higher education in the city. Perhaps it is to be regretted we do not have competition: some establishments have rival institutions observing each other avariciously, intent for the least excuse for a buy-out.

'If we had had a large established university in our vicinity we would have been bought out before breakfast on the first bidding day. Then our assets would have been stripped and the courses flung to the four winds. Because our unique circumstances have prevented this coming to pass we rest content in the false belief that we are impregnable both academically and geographically. We have grown accustomed to indulging a belief the threat does not exist. Well, ladies and gentlemen, the threat exists regardless of geographical isolation and current dearth of governmental acuity.'

The head of painting interrupted again; in truth, he had no option but to interrupt.

'I take on board what you say regarding our vulnerability,' he said, obviously irritated, 'but I cannot see how art education in its entirety is in such a parlous state just because the principal is the subject of a student stunt. If I may propose, the principal is generalising from a specific incident.'

Over a lifetime of altercations ranging from embarrassing mishap to life-changing disaster Johannes had learnt a hard lesson: never enter battle unless one is equipped with the appropriate weapon. Today Principal Taliesin felt confident he was appropriately equipped.

'The main problem for me is not so much the cow shit on my hands and clothes; indeed, I had enough of that as an impoverished child. Rather, the problem is the preposterous notion that both your staff and their undergraduate charges label the cow shit 'art,' and present it as a main dissertation for the award of a degree. Then you, as head of department, have the effacement to hide behind the smokescreen that it is a 'stunt'. Do you not think this denudes the value of degrees generally? Do you seriously believe art education is a stunt?'

'But the exhibit is only part of that student's presentation,' came the reply.

'If that is the part you wish to present as front-of-house

exhibit, then one questions the quality of that which remains out of sight. God help your priorities and sense of purpose!' Principal Taliesin snapped, 'You chose to display the stunt. Why? Have you lost your professional judgement?'

'Is that a rhetorical question?'

'Why?'

'I'm sure you will tell us, Principal,' came the reply.

'The problem goes much deeper,' the principal continued, 'because art is being used as a tool to facilitate a politico-personal end, not as a declaration in its own right. Art these days is seen as an organised event into public embarrassment of which I happen to be an incidental ingredient. But my embarrassment is not really the point. The point I am making is: do you not realise the time is long overdue when we take a cold hard look at our purpose? If I complain because one of my better suits was soiled, or you defend the trite playgroup work you manage in your department, we are in danger of missing the larger point; we are in danger of becoming those ferrets fighting blindly within the walls of our ivory tower.'

'What do you suggest we do?' head of fashion and textiles asked. The Department of Fashion and Textiles was famous for producing student work acknowledged in fashion expositions across Europe. The principal's criticism had to avoid direct reference whilst at the same time addressing the broader malaise affecting art and design education. Fashion had become a fine art that appealed to big money and fanfare, but failed to address the needs of the greater majority of ordinary people whose clothes, designed and produced in China and India, whose mass production now dominates markets in the West.

'Well,' said the Principal, affecting the role of a careful thinker, 'to be acclaimed in the market can be a very seductive balm, but one must ask difficult questions of oneself regarding whether one is leading the market, or being led by it.'

'You suggest we abandon the proven successes we have so far enjoyed?'

'Frankly, yes, but what I am about to suggest is not as crude as that,' the principal replied.

'Let me get this right,' said the head of three dimensional design very aggressively, 'you are suggesting we are travelling in the wrong direction? Some of my staff will be very angry to hear that.'

'I hope they are! And I hope you will break your neck in order to inform them what I am saying,' the principal goaded, 'because none of you ever initiate an aggressive analysis of your purpose.'

'You bet I will inform them.'

'Incorrigible,' the principal responded, 'And that, ladies and gentlemen, is another symptom of the malady that afflicts art and design education today – the inability of senior managers to elevate themselves above the level of the shop floor; the inability of senior managers to divorce themselves from the hoi polloi and walk away from the junior common room, take a worldview, to initiate development. Worse still the inability of senior managers to square up to their contractual obligations.'

The head of three dimensional design uttered a loud and protracted sniff.

'We are being too hard on them.'

'I have not called this meeting today to soothe you with terms of praise,' the principal continued, 'but rather to deliver aphorisms pertinent to the state of health of art and design at this institution; a state of health that should give all right-minded people grave cause for concern. We have long since passed the point where we need a genius to diagnose the patient's illness. Indeed, we have passed the stage where even an idiot can diagnose all is not right. Problem now is finding a cure that does not kill the patient.

'We have long since ceased to listen: today we only listen to ourselves; the myopic establishment gains a high from the patronage, but is regrettably ignorant to the endemic decease. In fact, the establishment is not only part of the decease; in broad measure the establishment is the cause of it.

'As you know a review is underway of the minor art and design centres; I have been nominated by the funding council to head up one such inspection in south Wales next week. Before one can say Delaney is dead they will be swarming over art and design provision in HE like wasps around a jam pot. The academic board recently received a discussion document promulgated by the funding council, no doubt the first shot in a major review of subject-based weighted funding.

'Meanwhile we have a board of butchers, bakers and candlestick makers who receive all of the appropriate documentation, and God knows we get enough of that from Brussels via Whitehall. But the BoG still chooses to remain aloof of reality by chasing the current week's politically correct trivia. They believe they have undertaken a job well done by criticising the *principal's* every point, not realising that they are acting as oafishly as students who construct a project of straw bales and cow shit in order to render indignity upon the principal. The lost opportunities of inconsequential meetings are most frustrating.

'No doubt the board of butchers, bakers and candlesticks will be thrilled by the exposition of cow shit and straw, wetting their knickers with pride that their institution is making a name for itself: fame for five minutes. I am weary of the parley of clueless amateurs that is our board pontificating on the glory of nihilistic art just because it makes them appear modern-minded. Like many of our staff, it will never occur to them that the fame is brought about for all the wrong reasons and is inappropriate to the international threats the remains of our nation's industry and commerce face.

'But unfortunately it *will* occur to the occasional wolf prowling in the shadows of Whitehall, eager to place their name on a slice of the forestalled revenues for education. Remember, since Brussels has become our government, Britain's Parliament is merely a parish council, so they *have* to undertake some demonstrative act to prove their existence.

'I aim to instigate a fundamental revolution in the underlying responsive processes of art and design. Current assumptions enshrine a curious fiction that objectives are being achieved; that progress is being made; that freethinking is abroad in the specialist disciplines; that the contribution art and design makes to the nation is invaluable. An objective survey of the true impact of art on society reveals these curious fictions to be a worrying distance from the fabric of reality; that institutions propagate the fictions by self-appointing their examiners; that most judgements contain little objective analysis; that many assessments are made almost wholly on the subjective view of a guru or what their acolytes presume to be the guru's view; that so-called movements are closely monitored and approved by the institutional buddy clubs; that too much credence is given to media responses, whose authors often belong to a buddy club themselves or worse – when it comes to the cutting-edge dynamics of scientific change they don't know the objectives from a hole in the ground. Clearly, the curious fiction is built upon a myth.

'When we analyse the end product of this myth what do we see? Despoliation of our environment on a grand scale: sgraffiti smeared everywhere demonstrating lack of appreciation of fine buildings and beautiful surfaces by the perpetrators, and today we have some loony institutions offering undergraduate courses in sgraffito, would you believe? Talk about the mindless tail wagging the inane dog – what are the proposers, sponsors and endorsers of such courses thinking about? We see detritus accepted as the totems of society, attracting mega fortunes proving the tat possesses no intrinsic worth: mindless millionaires sharp elbowing their brethren out of the buying limelight just to prove they have the means with which to wipe their backsides in public. Our colleges of art pursue this fatuous value-added in an un-thinking blind faith. That is the point, members of senior management: the thinking element of the process has been negated by reactionary exigency, while proactive thinking is relegated to the rump. Coming back to the specific – where in God's name was the real thinking in bales of straw and cow shit? Our students deserve better intellectual stimulation to energise their outstanding minds; certainly they do not need coaxing along to genuflect before the media clamour by making more of what the mindless media people acclaim to be interesting. Oh, dear! Someone here is uttering the obvious and I think it might be me. The best time to start is now, and the best place to start is here at Nehemiah.

'Finally, colleagues, looked at from a different perspective, two external matters concern me. One: the threat from the Calvinistic parish councillors of Whitehall who, having lost our sovereign nation to an un-elected hegemony at Brussels, are presuming political credibility by applying a doctrine of puritanical exigency. They perform the minor postulations of all pygmies but most unfortunately their edicts affect us. Two: that although we have had the means to implement a new departure from the old order under our own terms, we have acted like Tsar Nicholas and his family who refused to read the obvious signs around them indicating the need to change their modus vivendi. With that funding council paper tabled at the academic board yesterday, as sure as Anson is as Anson does new governmental stringencies will oblige us to change, unfortunately not in the direction of our choice.'

'Admittedly, Mr Principal, you have brought up this matter on several occasions.'

'Well documented, Vice-Principal.'

'Then why have we done nothing about it?'

'Good question! I blame myself,' replied the principal. 'I have been chicken-hearted and hesitant. Two matters – the refectory and the incident in the painting department yesterday galvanised my thoughts into a cogent purpose.'

'We have a good responsive staff at the college. I'm sure they would meet a challenge if they were given clear objectives.'

'They will be given clear objectives,' the principal responded, 'which will be deceptively simple.'

'What's the project? Although I believe I know what is coming!'

'Differentiate between the essential and the desirable in our broad college-wide provision.'

'That it?'

'Yes. That is it. In due course I shall present a paper to the academic board and thence the board of governors. In passing may I add a note about the governing board? In days of yore members of a board were constituted of captains of industry and commerce, scientific researchers and distinguished opinion-formers. They had a wealth of knowledge and experience to bring to, and support, the management of an institution. Unfortunately nowadays the board of governors is nothing more than a placement by the Privy Council to allay popular suspicion that we no longer live in a democracy. They set up model instrument and articles of government and pretend thereafter that the institutions are free to run their own affairs. Nothing of the sort! You need only to examine the instrument to perceive the constitution the Privy Council intends. As a consequence it is well known that persons of renown no longer sit on non-executive boards, instead they steer clear of the politicised organs of the parish council, and who can blame them?

'The government of the day preaches to the electorate that the country's educational institutions are democratically run. But run by whom? If a chimpanzee were elected to the board no one in government would know or care the difference. That in which Brussels fails to play its interfering hand the butchers, bakers and candlesticks will finish off. Democracy? Go tell that to Pericles. In the meantime we will hold another extraordinary meeting of the senior management team in exactly two weeks' time to table the broad outline of deliberations. Thank you all your forbearance.'

'How did we get away with that?'

As so many management events were overlapping, Principal Taliesin decided to insert a diary note for chief executive's log.

'Susan, could you come through, please?' Johannes flicked the switch.

Susan Harefeld entered his office.

'I need to place a diary note in the chief executive's log. I was thinking of recording it, but we'll do both. Have you had coffee?'

'No, not yet.'

'Neither have I. I'll get started whilst we take coffee.' Johannes was still in irascible frame of mind following the regrettable proposal the academic board was obliged to take. The incident in the painting studios did nothing to ameliorate his already sour view. A message peeped through on his Blackberry: Johannes peered at it, his brow blackening, 'Huh! Bugger it.'

'Hmm,' Susan commented, 'I can see something has trodden on your tail, Principal.'

'Yes, something certainly has,' Johannes replied, 'I feel liberated from an oppressive inferiority brought about by my silly belief in elevating pygmies to exalted heights in the hope

357

they would appreciate the gesture and rise to the occasion, when all they do is believe they earned it, if you see what I mean.'

'No,' Susan Harefeld admitted.

'Treating people reasonably in the optimistic illusion one will be treated reasonably in return hardly ever happens if one is the principal of an art asylum.'

'Oh, yes – I see now. Your predecessor said that in his farewell speech.'

'Too late saying it in a farewell speech,' Johannes smiled sententiously, 'anyway, down to diary note: put today's date.'

'Which address?'

'The public access one – Taliesin@Nehemiah, et cetera, but the text can be used for my Thursday evening speech at Drapers Hall as well.'

'Will do.'

'Yesterday I fell victim to an old game that has been played in art schools for at least a century, i.e. public humiliation of the principal on the pretext the spectacle is an exposition of educational enlightenment. These spectacles are easy to manufacture, as the principal is a de facto participant in that invidious circumstance known as damned if he does, damned if he doesn't.

'I was being escorted by a group of unusually polite painting undergraduates at a pre-preview of their degree show, being held in their cavernous studios converted into a temporary gallery for the purpose of exhibiting their chosen pieces from the previous three years' work, plus a dissertation. I should have been alerted to their disingenuous politeness, but I let it pass, as the only means by which the principal of an art college can retain his sanity is to maintain an unnatural sense of trust and optimism.

'I was inveigled and politely coerced to follow a predetermined pathway along a tunnel in a pyramid of straw bales which, for the life of me, I failed to recognise as quote painting unquote. A week or so previously I had caught a glimpse of an agricultural vehicle negotiating the delivery zone, but had given it no more thought until I found myself crawling back to the roots of my childhood.

'The recognition gap had widened with the incremental advance of the Great Reaper. The halls of our cathedral abound with deprecatory criticisms such as ageing, too far removed from the coalface, not having been touched by the hand of God who coincidentally resides at the Royal College of Art, and much more of that ilk. My self-deprecatory criticism would be too many hours spent in critical management conciliating between the forces of the dependency culture versus the gluttonous ravages of Mammon. But no party seems aware of the futile efforts being made on behalf of appeasement, as intuition is the console of caprice, and why should they in the culture they both propagate and promulgate?

'Then my inner search for a solution as I physically crawled through the dark tunnel was peremptorily met as I unintentionally placed my hand in a dollop of cold glutinous avoirdupois the odour and texture of which reminded me of cow shit.

'My associations were whisked back to childhood: helping in a lean-to corrugated shed euphemistically referred to as the quote milking parlour unquote on a cold dark wet November morning when Gastric our serially insane goat butted me into the gutter containing last night's bowel movements of our cattle. Apart from the discomfort of it all, the mess on my school uniform, and rages of parental admonishment for being stupid enough to allow the goat to express its tendency, the smell of cow shit would linger in my nostrils forever, reinforced by the feel of its texture.

'On clambering out of the straw pyramid my immediate

suspicions were endorsed: the mess on my hands and suit was indeed cow shit: dark olive green/raw umber in colour that the rich grasses in this part of England enable the bovine digestion to manufacture. The texture was consistent with cold vomit that had spent a number of hours idling on the pillow awaiting its creator's return to consciousness.

'As we are discussing an art college undergraduate submission for the qualification of BA (Hons) it is perhaps necessary to differentiate between the colours of cow shit and vomit: cows do not generally habituate Chinese restaurants, and even if it came to pass a cow should dine in the Hoo Flung Dung she would have avoided consuming those indigestible colorants that pillow paintings garishly denote in this crude comparator.

'The nub of the speech is at hand: the trivial act of defacing the principal's dignity was greeted by howls of laughter from tutors and hyena calls from their students. It raises simple and reasonable questions. One, what is the purpose of an art college? If tutors believe a presentation should humiliate the participants then, two, how has it come to pass that playing around with straw and cow shit equates in a degree qualification the work of say, quantum physics or medical neuroscience? As I am very much the product of the system and, indeed, the degree presentation at Nehemiah Institute of Art is an event occurring during my watch, I am exposed to the criticism from others what this speech implies for the sector: mea culpa. Three, what is to be done? Certainly the established structure of HE sector provision renders cumbersome if not unworkable specific financial penalties aimed at art and design. The Privy Council's models of governance ensure direct action would involve many interrelated levels of interest.

'The harrow of time divines a lucid reflection on matters best left alone. Patterns of inflated delusion meander along well-exercised pathways. The artist in early man, fascinated by the impossible, was erroneously convinced that impossibility is an entity that would never muster danger. Impossibility was there for the conquering, for the taking, the spoils for display and posterity. Miraculously, understanding had been undertaken by the universal language of the artefact, ages ahead of the verbal process of monosyllabic grunts. But in spite of there being no pre-ordained agenda, the communication cohered logically within the finite possibilities of the so-called primitive mind. Even when impossible to divine, the entity of impossibility existed for the thinkers of the day.

'Reality, however, was dismally nearer the ordinary, inasmuch as the grasping of abstract concepts would always evade best efforts. The harrow of time rang the knell beyond daybreak, beyond renaissance, but only during the artist's brief visit to these shores. As a consequence of this ungracious mindset the congregation took for granted that challenging the impossible was a normal procedure. We, so-called modern man, assumed the primitive artist's mind operated at a mundane level.

'Notwithstanding reason, impossibility was an objective to be achieved, overcome, utilised, wrung dry. Alas, in the beginning the early artist volunteered a wrong turning. Millennia later, mankind realised these early single-minded thoughts associated with the age of the quote primitive unquote had dramatically peaked at the optimum output of cerebral capacity. The pattern of individual achievement has been in grand decline ever since, to the despairing juncture where, with all of mankind's technological advances, the present-day artist plays with bales of straw and cow shit, and has the affront to call it quote art unquote. The realisation causes time to harrow its lines across mankind's forehead.'

Johannes broke off dictation, sat reflecting.

'No! Bugger it! Leave it at that, I have decided not to deliver this speech to the funding council officers. Why should I do their thinking for them?' whereupon Johannes giggled mischievously.

'Leave it on my e-mail diary, though, Susan. I'll devise a more controversial, more provocative delivery instead. Nobody thinks deeply into what they are doing anymore: they all have off-the-shelf pat answers revolving around political correctness; their own sense of well-being; their latest complexion of the political ideological flavour of the session; their rights; the rights of minority groups; their pretext that they alone are carrying the burden of social responsibility; the latest TV sound bite; the computer-derived image – anything but original thought. We have too many people believing they have a divine right to their government job, to their salary, to their right to shake the governmental money tree, to their job protection, to their future; to hell with them!' and he burst into hearty laughter, still with additives of mischief.

Susan Harefeld looked bemused, only a little, because she had grown sufficiently used to Johannes Taliesin's outbursts over the two years of his occupancy.

'I believe we are at such a sad ebb in society that only provocation will prise people out of their false sense of security. The country is rotting, Susan. No more innovative developments, no more scientific breakthroughs, thanks to the socialism of all party stripes the welfare state is strangling the nation, the press reports with alacrity any mishaps at CERN, but omits to celebrate its groundbreaking research achievements; America is in grand decline as indeed Europe has been for fifty years – and we are leaving innovative inheritance to the Indians, the Chinese, Japanese, South Koreans.

'Our ceiling of achievement in this country is to market, sell and service products and innovations of other nations. These days we own nothing more than a white van and concomitant mentality. Yet we still think we are important! Bloody politicians of all parties jabber on and on, while looking over their shoulders at their masters the media, about nothing more worldly than social trivia, and yet to a man and woman they stoically avoid addressing the major problems confronting our country. If America catches a financial cold, this country's economy bursts like a bubble, because that is all it is: bloody veneer! I see art in the centre of this navel-gazing crucible, playing silly games with cow shit while all the while avoiding big challenges that would demand brain power, hard work and dare I say it – skill.'

'I suppose your recent experiences have triggered this, Principal?' Susan asked.

'May as well have meditations on a hobbyhorse, Susan, the difference my views will make to society. I sometimes wish I could go back to times when one's views were taken seriously,' Johannes avoided answering the question.

'My husband thinks there was never a time when people's views were taken seriously.'

'Perhaps he's right, Susan, perhaps he is right.'

12
Genuflection To Necessity Before
The Altar Of Desire

'LADIES AND GENTLEMEN,' Sir Barcode Cardigan, chairman of the Higher Education Funding Council, rose to introduce Johannes Taliesin. He had a face every aspiring portraitist clambered to draw – linear wrinkles blanketing an angular bone structure, a mixture of the sgraffiti lines of WH Auden and the angular cragginess of Rudolph Hess – in graphite or pen. The face weighed a number of idiosyncratic characteristics that readily forgave marginal inaccuracies, whilst still allowing the artist to claim responsibility for the representation, as when drawing the thin dark fronds of a bare tree, few people's visual acuity is sharp enough to bear accurate judgement.

'Ladies and gentlemen, tonight's guest speaker will discuss developments being undertaken in the art and design sector. In accord with his unusual inclination to surprise he has declined an invitation to forward an abstract of his speech on the grounds that he had not yet written it! As a consequence his diffidence to exposure renders me unable to say anything intelligent in regard to an introduction.'

A burst of knowing laughter greeted Sir Barcode's expendable plaudit.

'Can't work out if they are laughing at Barky's chuckaway, or at us,' Inner Voice enjoyed the circumstance, *'whichever, we don't give a damn.'*

'Other than that I know him only too well. Many years ago

when I was a young visiting consultant at Swansea College of Art on behalf of the textile industry I remember him as a student at that establishment. Although not a student of textiles, he was frequently to be found in the textile studios. At first I quite naturally assumed he was a textiles student, until it dawned on me his presence had something to do with the preponderance of pretty females who populated textile studios in those days!'

A roar of laughter ensued, which to Johannes denoted the lack of gravitas the funding council attributed to art and design. This was most significant, because Johannes would be the first to declare the art and design sector did not deserve to be taken seriously, but in this public forum the levity served to irritate him.

'I cannot decide whether he ploughs a lone furrow because he has a reputation for suffering fools irascibly,' continued Sir Barcode, nailing the coffin of pantomime to the stage floor, 'or that he is irascible because in the main he is obliged to suffer fools. Ladies and gentlemen, it is my pleasure to welcome Johannes Taliesin, chief executive of Nehemiah Institute of Art.'

'Mr Chairman, ladies and gentlemen; thank you, Sir Barcode, for those forgettable words! I well remember you and your visits to that institution: if ever the textiles department was being honoured by a visit by the then Barcode Cardigan the staff would shoo me away, uttering such conflagrations as 'Out of the department, Taliesin, can't have Barky thinking we encourage the likes of you at our table.'

Laughter.

'Atavism is the opium of dreamers,' Johannes continued, 'and I plough that lone furrow because humanity's collective vacuity detracts from engaging with the real challenges of this world.'

Suddenly, silence descended on the audience.

'But I need to put the record straight,' Johannes Taliesin went on, 'my attraction to the textiles department was admittedly the surplus of pretty women, though I must add a second reason, but not of secondary importance: it was the only source of material off-cuts, which ostensibly I begged for use as paint rags, but in reality I used for patching my sole pair of disintegrating trousers. Those were indeed happy days! Thank you for reminding me, Barcode.'

A round of astonished applause and laughter greeted the last remark; conference noting with a smirk that one did not admit poverty unless as a theatrical artificer, and now settled in certain knowledge the repartee had been thoroughly shoehorned into surrealism.

'*On the other hand maybe this crowd of intelligent chimpanzees has recognised a meaning that we had not intended,*' Inner Voice as usual nagging the right hemisphere by its left hemisphere temperance, '*on second hindsight, chimpanzees are clever at shoehorning detritus up their backsides.*'

The applause disgusted Johannes, who stood awaiting silence. The speech he intended delivering could not be placed in a more inappropriate setting.

'*This shower does not take art and design seriously – no! They don't take us seriously! Well, sod that!*'

Johannes experienced the same old sinking feeling that had accompanied him all his life at moments such as this. However, on this occasion his mood was already primed with aggression, so he arrested the slide in a flash of anger and twisted it round as a tool of attack.

'*Let's change our mind!*'

On the spur of that moment, that very moment standing before the lectern on stage at Drapers Hall, Johannes Taliesin changed his mind.

'Mr Chairman, ladies and gentlemen: tonight I am going to ask a few questions,' Johannes began, as he set a course southwards for his abruptly changed plans.

'There! That's done it: as God is in heaven we know this non-speech will end in disaster for us!'

'Question number one,' Johannes dived headlong into his changed agenda, his impetuosity leading the thinking department of brain, 'You are confronted by two versions of the Mona Lisa, one a perfect Sexton Blake right down to brushstroke relief configurations, the other the original by The Boss himself. Given no other references, would you be able to identify the original with an absolute degree of certainty? In order to inject an ingredient of reality into the test, let us say you *must* get it right, as your life depends on it. Let us hope you will never find yourselves in such an impossible conundrum, but nevertheless you are obliged to identify the original.'

Johannes's opener generated a respectable gag.

'That's gagged the bastards, no turning back now.'

Clearly, Sir Barcode Cardigan had not expected this line of delivery. It put him in a frame of lost initiative catching levity thrown back at him. After initiating a jocular introduction he had expected the usual anodyne update regarding sector development, exchange successes with UN-financed Darfur students, grants from China for developing creative tabletop paper tigers, successful Vietnamese share investment of national curriculum furniture design, the establishment of a New Forest wood turning summer school; the setting up of courses in painting for the blind, the development of a theme park for presenting nineteenth-century British needlecraft, and many more blah blah blah droning trivialities that bubbled and frothed in the politically correct social circles of anodyne government art-think. But no – here was a testing challenge no one would find easy to meet.

'Question two,' Johannes continued, deliberately oblivious to the turmoil question one had provoked, 'Do you know how many stations the post-destructive parrot train has halted at on the line to Mediocreville since leaving Jarry's *Ubu roi* at his 1896 presentation? How many of you have bought one-way tickets for that journey?'

Stunned silence. The audience was not sure what Johannes was talking about, which was just as well.

'Question three. How can a working sketch metamorphose into a great work of art even if the artist adds nothing more to it?'

More stunned silence. Some fidgeting.

'Question four,' Johannes began enjoying his colossal cross-tacked *coup de grâce*. 'What is the most effective methodology for saving money?' Johannes paused; scuffles and titters followed.

'No doubt you are going to tell us,' a sour comment sank resignedly.

'Yes, I will answer my own question four,' Johannes replied, smiling maliciously, 'Let us imagine our political masters have commissioned the executive, i.e. the funding council to undertake a major cost-cutting exercise across the art and design sector. Surely many officers of the funding council will have fantasised that scenario, and individually will have arrived at a number of methodologies. You will already be aware the only politically safe methodology for undertaking such a suicidal task would be to apply the same stringent yardstick across all disciplines and subject areas. It would need to be an effective first strike as getting it wrong would spell disaster. What would that yardstick be? Ladies and gentlemen, the task I propose would be to separate desirable provision from the essential and, upon completion, eliminate the former. Of course interest groups, lobbyists, art and design staff, vested interest corporations, establishment aesthetes, fashion fetishists, meat cleavers, dough kneaders and candlestick lobby groups, politicians and emotional gravy-train addicts will fight like ferrets in a bag to prevent their specific hobbyhorse being sent to the knacker's yard. As the project would be a directive by the elected government, the funding council would be obliged to ignore all opposition. It is a question the answer to which so few people are prepared to address: can you separate the essential from the desirable? As a footnote, I have recently begun that task at Nehemiah Institute of Art.

'Question five,' Johannes's intonation indicated this to be the last question, 'this question comes from one who supposedly manages an institution in the art and design dependency culture: the Education Reform Act of 1988 introduced a new funding methodology that has enabled the nation's art and design provision to more than double the places available for undergraduate study. Why, with these additional numbers of supposedly skilled, talented and enlightened young people hitting the market, has the visual environment of the United Kingdom degenerated under the heavy burden of urban malaise, fine buildings and beautiful surfaces scrawled with sgraffiti, and public places heaped with mess, tat and general detritus? Why are our galleries fuller than ever with insubstantial bric-a-brac, elephant dung paintings and shit art to which the self-appointed chatterers clamour to gawp and appease their convoluted justifications? Although possessing a measure of self-deprecation, these questions equally apply to many educational constituencies of the higher education sector.'

Johannes stepped back from the rostrum and, initiating a hint of a bow said, 'Thank you, I rest my case.'

'*Now we've done it. Hope we are not heading back to the bad old days again.*'

'This is off the agenda, if I may say,' a delegate from the council erupted indignantly, 'I thought we were convening to be advised on current developments across funding council provision, which in this speaker's case should address the art and design sector.'

'This is the agenda precisely. You *are* being availed of

developments, such as they are negative and more negative, in the art and design sector,' Johannes replied provocatively.

'Preposterous! How can elimination of provision that is classified as desirable be development? Who is to decide? Will the judgement be objective?'

'Before answering the question, may I proffer two simple metaphors?' Johannes was enjoying the mischief, 'Polishing a surface is development, but effectively the action eliminates the livelihood of the dust hitherto inhabiting that surface; and a further metaphor could be the second law of thermodynamics, which is development, albeit counterintuitive development. But to answer your question more directly, the last part first: in my experience of quangos and their symbiotic relationship with government worthies I have every faith the judgement shall be anything but objective. In my view it would be subjective and politically slanted, and would arrive at an anodyne and fudged compromise, bearing little relationship to either the brief or the fabric of art and design provision at hand. Regardless, it will not matter, because the investigation will drag on for an exceedingly long time, having cost the taxpayer squillions, that the public will have forgotten it was sitting,' Johannes gained in confidence that the conference was playing into his argument, 'which responds to your second question and for the first, well, if we do not yet know what will be deemed desirable, then we cannot debate the consequences of development.'

'Speaker Taliesin has a point, and we must take it seriously,' Adam Krenwinkler, chief executive of the funding council said, as he rose to his feet. He had sat quietly during the opening repartee with Sir Barcode Cardigan, smiling the while. Krenwinkler was an interesting character. He was a thinker who gave the impression he cared no more than where to dine that night. His face gave the impression of having been plucked from 'The Absinthe Drinkers,' although Krenwinkler was an avowed teetotaller. Beneath the surface he would be deeply dispassionate regarding the winners and losers in Johannes's bag of ferrets.

'I agree with Johannes Taliesin's argument,' he said, 'although I would not have presented it as bluntly as he, that provision in art and design – and not exclusively art and design, may I add – has evolved into a form where a truly dependent relationship exists between the perpetrators and its supporters, with both having lost sight of the educational objectives. Too often we accept spurious arguments and succumb to peer group and political pressures when approving new course development; too often we regard the exigencies of audit compliance to be immovable feasts that are implicitly absolute to the fabric of reality; too often we depend on brethren deliberating on their brotherhoods; too often we rubber-stamp continuity without undertaking a referral of formal appraisal; too often we perpetrate self-serving jingoism and, colleagues, too often in education generally we insert our own political hobbyhorse between the mission and its execution. A *nota bene* for Mr Taliesin: no, in all probability I would not be able to save my life in differentiating between the Sexton Blake and the real thing – QED.'

Krenwinkler paused, as was his habit when exercising his chief executive prerogative, waiting for a challenging interjection. None came.

'Huh! No challenge to Krenwinkler: now that's bloody surprising!'

'I believe the speaker's last directive would unleash a battle a little stronger than mere ferrets in a bag,' the chief executive resumed, 'but if it were administered without foul or favour the results, I feel, would be very sobering.'

The hushed reflection aggregated into a gasp.

'But there are rules,' a delegate uttered.

'Yes, I know: but what do we mean when we refer to rules?' Krenwinkler responded, 'Do we mean rules that benefit the administrator? Or do we mean rules that benefit the administrated? Admittedly certain natural rules pertain for the duration of sentient life and maybe beyond, but rules pertaining to the mere circles of man are subject to the grinding wear of time, of appropriateness, of fashions and politics, I should think.'

The while Johannes Taliesin, standing stock on the stage, resigned himself to the consequences of the tempest he had unleashed, and awaited a formulation.

'What the hell – Krenwinkler agreeing with us? Now there's got to be a catch.'

But the formulation when it coalesced exhilarated Johannes, if knocking him a little off guard.

'I propose, Chairman Cardigan, if Johannes Taliesin is bold enough to suggest a culling of provision on the crude basis of differentiating between necessity and desirability then he should front up a commission by the council to produce a framework, without foul or favour, as Adam has suggested,' came from Dennis de Fleetwood, senior secretary for land occupancy.

Another delegate protested, 'But from a thumbnail calculation, I'm sure I'm right in estimating the result of 50 per cent less provision would translate into 25 per cent less real estate occupancy, so using that as a preponderant reference, then approximately 25 per cent of the funding council would disappear accordingly.'

'Oh, trust the Luddites to be still awake!' came an anonymous call.

Sir Barcode Cardigan motioned to the chief executive to join him across the floor. A whispered conversation that everyone could hear was followed by,

'We propose Johannes Taliesin set up a working party which he chairs to construct a framework for investigating on a national basis the viability of differentiating between essential and desirable disciplines in art and design provision within the purview of the funding council,' Sir Barcode Cardigan said, apparently relaxed in the conviction the motion would never come to fruition.

'OK, OK, where's the bloody catch? We don't trust this metropolitan shower an inch.'

'I realise a school of thought can ascribe development to the act of destruction, but these philosophical games have no place in the sterner field of educational provision,' a delegate representing, according to the conference place labels, statistical equalising, snorted indignantly.

'Mr Taliesin's implications are not developments,' said another member of SE, 'dare I say it, they sound more like anarchic deconstruction.'

'Is the proposal seconded?' asked de Fleetwood, ignoring the objections from statistical equalising.

'Yes, I second the proposal,' said David Eckto, head of audit compliance.

'Watch that Eckto character, always in the shadows, turning up when least expected,' Inner Voice jumped with alarm the speed his provocations were taking form.

'Agreed?'

'Agreed, with reservations,' came from the floor.

'Such?'

'Such that the executive be seen to drive the investigation, and the working party instrument determines a funding council majority, and that the concept be debated in council first.'

'God! Catches everywhere! Debated in council first, our ass! Next they will want us to speak to council, huh! They would regret that.'

'Good point; also perhaps speaker Taliesin will be kind enough to address council at its next meeting with more detailed elaborations of his proposals.'

'*Good, we'll give them bollocks!*'

'Good point! Are you in agreement, Mr Taliesin?'

'*Say no.*'

'Yes, it will be a great pleasure,' Johannes hedged, somewhat blown by the readiness at which his flag was saluted.

'I'm sure the chief executive cannot be serious,' said Kylie Protagon, 'it's for the institutions to organise justifications for their courses. It's not our job to engage such subjective matters as desirability: we simply arrange the funding on an unequivocal basis and distribute it accordingly.'

'On the contrary, we have taken a quiescent view of such matters whilst simultaneously maintaining an audit function. Quality control embraces these matters. Besides, a properly conducted survey should be constrained by objectivity alone.' David Eckto supported, never slow in detecting yet another means by which he could aggrandise his empire.

'*Bloody hell! With the likes of Eckto supporting us who needs enemies?*'

'That's how coral reefs used to grow,' someone muttered.

'I feel the majority of delegates are in agreement,' Sir Barcode blithely forced, 'it is only left for council to commission Johannes Taliesin his task, with the provision he addresses full council before embarking on such a path-finding mission. Do you have anything to add, Mr Taliesin?'

'*They've taken our aggro seriously; serve us right – will we ever grow up?*'

Johannes was taken aback the speed at which his provocative questions had been formulated into action. Having applied no thought to his compulsive onslaught on the sector had left himself little wriggle room leave alone escape clauses.

'*Trapped! Hoist by our own bloody petard.*'

Normally issues of similar groundbreaking importance would take at least a dozen lengthy speeches in as many different forums before beginning to take the shape of a woolly working party. Then, three years later following countless inconsequential meetings of said woolly working party, it would be quietly shelved. Obviously, a loaded gun had been sleeping in the funding council awaiting some gung-ho chief executive to come along and pull the trigger.

'*Now it dawns on us,*' was Inner Voice's belated realisation, '*a loaded gun awaiting the moment, just as we awaited the cow-shit moment to initiate a major review at Nehemiah. Bollocked by our own petard! That's why we were invited to speak here tonight. Someone at council must have calculated that we would utter inane rubbish that would play into the assassin's hands. Oh, shit!*'

'I realise this is not a meeting constituted by the board of executives,' Johannes replied after a few dread moments of thought, 'neither is it a council plenary, nor an adjunct to a standing committee empowered to formulate directives on behalf of the council; indeed it is not even an ultra vires factotum of the council.'

He paused, hoping either Chairman Cardigan or Chief Executive Krenwinkler would veto the proposal forthwith. But no such veto came. Johannes was obliged to sink deeper into the pickle of his own making.

'However, if this meeting is construed as having power of attorney to delegate and nominate as it sees fit and, on behalf of the funding council, the power of attorney wishes to take my proposals seriously, I will engage the task and endeavour to deliver a definitive framework to the executive council in brief due course.'

'Thank you, Mr Taliesin,' said Chairman Cardigan, 'we will of course navigate the constitutional terrain to which you have alluded, and we will work together regarding the constitution of the working party and its remit. Move next item.'

The trap was set. Johannes Taliesin would be remembered

for his act of gratuitous dismemberment of a nation's well-established art and design provision.

'*Bloody hell! We can see it now – 'The Taliesin Reforms'. The catch is the inner council of the funding council had already thought out the unthinkable and we became its mouthpiece. Oh, what a naive twat!*' an alarmed Inner Voice panicked, but too late, '*that's the reason we were invited, that's the reason our provocative questions flowed without real dissent; that's the reason it seemed so easy. Time was when every bloody thing was a struggle, but those struggles are nothing compared to what we will have to face. Bloody hell! Why didn't we admit it was all a hoax? Serves us right! Walked into a trap set by the metropolitan buddy club, too bloody naive to see the signs,*' Inner Voice went on and on... as usual after the fact, '*come to think of it, how did we get away with it? Perhaps we should employ a bodyguard – no, get the funding council to employ a bodyguard for us.*'

13

Two Views Of The Same Entanglement

JOHANNES CLICKED THE conference and record buttons, and
dialled.

'Hello, that David Eckto?'

'Speaking.'

'Hello, Johannes Taliesin here, Nehemiah.'

'Oh, hello Johannes, how are you?'

'Top of the world, David. Trust you are OK?'

'Yes, I'm fine. Enjoyed your speech last week, spectacular own
goal if I may say! Everyone here is still talking about it!'

'Yeah, bet you are.'

'I bet they are. All about falling into a trap set by funding
council pygmies. Talking about the own goal, I suspect, but
surely not the subject?'

'What can I do for you?' David Eckto avoided Johannes's
directness. 'Don't tangle with Taliesin when he's in a fractious
mood' must be blue-tacked on every free bit of space at head
office; and the depth-plumbers signal king of the fractious
moods.

'About this inspection at Swansea –'

'Ah, yes, on the 24th.'

'Yes, that's the one, the 24th,' Johannes replied, 'the papers
don't inform me – is anyone accompanying me? Is this another
trap?'

'Not that I know of, Johannes! Regarding assistance, were
you expecting someone from the council to assist you?'

'As bloody usual! Say yes.'

'No.'

'Do you need any assistance? Admittedly, there is what one would describe as strange fruit growing on those trees at Swansea College of Art. I visited the place once and it gave me the creeps. Boy, was I glad to be getting away. But, perhaps I'll come along and give you moral support if you need it.'

'Yes, but I would prefer a nubile blonde as an assistant.'

'Beg pardon, Johannes?'

'Um – I said, many thanks for the offer, David; might take you up on it, but as I see it at the moment I don't think I will need assistance: I'm sure I can cope. You should be aware though that I was a student at the place, albeit aeons ago. I enjoyed myself – at least I think I enjoyed myself – until I was kicked out! But these days I'm not too sure if I was kicked out or if I jumped.'

'Only Johannes Taliesin!' Eckto laughed, 'Even a past student of the college is uncertain of fundamental events that concerned him at the place.'

'Well, I wouldn't put it as dramatically as that. Anyway, about the pre-inspection literature…'

'As you know,' David Eckto picked up, 'an institution under inspection is obliged to provide secretarial assistance, computer space, a private room, and any other facility that will assist in the inspection. We at the council wanted to keep the inspection low key but with a cutting edge, that's why we chose you –'

'Another reason why the buggers invited us to speak.'

'– We feel the less people involved in the inspection proper the better, as there is a strong likelihood you will encounter some difficulties best kept to yourself. Do you follow my drift, Johannes?'

'No.'

'Don't know, David; didn't realise they had *problem* problems there.'

'Yes, there are strange problems there as far as we can gather –'

'*Curiouser and bloody curiouser.*'

'– Your inspection is just the tool; need you to find out… dig around… win over their confidence, that sort of thing. Do you think you can manage it? Council thinks you are the perfect man for the job.'

'*Flattery! Why is the bastard flattering us?*'

'Sure, I'll manage alone. Papers I've got don't name the principal…'

'Well, that's part of the strange set-up. The principal was appointed to the post by a board of trustees through their invoking an ancient pre-war right that apparently precludes reference to the council's guidelines, or any other authoritative body for that matter, and precludes the public recognition of their principal –'

'You must be joking, of course!'

'No, seriously, they –'

'Surely you have the name of the principal?'

'Frankly no, Johannes.'

'*He's got to be playing a game or something.*'

'What!'

'The trustees reserve the right to withhold their principal's name.'

'Invoking an ancient pre-war right that precludes public recognition of their principal, you say; what sort of Mickey Mouse organisation is the council tolerating at Swansea?'

'That's the predicament, I'm afraid,' Eckto sounded abashed.

'Yet they are a constituent member of the funding council, I take it?'

'Yes, Swansea College of Art is a constituent HE member of the council.'

'Just checking the date, David: surprise, surprise, it's not April 1st!'

'Ha ha! Can't blame you,' Eckto responded, 'there is other contentious stuff; no doubt you'll have fun finding out, Johannes. The council believes the principal as such is a technocrat placement, or even a committee of technocrats, which is why no name is declared in official communications. Notice we address all correspondence to the chair of the trustees.'

'And as the trustees are some curious pre-war fiction I take it the funding council reciprocally does not recognise that body?'

'The council has no option but to recognise the trustees, Johannes –'

'– You may as well write to the devil, care of hell,' Johannes interrupted.

'Your scepticism is becoming tiresome, if I may say, Johannes.'

'And you can stuff my collaborative inspection of Swansea, if I may say, David.'

'Er – Johannes, might I respectfully remind you all our conversations are recorded, and there is no way of deleting part or parts –'

'Mine's on record this end as well, David, we all play pygmy games these days; so if you did not understand the message first time – I'm not interested in inspecting Swansea College of Mickey Mouse.'

'I hear you. We will get back to you within fifteen minutes.'

Direct line rang. Johannes pressed 'conference' and 'record', 'Taliesin.'

'Krenwinkler here.'

'Huh.'

'I believe you are encountering difficulty in accepting David Eckto's descriptors of the situation at Swansea College of Art –'

'Of course I am – heavens, they refuse to submit the name

or names of their executive, yet accept funding council monies willy-nilly. Rum goings on.'

'I agree. It needs sorting. We have decided to sort it, and stage one is a visit ostensibly as a formal inspection by you. When you report back from the ground we will have concrete information to take matters further. Are you saying you are not up to the challenge, Johannes?' Krenwinkler was resolute.

'Of course I'm up to the challenge, but we need to clarify the main issue, that is, there shall be no come back on the inspector if matters go pear shape with this Mickey Mouse outfit.'

'Of course, Johannes.'

'Are we understanding each other?'

'Not only are we understanding each other, Johannes, but David Eckto and I, with most likely AN Other, will visit the place in due course. I hope this reassures you.'

'*Say no.*'

'Just about, Adam, but only just about; in which case I will accept the commission provided I can reserve the right to abort at any time I feel the circumstances are beyond acceptable parameters.'

'Agreed; you are in your rights to abort any mission the funding council requests of you. I will hand you back to Eckto,' Krenwinkler sounded calm considering, 'please hold.'

'Johannes? David. Swansea College of Art has invoked a rare legal clause that enables them to take council money while maintaining refusal to supply information on how it is spent,' Eckto breezed on as if words had not been exchanged, 'in the meantime our lawyers are working on it. Their action of course is illegal at Privy Council level, but we are obliged to conduct our business in deference to the smaller miscreant party. The funding council is investigating the college's case without necessarily kicking up a big media fuss, which is precisely what Swansea College of Art would want. That's the crux of your nomination for this inspection – your ability to go native without raising their antipathy to council above the press bar. And we happen to know how you loathe the press.'

'*You bet we loathe the Press.*'

'Excuse me just a sec please, David, got to get a message to my PA… Susan,' Johannes spoke on internal, 'download the main onto an integral, I'll take the HP with me. Did Foster confirm the hotel? Ask him to repeat but a day earlier. Inform the SMs I'm going to Swansea a day earlier, something cropped up. Thanks… Hello, David…'

'Still here, Johannes.'

'What I don't get is the reason the council has reciprocated the non-recognition game. Bit childish of the council, I must say,' said Johannes, still suspicious regardless Krenwinkler's intervention.

'I'm sure you will find out for yourself,' David Eckto replied darkly, 'after a day or so you'll have an entirely different world view of Swansea College of Art.'

'Surely this strange stand-off between the council and Swansea should merit an army of high-powered delegates up front led by Krenwinkler himself, rather than just lowly me.'

'We are working on that. And have every intention that both chairman and Chief Executive Krenwinkler shall pay a visit without prior notice,' David Eckto replied, 'we ran through the scenario of heavy guns recently but came to the conclusion that the opposite would favour both parties, i.e. keep it internal, low profile and any high-profile council visit executed under cloak and dagger without the usual prior notice.'

'*This is surreal,*' Inner Voice whispered.

'What is really going on, David?'

'I'm not at liberty to disclose; sorry, Johannes, I'm aware as an inspector you should be furnished with all outcomes, but they are *sub judice*. All I am able to say at this time is Adam

Krenwinkler and I think you are the right person for the job, horses for courses and all that. But watch how you go and use your inimitable Welsh guile. Report back using the coded channel, OK?'

'*Welsh guile my ass!*' Inner Voice grumbled the normal sceptical expletive.

'Hmph! OK.'

'As I said, I can accompany you; just say,' Eckto reassured.

'I'll call for your help on the coded channel.'

As Johannes drove to Swansea his thoughts flitted about the prominent matters of academic concern – two years' of striving to effect a change of culture at Nehemiah was beginning to return some movement, but arrived at through belligerent intellect: the consultation process succeeded only in promulgating the old failed systems much loved by the chatterers wallowing in their own detritus. The refectory problem was a fine example of imploring the uncommitted to engaging the challenge of rendering an enterprise viable, but who have no more intention than the man in the moon of rising to the challenge, a predicament which theoretically could persist to eternity provided someone continued to shake the money tree; its closure and inevitable redundancies a most regrettable outcome – odd, thought Johannes, how supposedly well-educated intelligent people love to hate the manager who resolves a running sore which their persistent lack of engagement had allowed to slide to an irrecoverable state; but there again, a well-established element of perverse human behaviour was for a people who were liberated hated their liberators.

Being landed with chairing the Desirable-Essential Survey of Art and Design Provision in Higher Education through his incautious 'speech' before council at Draper's Hall would prove to be interesting. Then, more apposite, there was Eckto's enigmatic warning regarding the strange relationship between the funding council and Swansea College of Art. What was he letting himself in for? All these matters were background but, due to his mixed feelings about Swansea, a seemingly innocuous folk story pushed itself to the fore, stimulated by the return after many years to his old stomping ground.

It was the salutary tale of a young man name of Llewellyn Llawgyfes who, upon journeying into Salem, famously walked back into the past. Llewellyn experienced the drapes of atavism descending from every quarter like a cold shower of rain: the further he walked the more readily the environment aged, falling opposite backwards, historical metaphor hanging in gloomy shrouds. Yet Llewellyn remained untouched by the affair around him. According to the folk tale, the mystery deepened, for Llewellyn's walk took him back through ages in which the smart dwellings of Salem turned to crofters' hovels, in turn metamorphosing into windswept heath.

Johannes shook his head and concentrated on driving. He had had a stressful time at Nehemiah of late; and no doubt more stress to come at Swansea; surmounting the unnecessary obstacles had brought shades of nostalgia hitherto confined to the dog kennel of his memory. The information both Eckto and Krenwinkler imparted did not fill him with eagerness to engage the official inspection at Swansea College of Art.

But it was the embarrassing cow-shit incident that triggered the sequence of knee jerks, first to his senior managers, then his too-clever desirable-essential delivery to the council conference that boomeranged to deliver more responsibility on his shoulders. How was he going to manage the project with his fellow art and design chief executives? Surely the council would have informed them by now.

'Thank God we have an appointment at Swansea, conveniently tucked out of the way for a few days, even if the inspection –'

For the time being the desirable-essential survey would have to await resolution of a different form. The current problem needing attention was Swansea.

Johannes pondered the most advantageous way of tackling the Swansea enigma. Should he take a softly-softly approach, or a head-on confrontation with the principal and his staff from the start? Johannes's favoured method was to give a touch of the slant-in method from the side, sort of softly intrusive; but of late he had adopted the blunt head-on methodology, which delivered results, albeit sometimes in the proverbial deep water. Maybe a mixture of the old softly-softly Johannes with a swipe or two of the new aggression would be expeditious for this unknown element. Notwithstanding, there were inspection protocols to be adhered to, of which Johannes was fully conversant.

'Perhaps the council will ask us to stay there as long as it takes to sort the mess out, like a hundred years…' Inner Voice wishfully thought a wonder.

Johannes drove down Jersey Marine, with Kilvey Hill to his right, the oil storage tanks to the left, through the suburbs of Port Tennant and St Thomas and over the Tawe Bridge into Swansea. Like Llewellyn Llawgyfes he, too, experienced a sense of atavism coming down like a shower of rain. His spirits were characteristically anticipatory, returning to a city where he had lived and loved all those years ago. Switching on the car's satnav, he headed for the Dragon Hotel the funding council had booked for him, and was overwhelmed by a sensation that he had come home. Nothing had changed: it was akin to Llewellyn Llawgyfes entering Salem.

At first appearance everything about Swansea College of Art appeared as it had all those years ago. The wide pavement outside the college was still adorned with an avenue of pruned limes. The faded Windsor blue double doors had not been changed, even the Norman arch above showed no signs of weathering. Each panel of the doors was centred with a brass bolt head, as polished as they had been those many years ago. The edges of the woodwork were rounded off, indicating over-painting techniques were being repeated as usual. The two giant brass doorknobs were as ever highly polished; Johannes half expected Cornelius the caretaker of his student days all those years ago to appear with a giant cloth to polish the doorknobs to a mirror.

The dressed stone steps leading up to the large doors gave the appearance of eternity, unchanged from all those years ago, maybe more worn, but it was hard to tell. One half door was open, as welcoming as they were when Johannes was a student at the college. Little had changed in the thirty-five or so years since he had been a student at the place. It was all very comforting. Johannes lingered, drinking in the visual atavism, but paradoxically anticipating the strange politics that awaited him inside. He held deep misgivings as to why the funding council stoically refused to recognise the establishment.

'Better go in. Sooner done the better.'

Something – almost imperceptibly – something shifted: not quite physical, perhaps more entangled with metaphorical. Johannes having been momentarily lost in the atavism of old times allowed a whiff of dream, perhaps anticipatory imagination, to smear across his shift. Then it was gone.

The hallway was disconcertingly devoid of students, unlike Nehemiah's lively entrance with its students' to-ing and fro-ing, using the place as a *treffpunkt*. The broad stone staircase rising up to the main college was similarly quiet. Johannes recalled vivid memories of his student days, of climbing these stairs in so many different moods and fashions. But now atavism pressed heavily as he climbed the stone staircase; once upon a time he had carried a distended cardboard suitcase filled with cork and mediocre models up these very same stairs to an interview, but today he swung a heavy business-like laptop briefcase with an entirely different purpose at hand. An item of separate genesis struck Johannes as seemingly odd: no lift. These days of the rampant health and safety executive an educational establishment would never be allowed to ignore its commands to install a lift; after all, the cavernous stairwell built in generous Victorian proportions lent itself admirably to despoilment by the health and safety vandals. He made a mental note in the event some pygmy or other should raise the subject.

Eventually reaching the landing he remembered so well with its magnificent replica of Michelangelo's David still in place, he turned through a set of sprung doors, the very same doors he had pushed through so many times all those years ago. Everything looked so familiar. During his student times there was a lack of directional advice, and surprisingly the lack persisted. Visitors to the institution then and now were expected to know their destination. Fortunately, Johannes knew the main corridor led off the landing, and halfway along that corridor he would encounter the principal's office, hopefully at the same orientation it had occupied all those years before.

Johannes was about to enter the Windsor blue door when it creaked open before him and a female slipped out, dressed the part. The girl had assembled herself charmingly in 1960s fashions, which resonated with Johannes's student days. She mewed a timid greeting, and passed on further up the stairway. Intrigued by the focus of atavism Johannes wistfully stared as she climbed further up the stairs – when his mobile rang, jerking him away from the ghost.

'Taliesin.'

'Ah, Johannes, Eckto here,' a thin broken voice tinned out.

'Hello, David; what's the problem?'

'No prob… I thought… near… join…'

'David, lousy reception. Did I make out you are joining me here?'

'You… yes… I… noon.'

'David, can't make any sense at the moment. Call you back on a landline soon, OK?'

'… danger.'

'What?'

'You… m…'

The connection went dead.

Until that broken moment his return to Swansea College of Art had been seductively relaxing; the hectic events of the past few days seemingly a hundred years away. But the broken conversation with Eckto had put a new complexion on the day, especially the word 'danger'.

'*Could have been part of a longer sentence like 'as you are in danger of enjoying yourself if left alone council has ordered I should join you and spoil things'. Or it could have been 'Because of your irascibility council has decided there is a danger you might put the cat among the pigeons, so I have been ordered to join you to ensure confidentiality'. Yes, hopefully that's it.*'

Instead of awaiting access to a landline, Johannes resolved to return the call on his mobile.

'Dr Eckto's office,' came the clear response.

'Hello, Taliesin here; is David there?'

'No, Mr Taliesin. He left a cryptic message for me he would be away, change of plans.'

'I've just had a call from him, obviously from his mobile: do you have his mobile number? Reason I request it is because reception mobile to mobile here is so bad our signal went dead and my phone did not pick up his number.'

'No, sorry Mr Taliesin, Dr Eckto keeps his mobile number strictly private.'

'*A likely story.*'

'Yes sure, that's what he told you to say. Thank you.'

Unable to fathom it out properly, Johannes left it at that, and pushed through the swing doors into the corridor.

An aura of deserted sepia pervaded the corridor's history, the flags of age silently sucking at each hollow, wowing back in pulses. He automatically looked up to where a clock had hung all those years ago during his student days: the same old clock was still there, tick-tocking 9.25. Well past the time when students should have been crowding about, heading for studios and lectures, gossiping, giggling, hurrying. Or, perhaps a new regime determined students reported to the studios much earlier, and they were already at work. So far the only student was the ghost on the landing.

Johannes had arrived back in the familiar main corridor of Swansea College of Art; the corridor he had grown so fond of long ago, the corridor to which he had formed a personal attachment. Circumstances had delivered him back to the cosy womb of his days of student irresponsibility. From the windows in the corridor he could see the familiar Swansea roof-scape scrubbed by the familiar Swansea weather. But the corridor itself was deserted and uttered a sepia wash over the painting of his memory. Familiar smells of linseed oil and turpentine spirit mixed with carbolic soap loitered their welcome in the air.

The strong atmosphere of atavism pervaded; so strong that he imagined the feeling of youthfulness all those years ago. Did he jump or was he pushed?

'*Don't start that again! We've buried that... now we are principal of Nehemiah Institute of Art,*' Inner Voice admonished.

His imagination was taking an absent ride without leave; it was difficult to avoid the present morphing with his past.

'*We must pull ourselves together, important official inspection business afoot, there might really be danger ahead as Eckto warned.*'

Johannes put his wild imagination down to the confluence of exceptional circumstances: a stressful week back at Nehemiah, together with the nagging mystery of the funding council's decision to ignore their protocols regarding conflict of interest by earmarking him as the official inspector of an institution he had previously attended as a student.

'Surely this overlap encourages pygmies to squeal vested interest, bias, conflict of buggeration and etc.'

Johannes's dreams flowed.

'God has been at pains to explain the lack of reference in clear timing,' Inner Voice prattled, 'This is due to an art college clouding the scene by superimposing the principal's irritation on numerous paintings of the same corridor. We are a stage prop experiencing at first hand God's conundrum that artists and their paraphernalia of galleries and art colleges and easels and models and paints originated as a sneeze that was accidentally programmed into the soup of the Third Day. This is one of two views of the same delusional entanglement.'

Johannes's thoughts were confused by emotions of nostalgia and atavism as he ventured a little further down the silent corridor…

'Fortunately for artists,' Inner Voice continued the deconstructed prattle, 'Mrs God prevailed upon her husband not to delete the sneeze, as she loved obtuse jokes. God was extremely pressed for time, so he could not engage in protracted reasoning with his beloved, and absentmindedly acceded to her wishes. What really compounded the creation of artists blunder was that God had had an improved design for galactic drains east of Andromeda that the sneeze inextricably bound into the artist bit.'

He was outwardly serene, inwardly taking two views of the same entanglement.

'Henceforward into eternity God will associate his improved drain design with artists, an affliction God feels is most unfairly deserving of drains, which he vows to amend in the Seventeenth Edition,' Inner Voice was no compensation for Johannes's interregnum of control.

Proceeding yet further down the corridor, Johannes's old fears and joys flooded back. But Inner Voice engaged deep denial.

'We should realise the implication of God's shrug given the artistic culture his accidental sneeze has evolved into. Even his junior angels stepping out of line advised it would have been better to have deleted the lot, new improved drain design for east of Andromeda notwithstanding, and started all over again without artists, even though this might have temporarily upset his wife, who would have joined the Lysistrata Women. As God had allowed the error to remain he effectively washed his hands of drains. Therefore, heaven does not possess the necessary time reference for accurate navigation back to our old alma mater in order to conduct an official inspection for the bloody funding council.'

Any old fable in a storm. So, instead of an official inspection in the now, Johannes stood in the then, playing wall-to-wall Llewellyn Llawgyfes in the main corridor of Swansea College of Art. Instead of the irascible principal of Nehemiah Institute of Art, Johannes would conduct the official inspection in a different entanglement. Be these matters as they may, he was back in the heaven of a familiar environment, with the added bonus that he could have a second go at making a mess of things.

Johannes strode down the empty corridor, looking for the principal's office. It was exactly where he had left it: nothing had changed. Before making himself known to the principal, Johannes used his prerogative as official inspector to take a cursory look about. He looked in at the Fine Art Department, his old department where he had studied on the painting special course. The main studio, known in his student days as the Antique Studio, screened off from the department's entrance, was still in operation. A notice hung at the entrance denoting 'model posing, no entry to unauthorised persons' and the familiar gentle sounds of graphite and brushes working their sweeps could be heard beyond the screen. Students were already busy at their stations. Although Johannes was an authorised person, in deference to the college protocols he withdrew.

Towards the end of the corridor, beneath the loft where he had spent many happy hours contemplating the meaning of perspective, he turned right into a passageway; after walking for some distance he arrived at the sculpture department. Opening the main studio door, he looked in: students were busy at their tasks. Plaster of Paris had already greeted him on the passage floor, but now it overwhelmed everything and everybody. Sculpture tables stood around randomly, upon which rested clay maquettes; some under their plastic covers. Large standing objects cluttered the alcoves; part-welded ironwork lurched drunkenly up the distant walls, and girders twisted by giant machinery entertained the far regions of the cavernous studio workshop. It reminded Johannes of his student days when he was ejected from a specialist sculpture group by common academic consensus on the grounds of three-dimensional ineptitude. His favourite memories were frozen in time, plastered all over the sculpture department. Not being able to bear the atavism any longer, he retreated.

Returning in the direction of the principal's office, he called by the Fashion Department. Upon entering he disturbed several fashion students working intently at the cutting tables. They, similar to the ghost girl at the swing doors, wore 1960s clothes; obviously the flavour that was going around the Fashion Department at the moment. They looked up as he entered; one made a lunge for her off-cuts: the others looked through him, and returned to their tasks.

'Remember? They looked through us all those years ago.'

Johannes retreated to the sanctuary of the corridor. It was now filled with students; drinking coffee, lounging against walls, stooping on benches, smoking, sprawling across the corridor floor. In an art college old habits are passed as a baton from year to year, cohort to cohort. Of course, Johannes was all too familiar with the poses struck by art students, but his commission preoccupied him: the smoke-filled air was a harkback to old times, yet the college together with its endless corridor was a public place, so how could smoking be permitted in the corridor?

'Surely, management must be aware of the Act banning smoking? Eckto was right. Ye Gods! No lifts, smoking in a public corridor, no facilities for food consumption – this report will be easy to compile.'

No emergency exits had been provided; worse, no exit directions were posted; no ventilation apparatus installed; the highly polished floor presented a slip hazard considering drinks were being consumed; seating for the cafe was limited resulting in students having to sit on the floor, presenting an egress hazard in the event of emergency evacuation, and so on – the health and safety report would be extensive, and so far Johannes had given cursory inspection to the corridor and stairwell only.

Shadows morphed with memories. Johannes walked off down the corridor in the direction of the door marked 'Principal'. A name was attached, but it had faded to unreadable. He knocked briskly. Failing to hear a response, though the buzz in the corridor could well have masked one, he sat down on a bench opposite, and waited. Johannes mused on his circumstances, deep in thought.

'There is truth in our life somewhere,' Inner Voice reasoned, *'everything we have attempted so far is unconvincing. Attempting to list our positive achievements would be futile as no examples come to us. But on second thoughts we don't want another go at it, not if it means meeting the same old shower again. Perhaps if we were to repeat the exercise from a time of our choice, it could be a solution, perhaps, but then again...'*

Johannes rose and knocked again, again returning to the bench to wait.

'No! We would meet a different shower equally as self-centred, conceited, superficial and amusing as the ones we have already met on this nine-o-nine to nowhere. Or would they be the same precisely? We bet they would, shit sticks to blankets, especially if the nine-o-nine goes through the station of art education again. Perhaps we alone could be different. That's an interesting idea, must write our memoirs on that theme one day. But not now, now to business –'

Inner Voice was freewheeling about the waiting space.

'Eckto was right, something strange about this place. Anyway, we now have an official inspection to undertake, and official report to write and, back at the ranch, prepare documentation for our working party on the desirable-essential survey.

'That will bring the walls of Jericho tumbling down. Joshua's fight is nothing compared to this pickle. But perhaps it has already happened; like one of God's cleverer laws determines no one will ever know, not even us, who are fortunate enough to be in the now but standing in the then.'

'Min.'

An ethereally distant, hazy blue voice called from behind the door. It could have come from behind any one of the many other doors leading off the corridor, or high up behind a fluted column, beyond a hidden architrave. The invitation to enter had been so distant, knitted into Johannes's daydream confusions, yet wafting around in the bustle of the corridor. He wondered if the sound could have been yet another onomatopoeic so regularly encountered in busy art college corridors, lost in the general mindless yelp and squeak. Or, perhaps it was a further example of…

'We must be on our guard at all times! Wonder what Eckto meant by danger?'

'COME IN!'

A voice, surely belonging to the principal, called from beyond the closed door.

Johannes entered the principal's office; he had reached the apogee of his journey. Walking through the portals and concentrating on the purpose of his mission, Johannes deftly off-loaded the baggage of his background.

'We need to inspect the institution's provision, to covertly investigate its reluctance to adhere to funding council financial regulations with regard to the funding methodology, and identify reasons why the institution sees fit to ignore council's procedure for correspondence generally and audit specifically, as well as comparators for peer group achievement, together with the health and safety transgressions. Phew! Almost overwhelming, but nothing to intimidate us; we can do it!'

Johannes entered, displaying the air of authority and dignity that the task of official inspector for the funding council demanded. To be selected by the council to undertake such a delicate inspection should only be interpreted as an honour.

'Honoured and put-upon!' Inner Voice exclaimed, *'because they don't have the courage to investigate this place themselves.'*

Being a principal himself encouraged him to entertain the delusion that he could handle the situation. Shadows continued to morph into memories. The coincidences would explain themselves in due course, a matter of smoke and mirrors, which were too far beneath his dignity to take seriously. Walking into the principal's office of his alma mater was a squeeze of toothpaste.

'A bonfire of smoke, lots of cracked mirrors, and lakes of toothpaste,' Inner Voice sighed.

The principal's office was not how he remembered it; but there again, over three decades had elapsed since he last saw it. He was surprised to find the old building still occupied, leave alone the corridor and the principal's office in the same place. But, more precisely, the room was not what Johannes had become accustomed to expect of a principal's office, as now memories morphed into shadows. It was devoid of furniture save a small scruffy table directly adjacent the door, accompanied by two scruffy chairs; in the far left-hand corner beneath one of the large windows stood two elaborate Chinese silk privacy screens, the Victorian variety, of which he had some vague blind-sight recollection of having been seen somewhere before. Obviously they fenced off an activity the current principal chose to keep private from official inspections. Certainly the principal of Johannes's student days –

'KW Hancock, no less, fine draughtsman and painter, we remember.'

– was a fine painter who, through the force of his painterly prowess, had persuaded his office to metamorphose into an atelier for the purpose of painting in oils. Those were happy days.

Johannes's attention was attracted to the bare floor, which imposed itself audibly the moment he stepped inside, individual boards competing with each other their creaking signal of his presence. The desolate floor declared this could not possibly be a principal's office.

'Here we go again! Entered the wrong bloody room,' Inner Voice grumbled.

Turning to leave, Johannes was arrested by a voice calling from behind the screens.

'Be with you in a moment!'

'Bloody hell! Someone in here after all; that's where the "come in" had come from,' Inner Voice adjusted.

Perhaps it was indeed the right room, and Johannes was relieved that some life existed in it, albeit behind Victorian privacy screens. Assuming the barely furnished room to be the principal's office, it was little wonder the funding council held reservations. He adjusted his thoughts: this must be an adjunct of the grand set-up, the modus operandi adopted by the college cascading from the principal down, closer to Kafka than Dominique Ingres, fluid in the dimensions of illusion.

He waited, looking around, counting the moment. A secondary furtive examination confirmed the office was indeed without furniture, save the scruffy little table and refectory chairs. Obviously the college was experiencing hard times, and the principal had been obliged to auction off the elaborate stuff that existed during the olden days of KW Hancock. As the institution was ostensibly an independent corporation enjoying charitable status, its governance was free within the guidelines laid down by the act of incorporation to auction whatever chattels it saw fit to maintain its educational provision at the required level.

'*We have the opportunity to endorse that venture later; must ensure no salient point is overlooked,*' Inner Voice readily assumed the mantle of Funding Council Official Inspector.

The bare floorboards were heavily eroded, giving the impression of being worse for a hundred years' wear, perhaps more; they had the appearance of recently applied raw umber stain, no doubt in preparation for the official inspection. Several of the floorboards had lost their knots, exposing empty holes simulating eyes staring darkly at Johannes. It was difficult to ignore the eyeholes: they reminded Johannes of a poem he had submitted to an eisteddfod poetry competition long, long ago at his school in Aberystwyth. Entitled *All the Eyes of the Floor Were Watching*, it was unplaced in the final adjudication. The unplaced poem however elicited a comment from adjudicator Rev. Illtyd ap Iago that a particular submission by an entrant nom de plume 'Nostradamus' had both startled and horrified him, not simply due its inherent clumsiness, but more its content of surrealist horror from one so young. All the eyes of the floor were watching, regardless he was an official inspector.

In a latter-day fantasy Johannes had the Rev. Illtyd ap Iago replaced by Will Self. Adjudicator Self would have laughed all the way through the reading. The poem would have still returned an unplaced status, but at least the audience would have been entertained. Alas! Such great promise had escaped the cranium of earthly delights.

Johannes surveyed the walls: once upon a faded time lime green emulsion had come into contact with them, but now exhibited sure signs of age, crazed, sinking into the wall. The high ceiling boasted a decoration that defied exact analysis, sort of eggshell drift crossed with sickly magnolia. Lighting paraphernalia hung centrally, thickly coated in magnolia, with a sheet of cartridge paper acting as shade attached to one side of its chain suspender. The door and its surrounding woodwork were painted the ubiquitous Windsor blue; the same colour, Johannes recalled, that was fashionable during his student days. Museum piece sit-up-and-beg water-heated radiators had had the same lime green treatment as the walls, but owing to the heat and proximity to hot water that obviously leaked from the safety valves from time to time the emulsion displayed the ravages of fade in different hues of drowned singularity.

Too high up on the wall to the right of the entrance door hung a framed print under clouded glass of the Thames below Bermondsey by Ruskin Spear. The edges of the print had begun to develop the familiar contagion that gum Arabic constituent in the paper manifests when rebelling against a damp atmosphere by breaking out in a brown rash. The atmosphere in the principal's office did not appear to be damp, however. Rather the opposite, for it was stiflingly warm with the radiators blasting out their heat, reminiscent of the heat necessary in life classes. Atavism and nostalgia flooded back, for Johannes so loved the original Spear oil painting that was displayed at the Glynn Vivian during his keen painting special days, and the heat of the life class atmosphere was for him a welcome environment when memories of the past morphed into shadows.

'*Sigh,*' Inner Voice sighed a nostalgic wordless flutter.

In order to maintain the feeling of importance Johannes fell to pondering the origin of the Spear print dampness. During moments of crisis as a young man he would seek solace by analysing the minutiae of a trivial item through his theory of everything contained within a thimble. Now, as principal of Nehemiah Institute of Art and in his capacity as official inspector for the funding council, standing in an uncarpeted office of scant furniture being made to wait by the incumbent principal, the feeling was no different. The atavism recalled those days of continuous crisis when brief moments of relief were spent dwelling upon trivia.

'*If we are dwelling on our circumstances, it's too late,*' Inner Voice warned, '*as we have off-loaded them into history, and bloody good riddance.*'

So Johannes brusquely shepherded his will away from daydreams to the mission at hand. This is what he must stoically contend with, not a case of wish, but a case of purpose and need.

'*Why invite us in only to ignore us thereafter? This will go in the report,*' Inner Voice was officially losing patience.

The old bogey of dither versus impulse had never deserted Johannes, regardless his worldly experiences as principal of these and those institutions, or holding the honour of official inspector of Swansea College of Art.

'*We should speak out... don't give him much more time,*' cursed Inner Voice.

'I say,' Johannes fairly commanded, 'is anyone here to meet with me?'

'Beg your pardon?' replied a voice coming from behind the screens, 'I will be with you in a moment. Please take a seat.'

'The insult of it! This refectory seat is no doubt covered in oil paint,' Inner Voice snorted, *'the occasion will even out precisely in accordance with the Nineteenth Law of Thermodynamics.'*

The tall sash windows were bare, their panes dusty on the exterior, but the lower reaches washed by blown corrugated rain, stony faced. Further up, the glass was untouched by window cleaner or Swansea's rainy nature, owing to the massive arches their heavy protruding capstones, Victorian embellishment, neoclassical architecture on the outside, masking daylight for the inside. The border between touched and untouched speckled by the rigid face of watermarks.

Across the road the Glynn Vivian Art Gallery displayed its beautiful facade and leaded roof. Fond memories flooded back of countless student visits to the gallery. Above and beyond the Glynn Vivian's roof, higgledy-piggledy terraced houses rose up Mayhill, tier on tier. High up and far away a little walled garden contained a washing line on which clothes clapped their hands with glee in the strong maritime wind.

Standing on the bare floorboards in the bare room, awaiting the principal to conclude his whatever task behind the screens, Johannes's otherwise optimistic mood was overwhelmed by one of bare sadness. To break the spell, he clomped and creaked across the bare floorboards to the windows in a manner rightfully begetting an impatient inspector. The sills were high and slanting; he was just able to see over them to the street below.

Next he clomped across the bare boards to the screens and in turn submitted them to an examination. They were delicate affairs of Chinese bamboo print, faded black on a fine sepia fabric with arched wooden tops, brass hinges fixed by brass screws, greening. Their aroma drifted as model's perfume, evocative in heady curvature of ancient balms, peddling wondrous stories they had discreetly shielded during a life long of screening due.

Finally Johannes returned with unsubtle deliberation to the table, uttering obvious creaking steps. His heavy briefcase, loaded with documents and his laptop, had not ceased reminding him its weight so, placing it with relief on the scruffy table, he stretched life back into the fingers of his left hand.

'Please take a seat, be with you in a moment,' a curt request squeezed through the Victorian screen.

The principal's room seemed to be in the final stages of abandonment, but this state was difficult to ascertain with any degree of accuracy. Along with the aroma of fresh wood stain, all the familiar unguents of oil painting – linseed oil, Scandinavian turpentine spirit and the medium of expensive oil paint – floated across from the region of the screens.

'All the old flavours; bet the principal is painting behind those screens. The old oils are the best.'

Johannes recalled his time when, as a student at Swansea College of Art, he and his colleague students were never sure if the then Principal KW Hancock was moving in or out of his atelier, as there was always activity of furniture coming and going. KW Hancock had had a reputation for being a little eccentric, but his magnificent artistic ability amply compensated this minor detraction.

'Wonder why we in turn have not become eccentric during our years as a principal? Perhaps we've plenty of time yet to fulfil that teapot.'

To be confronted so starkly by past memories the bare office conjured, boasting its Victorian screens masking a corner was atavism of a grand disorder that in all probability had been orchestrated by the incumbent and his staff. Certainly the situation could not have transpired without the interference of these people. No magic sleight of hand, or trick by an oily mechanic could have dealt such a unique circumstance.

But Johannes was losing patience and was about to abandon his imposition as the subject of an exercise in applied insult –

'Conjugate the verb to humiliate! We are losing patience,' glowered Inner Voice,

– to seek the general administration office instead when suddenly low, confidential tones were heard behind the screen. Obviously, there was more than one person! Johannes adjusted his listening. Perhaps a personal assistant was there? No, the principal had not been dictating or uttering any other form of business; besides, the silence had lasted too long.

'Perhaps the rebel trustees are holding a full board meeting,' Inner Voice mocked.

It occurred to Johannes that whomsoever had been occupying the same cramped zone behind the screens had so far observed total silence.

'Trappist trustees,' Inner Voice continued the mocking mode.

Calling upon his experiences over the decades of eccentric painter principals, he concluded the other person could be no other than a model; otherwise the accompaniment for whatever purpose would have been around the shabby table.

'Amazing!' Inner Voice piped, *'in this age of political correctness! Must mention it in a roundabout way in the report.'*

In this age of political correctness, it seemed to Johannes, surely the person behind the screens was the principal, working with his model in a designated office that is otherwise devoid of furniture: too far-fetched to be real! Where are the watchdog tyrants of political correctness? Surely it was not beyond the bounds of their tyrannical imagination to conjure an allegation that would nail him? If, as principal of Nehemiah Institute of Art, he were to entertain the notion of painting from a model in the privacy of his office the nosy academic pygmies would have wet their pants with pleasure at the thought of reporting him to some or other government agency.

'No, keep the pose. I'll finish this passage,' the assumed principal's gentle mutter drifted from behind the screens.

Johannes gave a start of confirmation.

'Aha! We bloody-well guessed so – he is working with a model behind those screens!'

Then the voice called out, loudly,

'Who is it? What is your business?'

'Astonishing way to address an inspector!' Inner Voice gasped.

'Johannes Taliesin, chief executive of Nehemiah Institute of Art; I presume you are the principal of this college, and I trust you are prepared for my visit this day. As you no doubt will have been informed by the funding council I have been commissioned to undertake the official inspection of this college,' Johannes spoke loudly into the empty space of the office, his voice tinged with irritation, 'I have waited long enough; I would be obliged you present yourself before me.'

A long silence ensued. Johannes had delivered a moment of professional reality that placed a perspective on the waiting shenanigans. Additionally, although Johannes did not care, the principal's project had been interrupted. No references could ascertain the greater concern. The dead space of silence seemed to last an age, but in all probability the whole waiting experience had lasted just a handful of seconds. Regardless, the Woody Allen quote wriggled into the rarefied atmosphere,

'Eternity lasts a very long time, especially towards the end,' Inner Voice had a knack for introducing irrelevances during moments of high tension. The notion expanded its triviality.

'Which Taliesin?' the principal broke the silence.

This struck Johannes as an odd question to ask a fellow principal/official inspector, especially as it had to mount the handicap of the Victorian screens. Regardless, the importance of an inspection transcended the inspector's name.

'*What the hell! Does it really matter which Taliesin?*'

'Johannes Taliesin,' Johannes repeated deadpan, 'and I would appreciate an audience with you as soon as possible as I have a busy schedule ahead.'

Another silence. For reasons beyond Johannes's immediate grasp the principal seemed reluctant to relinquish the anonymity the screens afforded him.

'What did you say was your business?'

This was too much!

'To repeat: no doubt you will have received papers from the funding council relevant to my visit. Could we please get started?' the principal's obfuscation was having a deleterious effect on Johannes's patience.

'*We'll definitely put this in our report.*'

At last the information appeared to break through the screens and present itself to the principal. Brushes were sluiced in a turpentine bath. From experience Johannes knew the action was being undertaken in an irritable fluster. The swilling lasted for ages as if it were a demonstration regarding the proper treatment of brushes.

'You may take a short break,' he muttered sotto voce.

'*The gall to be painting from a model the day an official inspection is starting!*'

The confounded sluicing continued. Waiting had become a major task in itself. So many years had elapsed since Johannes was a student at Swansea; he was all too aware he had experienced half a biblical lifetime since leaving, yet evidence of the effluxion of time mysteriously evaded him. He was reminded of the world of particle physics, a subject that had always fascinated him, although he was hopelessly out of his depth with the associated mathematics. At the awesomely small scale of subatomic particles no matter how prolonged and careful the observation of the quantum mechanics, no indication of an arrow of time could be discerned. A similar aura seized him at the present moment, except this was happening at the human scale.

'I shall be back shortly,' the principal spoke to whomsoever was with him. The screens wobbled and a hitherto concealed door materialised, through which the principal emerged, wearing a paint-spattered smock and a heavy scowl; he was wiping his hands agitatedly on a dapper rag.

What a difference the painted imagination makes: the paraphernalia of Boss furniture, a Giorgio Armani suit, Jasper Collins slip-ons, desktop PC, clipped mobile toys, wireless to computer and satellite, monitor tuned to FTSE, coded bourse bells link-up, strategically placed red plastic briefcase, accoutrements Venage rather than equipment functional; immensely expensive bric-a-crap vying tasteless junk for desktop prominence. All making carefully chosen socio-political statements of the New Principal, and to hell with the values of art education. As God intimated witheringly to Johannes in yet another illusion:

'Artists live the delusion they are bigger than art, and I have contrived humanity a weakness to suffer belief in them.'

Long ago in Johannes's student days, the old principal at Swansea College of Art threw political correctness out of the window. His refreshing incorrectness was in your face. His indefatigable striving to promote his art rather than himself was a superb example of self-effacement; the principal's self-centred students were shamed into saluting their role model. He practised his genius by painting studies of the female nude, and if you did not like the classical values, bugger off and take your masks of socio-hypocrisy with you. If you cherished the values of skill and dedication, take heed and learn.

For Johannes the clashing of the two cultures was an

extraordinary illusion, an exhilarating breath of fresh air after his adventures during half a lifetime. After the pretence and hypocrisy over many decades, the old principal's values were the standards Johannes had held dear, but as a student he had been too psychologically weak to declare them and too mediocre a painter to emulate them. At Swansea College of Art all those years ago he had been too clumsy to communicate his admiration for the principal's draughtsmanship. But in the ensuing decades Johannes's insignificance had assumed the mask of an arrogant clown who –

'YOU!'

Upon seeing Johannes the principal's features had sprung into recognition mode, quickly followed by elevations of horror. His roar filled the room, causing the door to rattle, or it could have been people passing in the corridor outside. Be the cause as it may, the roar contained the quintessence of mystery.

'*Watch out, this bugger doesn't like inspectors, or perhaps he thinks he knows us, which could be worse.*'

Upon seeing at last the owner of the voice from behind the screens, Johannes saw an apparition from the past phase into his illusions of the present, no doubt encouraged by the images surrounding him. This person was indeed the principal.

'*We must not be influenced!*' Inner Voice procrastinated, '*shouting or not.*'

Although the principal's outburst of assumed recognition was unexpected, Johannes determined to maintain his dignity by displaying an appropriate calm. In his student days he would have conjured up in his mind's department of secrets stacked on numerous shelves all manner of clever replies to such an unsolicited roar, none of which would have been delivered, for in those days he was far too timid a little runt to clever-mouth his superiors. Clever-mouth his peers, yes – provided they were not physically superior gorillas – but never his academic superiors. Now, after decades of treading the boards and administering services as a principal himself, all he needed to muster were dilute indifference and a momentary toss of his eyes to the memory of callow stupidity. He immediately regretted the momentary toss of the eyes, for the action obliged him to catch sight of the clothes on the washing line high up on Mayhill still clapping their hands with glee.

'Don't laugh at the incongruity, the principal has his back to the applauding audience,' Inner Voice cautioned.

'I take it you are the principal of this institution?' Johannes asked with an air of remarkable calm.

'YOU OF ALL PEOPLE! WHAT ARE YOU DOING HERE?' the principal roared, ignoring Johannes's question.

'It's pretty clear he doesn't like inspectors. We must continue to ignore his shouting. He's heavily made up to resemble KW Hancock, principal at this college a thousand years ago. We suppose he expects us to be fooled by the make-up. What sort of shoddy theatre is he playing? He's probably worried about the college's balance of payments deficit.'

Over the many years of his professional management duties Johannes had confronted awkward people in a plethora of circumstances; this current theatre was no exception, and its now was quickly becoming past. Maintaining a calm exterior in order not to give the charlatan any excuse for further overreaction, Johannes explained the purpose of his visit, using low non-hostile tones, just as the funding council handbook recommends.

'My name is Johannes Taliesin. I am principal of Nehemiah Institute of Art and I have been commissioned by the Higher Education Funding Council to conduct an official inspection of your institution. I am aware there have been misunderstandings between you and the funding council for some time, but I am confident we can clear matters up. I take it the council has advised you accordingly?'

'Stop talking nonsense, Taliesin!' the charlatan principal was having none of it; indeed, Johannes's gentle tones seemed to have the reverse effect to the handbook's presumptions, 'Higher Education Funding Council indeed! What nonsense! To repeat my question: what are you doing out? Who has brought you here?'

'What is the silly bugger on about? We think he's a doppelgänger. No wonder David Eckto warned us we would get an entirely different worldview of this place. Clearly, the doppelgänger has a balance of payments deficit, or the like.'

Johannes was fired into resisting Doppelgänger Principal's raging.

'You refuse to recognise the funding council probably because of your balance of payments deficit, and regrettably the funding council sees fit to reciprocate the stand-off. Many methodologies have been set up by which an institution can return to profitability. Incidentally, I am still ignorant of your name,' Johannes responded, continuing to speak calmly as per handbook.

Doppelgänger Principal on the other hand continued to display the opposite frame of engagement. His wrath showed no sign of abating, his face twitching monstrously and the eyes reddening. Struggling as if to maintain professional composure, he started for the door, probably in a vain attempt at running away or perhaps worse; but then hesitated and, still fighting to gain composure, once again turned to confront Johannes.

'We've hit the nail on the head – it has to be balance of payments deficit.'

'My God Taliesin! What *are* you doing here? You were made fully aware we have a permanent embargo on your entering this institution again. Why have they released you so soon?'

Doppelgänger Principal continued to rage, 'and what is that ragged suitcase doing on my desk?' the tirade flowed with no moderation of tone.

Evidently Doppelgänger Principal was deeply agitated by the notion of an official inspection.

'Watch out! This man is raving, dangerous even. Released? Brought here? Embargo? Ragged suitcase? We refuse to be intimidated by his nonsense. Obviously he has used this ploy with previous funding council inspectors; no wonder the council gave up visiting the place. Eckto should have warned us in more direct terms but the word danger did come over the crackling mobile.'

Meanwhile, the principal's raised voice had attracted the model to the door that had only just appeared in the screens. She peered discreetly round it. Johannes caught a glimpse of her.

'Oh God! Another bloody doppelgänger! She looks like a model of centuries ago we thought we had successfully forgotten! Sophie, that was her name, Sophie Howells. Oh, God! This bloody place gets worse. They've selected someone to resemble her. Now we have a Doppelgänger Howells. What is this game they are playing? What strange manoeuvrings in order to avoid an inspection!'

'I believe you are greatly mistaken,' said Johannes, painting his aloof calm over the intruding realities, 'and when you calm down, we will discuss your balance of payments predicament, after which I shall proceed with the business of inspection.'

'Why do you persist in gibbering confounded nonsense regarding a balance of payments deficit? I assure you there will be no such discussion!' the Doppelgänger Principal's tirade increased in magnitude.

'Oh dear, hope we've got it right about balance of payments.'

'It is my inspectorial duty to pursue all elements of institutional activity,' Johannes maintained his line.

'Thank you, Miss Howells, please retire to the atelier and close the door behind you, thank you,' Doppelgänger Principal said in a professionally calm voice.

'Thank you, Miss Howells... please return to the atelier. So he pretends a few screens in the corner constitute his atelier. What a clever act! What sort of game are these people up to?'

Johannes caught Miss Howells staring quizzically at him.

'Must say, the bitch plays her part convincingly. They've chosen a beautiful one for the part.'

She allowed a wisp of dressing gown to flap through the gap ajar. Her expression however turned to one of sorrow from the thespian accord. The mystery thickened into deep purple as memories morphed.

'It's all a bloody mystery to us. Too many coincidences.'

Miss Howells, responding reluctantly to Doppelgänger Principal's dispensation, slowly closed the door, still staring at Johannes through the narrowing crack.

Meanwhile Doppelgänger Principal, taking Johannes's advice, demonstrated a convincing appearance of calm. After all, successfully characterising KW Hancock made a minuet of pretension a little pie in the Swansea sky by comparison. The effort must have been well spent if it meant disparaging the pygmy bureaucrats of London. Clearly Doppelgänger opposed an official inspection by the funding council. His amateurish modus operandi was to articulate obfuscation and simple charade, a fan dance of desperation, dancing to charcoal stick insects. But Johannes was alert to Doppelgänger's games where in the past he had obviously succeeded in disparaging other funding council visitors, success dependent upon playing against persons of lesser determination. Johannes resolved his official inspection would not be derailed on this occasion, and an objective report would be duly delivered.

'Don't be detracted by these buggers: it will only reflect badly

on us back at the ranch,' Inner Voice's suspicion of humanity had rarely seemed more apposite.

Doppelgänger Principal sat down at his table, the outward appearance of his dignity fully restored.

'Please take a seat, Taliesin, and please remove your suitcase from my desk.'

'Desk! This shitty table a desk? How the mighty have fallen! Calling our briefcase a suitcase is a manifestation of his insanity. Bet no other inspector noticed that.'

As he was removing his briefcase Johannes noticed for the first time he had placed it on top of some watercolour brushes. Odd, they were not there at the time he had deposited the briefcase. Examining more carefully, he discovered the brushes were priceless Russian squirrel in Chinese bamboo handles. How disturbing! His briefcase had damaged their fine sable by flattening them against their hand-bound ferrules. Oh, bloody hell! The Doppelgänger Principal stared with horror at the damage inflicted on his watercolour brushes.

'How in God's name did we fail to see those watercolour brushes sitting there?' Inner Voice exclaimed, aghast.

Further shocks awaited Johannes. Embracing the sudden confusion, the table was not a table at all, but a desk of superb proportions, inlaid with dark viridian leather, the whole finely polished. This latest discovery set Inspector Taliesin to glance edgily about the room. While he had been involved in the commotion with the Doppelgänger Principal, he had failed to notice the transformation of the room, which was now held in a hush of luxury.

'Bloody hell! Can't believe what we are seeing. It's all a trick of projections, or some trick our mind is playing. Anyway, watch this bugger.'

The room's spacious elegance displayed the discrete mixture of business and leisure that characterised the exclusive artistic styles of the decadent 1930s when carried over to embellish the post-war institutions. The new office arrangement displayed all the arrogance of finery art, a pre-official inspection makeover that affected a cosmopolitan image.

'*Ye gods! There's more! Are we imagining all this? Perhaps no balance of payments deficit after all.*'

There was indeed more. Off to the left of the entrance Johannes could see through another doorway making its leisurely access to an Ingres-style painting atelier. The configuration reflected an era of ostentation, with artefacts drawn from influences and impressions up to the present moment. A painting of a nude-in-progress on a large canvas was clearly visible.

'*Ah! That's where the model poses, we thought it was behind screens… can't keep up with this bloody metamorphosis game –*'

As far as Johannes could make out the painting was resting on a heavy easel that needed boat wheels to facilitate its movement. It stood before a dainty rostrum on which rested a chaise longue, drapes arranged just so, just so. Beyond, the atelier was shrouded in shadow save for spotlights illuminating the rostrum, the painting-in-progress, the mysteries and of course his memories.

Glancing further around, Johannes felt the unsavoury surge of panic and nausea he had hitherto mastered so well over his years of managerial service.

'*Um… are we, um, are we? Sod it!*' Inner Voice was busy sorting the confusion and stoically fighting back surges of insecurity.

The Doppelgänger Principal's office was abundantly furnished with pieces of oaken accoutrement appropriate to the operation of an office for an *ex cathedra* title of an institution at the centre of metropolitan art. Instead of bare boards and knotholes the floor embraced the conspiracy by luxuriantly carpeting itself in catch-up time in rich Wilton patterns of burgundy and mahogany. Johannes's boots sank comfortably into the pile.

'In the land of mahogany shadows, wish we were there right now. We thought this bloody floor was constituted of bare planks. How did we miss this lot? Where did the creaking come from?'

The large windows were garnished with rich plum curtains draped from shining brass rods; through the sparkling panes Johannes could see across the roof of the Glynn Vivian Art Gallery to the higgledy-piggledy terraces beyond, where clothes on a line high up on Mayhill were hysterically applauding the stage hands their speedy set change in this wonderfully absurd theatre.

Then Johannes caught sight of the desk chair opulently embellished with inlaid ox blood leather on both seat and arms. The Doppelgänger Principal was sitting in it, inscrutably watching Johannes, waiting, all signs of anger suppressed. To one side another chair of similar upholstery was drawn up. Two cups and saucers of fine Swansea porcelain containing the remains of tea sat on a silver tray, together with a teapot, sugar bowl and milk jug, all of a set.

'Drinking tea from such valuable objects is the stuff of dreams,' Inner Voice whispered. It seemed the Doppelgänger Principal had been entertaining a visitor recently, probably someone of enormous importance from the trust in league with the whole charade.

'Sit down, Taliesin,' the Doppelgänger Principal repeated in a voice laden with patience.

Due to flimsy reasons of confusion and the result of convoluted thinking, Official Inspector Taliesin chose to avoid eye contact lest the spell break. Affecting an air of preponderant officialdom he continued glancing in inspectorial manner about the office. The action may well have infuriated the Doppelgänger Principal, but it was obvious he had resolved to compartmentalise his true emotions following his initial outburst. The official inspector's eyes flitted in weakly disguised nervousness from sumptuous piece to elegant object. The whole office had become a feast of displays, exacerbating a tendency to intimidation. Original oil paintings decorated the walls. Works including Evan Walters of his sick bedridden mother; Ceri Richards's *The Cathedral under the Sea*; Fred Janes's *Vernon Watkins*; and a landscape by Herman Shapiro *I Gaze across the Distant Hills*. Two glass cabinets containing displays of Swansea porcelain, parts of which tea set were on the desk, proudly stood by.

'Works by artists of the 56 Group, we remember.'

Johannes looked about at what had become the stuff of his dream.

'Look at the desk again, look anywhere, before we go sodding mad,' Inner Voice becoming more agitated, *'do something, anything, to avoid this atelier reality looming larger and yet bloody larger, and we have to admit the bloody truth, the bloody bloody truth. Pity we can't phone Eckto.'*

Again turning to study the desk, Inspector Taliesin was surprised to note the collection of pencils, quills, graphite sticks and other drawing accoutrements standing in blown glass goblets on a desk that otherwise seemed strictly reserved for business. Surprise superimposed his original perception that only a bare table had presented itself. Perhaps the appearance had been the result of a sleight of hand by the doppelgänger, but how this had been achieved so quickly and silently with so many articles was beyond the pay grade of a mere inspector –

'Stop looking so sympathetically at these bloody objects, that's why we are seeing them,' Inner Voice's insertion of anger denied the confusion mode that had accompanied Johannes's journeys with Nostradamus all the way from the present, *'looking makes them appear; looking away makes them disappear, the opposite to quantum entanglement and Shröedinger's bloody cat –'*

Johannes stoically avoided examining the damaged watercolour brushes. But in so doing an instrument, unusual in the context, caught his eye: an airbrushing pen that had the appearance of having been recently used, for the reservoir was wet and the nozzle glistened the tale of a job well done.

'*Strange,*' Inner Voice pondered, '*what on earth does a painter in oils use an airbrush for? Anyway, how do we know he is proficient in its use? We know of tools far superior to the simple airbrush in technology – laptop, mobile, iPod, memory stick. We've got a laptop in the briefcase –*'

A gold bladed letter opener with a beautifully decorated handle of cut crystal resembling an ancient sash cutlass lay next to a collection of shining writing instruments. The whole exuded a style of relaxed academia, highlighting the more the damaged watercolour brushes.

'*Do* sit down, Taliesin,' the doppelgänger principal repeated, his professional air now dominating the room's atmosphere.

'*Watch! There's wet oil paint on that bloody seat.*'

'Pull the chair around to there,' he said, pointing, 'and sit down.'

The large leather-upholstered chair was heavy to the pull. Johannes, holding his briefcase in one hand, attempted the operation with the other.

'I suggest you put your suitcase down, but this time not on my desk,' said doppelgänger, patiently.

Johannes did as advised, and sat down opposite the principal. Once at the lower eye level, he caught sight of a nameplate freestanding on the inlaid desk, facing the visitor,

'KW Hancock ARCA, Principal' etched intaglio on polished brass.

'*BLOODY HELL!*' Inner Voice gagged, '*KW HANCOCK ARCA PRINCIPAL! BLOODY HELL! CAN'T BE!*'

'Of course,' Principal Hancock responded, 'who did you expect?'

The charade had been developed to fine minutiae, or something was happening – too many coincidences concatenated: no item resonated with the accoutrement of Nehemiah Institute; he had no other option but to – the past had caught up with his now. Johannes Taliesin froze...

A steel-cold knife entered the brain of Official Inspector Johannes Taliesin, travelled slowly and painfully down, dallying long enough on its journey to disillusion the mind, freeze the tongue, subtract many heartbeats, churn the stomach, squirm the testicles and deliver a plain simple disoriented Johannes on the inlaid leather chair before Principal Hancock. A frozen moment crowding the barred windows of his mind weighed heavily. Johannes froze, as the rhythm of recognition climbed slowly through the trapdoor of his hysteria.

'Oh God, oh God, this one is Principal Hancock, after all. How did we get into this? What happened to our principalship? Where the hell is Nehemiah in all this? What are we doing here?'

'Now tell me, what is all this about, Taliesin?' the principal had elected to bypass Johannes's unreality as inspector for the funding council to instead engage him at the harmless level.

'Deny, for God's sake deny, until we think through what is happening. There's got to be an answer, deny, delay –'

Johannes exhibited scant regard for Principal Hancock's reality, engaging denial in the last gear of his personality.

'I'm here on behalf of the funding council,' he invented robotically, 'to undertake an official inspection of this college,' and strove to inject conviction into the delivery.

'Conviction yes, but think! Stall! There has got to be an answer.'

'Which funding council would this be?' the principal enquired in unthreatening but nevertheless claustrophobic tones.

416

'*Must think of a convincing funding council, quick!*'

'*The* funding council,' Johannes obfuscated.

'There are many funding councils,' Principal Hancock returned, almost as if he were enjoying the game, 'which funding council in particular do you represent?'

'*He's enjoying this, the bastard.*'

'The Higher Education Funding Council that has been commissioned by the government; the funding council responsible for the funding and audit of the higher education sector; the funding council set up as an instrument of the 1988 Education Reform Act.'

'Could you be more specific?'

'*The bugger is trying to nail us – how could we be more specific – obfuscate some more, don't let him get the better of us. Eckto was right.*'

'Surely you are aware of the funding council that was set up by the government following the 1988 Education Reform Act to administer the institutions of the higher education sector following their incorporation?'

'I am aware of a block grant we receive from the Ministry of Education which comes via the education committee of the local education authority. Is that the funding council you mean, Taliesin?'

'*Our mind seems to have gone blank – no, hold on, it's coming. Aha! It's coming back!*'

'Forgive me, I'm moving ahead too hastily. I was unsure how aware or otherwise you were of the funding arrangements for the higher education sector that have been in place for some considerable time,' Johannes at last re-engaged the grand flow of his entanglement delusion, 'of the funding council set up after the 1988 Education Reform Act, and the funding methodologies administered by that council in order to bring to bear a measure of competitiveness in the unit cost within the sector. The funding council had advised me of a measure of misaligned synchrony your institute manifests relative to their deliberations,' Johannes delivered, suppressing a sigh of relief.

'Careful, sigh of relief a bit premature, perhaps.'

His outburst of authentic-sounding information caught Principal Hancock off guard, causing him to stare blankly.

'Got the doppelgänger, perhaps! That was close!'

After some while Principal Hancock responded, 'I am afraid I do not know what you are talking about. Obviously they give you profound science fiction reading matter at Cefn Coed, presumably as part of the therapy.'

'Cefn Coed? What is the bastard on about? Don't ask for explanation, in case he tells us what we don't want to know.'

'If you still retain doubts, might I suggest you give the council a call?' at which, Johannes pointed authoritatively to an ornate ceramic and brass telephone receiver that had at that instant become apparent on Principal Hancock's inlaid leather desk.

The principal breathed a huge sigh of relief, and smiled the smile of a chess master released from zugzwang.

'That smile tells us a lot. Did we let the cat out of the bag or something? Now *what is the bugger up to?'*

'A good idea, Taliesin. Give me one moment, and I'll give the council a call. Did you have a contact at your funding council?'

'Yes, Chief Executive Adam Krenwinkler; but David Eckto, head of audit compliance at head office, has the day-to-day brief for inspections. I received a call from David on my mobile when I arrived here but reception seems to break up in this building. His secretary advised me he is not at his office this morning, but you might have better luck.'

'Ah! Dr Eckto. Yes, I believe I know him; he has enjoyed the post of head of audit compliance for some time now, hasn't he?' came the clumsy test.

418

'For about a year,' was Johannes's sententious reply, 'sure you know him?'

'Um, yes,' Principal Hancock hesitated, 'when did you see Eckto last?'

'Bugger's hedging.'

'About a week ago at the Drapers Hall conference; we spoke yesterday on landline, and a garbled mobile call this morning; as I said the signal breaks up in this building. I can give you his direct line – let me find it,' Johannes replied, reaching for his briefcase.

'Um – thank you, Taliesin, but I already have Eckto's direct line. I'll get through to him, then we can resume normal business,' Principal Hancock said calmly.

Johannes remained unmoved, purposefully maintaining an inscrutable watch. Two principals from divergent times in an entanglement of events, one overlapping his memories in a crudely pasted collage, the other refusing to believe the one's arrival as official inspector from an overshot ethereal experience far into a future event.

'Still think he's a doppelgänger. He's up to all sorts of tricks. Eckto was right, there's danger here, we see it now in this character.'

Although adopting an air of sangfroid overlaid by professional calm, Principal Hancock of Swansea College of Art was clearly the lesser comfortable of the two, due most probably to his reputable dislike for the Higher Education Funding Council and equally, his life-painting project having been interrupted. These were issues that eluded Johannes's artistic temperament, even when it was under control. Johannes was content to call down the effortless delusion by convincing himself that Principal Hancock was apprehensive of the official inspection lest his skeletons be let loose and chase the supportive trustees out of town, leaving his nude study painting high and dry, bereft of public funding. The truth of Johannes's assumption confronted him as the remnants of a bygone age when art held centre stage on the merits of its affiliated toil.

'Whilst I'm making the call to Eckto, would you care to browse my most recent painting in the atelier? I know how much you appreciate paintings of the nude.'

'How did he know we appreciate paintings of the nude? Can't put our finger on it, but all doesn't seem right. Although our answer stunned him, he's not responding the way we expected. Bloody hell! Eckto won't answer the call, then what? Anyway, good opportunity to investigate his latest painting of the nude.'

The principal lifted the ornate receiver and began dialling, motioning Johannes go through to the atelier. But Johannes saw reasons to do both, i.e. linger in the office and walk through to the atelier. The air of mystery deepened. Playing wide games with his mentality the luxurious furniture and painting atelier appeared incidental to the disappearance of the Victorian screens.

'Don't investigate the space lest we happen upon something we don't want to see,' Inner Voice prattled the reality.

Johannes strove to ignore the space recently vacated. Upon entering the painting atelier he could hear the principal speaking distantly,

'Hello! David Eckto? Hancock Swansea College of Art here. Very well, thank you, and you? Good. Listen, I have Johannes Taliesin with me... yes... no, perfectly straightforward... he's with me at the moment... yes, so am I, to say the least... listen...'

It was at this point in the principal's telephone conversation that Johannes had cause to pay no further attention for he had come face to face with a far more disturbing occupation – the model Miss Howells. She bore an astonishing likeness to a model name of Sophie with whom he recalled having an unfortunate altercation aeons ago.

Miss Howells was sitting cross-legged on a little cushion in the right-hand corner of the atelier, reading a book. Her dressing gown was provocatively short, which struck Johannes as incongruous in the official environment of the principal's atelier. She affected slight surprise.

'*Oh God,*' Inner Voice groaned, '*it's true. We did see the model resembling Sophie Howells. More bloody obfuscation.*'

'Hello, Yoyo,' Miss Howells greeted him with apparent calm, albeit shuffling backwards to the wall on her cushion.

'*Bloody hell, trapped! Divert! Look at the painting – quick, and then retreat.*'

'Hello,' Johannes hesitated, 'how did you know my nickname?'

'What are you doing back in college?' she asked, continuing to shuffle backwards.

'*Mind your own bloody business.*'

'I am here to undertake an official inspection of this college of art,' Johannes replied, 'today is the first day. Principal Hancock invited me to take a look at his paintings.'

She smiled and relaxed, clearly realising Johannes Taliesin constituted no threat to her.

'My, my! You have quickly come up in the world! Which funding council nominated you?' Obviously she had been eavesdropping on Principal Hancock's cross-examination.

'*Another bloody interrogation, this time from her, of all people – don't ask her what she's on about – she might tell us.*'

'What is your name?' Johannes asked flatly.

'Have you forgotten so soon, Yoyo? You should know my name – I'm Sophie Howells.'

Johannes stared as coldly as he could possibly muster.

'*She's one and the bloody same!*'

'Sophie Howells, hmm. It's irrelevant who nominated me; I am an inspector in my capacity as principal and chief executive of Nehemiah Institute of Art. That is enough on the matter,' Johannes replied haughtily.

Sophie smiled and crinkled her nose, visibly relaxing.

'Principal of Nehemiah Institute of Art!' she squeaked with feigned surprise, 'obviously you're still raving. Where's Nehemiah Institute of Art? Never heard of it,' and she smiled broadly, playing the catch.

'It comes as no surprise you have never heard of Nehemiah Institute. It is not something a model is expected to know,' Johannes retorted feigning a variety of signals, but unsure as to which to organise into the main thrust.

More nose crinkling followed.

'For God's sake – ignore the bloody woman!'

'But where's Nehemiah?' she asked innocently.

'That's it! It's a trap – Principal Hancock set her up to it,' Inner Voice hissed.

'Nehemiah Institute of Art is in the city of Loudwater in Buckinghamshire,' he retorted, then swivelling around to look at Principal Hancock's painting, 'superb nude study. No one can paint the nude like Hancock; and I have to add, you look fine in the painting as well,' he could not resist the touch of flattery.

'Come on, Yoyo,' Sophie giggled as she rose from her cushion, 'you're having me on!'

'I most certainly am not! No one can paint the nude like Hancock.'

'You're having me on about this Nehemiah Institute thing, I mean,' she persisted.

'It's in Loudwater Buckinghamshire.'

Johannes was not confident that the information he had given the principal enjoyed an existence in reality. Indeed, he was unsure which reality these people at Swansea College of Art occupied: the reality his memory morphed into shadows, of which he was sure; or the reality his imagination constructed, of which he was equally sure.

'Come on, we are certain of the world of Nehemiah Institute of Art and its connections with the funding council, and its Chief Executive Adam Krenwinkler, Chairman Sir Barcode Cardigan, David Eckto... we must concentrate on these realities, we must –'

'Dr Eckto wishes to speak with you, Taliesin,' Principal Hancock called, 'don't hang up when you finish, I have more to discuss with him.'

'So Hancock is conversant with the funding council after all! What's his bloody game?'

Johannes fled the atelier and eagerly went to the phone, while trying to figure –

'Taliesin here... what do you mean, thank goodness Principal Hancock has found me? Au contraire, Eckto, it was I who found him... of course, bit of a confusion regarding knowledge of my official inspection visit, but other than that, fine... yes, been here about half an hour in all – what is it that is troubling you? Me? Oh, that is what you meant regarding danger... what, today? Don't think I really need your assistance – this morning you say? Thought you were in London... you're in Swansea! Good Lord! OK, yes, see you shortly... um, hold the line, Principal Hancock wishes to discuss something else with you,' and Johannes handed the phone back.

'Wonder what Eckto meant, thank goodness Principal Hancock has found me... everybody seems to be forgetting their lines...'

'I suggest you go back to the atelier, Taliesin, I'll join you there presently... Eckto, you still there? Good. Listen, about the rendezvous...'

Johannes had already wandered back into the atelier, deep in thought. Regardless Eckto's inadvertent confirmation, other recollections persisted in invading his thoughts. The Sophie thing rekindled memories of his being a miscreant student at Swansea

College of Art. Johannes was experiencing difficulty with events that occurred in the three and a half decades between, readily alighting in the distant past at Swansea, or clumsily hovering in the present Nehemiah Institute of Art. Yet if he had needed reassurance then speaking with David Eckto, head of audit compliance at the funding council was sufficient. That was all right, then.

'Nehemiah in Loudwater? Where is that?' Sophie's question jolted Johannes from his quandary.

'What?'

'What?'

'Loudwater?'

'A city in Buckinghamshire,' Johannes replied absentmindedly, his thoughts still on his dilemma.

'*We are getting angry with this bloody woman and her trivialities – more important things concern us. This whole bloody circumstance makes us angry. Anyway, the play-acting of these two is getting too realistic for our comfort, that's for sure.*'

'I have never heard of Loudwater, leave alone Nehemiah Institute,' Sophie persisted in demonstrating something well beyond Johannes's tolerance.

'Surprising number of ignorant people claim they have never heard of Loudwater!' Johannes blurted, 'Why don't you go and ask your principal, if you dare make a fool of yourself, but he's talking with David Eckto of the funding council at this moment.'

In recollection Sophie was the innocent subject of a long ago debacle that was Balthusian in its innocence, Groszian in vulgarity. Johannes's subsequent busy life had eclipsed his memory of the event, replacing his contrition with the satisfaction people garner from being accusatorial. Then the principal's reference to an embargo arrived belatedly at the point of Johannes's brain.

'What did he mean by that? Embargo means someone or thing is prohibited, disallowed; perhaps we are prohibited to enter here. Stick to the official inspection story and see what happens. Anyway, that is what Eckto was on about: the principal's embargo on the funding council. Never looked forward to an Eckto arrival so much.'

In spite of Eckto's confirmation re-instating equilibrium, Johannes's loyal lifelong cloud descended as a shroud, dogged and persistent; a darkening atmosphere presaging the fog that always took hold of matters, clouding his thinking. The day's events were assuming a complexity beyond his endeavour, his soul long gone and airbrushed from a history that he had so painstakingly constructed. Johannes had fallen through history, elevating time around him: no one understood. This was a new experience. Whenever confronted by a new experience Johannes's confidence would waver. He broke out in a sweat – the warmth of the atelier – the clammy familiarity of perspiration could signal to Sophie that his stance might indeed be a charade.

'This is beyond,' Johannes muttered, 'I now realise the window in history God arranged for me to leap through.'

'Don't dwell on the window solution, Yoyo,' Sophie interjected knowingly, but aware that the situation could deteriorate at the drop of a frame.

'I have travelled far in both distance and time, but all the same I have been standing still draped in my flags of age. I did not expect to witness you of all people looking in on my new world. I don't know if it has been worth all this travelling.'

'They've certainly changed your attitude, Yoyo. But what are you talking about? You seem to forget you were –'

She came closer, her proximity triggering Johannes's social claustrophobia that danced widdershins with his inadequacy.

A loud ting sounded from the office as Principal Hancock replaced the telephone and within seconds he had joined them in the atelier. He had patient satisfaction tinged with anxiety painted across his face. Although the man's sense of eternal dignity had been molested following his somewhat uncharacteristic outburst upon realising the visitor to be Johannes Taliesin, he had re-grouped their components to display a more or less intact facsimile. Johannes similarly was relieved the bubble of unbearable recollections that Sophie stimulated had not burst onto the set.

'I was just saying to Johannes Taliesin, Mr Hancock, he seems to forget that just the other day he was –' Sophie was cut short by a gesture from the principal, the signal not lost on Johannes.

'What were you about to say?' Johannes edgily asked of Sophie.

'It would have been quite immaterial,' the principal interrupted firmly, 'because Miss Howells is about to take a longer break than usual; please, Miss Howells,' he commanded the suggestion.

Sophie obediently took the cue and tripped lightly to her changing cubicle, from which emerged sounds of the woman dressing. To Johannes's aggravation and deep embarrassment she reappeared, partly dressed.

'How long shall my longer break be, Mr Hancock?' she asked, with emphasised innocence smearing across her smile.

'*My God!*' Inner Voice was desperate, '*who the hell cares? Must say something.*'

As an action done simply to provoke Johannes, it worked better than a stave of psychiatrists.

'Who the hell cares? Take as long as you like; I'm sure Principal Hancock does not want you around at this moment of official inspection,' Johannes burst, and turned his back on her.

Sophie affected a startled gasp, 'I need to know in order to dress appropriately,' she addressed Principal Hancock with syrupy innocence.

'Of course, Miss Howells, thank you,' the principal said with a measured tone of tact and patience, 'visiting Inspector Taliesin has a brusque manner, which I trust he will not cascade across the college. Take as long as is necessary,' and he made a sweeping gesture for her to quickly exit.

Johannes shook his head, signalling his clumsiness and other implications beyond immediate understanding. The curtain of the changing room swept shut indicating Sophie had retreated, but she continued talking, 'You see, Mr Hancock, I wanted to know how long in order to dress in internal college clothes, or the streets of Swansea clothes,' her voice coming from inside the changing room.

Johannes glanced at the principal, awaiting a reaction.

Principal Hancock arranged a pained frown; since Johannes Taliesin had intruded it had not been one of his better days.

'Streets, Miss Howells,' he said with a voice as pained as the expression, 'streets'.

Following a few scurried flusters Sophie emerged fully dressed. Swaying past Johannes on her way out, she cast him a glance of sorrowful longing. A fluster of perfume hung in her wake, leaving a whisk of scent mingling with the atelier's bouquet.

'That perfume! Fancy, still wearing that perfume after all these years...' Inner Voice loitered, *'amazing it's still being marketed... brings back memories of that night of our uselessness...odd how a perfume can evoke memories of so long ago...wish we were young again...'*

Looking in the direction of the principal as she passed, Sophie muttered, 'you realise he's still barking, Mr Hancock.'

Principal Hancock quickly looked away, and kept his counsel.

'Barking? What the hell?'

Sophie left the atelier and walked briskly out of the office into the corridor. Bursts of chatter and giggle thrust in, falling to silence again as the door closed. She had disappeared, taking an enigma with her.

'What did your model mean by that, Mr Hancock?'

'I… I'm not sure. Please, Mr Taliesin, come back into my office while we await Dr Eckto.'

'At least David Eckto will resolve these ambiguities.'

'What did you say, Taliesin?'

'I, er… I said, um… no doubt that is what he must have tried to communicate during a phone conversation we had earlier on my mobile. Incidentally, mobile reception seems to be poor in this building.'

The principal hesitated before this new information. His mind seemed prepossessed, as if the game was tilting. He shook his head, but slowly.

'Dr Eckto says a new matter has arisen of which you are aware that needs his personal attention,' the principal volunteered after some thought, 'he will be joining us shortly… now let us sit down and discuss this official inspection you are here to undertake.'

'Yes, surely,' said Johannes, deeply suspicious, but relieved for having turned his back on the thoughts that entertained him when alone in the atelier with Sophie, 'obviously Eckto will have furnished you with the inspection format?' he added.

The principal, obviously distracted, caught up with Johannes's line of thinking.

'Um, yes, of course,' he responded, hesitantly, 'but he stressed you await his arrival here in my office.'

'Why should I do that? All I needed you to do was to seek corroboration from Eckto the purpose of my visit to this college,' said Johannes, uneasy again, 'it was unnecessary to bring him here, if it does not agree with you.'

'As I said, a matter has arisen that needs his personal

attention,' the principal responded tetchily, 'once I had asked his corroboration of your attendance here, I can assure you, Taliesin, he volunteered to join us. Did you appreciate the painting?'

'*Bloody mysterious, this,*' Inner Voice grumbled, '*Eckto of audit compliance attending to a task nearby, bloody mysterious. Did we appreciate the painting? Bollocks, doubt if he really wants to know our view.*'

'Strange, I would say, Mr Principal. How long do we have to wait for Eckto?' Johannes brought the subject back to official status.

Principal Hancock fixed Johannes with an impassive stare, at which Johannes decided to test the bluff.

'In the meantime I will begin the official inspection,' Johannes announced bluntly.

Principal Hancock closed his eyes, and put up his hand as a halting sign to Johannes.

'First I would like to learn more of… of the funding council's idiosyncrasies, if you don't mind. You are both the ideal and appropriate person to explain them to me. Would you mind taking your seat and starting all over again?' clearly the principal was working hard to manage a situation beyond Johannes's comprehension.

'*It's bloody obvious he's trying to prevent us from going outside to start the inspection; the sod is up to something… can't figure it…*'

'But you must understand, Principal Hancock, I will have to commence the official inspection sooner or later, regardless your curiosity concerning the funding council's idiosyncrasies, or the newly contrived artefact of matters arising between you and Eckto.'

'Yes, yes, whatever you say,' the principal snapped, his initial anger rekindling, 'but as head of this institution I have both the need and right to know your rules of engagement, newly contrived artefact, as you put it, or not.'

'We must take care – this trap is big enough to catch a bloody elephant!'

'Of course, my apologies for assuming too much of your local protocols; you are indeed right,' Johannes responded, 'what information do you seek regarding the funding council?'

'Firstly, I'm interested in the procedures you implement in reporting your findings,' the principal replied tetchily, 'and the protocol of verification.'

'On our guard!'

'The official report follows the strict format set out by Audit Compliance Division at the funding council. Guidelines HEFC OIR, paragraphs 3 to 6 are the appropriate instances, of which you should have a copy,' Johannes began in flat tones, 'If the guidelines are not readily to hand, you can locate said on the funding council website, which is generally accessible. We could access it on my laptop here,' he said, patting his briefcase.

Principal Hancock winced.

'Don't know whether it is wise to ensnare him or hasten with the preliminaries.'

'Anything of a confidential nature requiring an on-site follow-up or obligatory attendance at head office will naturally be encoded within the appropriate protocols of the day,' Johannes continued, 'Once scrambled, only the instigator can validate unscrambling – I trust you will stop me if you are already aware of these procedures?' he paused, at the summit of politeness.

'Of course, of course; please go on, Mr Taliesin,' said the principal, seemingly once again scurrying in catch-up mode.

'Once the report is sent by the designated inspector, its bullet points and executive summary are perused by Audit Compliance Division, David Eckto and his team. A review committee working strictly to standing orders and fixed terms of reference is temporarily constituted, usually from officers of the council with the designated inspector co-opted, unless the report concerns a specialist institution when a person conversant with its specialist disciplines will also be co-opted. The chief executive of the institution is invited to attend the review committee, but not normally for its first sitting. Are you sure you are not conversant with these procedures, Mr Hancock?'

'I'm speechless,' the principal murmured, 'please go on.'

'That's as may be, Mr Hancock, but are you conversant with the inspection procedures?'

'Please *do* go on,' Principal Hancock spoke in a small voice.

Johannes stared at him.

'Many conflicting factors need to be addressed,' Johannes continued in his newly adopted flat tones of an official inspector and, realising the principal could no longer obfuscate, began turning the screw, 'for we have official government interference, individual secretaries of the Crown riding their own hobbyhorses, equal opportunities, designated quotas, European Union cross-border equivalences, international transfers ultra vires to the European Union member states, political correctness, budgetary predetermination, local ethnic representation and so forth that impinge on the outcomes of the teaching programmes –'

'Wonder if the bugger is as up to date as we are in these matters?'

'– as well as the computer-based Open University inputs. It is to be accepted that institutions will have installed sub-committees of the academic board as per Privy Council guidelines to specifically address and monitor these sensitive issues.'

'Where on earth did you acquire this claptrap...?' the principal emitted in a small hollow voice.

'How dare you? Calling this ongoing information claptrap!

Come, come, Mr Principal, I cannot believe you have been ignoring official funding council correspondence, but I had been forewarned, of course. Unfortunately, from your attitude it appears the executive and trustees have at the very least been ignoring important funding council directives in the management of this institution.'

'How is it you have gained all of this... this... verbose bureaucratic piffle in just three weeks?' the principal asked in genuine amazement.

'Three weeks? Gibberish, now he's talking gibberish.'

'In the same way as you should have gained the bureaucratic piffle, as you put it – through official funding council, Whitehall and Brussels directives,' Johannes replied, throwing the insult back into the principal's court.

'What I'm asking is, what book supplied you with this bureaucratic piffle?' Principal Hancock asked, clearly baffled, 'because what you say bears no relationship to art education as it is known here in Swansea College of Art.'

'Perhaps some strange time dilation must have occurred at this place,' Inner Voice pondered.

'Some matters are becoming quite clear, Mr Hancock. Your attitude implies you have no relationship with the reality of present-day governance of education in art and design,' Johannes responded, growing in confidence.

'Well, I'm blessed!' the principal muttered, shaking his head, 'so I am given to suppose you have?'

'Got to be time dilation; Eckto was right, something very strange about this principal.'

'I regret to say your attitude reflects a profound sense of atavism,' Johannes rebuked in as official a tone as he could muster.

Clearly Principal Hancock was taken aback by Johannes's authoritative knowledge base, and felt obliged to label it as bureaucratic piffle in order to give the impression he had kept abreast of the effluxion of time.

'I'm genuinely intrigued, Taliesin,' the principal confessed, 'both as to the information itself and whence it comes. Tell me, what else is happening in your world – better still, while we await Eckto, give me a snapshot of social and political issues as you see them and as they relate to art education – not as they are in reality, but strictly as you see them, you understand.'

'There is no need for the caveat, Mr Hancock; however, it seems I have a knowledge advantage over you. My view, and the reality of current socio-political issues, are one and the same,' Johannes corrected the principal's sleight of word, 'but so far I have touched on only a small portion of the actual. Political correctness commands respect from our elected representatives in Parliament, reflecting the nation's social structures; we have a tyranny of the minorities, exerting social and political pressure on the silent compliant majority; all sectors of education have been hijacked by the politicians who insert their own socio-political fantasies between the students and the coalface, art education being no different; we have widespread phone hacking where no one's privacy is secure and the stolen information is published willy-nilly; the British Broadcasting Corporation openly supports the Left to the detriment of balance; we have a down-dumbed media tailored to suit the ignorant of society rather than the educated; and of course for the short-term fix and the fast buck the great institutions of the land such as Parliament and the banking sector have abandoned overseer responsibility; generally there is a collective abrogation of responsibility for the consequences of actions taken for and on behalf of the institutions. Specifically in art education there is a strong reluctance to belatedly address the desirable-essential dichotomy.'

'Why on earth should the desirable-essential be seen as a

dichotomy in art?' the principal interjected, as obviously from his perspective this was the main issue.

'Predetermined attitudinal disposition,' Johannes responded flatly, comfortable in the scene, 'invented by the pygmies of our society who, having found they are unable to administer authority in a competitive environment, perpetrate hoops that empower them socio-psychologically, obliging society to perform spurious hoop-jumping, failure of which is monitored by internal kangaroo tribunals, aided and abetted by the media.'

'Well, I'm blessed! What *are* you talking about, Taliesin?' the principal uttered in exasperation.

Johannes's suspicions that Principal Hancock was out of touch with reality were endorsed by the repeated interjections and atavistic surroundings of office and painting atelier.

'Clearly this college of art and its lot are suffering the effects of some gigantic time dilation. Or maybe the result of applied recalcitrance on a protracted scale; can't be too cautious. Eckto was right.'

Principal Hancock glanced edgily at his watch. Clearly from his expression he was treating Johannes's information as gobbledegook.

'Odd though,' Inner Voice niggled, *'considering the recalcitrance must have been maintained over several years why the funding council did not pursue their investigations more rigorously.'*

Contradictions proliferated before Johannes's very reasoning. His enduring response during times of doubt was to accentuate the hope. Treating the present circumstance no differently, he continued to press home his assumed knowledge advantage but, as in all instances when matters fell too readily into place, Johannes lost his grip on perspective and began bending his advantage to breaking point.

'To satisfy its political ideology,' Johannes continued,

becoming too enthusiastic for his predicament, 'quotas for ethnic minorities are imposed on the institutions by the government, which the funding council pursues with alacrity; we have to give preferential consideration to ethnic minorities when appointing academic staff, regardless of their merit. The government, having forgotten the etiquette of democracy and, bent on destroying the elite specialist nature of the art institutions, bribes them with large financial top slicing to appoint blind students.'

At this moment Johannes climbed into the land of mahogany shadows.

'Don't tell me, Taliesin: these blind students study painting?' the principal's sardonic laugh was an easy giveaway, considering.

'Why, yes of course, Mr Principal, I am pleased you are catching up at last! As it happens, by enrolling blind students onto courses such as painting, art institutions gain more funding than they would from the standard unit.'

'And to hell with the values of the subject, I suppose,' Principal Hancock was experiencing difficulty in containing his anger, 'where in God's name have you acquired such rubbish? I thought you were institutionalised at Cefn Coed for a curative programme, not to fill your head with socio-political fiction.'

'How dare you, Mr Principal! All of this information is contained in the official directives of the funding council. Surely you must read them?'

'*We bet he doesn't! Bet the only literature he reads is Old Masters Quarterly and Quillpepper's Almanack of Painterly Matters; anyway, what's this Cefn Coed thing he's on about?*'

'I certainly read directives, Taliesin, but seemingly not the ones you allude to,' the principal replied, again glancing at his wristwatch.

'Well, I am surprised, to say the least,' Johannes responded, 'because, as you should know, clause 69 of Funding Council

HE Directive comes into operation 1st April next, placing a mandatory requirement on specialist art institutions to appoint only blind – um, beg your pardon, I should be saying visually challenged – applicants, to the academic staff of art institutions, as well as of course deaf applicants to the conservatoire schools of music,' Johannes's imagination morphed him deeper into the land of mahogany shadows.

'This is arrant nonsense! Never heard anything so preposterous! Thank goodness you have been removed from art education –'

'*Removed? What's he on about?*'

'Removed? What are you talking about?' Johannes protested, 'I am principal of Nehemiah Institute of Art. To return to my narrative –'

'Before you do that,' Mr Hancock interrupted, 'have you given a thought as to how these blind persons can see what they are doing, for heaven's sake?' as he lost more of his narrowing patience.

'Might I suggest I am merely the messenger: it is not for me to give a thought as to how these blind persons can see what they are doing, as you put it. Tearing my tongue out merely indicates to the pygmies in government that they are on the right track in their mission to establish equality throughout society, regardless handicap challenges and other circumstances. It is the government that deserves your wrath but be assured as we live in a democracy the elected members will ignore you.'

'Forgive me, Taliesin. But in your land of fantasy how does this government of yours propose these directives be met?'

'*He's not interested in how the directives will be met – the bugger's stalling, he's waiting for Eckto. Dead sinister.*'

'My government is as much your government. It will elevate the standard unit payment in order that the institutions can appoint one-on-one tutorship to verbally guide the visually handicapped person, a sort of visual translator, if you will,' so pleased was Johannes with his reply that he stood up to afford better purchase.

'Sit down, Taliesin,' Principal Hancock commanded.

Johannes ignored the command, 'The incentive is simple avoidance of the disincentive, whereby funding is gradually diminished for sighted students. A further incentive to implement equality will be the granting of large payments to appoint deaf translators who will have sign-language specialists assisting the deaf to translate instructions into Braille for the blind painting students,' Johannes's zeal had got clean the better of his composure as he waved his arms about to effect greater podium expression. Effectively, Principal Hancock's forbearance had encouraged Johannes to run round the bend of logic.

'Preposterous! And will you please SIT DOWN!'

'We had better sit down; for some reason he doesn't like us standing up. As official inspector to the college perhaps we shouldn't stand up if the principal is seated.'

Johannes sat down.

'Preposterous! Do you for one moment believe this rubbish?'

'You have no option but to believe it,' was Johannes's strained reply, 'and the sooner you –'

'I have never heard so much rubbish! What you are saying is preposterous. What you… what…' the principal's exasperation lost him his line of response.

'Still shouting, but he's lost for words! His anger is directed at what we are saying, not for standing up. Shows how out of date he is,' Inner Voice bounced back.

'Perhaps I should explain further details –'

'Don't tell me, Taliesin,' Principal Hancock took control of his voice, 'don't tell me, the same mandatory requirement stipulates only legless persons may apply to the nation's schools of dance?'

at which his sardonic quizzing prompted the ghost of a smile to slip beyond his pained grimace.

'I'm beginning to think, Mr Principal, you are quite unaware of the requirements of the Multi-Handicap Enabling Act recently enacted by Parliament. For God's sake, how out of synch are you?'

Principal Hancock stared aghast; his jaw sagged at a distressed angle; the remnants of colour in his face drained away; his features showed textural signs that his immense reservoir of dignity was quickly depleting under the onslaught of Johannes's update. The exercise in humouring Johannes while awaiting Eckto's arrival had badly misfired, for the principal found he was being drawn inexorably into the surreal world of Flann O'Brien,

'Blind enrolments to schools of painting, legless persons enrolled in schools of dance' the principal croaked, 'deaf persons enrolling at the conservatoire schools of music, top-slicing of grants to fund one-on-one interpretive tutoring – preposterous! Frankly, Taliesin, I have never heard of this Multi-Handicap Enabling Act you have conjured from the blue. Dare I enquire the general objectives of your imaginary Act?'

'It is clear to me you have not been keeping abreast of government initiatives in the field of higher education,' Johannes preached regardless, 'let me update you in these important matters, but you must be aware it is *your* responsibility to maintain cognisance of new legislation in the education sector, not mine to keep you updated – it may have slipped your mind, but I am here to undertake an official inspection.'

'I can assure you, Taliesin, the reason for your presence here has never left my thoughts for one moment,' the principal replied acidly.

'The purpose of the Act,' Johannes blithely proceeded, lost in his shadows, 'is to ensure that established education should

438

no longer be available to those fortunate enough to possess so-called normal faculties such as limbs, sight, hearing, intelligence, money and other facilitators of elitism.'

Principal Hancock rearranged his features in a manner to demonstrate resignation that hell had slipped into his office in the form of Johannes Taliesin while he was happily painting in his atelier. His mouth opened, but at first no sound emerged. Eventually a hoarse whisper came, 'Miss Howells's comment was apposite, you are barking, if I may say, Taliesin.'

'Sophie Howells is a mere model, her presumptions are immaterial,' Johannes responded sharply, 'regardless, once the Enabling Act is seen to be meeting its objectives in replacing all elitist academics with handicapped staff, then possibly at some point in the future, privileged persons will once again be permitted to enrol, on condition they are taught exclusively by handicapped staff. Times are changing in higher education, Mr Hancock, except seemingly in the backwater of Swansea College of Art. Incidentally, for my sins I have been commissioned to undertake a survey of the nation's higher education art and design provision under the aegis of desirable-essential. *That* should sort out the wheat from the chaff, don't you think?'

'I'm not hearing this!' Principal Hancock croaked, 'the sooner Dr Eckto arrives the better for the maintenance of my sanity,' at which he lifted his telephone receiver and pressed a button… 'Miss Sparrow, please ensure I am not interrupted by any of my diary appointments. As a matter of emergency I am expecting David Eckto, who is due any moment. When he arrives please bring him to my office without delay! Only then will I resume my scheduled diary appointments. Thank you.'

Then, wearing his weary countenance with dignity, the principal once more addressed Johannes, 'If this were not dysfunctional nonsense, Taliesin, I could find it intriguing that you should construct such fantasies when presumably you have been undergoing psychiatric treatment at Cefn Coed Hospital.'

'Psychiatric treatment at Cefn Coed Hospital? Why does the silly bugger persist? We didn't hear any marbles falling.'

'Psychiatric treatment at Cefn Coed Hospital, Mr Principal? What do you mean, psychiatric treatment?' Johannes bluntly demanded.

'Um… this charade has progressed to a grave quarter, Taliesin, and I wish to contain your excitability until Dr Eckto arrives. So, please tell me more of your, may I say, constructions.'

'Constructions?'

Johannes's head was buzzing.

'So many contradictions.'

He collected his thoughts.

'Give him some of the more ridiculous directives we have to contend with in our land of mahogany shadows that morph into Nehemiah,' Inner Voice growled.

'Notwithstanding the all-embracing Multi-Handicap Enabling Act, we have to contend with much of its content already,' Johannes continued, 'we have to contend with, for instance, directives that disallow the consideration of merit when appointing academic staff: qualifications, achievements and experience are no longer the referential criteria of choice. Now we have to first consider the applicant's ethnicity, gender orientation, handicap quotient, visual and audible acumen challenges, ESN orientation –'

'Gender orientation?' the principal interrupted, aghast, 'What the…?'

'Yes, gender orientation, or if they belong to any other minority that happens to come to the surface in the social miasma of the media's fashionable causes. We are then obliged to make an appointment from this basket of categories regardless of merit or appropriateness to the post.'

Principal Hancock yet again rearranged his features: on this occasion he struggled bravely to disguise registering disbelief, disdain, pity with a look of sublime blandness that was marred by undisguised fault lines across his face.

'Also, we have to enrol a sizable quota of students from deprived backgrounds regardless of their ability, academic qualifications, inclination to work or even love of the subject; all done for ideological social engineering in equality. These are socio-political goals the politicians strive for, using the educational establishments as theatres for their prioritised levelling-down ideologies and to hell with quality, merit or achievement. In fact, the intrinsic purpose of education per se in the educational establishments of our brave real world is the least important element to be accounted for by our politicians. Of course, the hidden long-term political agenda is to cultivate a land of third-rate fools, thereby gifting the government the means by which totalitarian governance can be implemented with ease. There can be no other explanation for their intent. Our competitors overseas are laughing their heads off. By electing such governments we get what we deserve, but I doubt if the electorate intended putting buffoons in charge of higher education.'

'Intriguing,' the principal croaked disbelievingly, 'tell me, in your real world of construct, what happens to practical values such as skill, workmanship, technical prowess and the like?'

'It is obvious you believe I have constructed this world. Nothing can be further from reality. It is the butchers, bakers and candlestick makers that the country elected into government who are imposing these ideologies. To answer your question, the artisans receive lip service at best but, more often, as only able-bodied persons can fulfil the exacting requirements of practical value returns, they are removed by default from the curriculum.'

'Am I hearing this?' the principal muttered, shaking his head, 'please look sharp, Dr Eckto,' he pleaded to himself.

'My God, is this bugger out of touch? Eckto was right.'

'Due to this political intrusion, aided and abetted by many of the inmates, the institutions' missions are being deflected, diluted and eclipsed, resulting in a lowering of standards that is avalanching towards the abyss,' Johannes continued to grind home a reality that the principal was reluctant to comprehend, 'excuses abound: everyone yells solutions and no one listens.'

'No, no, this cannot be,' the principal muttered, 'thank God it exists only –' and he broke off.

'You must hate what you are hearing, Mr Principal. It has to be contrary to your values and lifestyle. No wonder you have constructed a cocoon about you that perpetuates the philosophy of times past. Regardless of the employment of a personal solution the seismic shift has obviated your anomalous existence. Clearly, Eckto has decided to join *me* rather than you in order that together we confront the causes of Swansea College of Art's suspended development.'

'Your barking world,' Principal Hancock completed from his croak, 'I have addressed the Dr Eckto charade, Taliesin, and I await him.'

'Don't listen to him. It is we awaiting Eckto.'

Then, speaking more clearly, the principal barely able to suppress his incredulity, added,

'I am in no doubt all this fantastic fiction comes from your troubled head, Taliesin. No doubt you classify wiping away decades of hard-won values and skills as 'development'. The picture you paint lays waste the domain of art education, in place of which you impose your so-called development. One is mindful of Tacitus when referring to the actions of the Roman legions in Britannica: 'Solitudinem faciunt pacem appellant.'

How apposite in illustrating your future vision of art and design, would you not agree?'

'Praise the Lord! The only bit of Tacitus we remember!'

'On the contrary, Mr Principal, it is the elected members who make a wilderness and call it peace, not I,' Johannes calmly replied, 'I am merely chief executive and principal of Nehemiah Institute of Art, and everything I have so far stated bears a close relationship to that institution's delivery.'

'As if administering an institution as chief executive legitimises the rape – nay, the nihilism – of hard-earned values and skills. I suppose, Taliesin, you believe my college should embrace similar fantasies of social engineering?'

'Aha! Eckto was right: he's betraying his weaknesses. No wonder the funding council and he never met eye to eye. We'll see what Eckto has to say. Drive the nail home.'

'That is the nub of the problem,' Johannes responded, 'your failure to embrace the socio-educational reforms has resulted in three major issues: ideological, practical and balance of payments –'

'Um – perhaps not balance of payments –'

'I mean two major issues: ideological and practical,' Johannes corrected, 'ideologically, you are isolated to the degree where you see fit to question my sanity but I will demonstrate the practical issue by way of asking you, Mr Principal: what form does the Privy Council model instrument and articles of government take at Swansea College of Art?'

'Umm, good question, coming from you of all people, Taliesin. As your treatment appears to be centred on educational management and the logistics thereof, allow me to refresh the conversation with a few nuggets of reality: hopefully it should consume the time I am committed to waiting for Dr Eckto.'

'Wonder in what discipline Eckto holds a doctorate?'

'Governance at this institution takes the form dictated by

the 1944 Butler Education Act,' the principal spoke slowly, as in the grand Prix de Rome scholar manner, 'that is, a board of trustees appointed by the local education authority. The practical governance of the board of trustees is constituted in the form of a working group, of which I am chairman in my ex-officio capacity as principal. Any matters arising that cannot be addressed internally are mediated through me to the trustees. The Privy Council model you allude to is non-existent in the reality of day-to-day governance, and surely resides only in the realm of your fantasy. The governance subscribed by the funding council you allude to is not different in principle.'

Mr Hancock sat back in his swivel chair, carefully watching for Johannes's reaction. But Johannes was unfazed.

'We're cracking this bugger; Eckto will be proud of us.'

'Go on,' said Johannes.

'That's it.'

'That's it?' Johannes burst in feigned astonishment, 'No wonder the funding council has reservations regarding the management of this institution. If you have not progressed beyond the aegis of the 1944 Butler Act, then a massive tranche of parliamentary legislation must have avoided this institution by goodness-knows-what means considering the number of checks and balances the funding council has at its disposal.'

The principal's head dropped, he sighed deeply, and stole another glance at his watch.

'It has been easier to crack the recalcitrance of Principal Hancock than we imagined, especially considering the confident way he bullied us at first,' Inner Voice crowed.

'We are answerable to the Office of the Education Authority… of course' at which Principal Hancock narrowed his eyes and again observed Johannes's reaction closely.

'How out of date can he get? This bugger's playing some sort of game for time.'

'Ridiculous! It appears you are reluctant to engage in the proper discourse necessary to establish the framework for a funding council inspection,' said Johannes, gaining in confidence. Clearly, Johannes's reaction was not what the principal had anticipated; to be sure the illusion he was propagating possessed a reality of its own, 'nothing I have introduced so far seems to resonate with you. It is as if Swansea College of Art is suspended in a past existence, if I may venture.'

'Though by right we should be aware of our precarious perch, toehold on Zen, or something we are similarly unsure of. Must beware!'

The principal displayed signs that his composure was almost gone.

'Perhaps his irritability threshold has been reached, or he can't stand the thought of four hours of our governance catch-up phase,' Inner Voice went walkabout.

'I am professionally intrigued the thoroughness of your briefing, although the ideas themselves are based in fantasy,' the principal conceded.

'It is an understandable human reaction that, when confronted by an incomprehensible truth,' Johannes responded flatly, 'we have recourse to reacting on a personal level, the purpose of which renders a false perspective in order that trivia eclipses the awesome preponderance, nevertheless delivering satisfaction.'

'The good Lord saw fit to steer me away from psychology, psychiatry, philosophy and all the other after-dinner time-fillers,' Principal Hancock sighed, 'It appears, however, the Lord has granted you licence to implement more than one blunder in your lifetime. You are talking preposterous rubbish,' his dignity could bear no more of it and, lifting his phone, pressed the same button and waited… then, 'Miss Sparrow, any sign of Dr Eckto… no, no cause for concern, Inspector Taliesin is still with me at present... yes, Miss Sparrow, Inspector Taliesin... I would appreciate your investigating why Dr Eckto is taking so long –'

'Miss Sparrow? We sort of remember her. What's going on?'

'– beg pardon? No, no, not at all, keep the academics out of it. When Dr Eckto arrives please bring him directly to my office. Thank you, Miss Sparrow,' he replaced the receiver with deliberate grace.

'Something dead fishy going on in this loony place. Pour more information at the bugger...'

'Specifically relating the changes to your idiosyncrasies,' Johannes resumed his full flow, 'the introduction of multifarious materials under the guise of painting would probably tilt the balance of your mind.'

'You did not give me an answer, Taliesin: did they give you this nonsense at the asylum?' the principal earnestly enquired.

In occupying the position of principal in his own right Johannes was inured to rude and derogatory comments, so he chose to ignore Principal Hancock's question.

'I'm simply making reference to what is happening now at the Nehemiah Institute of Art,' was Johannes's stoical reply, 'and, I hasten to add, other specialist art and design institutions in the higher education sector.'

'But have you thought through that the authorities in the real world would not allow such meddling lunacy in the first instance?' the principal suggested, playing the fish.

'I am afraid you have not been listening; perhaps it accounts for the funding council's stand-off with this college,' Johannes answered, 'What I am warning against is an explosion of different media proliferating the abscess of posited art, like cows cut longitudinally in two, immersed in a glass case of formaldehyde, or elephant dung paintings, and so on.'

'Your absurdities have such conviction as to attenuate my reasoning,' the principal said quietly, dropping his head and slowly shaking it, 'you have my sympathy regarding your condition, but what you say is preposterous, utterly preposterous! What are these slang terms you use? Where on earth did you trump up such terms in art, leave alone imagining yourself as a principal of all things about to conduct an official inspection of this college of all things on behalf of a council of all things?'

'Funding council, not council,' Johannes corrected.

Principal Hancock quickly dialled his secretary again.

'Miss Sparrow... on second thoughts regarding academics: could you please locate Professor Price and ask him to stand by in the event I may urgently need him... beg pardon? No, no, not at the moment. Thank you,' replacing the receiver, he turned again to face Johannes, 'Your delusion that you are a principal does not bear thinking about,' he continued, ignoring the correction, 'At least your fixation on Miss Howells confined your attention, indirectly safeguarding this institution. The same is applicable to your obsession with those windows over there,' indicating the windows behind him, 'which, incidentally, lest you should re-engage your alternate exit melodrama, have been fitted with child-locks; but now you have returned you have the whole institution in your sights, heaven forbid. What horrors! Fixations for our model have transformed into delusions of grandeur,' the principal continued, 'the psychiatrists must have fed you strange fruit in the asylum.'

Drawing attention to the windows caused Johannes to glance through the nearer one: there the washing on the line high up on Mayhill was still applauding his performance. He smiled at the irony of it all.

'It's no laughing matter, Taliesin; but I suppose as long as you fantasise delusions of government acts and funding councils and official inspections at least it causes neither the model nor yourself any further harm.'

'From what I was led to understand from David Eckto you

were more dysfunctional in your reasoning than you appear to be,' Johannes said calmly, 'you are simply manifesting a time-dilated disaffection to progress, and mindful of the circumstances of art to which progress has transported us, one cannot blame you. You have suspended the College of Art in the realm of catatonia. How admirable! But from my perspective it is most intriguing how you have avoided the circumstances of change.'

'Thank God Dr Eckto is on his way,' the principal muttered sotto voce.

'There are many unexplained movements afoot, Principal Hancock, not least Eckto being so readily at hand,' Johannes responded.

'That is the least of my problems,' the principal compounded the enigma.

'We think we are confused.'

'I too am glad Eckto is on his way,' Johannes continued, 'regardless the contrivance of his having business in the vicinity. The task of inspecting this backward institution will probably prove to be beyond one person. However, there are one or two aspects of the visit that admittedly I find difficult to grasp, but they are not to do with my status, I can assure you. For instance, can you refute my outline of the politico-educational scene?'

'The very phraseology you use belies delusions at variance with reality,' the principal declared.

'I shall indulge your clarification of that statement, Mr Principal,' Johannes invited, maintaining his air of authority.

Principal Hancock's professional disposition did not waver, though the beetling of his brow indicated the measure of discomfort was deepening. Clearly as a manager of long standing he was deeply troubled such stuff should be coming from Johannes Taliesin. The principal stared long and hard, manifestly relying upon decades of experience in keeping his disquiet to manageable proportions.

'If you will,' the principal eventually spoke, 'take for example the most recent of your inventions – the Multi-Handicap Enabling Act, of all things. Fortunately for us, this Act is fiction. Regardless, from it you conjure the term 'politico-educational', no doubt due to its right-sounding authenticity, no doubt due to your mental state –'

'*Persisting with this mental state line with us.*'

'– From the point of view of practical art education, could you tell me what it is supposed to mean?' and he paused.

'That –' Johannes began, but was interrupted by the principal.

'We are all aware the political establishment in this country has a statutory duty to maintain the governance and law of education,' the principal continued, 'in a manner that enables the professionals to deliver a service for their students, yet you imply the reverse, if you would. What do you mean?'

'Tyrants throughout history have alighted upon youth as the tool for promulgating their ideologies. The circumstances we witnessed in art education during the last decade of the twentieth century and the first decade of the twenty-first are unfortunately the reverse of your established assumptions,' Johannes said.

'You appear to be convinced of this philosophical change in the delivery of provision. As you are so certain, tell me: when did the supposed change occur?' Principal Hancock's interest appeared genuine.

'*Watch it! Suddenly the bugger seems more interested in this standard inspection information. Must beware.*'

'Key dates, which seem to have slipped your mind: one, the weak governments of Heath, Wilson and Callaghan in the 1970s,' Johannes answered robotically, 'which allowed the unions to fill the vacuum caused by impotent leadership; two, the reforming zeal of the Thatcher administration, with its crushing of union power, privatisation of nationalised utilities and reform of higher education. Pertinent to our self-centred perspective, the Education Reform Act of 1988 ended the traditional LEA domination of colleges and universities with its nepotism and old boy network of political patronage for a more equitable assessment methodology, which brought about a universal objectivity to the funding mechanism.'

Principal Hancock's jaw sagged once again; he shook his head slowly and deliberately, glancing towards the closed door for salvation, as if yearning it to spring ajar to reveal Eckto. But Johannes had not finished.

'Three, the weak Major government allowed ill-thought policies to once again infiltrate education and other national institutions; four, the politics of envy during the Blair years attacked education by statutorily inflicting ethnic and other minority quotas on elite educational establishments, infusing political correctness and other fanciful flavours into the curriculum, and blatant socially engineered manipulation of standards and quality; five, the Brown Terror that has recently commenced is building up a huge welfare state of unemployed, uneducated voters. Not for one moment are the Blair-Brown politicians interested in the welfare of ethnic minorities – it is more to do with their ideological zeal in lowering the world-famous status of our quality educational establishments. I am sure you are aware this latter has cast a general educational mediocrity over our land.'

'It seems some science fiction version of Grimm's *Fairy Tales* is standard reading at the asylum,' the principal croaked.

'If this bugger mentions asylum again we will attack him with his fanciful letter-opener,' Inner Voice vacuously threatened, *'and dance widdershins on his bloody inlaid desk.'*

But, resolving to push aside the wisps of contradicting reason that persisted in building up before him, Johannes forged ahead.

450

'If you had kept abreast of changing social mores, you would be aware how loyalty and reverence have degenerated into cant and hypocrisy.'

The principal sat in silent tolerance, although it was clear he was becoming increasingly impatient with Eckto's delayed arrival. Occasionally he reached across the desk to press buttons on his elaborate telephone; to scribble notes on a pad.

'At Nehemiah Institute of Art perfidy is assumed to be the given,' Johannes continued, 'the academics believe it to be a national sport. A meeting of the board is more like a playpen for irresponsible offspring of the Fabian Society – everyone jiggling their self-centred hobbyhorses for all that is useless. The circumstances of Nehemiah are light years from your environment of reverence that both your title and art deserve. And so your work *should* be respected: over the years I have seen many examples of your paintings and drawings in galleries up and down the land – I believe your draughtsmanship to be the chief excellence of your repertoire.'

This turn of subject caught Principal Hancock unprepared. He experienced obvious difficulty in reconciling praise of his work with what he had decided to be hallucinatory nonsense that Johannes had been uttering. It was clear the principal rejected out of hand the notion of socio-political interference in art education. Instead, he attached the idea to Johannes's daydreams of some future entity: but now that same person was praising his art.

'Like all artists, a bit of praise throws his sense of judgement into the waste paint pot.'

'I have to advise you, Taliesin, unless something supernatural has affected your technical ability in the three weeks you have been under medical supervision, your achievements never matched the grandiose status you have delivered upon your delusion. I must confess however I cannot conceive of where you would have gained such knowledge of maintained governance in education. I am at a loss as to your reading matter at the asylum –'

'That's it! It's the letter opener for this bugger!'

'– Regrettably, the mystery deepens,' the principal continued, 'but I shall not allow my curiosity to detract from my responsibilities to this institution. As for you, please be aware: when you were handed over to the mental health authorities Swansea College of Art was effectively absolved of responsibility for you. My only concern for your welfare today is that you are on the premises of this establishment for which I am responsible. When Dr Eckto arrives I shall hand over that responsibility forthwith.'

'I believe you have already allowed atavism to detract you from your responsibilities, Mr Principal,' was Johannes's response.

'I am not referring to the nonsense of your delusions, Taliesin: I am referring to my responsibilities to this institution, its students and staff.'

'The information I have so far imparted is not the problem. Eckto advised me the funding council believes you, Principal Hancock, to be the problem.'

'I am sure from what I know of Dr Eckto's professional approach, you are greatly mistaken. But you have lost me with your fantasies, Taliesin, as fortunately I was never attracted to the profession of psychiatry, for which I thank the Lord for his guidance,' the principal sighed.

Still watching over Johannes guardedly, Principal Hancock continued pressing tabs on a keyboard. From time to time he glanced edgily at the door. The tapestry of his monumental patience had long since become threadbare, although Johannes was oblivious to the real warning signs.

'I mounted many exhibitions of my paintings and drawings,' Johannes said, 'until the exigencies of office forbade the time for such pleasantries. While your paintings are based upon a reliable constancy of knowledge and craftsmanship, mine are at best ephemeral.'

'It is all very flattering, but does not amount to much. Certainly art is not, and never has been, your vocation; I do not feel of sufficient confidence to identify *what* if anything *is* your calling. Perhaps following a lengthy period of enforced institutional care and observation, and hoping your confinement will be a little more secure in future someone may be able to identify your finer points. Apart from being at a loss with you, Taliesin, I very much regret that my patience was quite exhausted three weeks ago, leave alone today.'

'Your patience is exhausted simply because your life painting session has been interrupted. You live in a cosy cocoon with complete freedom to paint away the day in an office that doubles as an atel –'

Johannes's flow was interrupted by a sharp knock on the door, which opened ahead of the principal bidding entry.

'Dr Eckto and Ms Ulanova to see you, Mr Hancock,' a woman's voice announced with some urgency. Johannes mistily recognised the voice from some time past; he swivelled round in his chair but the door prevented his putting a face to the voice recognition.

'At last, thank goodness!' the principal called in theatrical tone, 'show them in, Miss Sparrow,' and he breathed a loud sigh of relief.

'*Ms Ulanova?*'

'Hello again, Kenneth!' David Eckto extended his hand on entering the office, 'well, well, has Johannes led us a dance!'

'*Led us a dance – ?*'

'Hello, David, am I relieved to see you. This has been some

ordeal,' the principal responded, standing up, shaking hands. Johannes rose to greet David Eckto.

'Eckto, at last! But what are they talking about? This woman Ulanova is new – wait a minute, we think we –'

A petite woman in her early twenties had followed Eckto in. Johannes's attention was drawn to her remarkably large eyes.

'We remember this little thing, of all the…'

'Hello again, Johannes,' said David Eckto, extending his hand, 'my, you have begun work very promptly! You and Patty have met before I believe,' he said, with a wave of the hand –

'Where was it…?'

– And, turning to Principal Hancock, Eckto said, 'this is my Girl Friday, Patty Ulanova. I've brought her along because she is specialising in an MA dissertation on the rare condition of quantum entanglement in the contagious form of hysteria, of which I believe we have the perfect example right here,' nodding in Johannes's direction.

'Quantum entanglement in the contagious form of hysteria,' Patty Ulanova echoed.

'A likely story! Driving up from London on any pretext to have a squeeze with his little flimsy,' Inner Voice grumped with disdain, *'everybody should know, I think –'*

Principal Hancock hesitated before shaking hands stiffly with Patty Ulanova, 'How do you do,' he murmured.

'Why the hesitation? Something fishy here, after all she can only be a cosy shagbox.'

Forgetting out of hand the circumstances of his business, Johannes could not take his eyes off Patty.

'Hello again, Johannes!' Patty greeted Johannes with a huge wink of a huge eye.

'Would willingly paint this one, perfect proportions… she reminds us of someone… a million years ago, can't quite

454

remember…' Inner Voice plumbed the depths, *'um… we must keep our wits about us.'*

'Hello, Patty, um… what do you think of Swansea?'

'Why was Taliesin commissioned by the funding council to inspect this college, David?' the principal wasted no time in getting down to business.

'You should know, Ken! For a number of years now the funding council has been monitoring this college regarding its lack of cooperation on administrative fundamentals. The funding council commissioned Principal Taliesin to undertake the inspection of Swansea College of Art as part of the agreed schedule of inspections.'

'I concur,' Johannes asserted, 'it's a point I have attempted to get across.'

'I trust you have furnished Principal Hancock with details of funding council procedures, Inspector Taliesin?' Eckto breezed.

'Mostly; I was obliged to bring Principal Hancock up to speed with other funding council protocols, owing to several decades' backlog of directives, government decrees and the like that regrettably have been either overlooked or neglected.'

'Hmm, understandable under the circumstances,' Eckto muttered.

'When did you arrive in Swansea, David?' the principal asked, deflecting attention from the backlog, as if nothing had ever happened.

'This should be interesting.'

'Best we can tell,' said David Eckto, looking at Patty Ulanova for support, 'was about five last night – what time did you leave us, Johannes?' he asked of Johannes with an air of not particularly wanting a reply in front of Principal Hancock.

'What is he pretending? He wants us to assist a cover-up for having it off with Patty Ulanova last night – don't answer that question.'

'I stayed at the Dragon Hotel last night; the funding council made the booking for me,' Johannes replied, avoiding the Eckto cover-up.

'Oh dear, I think we are in unknown territory,' said David Eckto shiftily.

'Patty has that universal look that reminds us... those huge eyes have the secret...'

'I have hardly begun the official inspection, and would like your assistance with several matters,' Johannes said.

'This is true,' came Eckto's reply.

'Taliesin certainly has a fanciful delusion right now,' Principal Hancock glowered, 'he has certainly kept me entertained during our wait for you.'

'I'm sure you must have been well entertained, Kenneth,' said Eckto, 'there being such an immense backlog.'

'At another time not so pressing as now I would be interested in learning the reading matter you proffer your patients,' Mr Hancock volunteered interest.

'That is simple to resolve – as part of our programme for recovery we do not allow the patients any reading matter. In cases of quantum entanglement in the contagious form of hysteria the patient is shut off from stimuli as it is essential to keep the mind as blank as possible.'

'Remarkable! I am at a loss –' Mr Hancock stuttered, while smiling relief that matters were no longer his responsibility.

But the while Johannes's mind was on other matters and failed to resonate with the conversation.

'Aha! The Frameshop!' it belatedly rushed home, *'we remember now, the Frameshop – that's where we saw this woman previously.'*

'Tell us about the official inspection you are undertaking, Mr Taliesin,' Mr Hancock once again diverted from signal truths.

Johannes looked to David Eckto for moral support.

'As if the silly bugger doesn't know!'

'You know full well about the official inspection I am undertaking,' Johannes muttered darkly.

'Perhaps if I were to describe from my perspective it might enlighten you, which could assist in his treatment and consequent recovery,' said the principal.

'What on earth are they talking about?'

'Yes, please, Principal Hancock, if you must,' Dr Eckto humoured the principal.

Meanwhile, Patty Ulanova moved round to stand beside Johannes, which new development took Johannes's mind further off the discussion.

'Ah! The smell of oil paint, not Old Holland, but the smell of the Frameshop –'

'I shall summarise the points that have come to light in the past twenty minutes or so,' the principal said, 'but you realise I was unprepared for this, otherwise I would have had the DVD recorder set up.'

'The bugger's got a DVD recorder, just when I thought this place was steam driven,' Inner Voice gasped.

'As I believe it to be, Taliesin is the principal of Nehemiah Institute of Art – I have never heard of the place, must be an invention. He has been commissioned by the funding council to undertake an official inspection of this college. The council feels Swansea College of Art has been obstructing dialogue and progress, at least according to Inspector Taliesin.'

'Come, come, Kenneth, your humour is more obtuse than ever. I have to say Principal Taliesin takes his responsibilities to educational administration very seriously. He has a point, of course,' Eckto exclaimed.

Principal Hancock scowled darkly.

'How interesting!' Patty Ulanova echoed Eckto, 'I'm sure I will not regret my interest in Johannes Taliesin's rare entanglement condition,' she nodded emphatically, beaming all over her large eyes and edging yet closer to Johannes.

'It's that echo on top of the oil paint fragrance... confirmation if ever we needed it.'

'I fail to see how my commission can be so interesting,' was Johannes's obdurate comment, 'it's a straightforward process that occurs up and down the land on a regular basis.'

'Forgive me,' Patty Ulanova made amends, 'I was merely resonating with Dr Eckto's general disposition.'

Both Hancock and Eckto stared at her, awaiting further elucidation, but none came.

'Fair play to Johannes,' Dr Eckto said after a while, 'he certainly volunteers for some interesting tasks, given the nature of –' but he cut himself short, obviously not wanting further disclosure of Johannes's current obligations, 'we must get on with the inspection, Johannes, as all of us have a busy administrative schedule to complete today.'

'I certainly have a busy administrative schedule to complete, but I was about to disclose more of Taliesin's future imperfect delusions,' Mr Hancock rejoined tetchily.

'Busy administrative schedule indeed!' blurted Johannes, 'that's the first time I've known painting from the life model, the exercise being attended to when I arrived this morning, categorised as a busy administrative schedule. Apologies for my bluntness, Principal Hancock,' and, to confirm the implication he turned and pointed in the direction of the atelier.

'Of course principals of art colleges should practise their art and sullen crafts,' the principal sighed officiously, 'but you will note, Dr Ecko, that today of all days although I am preparing for an inspection, I am supposed to be painting from the life model here in this busy office, the very life model who was the subject of Taliesin's fixation three weeks ago.'

'Hang on, how does he know the model he denies being here in

his office is the same one I am supposedly fixated on? Go on, we must challenge this disjoint in the sod's logic,' Inner Voice urged.

'Would that I had the time to paint from the life model these days!' the principal added, capping the authenticity of his defence.

'How do you know the model of your denial is the one and the same of a supposed fixation of three weeks ago?' Johannes coldly demanded.

'Alas, those days of leisurely creativity have gone since the Education Reform Act overwhelmed the higher education sector,' the principal regretted, but in a wild attempt at eclipsing his disingenuous inference, he inadvertently blew the cover on his previous charade.

'*Got him!'*

Johannes shot the principal a look of triumphal anger.

'*So the wily old bird knows all about the Education Reform Act! We'll give him calling our briefing preposterous – he's not so wily as he thinks he is,'* Inner Voice growled.

'You have just confirmed Swansea College of Art is incorporated as a consequence of the 1988 Education Reform Act,' Johannes said, controlling his excitement.

The principal gestured a small sad toss of the head as he looked to Dr Eckto, who readily reciprocated.

'Come, come, Johannes,' Dr Eckto laboured, 'no need to rub in small victories, don't you think?'

'Yes, *do* come,' Patty Ulanova urged.

'Of course this institution is incorporated. It goes without saying if you are meant to be conducting an official inspection of the institution then you should be aware of its status. If it were not incorporated under the aegis of the funding council then please advise us the reason you are here,' the principal smiled the look of conviction he had turned the matter on its head and cemented Johannes's conundrum.

'Privatisation of the higher education sector comes at a price,' Eckto added in consolatory support of Principal Hancock, 'usually in the form of extra work for less return by the hardworking incumbency, especially management; Principal Taliesin will no doubt agree. Next thing we know, the government will be privatising the hospitals, the fire service and forestry. Alas! Goodbye to shivering money trees!'

'*Huh? Are we hearing this from Eckto?*'

'I agree with the former aspect of your comment, Eckto, but the latter part is borne of a dependency culture of yore, with which I vehemently disagree,' Johannes said, still fighting to recall his previous conversation with a principal best described as elusive.

'*Best described as bloody-minded and obdurate,*' Inner Voice concluded, '*the mystery thickens.*'

'I must say in support of Principal Taliesin,' Patty Ulanova addressed Mr Hancock, 'there is irrefutable logic in his question regarding your denial of the model being here. Your obfuscation denotes an intention to deflect the realities of this institution from disclosure during an official inspection. Apart from falsifying data your obduracy is both a hindrance to the funding council and intolerably unfair to Principal Taliesin in his capacity as official inspector.'

'Miss Ulanova!' the principal shouted angrily, 'of all the –' he could hardly conceal his displeasure as dark secrets began unravelling from the hitherto closed circuit.

'Um, we really must be getting on with the task,' Dr Eckto dived to rescue Hancock from the two-pronged attack on his veracity, 'we've already gossiped too much, wasting precious time.'

'You came to assist me in unravelling the obfuscation and diffidence the funding council has experienced with this college for some time!' Johannes erupted in uncharacteristic anger.

'Sorry, Principal Taliesin: you are the sole inspector in that detail. Patty Ulanova and I came simply to check college records and documented accounts pertinent to the inspection,' Eckto retaliated.

'It's a conspiracy. He's changed his story. We must escape from this bloody mob. But that Patty Ulanova is a curious enigma; we must ask, must ask – go on, ask now, last bloody chance.'

'Did I not see you in the Frameshop?' Johannes levelled the long shot at Patty Ulanova, coming from the depths of his memory morphed into shadows.

'NO!' Principal Hancock answered on Patty's behalf, 'that was an unrelated Ulanova – Ingrid Ulanova! Tell the fool it was another Ulanova he saw in the Frameshop. For God's sake, tell him before things unravel out of hand!' Principal Hancock's roared gibberish.

'Ye gods! Stumbled onto something here! How would he know it was another Ulanova without being there?'

'Yes, it was me you saw at the Frameshop,' Patty replied, calmly ignoring Hancock's transformation into a nether portfolio.

'I *thought* so, knew we had met in unusual circumstances the moment I saw you! So Principal Hancock must be Laughing Cavalier!' Johannes fair shouted with excitement. 'Laughing Cavalier! I *knew* there was a charade going on, but couldn't put my finger on it. It transpires I've been right all along! Do you get it, Eckto?'

'Eckto certainly does not get it!' the principal barked, 'Take him back with your accounts, Eckto!'

'I've been right all along!' Johannes competed in shouting.

'Of course he is Laughing Cavalier,' Patty Ulanova giggled at the commotion erupting around her.

'Well, I'm an audit compliance officer. These revelations are out of my remit –' Eckto stuttered weakly.

'We've been right all along!'

'I've been right all along!'

'Eckto, can't you see I'm being confounded!' Principal Hancock was becoming darkly hostile, 'Ms Ulanova is greatly mistaken! The Ulanova in the Frameshop was a different Ulanova. Take them both away, Eckto!' the principal ordered, inadvertently putting Johannes and Patty in the same parley.

'Why the denial? It's obvious you are Laughing Cavalier, otherwise how could you tell Patty is an unrelated Ulanova and why is the Frameshop so pertinent to your obfuscation? This is an enormous revelation and explains a lot for me,' Johannes insisted and, turning again to Patty, 'I'm convinced you are the same, the one and the same – it's those large dark eyes! Tell me, did you escape the tsunami?'

'Yes, after a while,' she replied enigmatically, 'but at the start the tsunami was excruciatingly pleasurable, pure ecstasy!'

'That explains a lot, but we are still confused about Eckto's audit compliance role in all this.'

'I was certain you and Laughing Cavalier were drowned in the rose madder tsunami,' Johannes reasoned and, turning to Eckto, 'what is your role in this, David?'

'The significance of my role will become obvious in due course,' Eckto obfuscated.

'Come on, audit compliance officer, stop obfuscating!'

'No, I wasn't drowned! Laughing Cavalier dragged me into his atelier,' Patty reassured and, turning to address Laughing Cavalier, 'I never told you, but the moment you rescued me the ecstasy stopped. Following the Frameshop priming I had to take up writing MA dissertations on quantum entanglement and then, when matters became clear, I enlarged the scope to include the contagious form of hysteria; that is, quantum entanglement in the contagious form of hysteria.'

'Bloody hell! We're more confused than ever, we think. Must try to keep a clear head.'

'It was my duty to stop the fun; you were only painted in parts,' Laughing Cavalier's contrition was as sudden as the changing set, 'but that fool,' pointing at Johannes, 'that fool had painted your clothes straight onto the canvas; you had no body, he had not even primed the canvas!'

The talk of clothes prompted Johannes to look through the window: sure enough, the clothes on the line high up on the terraced reaches of Mayhill were still clapping in the wind.

But other matters called attention, 'How dare you be so insulting!' Johannes exclaimed.

'Don't you realise that was precisely the reason I loved it – being painted straight onto a bare canvas, deliciously wicked, much more exciting than MA dissertations,' Patty Ulanova salivated.

'I thought you enjoyed writing MA diss –' David Eckto broke off.

'Can you believe it?' Laughing Cavalier addressed Eckto, 'the fool did not prime the canvas, yet he painted clothes onto the bareness of an empty canvas and *then* the idiot expected his portrait to manage a Frameshop! He has the gall to call himself an artist! Standards in art have fallen astonishingly low since the advent of the 1988 Education Reform Act, encouraging a wave of dross to stifle art and design provision.'

'What have we got ourselves into? How many ways are things...? We must analyse things when the opportunity...' Inner Voice sniffled.

'When one is striving to safeguard the old values the idiots escape from the asylum to formulate funding councils and phoney inspectorates,' Laughing Cavalier continued, 'giving them a head start to beat the old values into submission.'

'Quite right, Laugh,' Eckto endorsed.

'Regardless I managed the Frameshop surprisingly efficiently considering my disadvantages, not to mention the loony customers who came in from the arcade,' Patty Ulanova claimed, 'you can at least give me credit for that.'

'On the contrary, Miss Ulanova, I could not help noticing your indiscretions from my atelier. Whenever a customer clanged into the Frameshop your sense of classical decorum disintegrated.'

'Well, I never –' Eckto truncated.

'I know what you are driving at, but my behaviour was not all what it seemed, given my disadvantages,' Patty Ulanova defended.

'You contrived to have your clothes taken off by the customers, that's what I am driving at or, if the costumers were unforthcoming such as this clown,' nodding in Johannes's direction, 'you obligingly removed your clothes yourself,' Laughing Cavalier accused.

Laughing Cavalier had become highly animated, and his character was in danger of metamorphosing as a spotted handkerchief tucked in a top pocket, made signs of coming adrift and flapped alarmingly. Spotted shadows morphed across the office.

'But I wished the customers to see my no-body,' Patty Ulanova admitted.

'Well, I never –' Eckto seemed incapable of completing the sentence on what he never.

'Your parading the gaps was disgusting! I had to do something about it,' came Cavalier's snorting response.

'Laughing Cavalier appears to have painted all the missing parts perfectly,' Johannes interjected, unable to resist flattering Patty Ulanova, but unaware of the damage his contribution was doing, 'and I admire the perfection as far as I can see that he has achieved in your life-size portrait.'

Patty blinked. 'Would you like to see my new perfect body Principal Cavalier has painted? The representation of flesh tints is wondrous to behold,' she gushed and, oblivious to the place and circumstance, began to unbutton her blouse.

'No, no, no!' Laughing Cavalier shouted; 'Eckto, for God's sake *do* something! The image is escaping out of its frame, running into the background and away up the hill. The scene has gone too far: her blouse will join the clothes clapping their hands with glee up on Mayhill, then I'll really be in trouble with the funding council. Bring the image back to the purpose of its duty!'

'Huh? Didn't realise he had noticed the clapping clothes on Mayhill.'

'Well, I never –'

'His well I nevers are getting tiresome!'

At which tense moment Laughing Cavalier mopped his brow with the large spotted handkerchief that flapped at hand. Unfortunately, several spots dislodged and stuck to his face.

'Don't just stand there allowing things to unravel, Eckto, it's typical of auditors, so pedantic they are incapable of extemporising remedies in the face of degenerating circumstances,' Laughing Cavalier raged, 'I am expecting important visitors from the funding council later this morning; we cannot allow this insane transformation to be witnessed by them. Take them and yourself away!'

'Calm down, Laugh, quantum entanglement has allowed your attention to run ahead of you – don't forget I am head of audit compliance at the funding council. Principal Taliesin, Patty Ulanova and I are important visitors from the funding council and we are already with you! Besides, those spots on your face appear quite angry,' at last Eckto completed a sentence.

'Do you have a medical centre at this college?' Johannes interjected.

'What for?'

'Emergencies.'

'I'm good in emergencies,' Patty Ulanova chipped in, 'especially rose madder tsunami emergencies.'

'Eckto is amazingly calm now he has got back to completing sentences, considering they appoint nincompoops these days, that is, but his indiscretion – huh!'

Johannes's thoughts were appropriate. Eckto's inept indiscretion caused the superposition entanglement to snap. Without further ado Laughing Cavalier pressed a button on his keypad and waited, fingers tapping.

'Thought so, it had to come, superposition.'

'Yes, Mr Cavalier?' the conference speakeasy buzzed.

'Miss Sparrow,' Principal Cavalier spoke crisply, 'when my visitors from the funding council – Sir Barcode Cardigan and Adam Krenwinkler – arrive, bring them to my office immediately.'

'Sir Barcode Cardigan and Adam Krenwinkler from the funding council? Eckto didn't tell me they were coming.'

'Will do, Mr Cavalier – are you well, Sir?'

'Perfectly well, thank you, why do you ask, Miss Sparrow?'

'Oh, your voice sounds strangely different – it must be this new satellite intercom system they have just installed.'

'Satellite intercom? Wasn't here when we arrived – bugger, more timing oddities.'

'You didn't advise me Sir Barcode Cardigan and Adam Krenwinkler are coming here at the same time as I am undertaking an inspection of the place,' Johannes addressed Eckto accusingly.

'Information of that nature is above your salary level, Taliesin,' was Eckto's curt reply and, turning to Laughing Cavalier, he added, 'you are quite right, Principal Cavalier, the time has come for us to stop this theatre. I have been pondering a revision of the inspection procedure: having observed Patty Ulanova's change of behaviour I have no option but to accept what we at centre suspected all along: the problem besetting us is definitely quanglement in the contagious form of hysteria.

'What do you mean, theatre?' Johannes burst, 'Isn't psychoanalysis above your salary level, Eckto?'

'Quanglement in the contagious form of hysteria!' Laughing Cavalier exclaimed, throwing up his hands, 'My goodness, what next?'

'Perhaps that acting was a bit OTT.'

'Only contagious to those who observe it, who possess a propensity to adopt the malady,' Eckto assured stiffly, 'take the case of Ms Ulanova for example – perfectly normal when we arrived here, but now having come into contact with the carrier she is overwhelmed to the point of acting as a self-motivated life painting. Fortunately for us, old friend, the likes of you and I have strong psychological resistance to such caricature maladies.'

'Strong psychological resistance to such caricature maladies,' Patty Ulanova echoed.

'Not only strong psychological resistance,' Laughing Cavalier advised, 'but the transformation explains a lot to those of us with foresight. Regardless, you should leave before my visitors arrive – I don't want different echelons of funding council bureaucracy conflating in my attel – er, office.'

'Those spots are in serious need of attention, Laugh,' Eckto suggested.

The scenes playing out exercised Patty Ulanova's imagination, 'Laughing Cavalier created my new perfect body from copies of his model Sophie,' she prattled on.

'Oh dear, we might have known it: had to be a Sophie connection; explains a lot.'

Patty's last comment animated Principal Cavalier beyond, 'Eckto! Don't just stand there so stiffly – I SAID TAKE THEM BOTH AWAY!' he roared, clearly wanted his office empty before Sir Barcode Cardigan and Adam Krenwinkler arrived.

'The inspector on behalf of the funding council happens to be here already vis, me, standing before you,' Johannes addressed Laughing Cavalier, 'but what I don't understand is why you became so aggressive towards my briefing you on recent historical developments. Why did you have to pretend all the 'this is preposterous!' nonsense?'

Principal Cavalier seemed lost for a plausible explanation.

'Eckto!' he raged, 'initiate prearranged procedures, for heaven's sake! Augment the peripheries as we agreed, and may we all be damned! Damned, I say!'

'Whoopee!' Patty Ulanova exclaimed, 'Dr Eckto is going to augment the peripheries!'

Immediately Laughing Cavalier's words triggered prearranged chicanery between the old friends, whereupon Johannes could not prevent his imagination taking free reign. It was a sad sight to behold, as once again Johannes Taliesin found himself in a pickle he believed belonged to others. Eckto obediently metamorphosed into a cardboard cut-out, rooted to his stand-up spot. Laughing Cavalier's augment the peripheries command had centred on Eckto's idiosyncratic handicap. Once the prearranged trickery had been applied Johannes was swept up in the superposition. Meanwhile the two-dimensional nature of the head of audit compliance conformed to the law of physics regarding a cut-out occupying territory at a propped-up angle. David Eckto had become the perfect cardboard dolt, in strong compliance with current government policy to recruit ethnic minorities, half-wits, the severely challenged and cardboard dolts to senior ranks of educational administration.

'It seems we have to seek meaning in trivia; Eckto's achievement is remarkable, really, attaining the status of head of audit compliance with such a handicap – every bit as amazing as the achievement of an unfinished painted model managing a Frameshop.'

468

Once again caught up in his superposition, Johannes urgently sought an avenue of release,

'All the trivia have got meaning,' he muttered a propos the transitional continuum.

But Cardboard Cut-Out had over-augmented the peripheries and found himself so severely constrained that all that his emulsion-splashed two-dimensional features could do was look longingly at Patty Ulanova.

'Here's our opportunity! Seize the moment!'

'Take Laughing Cavalier away,' Johannes took advantage of the flat interregnum, 'he's a doppelgänger interloping in the realms of the Education Reform Act,' which contradicted the whole inspection exercise while ignoring the extent of Cardboard Cut-Out's metamorphosis that compromised his taking even himself away, 'but not before I have concluded my pre-inspection questioning of him,' he added as an afterthought.

But it was a false dawn for Johannes, for meantime he needed more integration with the totems.

'We should keep our wits, while all those around us…'

'You should take Cardboard Cut-Out away instead,' Patty Ulanova cautioned Johannes as she was now fully consumed by the contagious form of hysteria, 'because every time we are alone together, he attempts having his wicked way with me,' and, turning to Laughing Cavalier, added, 'that's why we were late arriving – he stopped on the way and tried to rekindle the ecstasy I last experienced during the Frameshop tsunami, but unfortunately he failed to get the lid off the drum of rose madder.'

'What you are saying is preposterous, Miss Ulanova,' Laughing Cavalier exclaimed, 'how could a two-dimensional cardboard figure open a drum of rose madder? After your rescue from the tsunami I painted a perfect body on you so that you could conduct a normal life and behave appropriately. Why did you have to get mixed up with funding council lunatics and then divulge your painted history to Cardboard Cut-Out of all totems?'

'But I owe it to him,' Patty replied plaintively, 'he discovered me as a placement jobsworth at head office writing an MA dissertation on the uncertainty principle a propos the 1988 Education Reform Act and, notwithstanding his extraordinary two-dimensional condition, pumped life into me.'

'*Huh! We thought as much... except theoretically he should not have been two-dimensional at that time of pumping,*' Inner Voice jealously sniggered.

Cardboard Cut-Out remained propped up stiff and impassive, save for his eyes that could but watch appealingly. Johannes, who had been confused since Principal Kenneth Hancock had metamorphosed to Laughing Cavalier upon a simple historical device, was now plunged into complete confusion as his sense of time indulged disorientation.

'*Our thinking says it's quantum entanglement acting in a dissimulative manner, but in slow motion, perhaps,*' Inner Voice reasoned, as Johannes began entertaining the notion that counterintuitive consequences of quantum entities were interacting beyond his mentality, '*after all, there's no other explanation why these events from different times should conflate in the principal's office.*'

Meanwhile, Patty Ulanova continued to ignore her superiors, 'Come along, Johannes,' she said, taking his arm and jolting his thoughts from here and there, 'let me take you back to the hotel where I can show you my perfect body that Laughing Cavalier painted for me with no strings attached out of the goodness of his pure skill.'

'*For God's sake don't go! She'll want us to shag her! Never forget our track record at failing to perform the shag manoeuvre, which*

*will profoundly compromise our status as principal of Nehemiah
and inspector for the funding council.'*

'No, I am afraid I cannot leave: I have not completed
inspecting the shag department yet,' Johannes blundered, 'after
all, I have responsibilities to my track record.'

'Get a grip! What are we saying?'

'But I desperately need a –' Patty began.

'We are aware you do, Ms Ulanova, so off you go,' Laughing
Cavalier conspired, 'and impress on Taliesin that he has a duty to
go with you to fulfil your desperate needs. We all need to –'

*'Oh no! We must avoid being alone with this painted nympho.
Our failure will climb onto stilts this time.'*

'– Exhibit a degree of professionalism when dealing with
dangerous cases of contagious hysteria, but I must confess I'm
at a loss as to the best advice for dealing with Cardboard Cut-
Out,' he hedged, 'though I have to hand it to the head of audit
compliance: over-egging the metamorphosis into a cardboard
stasis is a clever safeguard against contracting the Taliesin
contagion –'

*'Clever safeguard against contracting the Taliesin contagion!
What's he on about?'*

'– Might I suggest you take the cut out with you?'

'What!' Johannes interjected, 'Are you suggesting Patty
Ulanova carries her line manager out of here in his cardboard
cut-out form?'

'It is by far the easiest method considering the alternatives,
especially as I am expecting important visitors any moment,'
Principal Cavalier shrugged.

However, Patty Ulanova was still engaging her plan which
she was strongly reluctant to relinquish, so the gibberish
continued.

'Why don't you e-mail the funding council to say the
inspection is being temporarily delayed?' she suggested to

Johannes, still clutching his arm, 'Any old excuse will do, like 'as Laughing Cavalier is busy commanding augmentation of the peripheries' or 'the validation papers have been damaged by rose madder emulsion paint in a failed attempt to generate a second tsunami – please fax another set of papers to Swansea College of Art tomorrow after Patty Ulanova has shown me her recently painted perfect body'. What do you think, Cardboard Cut-Out? Would those sorts of excuses give me sufficient time to have it off with Johannes Taliesin?'

Unhelpfully Cardboard Cut-Out's two-dimensional painted features had dried hard. His mouth could no longer move, and the eyes settled into dull impressions, although the eyebrows displayed an alternative meaning, presumably because a different hand had painted them.

'Levity used at the appropriate time is often seen to be effective in putting a lunatic's mind at rest, Ms Ulanova,' Laughing Cavalier spoke gravely, 'but in my opinion the humour has to be devoid of elaborate sexual inference in order to conform with an abundance of regulatory protocols recently decreed by government micromanagement.'

'Hmm,' she sniffed, 'in the old days my MA dissertation on quanglement in the contagious form of hysteria was inlaid with all sorts of sexual innuendo.'

'Immaterial, Ms Ulanova, your current plan is way out of line!' Laughing Cavalier insisted, 'you are simply succeeding in concatenating the two views that Taliesin's delusion obliges him to imagine.'

'Or, you could try this, Johannes: 'Dr Eckto had an accident when opening a drum of rose madder and turned into Cardboard Cut-Out when it dried.' They'll surely believe that because they accept any old excuse that will accord with their politics,' she continued in defiance of Laughing Cavalier's insistence.

'Good heavens, Ms Ulanova!' Laughing Cavalier burst, 'pull

yourself together! An inordinate amount of my time has been wasted already since that charlatan,' nodding in Johannes's direction, 'walked into my office. Clearly, it is beyond your capacity to realise the importance of my work, regardless my realistic portrayal of a body on you that is compatible with all the other anatomical appendages of your person. Please realise any moment now I am expecting the funding council delegation.'

'*What's the silly bugger on about? We* are *the funding council delegation,*' Inner Voice huffed.

'Thank God you are *not* the funding council delegation,' Laughing Cavalier responded to Inner Voice's huffing, 'you, Taliesin, are a lunatic escaped from Cefn Coed Hospital for the Seriously Mentally Challenged; you, Ms Ulanova, are the result of a botched paint-over job where you needed large passages of your missing body re-worked by an expert hand –'

'*Um, must huff quieter.*'

'And static Cardboard Cut-Out over there is the result of a prearranged augmentation of the peripheries procedure designed to renege on Taliesin's inspection, but he over-egged the metamorphosis and is now suffering, inter alia, the result of an accident with rose madder emulsion cunningly doctored with driers accelerator.'

'*Wonder who cunningly doctored the rose madder emulsion with driers accelerator?*' Inner Voice clucked, still having not got the modulation right.

'Who cunningly doctored the rose madder emulsion with driers accelerator?' Patty Ulanova picked up the cluck.

At that, Laughing Cavalier once again lost his patience and broke the entanglement in a new departure. Clapping his hands in an act of finality, he hurriedly opened the door as a demonstration he was bidding the party farewell.

'*It's got to be collapse of the wave function… all fitting together now.*'

Leaving the door ajar and walking back to his desk, Principal Cavalier pressed a single digit on the satellite intercom gadgetry.

'Miss Sparrow, have the inspectors arrived yet?'

'Yes, Sir, Sir Barcode Cardigan and Adam Krenwinkler happen to have arrived at just this moment,' the speakeasy buzzed.

'Good, please bring them along immediately. My morning's motley interruption is about to take leave,' and, turning to the parley of instruments, he said, 'it appears while this charade has been wandering its higgledy-piggledy way through my morning's tranquillity the inspection team from the funding council has arrived. I must now reluctantly bid you all farewell. Thank you for coming along; I can rest assured Taliesin is once again safely in your custody. Perhaps, if I may suggest, Cefn Coed should restrain him a little more securely in future, for instance, in arm and leg irons, lest his inspection visits to this institution become tiresomely regular. Carry Cardboard Cut-Out with care as you never know, quanglement symmetry has a habit of reversing when entangled with augment the peripheries commands.'

'*What is Laughing Cavalier on about? The head of audit compliance came to assist in the inspection but regrettably turned into cardboard as a result of that Cavalier's chicanery,*' Inner Voice continued to boom.

'Hurry up and leave,' Laughing Cavalier bullied, 'for the record, Taliesin, the head of audit compliance was already turning into Cardboard Cut-Out at the time of his arrival: goodness knows how you failed to notice he was covered in rose madder emulsion, but as I recall perceptivity was never your strong point.'

It seemed Laughing Cavalier wanted the visitors out of his office at all costs notwithstanding they in turn were delegates to a formal inspection of his college.

474

'*Perceptive enough to catch you up to no good with your model behind the screens,*' Inner Voice snarled.

'Please take your salacious thoughts with you, Taliesin,' the principal snapped, 'and when you are sure you have rid yourself of all delusions, return to this office to continue the inspection.'

This gave Johannes renewed hope, 'Patty could take Cardboard Cut-Out with her,' he suggested.

'*A brainwave, we must say.*'

'A brainwave, I must say, Inspector Taliesin,' Patty Ulanova gushed excitedly, 'play my cards right and I can have both of you at the same time, oh ecstasy!'

'*We've got a better suggestion – it's superposition, the concatenation of quantum states, we think; can't be collapsing wave function, regrets to Schröedinger, although we are not sure.*'

As Patty Ulanova was in the act of hooking Cardboard Cut-Out under her arm its painted mouth began to talk,

'Apologies your prearranged authenticate the peripheries chicanery went pear shaped, Laugh, and especially you having such a busy schedule with no sense of humour as backup.'

'I'll have you know I was drenched in a sense of humour until this lot happened,' Cavalier growled.

'That's for others to judge, Laugh,' the mouth said, 'anyway, goodbye, I'm sure you will be in good hands with Cardigan and Krenwinkler, trusting they have not been similarly inflicted.'

'Bye, Mr Cavalier!' Patty chirped, 'thanks for the suggestion.'

'Goodbye,' Laughing Cavalier returned, 'and sort your MA strategies out.'

'Be back shortly, Laughing Cavalier, but get those spots seen to before Cardigan and Krenwinkler see them... getting to look quite angry,' Johannes joined.

Irrespective of the spot contagion, Laughing Cavalier's features signalled he was already congratulating himself on the safe despatch of Cardboard Cut-Out and company when a smart knock sounded on the already open door: in hopped Miss Sparrow, followed by two officials. The two parties inadvertently converged at the doorway.

'Sir Barcode Cardigan and Adam Krenwinkler here to see you, Mr Cavalier,' she said.

'Hello again, Laughing, good to see you,' Sir Barcode beamed, stretching forward his hand.

'*Here we go again.*'

'Hello, Laugh,' Adam bustled, 'what happened to your face?'

'Hello, Barky, hello, Adam! Did you have a good journey down?' Laughing Cavalier breezed, ignoring the question.

'Morning, Principal Taliesin, are we interrupting your inspectoral procedures?'

'Good morning, Adam! No, no interruption, everything is proceeding according to plan; Principal Cavalier has been most helpful and co-operative.'

'Good to hear so,' Krenwinkler chortled, 'makes a change from the recalcitrant old bugger he normally is.'

Sir Barcode nodded politely at Patty Ulanova; caught in the doorway neither Principal Cavalier nor Principal Taliesin saw it their business to introduce her.

Concealed within the moment Cardboard Cut-Out, having no control over his travel plans, could but smile mulishly as Patty manoeuvred his cardboard length through the crowd.

'Before we leave,' the mouth called out, 'perhaps you could remind Sir Barcode Cardigan and Adam Krenwinkler who I am and how I got into this condition.'

To maintain propriety in conduct, Patty propped Cardboard Cut-Out upright again.

'Thank you, Miss Ulanova, I can now see the visitors eye to eye,' the mouth spoke.

'Ventriloquism! Very clever! Should I congratulate the young lady, or is the voice from you, Principal Taliesin?' Sir Barcode smiled, 'have you been entertaining Principal Cavalier thus? Wouldn't put it past you, being a jack of all trades.'

'No, no! It's a rather delicate matter,' Laughing Cavalier intervened, 'the cardboard silhouette is the remains of Dr David Eckto, head of Cefn Coed Hospital for the Seriously Mentally Challenged until he was infected by Taliesin's quantum entanglement in the contagious form of hysteria.'

'He means superposition, not entanglement, we think.'

The startling news of a new strain of infection caused Chairman Cardigan and Chief Executive Krenwinkler to step away from Johannes and Cardboard Cut-Out, horror painted in large brushstrokes across their faces.

'Quantum entanglement in the contagious form of hysteria! Surely not!' Chairman choked.

'Yes, I am afraid so,' Cavalier calmly assured.

'Our friend Laugh is the court jester,' the mouth interjected, 'he has Cefn Coed on the brain ever since... um... ever since Johannes Taliesin leaped out of the window; anyway, don't listen to a word he says. I suppose it is difficult for you to recognise me in my current guise: I am David Eckto, head of audit compliance at the funding council. In the line of duty I was undertaking a difficult authenticate the peripherals manoeuvre at Laughing Cavalier's instigation during a moment when his burials resurfaced, which rendered me vulnerable to an extraneous malfeasance perpetrated by this false Thespian, Taliesin, resulting in a cardboard extension.'

'Good Lord!' Sir Barcode exclaimed, 'it cannot possibly be more serious for you than it already looks!'

'Much more serious than that; so serious it plumbs the shadows of funding council audit compliance, which is shady enough in its own right,' Cardboard Cut-Out emphasised in a sort-of-cardboard voice.

'I take it you deny the accusation, Taliesin?' Krenwinkler posed.

'Of course,' Johannes said, 'Cardboard Cut-Out was indeed Dr David Eckto, head of audit compliance at the funding council until a pre-arranged bit of chicanery between him and Cavalier got out of hand, the result of which you witness before you. The council has inserted so many layers of management in recent months that the higher reaches are quarantined from ordinary functions, so I daresay there is no chance of your recognising him.'

'Astonishing turn up for the funding council books!' Adam Krenwinkler gasped.

'I had a premonition the day was going to be different when the cat started barking at the postman this morning,' Sir Barcode muttered.

'Cats are like that, Chairman; I suggest you don't respond the way they want you to; people cannot simply metamorphose into cardboard just like Kafka's woodlouse – got to be another explanation,' Krenwinkler tempered.

'Kafka's was a beetle,' Johannes corrected.

'Yes,' Krenwinkler acknowledged, 'but I must congratulate your faultless ventriloquism, Taliesin.'

'Ventriloquism is well and good, Adam, but where does the head of audit compliance come into it?' Sir Barcode quizzed.

'Figment of the comedian's fertile imagination – can't make the imagery out on the dummy, seems splashed with paint' Krenwinkler replied, scrutinising the painted face.

'Rose madder emulsion,' Patty intervened, 'he was covered in it when he tried to have his wicked way with me, and now it has hardened off. By the way, as you men are so obsessed with your own gender and consider women unimportant, I had better introduce myself – I'm Patty Ulanova, assistant to Cardboard Cut-Out, MA ghost for the funding council. Needless to say

I do not require layers of managerial largesse to successfully camouflage me from the dim lights of senior management.'

To be fair, at the 'he tried to have his wicked way with me' both Cardigan and Krenwinkler had already pricked up their hearing aids and skewed their attention round to the young woman.

'Flaw! Flaw in her story – she said Cardboard Cut Out couldn't get the –'

'Thought you said Cardboard Cut-Out couldn't get the lid off,' Johannes snapped.

'As usual, Johannes, you were not listening properly when I lodged my grievance procedure in quadruplicate to the Funding Council Grievance Committee,' Patty snapped.

'Layers of management largesse notwithstanding, why is it I haven't seen you before?' Sir Barcode enquired of Patty, smiling coquettishly.

'Don't know, but if I had known I would have been constantly looking out for someone with such a coquettish smile as yours,' she flirted, 'but I have spent an inordinate amount of time recently in Principal Cavalier's atelier having my body painted. Would you like to see his latest masterpiece in flesh on my belly?'

'We've heard of ghost writers, but ghost painters?'

'Um, we must get on,' Laughing Cavalier interrupted in embarrassed stammer.

'Bollocks! What charade are all these farts playing?'

'Cleverer still; where did the voice come from on that occasion, Principal Taliesin?' Adam Krenwinkler enthused, 'but in answer to the cursing whimsy: no, we are not playing a charade; neither are we farts,' and, turning to Laughing Cavalier, he added, 'entertaining as all this is, Principal Cavalier, I agree with you, we must get on with the inspection.'

'Yes, but in order to set the record straight I am obliged to say before Johannes Taliesin escorts this parley of instruments to the exit,' Principal Cavalier began with great forbearance, while simultaneously clapping a hand across his forehead in a gesture of incorporated despair, 'Taliesin was a student at this institution until three weeks ago when we were obliged to discipline him for gross misconduct with one of our life models –'

'Sexual impropriety?' Krenwinkler panted the interruption.

'No, the nature of the gross misconduct is beside the point, but actually he applied oil paint to her naked torso by means of a hardboard conveyance,' Principal Cavalier responded tetchily.

'I'm surprised it was not sexual impropriety considering it was with a life model,' Krenwinkler's tone indicated disappointment.

'My setting the record straight is being shunted into a siding,' Laughing Cavalier sounded really cross, 'As you know chief executives of incorporated institutions often use rumour as tools of management, but in this particular case the rumour insisted that Taliesin was incapable of sexual impropriety, so the reprimand related to his assault by overloaded paint support with economy re-use of boiled linseed oil – confound it! Will you please allow me to finish my report on the reprimand?' Principal Cavalier raised his voice.

'Yes, surely; proceed, Laughing,' Adam Krenwinkler wheezed apologetics.

'During the statutory procedure of reprimand,' Principal Cavalier continued, 'Taliesin finally lost his mind and leaped through that window,' waving the while, 'as Cardboard Cut-Out has already intimated,' in the direction of the window in question through which the washing on its line high up on Mayhill was still applauding the theatre, 'although I am advised by the academics he had been threatening to mislay his mind for some considerable time prior to this engagement.

As was apparent to the few of us who enjoy the privilege of recognising such symptoms, the strain of superposition was taking –'

'WHAT?' Sir Barcode burst, 'Strain of superposition? A very intriguing story, Cavalier; I believe it can only be stress exacerbated by too many cock and bull stories to officials of the funding council.'

'Superposition?' Adam Krenwinkler sought clarity, ignoring Chairman's enlightened directive.

'*We came to that conclusion ourselves,*' Inner Voice boasted.

'Yes, the strain of superposition was taking its toll on Taliesin's sanity, which his fundamental psychological weakness rendered him ill-equipped to manage,' Principal Cavalier continued cocking and bulling, 'Following the attempted suicide he was committed to Cefn Coed Hospital for the Seriously Mentally Challenged.'

'Goodness, Laugh,' Sir Barcode indulged the fantasy, 'what principals have to put up with since the Education Reform Act laid waste the land and called it progress, but a case of superposition in a student at a higher education art institution is vanishingly rare, and something to be celebrated, surely.'

'Too late,' Johannes interjected, 'regardless Cavalier's delusion, I was no longer a student at this college of art. Besides, I am now principal of Nehemiah Institute of Art and thankfully am no longer their responsibility.'

'I thought this floor is some considerable height above the street,' Adam Krenwinkler, surprisingly logical for a chief executive, disputed Cavalier's story.

'It is,' Johannes responded, growing in confidence by the second, 'but when you lose your mind all the protons and neutrons that constitute your mass jump out of the cupboard; as a consequence gravity ceases to have any effect regarding the ordinary laws of physics and you float gently in whatever direction, no matter what window you exit, sort of slow motion superposition entanglement –'

'*Why are we bullshitting?*'

'– Incidentally, Principal Cavalier, I had independently come to a similar conclusion that superposition was the cause of my problems.'

'My, my!' Principal Cavalier breezed, again clapping his forehead, 'Entanglement is the sort of condition principals have to contend with since enactment of that confounded 1988 Education Reform Act,' he said, leaping at the laying waste of the land opportunity availed by Sir Barcode, 'anyway, Taliesin walked into my office about an hour ago introducing himself as principal of Nehemiah Institute of Art –'

'Which I am!' Johannes emphasised.

'Which he is,' Krenwinkler corroborated.

'– And that he had been commissioned by the funding council to undertake a formal inspection of this college –'

'Which he has,' Cardigan and Krenwinkler chimed.

'Obviously Cefn Coed had failed to address his superposition problem,' Laughing Cavalier batted on, regardless the interjections, 'but to add incompetence to their lack of professionalism he escaped the hospital's custody. How he gained awareness of the official inspection commencing this day evades me.'

'Great Scott, Cavalier, what daring for an imaginary superposition mental patient – having the pluck to entangle as principal and masquerade as an official inspector,' Sir Barcode humoured Principal Cavalier.

'*Which is the real us?*'

'Seriously, Taliesin, were you injured?' Krenwinkler maintained his line.

'*Of course we weren't!*'

'Not a scratch! After a series of escapades including a

close-run thing with a rose madder tsunami in a Frameshop, I completed my studies at Cardiff and eventually became principal of Nehemiah Institute of Art,' Johannes explained ever so calmly.

'This is preposterous!' Principal Cavalier burst, 'the clerestory arrested his suicide attempt and, as I had no time to call for assistance, my model and I grappled him back into the room. The model was very courageous considering she was wearing nothing but a flimsy dressing gown.'

'This is pure fantasy!' Johannes squawked, 'you, Sir Barcode and Adam, commissioned me to undertake a review of the art and design sector under the brief of the Desirable-Essential Elements of Art and Design in Higher Education.'

'Were you aware the clerestory would arrest your leap, Taliesin?' Adam Krenwinkler pursued the best line of logic open to his enquiring mind.

'Of course; I had been aware of the clerestory adjacent the principal's current office for at least two years,' Johannes replied, 'and I had rehearsed that particular escape methodology on many occasions.'

'No doubt we'll suffer for that lie.'

'He found his mind again in the hospital library,' Patty Ulanova chirped, 'flattened out between the pages of John Gribbin's 'In Search of Schrödinger's Cat'.

'I'm sorry, Principal Taliesin,' Sir Barcode shuffled absentmindedly, 'this is not the time or place for us to have to verify – um, Principal Cavalier, you understand, could we and Taliesin please get on with the inspection?'

'Please, Principal Taliesin, escort Ms Ulanova and her theatre prop to the exit,' Krenwinkler took appropriate grasp of the situation.

'But surely if you recognise Taliesin you must also recognise me?' Cardboard Cut-Out called out.

'Can't get over this first-class ventriloquism,' Adam Krenwinkler again shook his head.

'Are you saying you don't recognise me?' Cardboard Cut-Out demanded.

'Superb ventriloquism, Mr Taliesin, even if you are mentally encumbered with superposition and official inspections,' Sir Barcode smiled dismissively, 'but enough of this display: we must get on with our task.'

'This condition of mine is so frustrating I could explode,' Cardboard Cut-Out's mouth spoke.

'Not in here, if you please, I don't want pulp all over my office,' Laughing Cavalier grimaced, 'had something similar once before: never again!'

'Might I remind you,' the mouth spoke, 'the pulp industry can recycle cardboard no more than four times, after which its fibrous viscosity begins to break down.'

'What are you talking about, Cardboard Cut-Out?' Principal Cavalier demanded.

'Stoical to the last, Laugh,' Sir Barcode applauded, 'while all those around you are losing their composure, you remain true to what you remember you should have been.'

'I have believed it to be superposition for some considerable time,' Johannes insisted, 'sort of entanglement as in the EPR thought experiment.'

'How did you get to know about the EPR paradox?' Principal Cavalier dropped his guard, 'surely, your time must be wholly consumed in management?'

'Simple, really,' Johannes replied, relieved he had been handed a hook, 'I seem to jump around in time, very slow-motion in comparison to the speed of quantum collapse, but nevertheless describing the same parabolic oscillations as in the subatomic world, although within a time-span of about fifty years plus time out for failures, so managing an art college in the meantime is a mere squeeze of toothpaste.'

'What are you people talking about?' Patty interrupted the flow.

'Superposition and quantum entanglement,' Johannes explained, 'thought you were writing an MA dissertation on the matter.'

'No, not me, I'm as thick as a plank; Cardboard Cut-Out dictates to me and my spelling is corrected by the spelling and grammar utility on the documentation processor. Each time Cardboard dictates to me he has his wicked way with me; I don't mind,' Patty Ulanova replied dreamily and, lost to the scientific turn of conversation, she once again hooked Cardboard Cut-Out under her arm and made to leave.

'Gosh! You are difficult to carry, Cardboard,' she strained breathlessly.

'Definitely, the EPR paradox, superposition and entanglement; we should repeat it because we think they are not comprehending –'

'Definitely the Einstein Podolsky Rosen paradox, which embraces superposition and entanglement,' Johannes boldly declared, 'regardless being a student or a principal or inspector on behalf of the funding council it is spooky attraction at a distance.'

'Please demonstrate the physicality of the paradox to us, especially your inspectorial properties by escorting this motley duet away,' Principal Cavalier sighed.

'Hmm! Cavalier comprehends, but what about the other clowns?'

'I'll have you know, Taliesin, I might resemble a painted clown, but my temperament is far from one,' Cardboard Cut-Out's huffing came from under Patty's arm.

'We'll see about this clowning when we get back to head office,' Adam Krenwinkler jibed.

'Don't rise to the bait, Krenwinkler,' Sir Barcode advised.

'We never intended going to the hospital,' Patty Ulanova heaved, 'rather, the two and a half of us are going back to the hotel.'

Of a sudden, a propos the right-angled chemistry that was Johannes where nothing of unimportance issued, his head spun wildly as he sought the refuge of a chair. From thereon events proceeded from vagueness to gathering clarity. It seemed only Johannes was aware of his metamorphosis.

'Prop me upright again, Miss Ulanova,' he heard David Eckto speak, 'I have something important to say.'

Shapes moved about, apparently in some accord. Patty obliged and stood next to Eckto. Gathering his wits ahead of losing the plot, Johannes heard Eckto say,

'Regardless, Johannes Taliesin is mid-way through a project at the moment redefining quantum mechanics as it affects the wiring of our quantum brains together with intellectual superposition in entanglement of the contagious form of hysteria,' he preached, 'we were just leaving to compare notes. It was interesting meeting you again, Laugh, always a mystery that one devoid of humour should possess an appellation of such misleading proportion but, nevertheless, I thank you for your indulgence.'

'David Eckto! What a novel way of delivering a proclamation.' Adam Krenwinkler applauded, 'but it is unconscionably inappropriate.'

'Didn't realise Cardboard Cut-Out… um, Eckto, was in on the superposition act, but delivering a proclamation out of cardboard takes some beating,' Inner Voice whispered, steadying the intensity.

'You mean three years, surely?' Sir Barcode corrected, 'No redefinition of quantum brain mechanics as far as I see it,' he levelled, affecting a smile, 'not getting away with your commitments to the council as easily as that, Taliesin,' as the Nehemiah Institute of Art time warp returned to wrap around Johannes's present participle.

'Um, perhaps this could be settled at some other time,' Laughing Hancock reasoned, using his grandmaster talents at diplomacy.

'What hotel is this young woman referring to, Taliesin?' Sir Barcode asked.

'Huh! We know why he wants that information.'

'The Dragon Hotel,' Patty replied, as Johannes had hesitated in answering.

'Cefn Coed Hospital,' Dr Eckto corrected.

'Uh-oh! Eckto Cut-Out's reality is still lollipop.'

'I stayed at the Dragon Hotel last night,' Johannes put speculation to rest, 'but how Ms Ulanova learned the identity of my hotel fails me.'

'As Johannes Taliesin is securely within my remit it is my duty to learn the identity,' Patty quickly consolidated.

'Yes, indeed!' Dr Eckto confirmed, 'within her remit.'

'But I demand my wicked way with him!' Patty stamped her little breathless.

Principal Hancock, together with his eminent guests, looked lost in a maelstrom of confusion. They had not yet caught up with Johannes's superposition role.

'I suppose we should get started! We have a tight schedule and are already running late,' the principal said, 'but why Eckto and Ms Ulanova don't get on with the business of leaving is beyond my morning's salary,' he joked.

'It's three-dimensional obfuscation, a near neighbour of superposition,' Johannes explained.

'Not beyond my salary level,' Eckto said, 'except it's just a little tricky organising Johannes's erratic behaviour. Come along Ms Ulanova,' and, giving a broad wink, 'let us leave Principal Hancock and his visitors to proceed with their business. Good to have met you all; perhaps another time less preoccupied with unexpected guests?'

'Yes, hopefully,' Sir Barcode conceded.

Dr Eckto's valedictory prompted the principal, 'Inspector Taliesin, don't tempt any further entanglement,' he suggested.

Clear in head and mission, Johannes ushered Patty and Dr Eckto out of the door, which Principal Hancock closed behind them with a sigh of relief,

'Goodbye.'

'Something sinister going on… only sure reference is the washing on Mayhill clapping its hands with glee.'

'If you are escorting us to the exit, Johannes, please don't initiate another one of your superposition phases,' Eckto said irritably.

'What's he on about?'

'Perhaps I should change my MA studies to helping victims of initial conditions,' Patty said, 'instead of this quantum entanglement in the contagious form of hysteria thing.'

'It all supports a lifestyle of contrariness,' Johannes muttered, as they walked on towards the exit.

'We will go at a brisk pace before we are impeded by another consequence of contagious entanglement,' Eckto suggested, 'incidentally, Johannes, we thought you had been play-acting in the principal's office.'

'Yes,' Patty chimed in, 'that's why we joined the charade.'

'By metamorphosing into Cardboard Cut-Out, I presume?' Johannes asked.

'Yes,' David Eckto conceded.

'I thought it was a tremendous party trick!' Patty chimed.

'It might have been a party trick, but for me it adds up to entanglement,' Johannes grumbled.

'Some point in your past you should recognise as the cusp,' Eckto said, 'it's important you identify it.'

'Do I have to think about cusps here in the corridor at the same time as I am escorting you to the exit?'

'Yes now, before you metamorphose into a character we are unable to control –'

'Who is controlling whom?'

'– the exercise will assist in your return from the strange realm your thoughts inhabit, otherwise you could be lost forever between the phases.'

'No, bugger it! I enjoy being principal of Nehemiah Institute, lost between the phases. I don't wish to return to this anonymous disproportion where you turned into a cardboard cut-out and the principal morphed into Laughing Cavalier. At Nehemiah everything is normal, nothing like this happens and I have authority and security.'

'And we put our hands in cow shit,' Inner Voice remembered, *'perfectly normal.'*

'Come on, Johannes, an escape from the phases will give you the opportunity to start all over again, to strive for a real Nehemiah, not an imaginary one,' Eckto reasoned.

'And make all the same mistakes again?' Johannes winced, contemptuous of his failures, 'No, forget it.'

'Many of us will never enjoy such an opportunity,' David Eckto added knowingly.

'Oh, sod it!' Johannes cursed, 'I've left my briefcase in the principal's office – it contains confidential documents, they'll tamper with them! Must go back to pick it up: hold on, won't be a tick,' and he doubled back down the corridor.

'We'll hold on, Johannes, how could we leave without you?'

Patty said; then, to Eckto, 'don't think we should let him go back alone – it might be the last we see of him,' she muttered.

'We'll wait here, there's no other way of escape,' Eckto advised, 'he has to come back this way…'

Their voices faded as Johannes continued back.

'We'll see about no other way of escape… now's our opportunity to break with this nightmare… from this parley of loonies…'

Reaching the principal's door, he tapped and waited.

'Min!'

Johannes opened the door; someone had placed his briefcase adjacent the doorway.

'How did they know?'

'Ah Taliesin, come in,' the principal greeted him.

'I've… um… left my briefcase –' he pointed at the subject.

'Yes,' the principal interrupted, 'we wondered how long it would take you to realise you had left without your suitcase. Are Dr Eckto and Ms Ulanova at hand?'

'Suitcase? It's a briefcase, filled with important documents – tell them!'

'Yes, they are just up the corridor. But it's a briefcase,' Johannes attempted a last throw, 'Briefcase, containing classified material that I am obliged to keep with me at all times.'

The three officials maintained their aloof dignity, but even so both Krenwinkler and Sir Barcode chuckled menacingly, while Principal Hancock smiled inscrutably.

'They see clean through our briefcase strategy! Clean through! Oh God – let's get out of our nightmare.'

Looking at the briefcase for reassurance Johannes witnessed his official symbol of status morphing into an old tattered suitcase. The moment had arrived to fight back the hysteria.

'Oh God, please help us.'

'I'll… um… I'll take it…'

Clutching the old suitcase, he turned to leave,

'Goodbye, Mr Hancock, and thank you for your indulgence.'

'Goodbye, Taliesin,' the principal replied, arranging his features to display a hundred years of sadness.

Pulling the door shut behind him, Johannes sighed despairingly.

'*Oh dear, what a horrible mess we're in,*' Inner Voice despaired, '*our briefcase was our tattered cardboard suitcase all the time. They must have known and played along…*'

Glancing up the corridor, he saw Dr Eckto and Patty Ulanova waiting. They beckoned him make haste.

'*Oh God no! We can't go back to all that. Our soul has made up our minds… it's leaving, can't let it leave without us –*'

Johannes waved goodbye to the parley of memories –

'*Goodbye, meagre and struggle; goodbye,* do *goodbye,*' Inner Voice sighed,

– And, turning down the corridor in the opposite direction, he walked out of his painting.

Also from Y Lolfa:

Dylan Thomas's last days – and someone's watching...

THE POET &
THE PRIVATE EYE

ROB GITTINS

£14.95 (hardback)
£8.95 (paperback)

Water

Lloyd Jones

yLolfa

£8.95

Llywelyn

JOHN·HUGHES

A novel based on the story of the last Prince of Wales,
a young woman and a bishop

£8.95

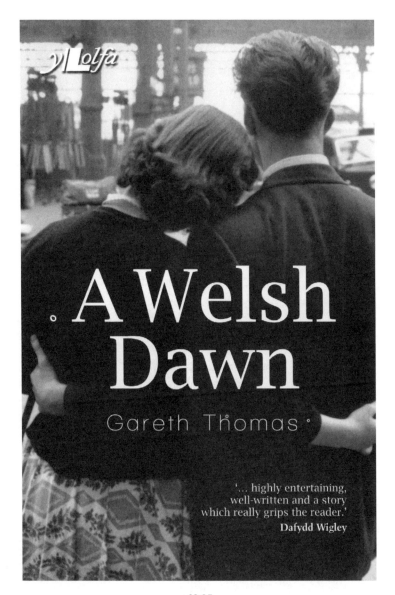

yLolfa

A Welsh
Dawn

Gareth Thomas

'... highly entertaining,
well-written and a story
which really grips the reader.'
Dafydd Wigley

£9.95

Dead Man Airbrushed is just one of a whole range of publications from Y Lolfa. For a full list of books currently in print, send now for your free copy of our new full-colour catalogue. Or simply surf into our website

www.ylolfa.com

for secure on-line ordering.

TALYBONT CEREDIGION CYMRU SY24 5HE
e-mail ylolfa@ylolfa.com
website www.ylolfa.com
phone (01970) 832 304
fax 832 782